# DEAD HEAT

## DICK FRANCIS
### AND FELIX FRANCIS

BERKLEY BOOKS, NEW YORK

**THE BERKLEY PUBLISHING GROUP**
**Published by the Penguin Group**
**Penguin Group (USA) Inc.**
**375 Hudson Street, New York, New York 10014, USA**
Penguin Group (Canada), 90 Eglinton Avenue East, Suite 700, Toronto, Ontario M4P 2Y3, Canada
(a division of Pearson Penguin Canada Inc.)
Penguin Books Ltd., 80 Strand, London WC2R 0RL, England
Penguin Group Ireland, 25 St. Stephen's Green, Dublin 2, Ireland (a division of Penguin Books Ltd.)
Penguin Group (Australia), 250 Camberwell Road, Camberwell, Victoria 3124, Australia
(a division of Pearson Australia Group Pty. Ltd.)
Penguin Books India Pvt. Ltd., 11 Community Centre, Panchsheel Park, New Delhi—110 017, India
Penguin Group (NZ), 67 Apollo Drive, Rosedale, North Shore 0632, New Zealand
(a division of Pearson New Zealand Ltd.)
Penguin Books (South Africa) (Pty.) Ltd., 24 Sturdee Avenue, Rosebank, Johannesburg 2196,
South Africa

Penguin Books Ltd., Registered Offices: 80 Strand, London WC2R 0RL, England

This is a work of fiction. Names, characters, places, and incidents either are the product of the author's imagination or are used fictitiously, and any resemblance to actual persons, living or dead, business establishments, events, or locales is entirely coincidental.

DEAD HEAT

A Berkley Book / published by arrangement with the authors

PRINTING HISTORY
G. P. Putnam's Sons hardcover edition / September 2007
Berkley international edition / May 2008

Copyright © 2007 by Dick Francis Corporation.
Cover design copyright © 2007 by RBMM/Brian MeAdams.

ISBN: 978-0-425-22224-9

BERKLEY®
Berkley Books are published by The Berkley Publishing Group,
a division of Penguin Group (USA) Inc.,
375 Hudson Street, New York, New York 10014.
BERKLEY® is a registered trademark of Penguin Group (USA) Inc.
The "B" design is a trademark belonging to Penguin Group (USA) Inc.

PRINTED IN THE UNITED STATES OF AMERICA

10  9  8  7  6  5  4  3  2  1

*Our thanks to*

*Dr. Tim Brazil, equine veterinary surgeon*
*Allen Handy, principal trumpeter*
*Andrew Hewson, literary agent*
*John Holmes, resident of Delafield, Wisconsin*
*Newmarket Racecourse*
*Gordon Ramsay, restaurateur*


*and to*
Debbie
*for the title*

# 1

I wondered if I was dying. I wasn't afraid to die, but, such was the pain in my gut, I wished it would happen soon.

I'd had food poisoning before, but this time it was particularly unpleasant, with agonizing cramps and long bouts of retching. I had already spent most of Friday night kneeling on my bathroom floor with my head in the toilet, and, at one point, I became really concerned that the violence of the spasms in my abdomen might result in me losing my stomach lining altogether.

Twice I resolved to get myself to the telephone to summon help, only again to be doubled up by a fresh round of dry-heaving. Didn't my bloody stupid muscles realize that my stomach was already empty, and had been so for ages? Why did this torture continue when there was nothing left in me to throw up?

Between the attacks, I sat sweating on the floor, leaning up against the bathtub, and tried to work out what had brought on this misery.

On Friday evening, I had been to a black-tie gala dinner

in the Eclipse tent at Newmarket racetrack. I'd eaten a trio of cold smoked fish with a garlic mustard dill sauce for a starter, followed by a sliced black cherry stuffed chicken breast wrapped in pancetta with a wild chanterelle and truffle sauce, served with roasted red new potatoes and steamed snow peas, as the main course, and then a vanilla crème brûlée for dessert.

I knew intimately every ingredient of the meal.

I knew because rather than being a guest at the function, I had been the chef.

FINALLY, as my bathroom window changed from black to gray with the coming of the dawn, the tight knot in my stomach began to unwind and the cold clamminess of my skin slowly started to abate.

But the ordeal was not yet over, with what remained in my digestive tract now being forcefully ejected at the other end.

In due course, I crawled along the landing of my cottage to bed and lay there utterly exhausted; drained, dehydrated, but alive. The clock on my bedside table showed that it was ten past seven in the morning, and I was due to be at work at eight. Just what I needed.

I lay there, kidding myself that I would be all right in a little while, and another five minutes would not matter. I began to doze but was brought back to full consciousness by the ringing of my telephone, which sat on the table next to the clock. Seven-twenty.

Who, I thought, is ringing me at seven-twenty? Go away. Leave me to sleep.

The phone stopped. That's better.

It rang again. Damn it. I rolled over and lifted the receiver.

"Yes," I said with all the hurt expression in my voice from a night of agony.

"Max?" said a male voice. "Is that you?"

"One and the same," I replied in my more usual tone.

"Have you been ill?" asked the voice. It was his emphasis on the word *you* that had me worried.

I sat up quickly. "Yes I have," I said. "Have you?"

"Dreadful, isn't it. Everyone I've spoken to has had the same." Carl Walsh was technically my assistant. In fact, these days he was as often in charge of the kitchen as I was. The previous evening, as I had been working the tables and receiving all the plaudits, Carl had been busily plating up the meals and shouting at the staff in the kitchen tent. Now, it appeared, there may be no more plaudits, just blame.

"Who have you spoken to?" I asked.

"Julie, Richard, Ray and Jean," he said. "They each called me to say that none of them are coming in today. And Jean said that Martin was so ill that they called an ambulance and he went to the hospital."

I knew how he felt.

"How about the guests?" I asked. Carl had spoken only to my staff.

"I don't know, but Jean said that when she went with Martin to the hospital the staff there knew all about the poisoning, as they called it, so he can't have been the only one."

Oh God! Poisoning two hundred and fifty of the great and the good of the racing world the night before the 2000 Guineas was unlikely to be beneficial to my business.

Being a chef who poisons his clients was not a reputation to relish. The event at the racetrack was a special. My day job was my restaurant, the Hay Net, situated on the outskirts of Newmarket in Ashley Road: sixty or so lunches a day, from Sunday to Friday, and dinner for up to a hundred every night. At least, that's what we'd served last week, prepoisoning.

"I wonder how many of the other staff are affected," said Carl, bringing me back to the present. My restaurant had been closed for the evening, and all eleven of my regular employees had been working the dinner at the racetrack, together with twenty or so part-timers who had assisted in the kitchen and with waiting on tables. All the staff had eaten the same food as served at the function, while the guests were listening to the speeches.

"I've arranged five to do the job at the racetrack today," I said. The thought of having to prepare lunch for forty of the sponsor's guests sent fresh waves of nausea through my stomach and caused the reappearance of sweat on my brow.

I was due to provide a three-course meal in two of the large, glass-fronted private boxes in the grandstand. Delafield Industries, Inc., an American tractor-manufacturing multinational from Wisconsin, was the new sponsor of the first Classic race of the year, and they had offered me more money than I could refuse to provide their guests with fresh steamed English asparagus with melted butter, followed by traditional British steak-and-kidney pie, with a summer pudding for dessert. Thankfully, I had talked them out of the fish-and-chips, with mushy peas. MaryLou Fordham, the company marketing executive who had secured my services, was determined that the guests from "back home" in Wisconsin should experience the "real" England. She had been deaf to my suggestions that pâté de foie gras with brioche, followed by a salmon meunière, might be more appropriate.

"I'll tell you right now," MaryLou had declared, "we don't want any of that French stuff. We want English food only." I had sarcastically asked if she wanted me to serve warm beer rather than fine French wines, but she hadn't understood my little joke. In the end, we had agreed on an Australian white and a Californian red. The whole meal had boredom written all over it, but they were paying, and paying very well. Delafield tractors and combine harvesters, it seemed, were all the rage in the American Midwest, and they were now trying hard to grab a share of the English market. Someone had told them that Suffolk was the prairie country of the UK, so here they were. That the "Delafield Harvester 2000 Guineas" didn't have quite the right ring to it didn't seem to worry them one bit.

As things stood at the moment, they would be lucky to get anything to eat at all.

"I'll call around and get back to you," said Carl.

"OK," I replied. He hung up.

I knew I should get up and get going. Forty individual steak-and-kidney pies wouldn't make themselves.

I was still lying on my bed, dozing, when the phone rang again. It was five to eight.

"Hello," I said sleepily.

"Is that Mr. Max Moreton?" said a female voice.

"Yes," I replied.

"My name is Angela Milne," said the voice formally. "I am the environmental health officer for Cambridgeshire."

She suddenly had my full attention.

"We have reason to believe," she went on, "that a mass poisoning has occurred at an event where you were the chef in charge of the kitchen. Is that correct?"

"Who are 'we'?" I asked.

"Cambridgeshire County Council," she said.

"Well," I said, "I was the chef for a gala dinner last night. But I am unaware of any mass poisoning, and I would seriously question as to whether my kitchen would be responsible for one even if it existed."

"Mr. Moreton," she said, "I can assure you that a mass poisoning has occurred. Twenty-four persons were treated overnight at Addenbrooke's hospital for acute food poisoning, and seven of those were admitted due to severe dehydration. They all attended the same function last evening."

"Oh."

"Oh indeed," said Ms. Milne. "I require that the kitchen used to prepare the food for the event be closed immediately and that it be sealed for inspection. All kitchen equipment and all remaining foodstuffs to be made available for analysis, and all kitchen and waitstaff to be on hand to be interviewed as required."

That might not be as easy as she thought.

"How are the seven in the hospital doing?" I asked.

"I have no idea," she said. "But I would have been informed if there had been any fatalities."

No news was good news.

"Now, Mr. Moreton"—she sounded like a headmistress addressing a miscreant pupil—"where exactly is the kitchen that produced the food for the event?"

"It no longer exists," I said.

"What do you mean it no longer exists?" said Angela Milne.

"The dinner was held in the Eclipse tent at Newmarket

racetrack," I said. "The tent will be used as a bar during the race meeting today. The tent we used for the kitchen last night will be being used to store beer by now."

"How about the equipment?"

"Everything was hired from a catering supply company from Ipswich. Tables, chairs, tablecloths, plates, cutlery, glasses, pots, pans, ovens, hot servers—the lot. My staff helped load it all back on the truck at the end of the event. I use them all the time for outside catering. They take everything back dirty and put it through their own steam cleaners."

"Will it have been cleaned yet?" she asked.

"I've no idea," I said, "but I wouldn't be surprised. I have a fresh truck of equipment due to arrive at the racetrack today at eight o'clock." I looked at the clock beside my bed— in precisely two minutes.

"I'm not sure I can permit you to prepare food again today," she said rather sternly.

"Why not?" I said.

"Cross contamination."

"The food for last night came from a different supplier than I am using today," I said. "All the ingredients for last night's menu came directly from a catering wholesaler and were prepared at the racetrack. Today's ingredients were ordered through my restaurant, and it's been in the cold-room there for the past two days." The cold-room was a large walk-in refrigerator, kept at a constant three degrees centigrade.

"Did you get anything from the same wholesaler for the dinner?" she asked.

"No. The dry provisions would have come from the cash-and-carry near Huntingdon, the meat from my butcher in Bury St. Edmonds and the fresh fruit and vegetables from the wholesale greengrocer in Cambridge that I use regularly."

"Who provided the food for the dinner last night?" she asked.

"Something like Leigh Foods, I think. I've got the details at my office. I don't usually use them, but, then, I don't often do a function for so many people."

"How about the equipment company?"

"Stress-Free Catering Ltd," I said, and gave her their telephone number. I knew it by heart.

The digits of my digital clock changed to 8:00, and I thought of the Stress-Free Catering truck arriving down the road with no one to meet it.

"Look, I'm sorry," I said, "but I have to go now and start work. If that's all right by you?"

"I suppose so," she said. "I will come down to the racetrack to see you in about an hour or so."

"The track is in Suffolk. Is that still your territory?" Actually, there were two racetracks at Newmarket; one is in Cambridgeshire and the other in Suffolk, with the county line running along the Devil's Dyke between them. The dinner, and the lunch, were in Suffolk, at the Rowley Mile course.

"The sick people are in Cambridge, that's what matters to me." I thought I detected the faint signs of irritation, but maybe I was mistaken. "The whole area of food hygiene and who has responsibility is a nightmare. The county councils, the district councils and the Food Standards Agency all have their own enforcement procedures. It's a mess." I had obviously touched a nerve. "Oh yes," she went on, "what exactly did people have to eat last night?"

"Smoked fish, stuffed chicken breast and crème brûlée," I said.

"Perhaps it was the chicken," she said.

"I do know how to cook chicken, you know. Anyway, the symptoms were too quick for salmonella poisoning."

"What happened to the leftover food?" she asked.

"I've no idea," I said. "I don't think there was much left over. My staff are like a pack of wolves when it comes to leftovers and they eat whatever remains in the kitchen. Food left on people's plates goes into a bin that would normally be disposed of by Stress-Free."

"Did everyone eat the same?" she asked.

"Everyone except the vegetarians."

"What did they have?"

"Tomato and goat's cheese salad instead of the fish starter, then a broccoli, cheese and pasta bake. There was one vegan who had preordered grilled mushrooms to start, roasted vegetables for main course and a fresh fruit salad for dessert."

"How many vegetarians?"

"I've no idea," I said. "All I know is that we had enough of the pasta bake."

"That seems a bit cavalier."

"We did two hundred and fifty covers. I ordered two hundred and sixty chicken breasts, just in case some of them were a bit small or damaged."

"What do you mean by damaged?"

"Bruised or torn. I didn't know the supplier very well, so I decided to order a few more than I normally would. In the end they were all fine and we cooked the lot. Then there was enough vegetarian for at least twenty, plus the vegan. That should be about thirty to thirty-five extra meals over and above the guests. That feeds my staff. If there are only a few vegetarians among the guests, then my staff have to eat more of that. Look, I really must go now, I'm late already."

"OK, Mr. Moreton," she said. "Just one more thing."

"Yes?"

"Were *you* ill in the night?"

"As a matter of fact, I was." Horribly.


BY THE TIME I finally arrived at the racetrack, the man from Stress-Free Catering was well advanced with the unloading of the truck.

"Beginning to think I'd got the wrong day," he said sarcastically by way of welcome. He rolled a large wire cage full of crockery out onto the hydraulic tailgate and lowered it to the ground with a clatter. Perhaps he could use the tailgate to lower me onto a bed. I worked out that I had been awake for more than twenty-six hours, and remembered that the KGB had used sleep deprivation as their primary form of torture.

"Was it you that collected the stuff from last night?" I asked.

"No chance," he replied. "I had to leave Ipswich at seven

and had to load everything before that. I've been at work since five-thirty." He said it in an accusing manner, which was fair enough, I suppose. He wasn't to know that I'd been up all night.

"Will it still be on the truck from last night?" I could see that today's was a much-smaller version, for a much-smaller function, and there was no kitchen equipment.

"Doubt it," he said. "First thing that's done after a late function is to unload and steam-clean the lot, including the inside of the truck."

"Even on a Saturday?"

"Absolutely," he said. "Saturdays are the busiest day of the week for us. Weddings and all."

"What happens to the food waste bins?" I asked him. Perhaps, I thought, some pig farmer somewhere is getting the leftovers delivered for his charges.

"We have an industrial-sized waste-disposal unit. You know, like those things in kitchen sinks, only bigger. Liquidizes all the leftover food and flushes it away down the drain. Then the bins are steam-cleaned like the rest. Why do you want to know?" he asked. "Lost something?"

Only my stomach, I thought. And my pride.

"Just wondered," I said. Ms. Milne was not going to be happy. No kitchen to inspect and no leftover food to test. I wasn't sure whether I should be pleased or disappointed. With none of the offending material to analyze, it couldn't be proved that my food was responsible for the poisoning. But, then again, it couldn't be proved that it wasn't.

"Where do you want all this stuff?" he asked, waving a hand at the row of wire cages.

"Glass-fronted boxes 1 and 2 on the second floor of the Head On Grandstand," I said.

"Right." He went in search of the elevator.

As the name suggested, the Head On Grandstand sat near the finish line and looked back down the track, so that the horses raced almost directly towards it. The boxes had the best view of the racing and were the most sought after. The Delafield tractor makers had done well to secure a couple of boxes side by side for their big day.

I wandered past the magnificent Millennium Grandstand towards the racetrack manager's office. The whole place was a hive of activity. Last-minute beer deliveries to the bars were in progress, while other catering staff were scurrying back and forth with trays of smoked salmon and cold meats. The groundsmen were putting the finishing touches to the flower beds and again mowing the already-short grass in the parade ring. An army of young men was setting up tables and chairs on the lawn in front of a seafood stall, ready for the thousands of racegoers who would soon be arriving for their day out. Everything looked perfect, and normal. It was only me that was different. At least, that's what I thought at the time.

I put my head through the open door of the manager's office. "Is William around?" I asked a large woman who was half standing next to and half sitting on the desk. William Preston was the racetrack manager and had been a guest at the function the previous evening.

"He won't be in 'til eleven, at the earliest," she said.

That sounded ominous, I thought. The racetrack manager not being in until eleven o'clock on 2000 Guineas day.

"He's had a bad night, apparently," she went on. "Something he ate didn't agree with him. Bloody nuisance, if you ask me. How am I meant to cope on my own? I don't get paid enough to cope on my own."

The telephone on the desk beside her ample bottom rang at that moment and saved me from further observations. I withdrew and went back to the delivery truck.

"Right," said the man from Stress-Free, "all your stuff's up in the boxes. Do you want to check before signing for it?"

I always checked deliveries. All too often, I had found that the inventory was somewhat larger than the actuality. But today I decided I'd risk it and scribbled on his offered form.

"Right," he said again. "I'll see you later. I'll collect at six."

"Fine," I replied. Six o'clock seemed a long way off. Thank goodness I had already done most of the preparation for the steak-and-kidney pies. All that was needed was to put the filling into the individual ceramic oval pie dishes, slap a pastry cover over the top and shove them into a hot oven for about thirty-five minutes. The fresh vegetables had already been blanched and were sitting in my cold-room at my restaurant, and the asparagus was trimmed and ready to steam. The individual small summer puddings had all been made on Thursday afternoon and also sat waiting in the cold-room. They just needed to be turned out of their molds and garnished with some whipped cream and half a strawberry. MaryLou wasn't to know that the strawberries came from southwest France.

As a rule, I didn't do "outside catering," but Guineas weekend was different. For the past six years, it had been my major marketing opportunity of the year.

The clientele of my restaurant were predominantly people involved in the racing business. It was a world I knew well and thought I understood. My father had been a moderately successful steeplechase jockey, and then a much more successful racehorse trainer, until he was killed in a collision with a truck carrying bricks on his way to Liverpool for the Grand National when I was eighteen. I would have been with him if my mother hadn't insisted that I stay at home and study for my A level exams. My elder half brother, Toby, ten years my senior, had literally taken over the reins of the training business, and was still making a living from it, albeit a meager one.

I had spent my childhood riding ponies and surrounded by horses, but I was never struck with Toby's love of all things equine. As far as I was concerned, both ends of a horse were dangerous and the middle was uncomfortable. One end kicks and the other end bites. And I had never been able to understand why riding had to be done at such an early hour on cold, wet mornings, when most sane people would be fast asleep in a nice warm bed.

More than thirteen years now had passed since the fateful day when a policeman appeared at the front door of our house to inform my mother that what was left of my father's Jaguar, with him still inside it, had been identified as belonging to a Mr. George Moreton, late of the parish of East Hendred.

I had worked hard for my A levels to please my mother and was accepted at Surrey University to study chemistry. But my life was changed forever, not only by the death of my father but by what should have been my gap year and turned out to be my gap life.

I never went to Surrey or to any other university. The plan had been that I would work for six months to earn enough to go traveling in the Far East for the next six months. So I went to work as a pots-and-pans washer-upper, beer-crate carrier and general dogsbody at a country pub/restaurant/ hotel overlooking the river Thames in Oxfordshire that belonged to a widowed distant cousin of my mother's. The normal designation for such an employee is *kitchen porter,* but this is such a derogatory term in catering circles that my mother's cousin referred to me as the *temporary assistant undermanager,* which was more of a mouthful and less accurate. The word *manager* implies a level of responsibility. The only responsibility I was given was to rouse the chambermaid each morning to serve the early-morning teas to the guests in the seven double bedrooms. At first, I did this by banging on her bedroom door for five minutes until she reluctantly opened it. But after a couple of weeks the task became much easier, since I simply had to push her out of the single bed that we had started sharing.

However, working in a restaurant kitchen, even at the kitchen sink, sparked in me a passion for food and its presentation. Soon, I had left the washing up to others and I started an apprenticeship under the watchful eye of Marguerite, the fiery, foulmouthed head cook. She didn't like the term *chef.* She had declared that she cooked and was therefore a *cook.*

When my six-month stint was up, I just stayed. By then, I had been installed as Marguerite's assistant, and was making everything from the starters to the desserts. In the afternoons, while the other staff caught up on their sleep, I would experiment with flavors, spending most of my earnings on ingredients at Witney farmers' market.

In the late spring, I wrote to Surrey University, politely asking if my enrollment could be deferred for yet another year. Fine, they said, but I think I already knew I wasn't going back to life in laboratories and lecture halls. When, in late October of the following year, Marguerite swore once too often at my mother's distant cousin and was fired, my course in life was set. Just four days short of my twenty-first birthday, I took over the kitchen, with relish, and set about the task of becoming the youngest chef ever to win a Michelin star.

For the next four years, the establishment thrived, my confidence growing at the same spectacular rate as the restaurant's reputation. However, I was becoming acutely aware that my mother's cousin's bank balance was expanding rather more rapidly than my own. When I broached the subject, she accused me of being disloyal, and that was the beginning of the end. Shortly after, she sold out to a national small-hotel chain without telling me and I suddenly found I had a new boss who wanted to make changes in my kitchen. My mother's cousin had also failed to tell the buyers that she had no contract with me, so I packed my bags and left.

While I decided what to do next, I went home and cooked dinner parties for my mother, who seemed somewhat surprised that I could, in spite of reading about my Michelin success in the newspapers. "But, darling," she'd said, "I never believe what I read in the papers."

It had been at one of the dinner parties that I was introduced to Mark Winsome. Mark was an entrepreneur in his thirties who had made a fortune in the cell phone business. I had joined the guests for coffee, and he was explaining that his problem was finding good opportunities to invest his money. I had jokingly said that he could invest in me, if he liked, by setting me up in my own restaurant. He didn't laugh or even smile. "OK," he'd said. "I'll finance everything, and you have total control. We split the proceeds fifty-fifty."

I had sat there with my mouth open. Only much later did I find out that he had badgered my mother for ages to organize the meeting between us so that he could make that offer, and I had fallen into the trap.

And so six years ago now, with Mark's money, I had set

up the Hay Net, a racing-themed restaurant on the outskirts
of Newmarket. It hadn't especially been my plan to go to
Newmarket, but it was where I found the first appropriate
property, and the closeness to racing's headquarters was
simply a bonus.

At first, business had been slow, but, with the attendees of
the special dinners and lunches around the race meetings
spreading the word, the restaurant was soon pretty full every
night, with a need to book more than a week in advance for
midweek and at least a month ahead for a Saturday night.
The wife of one major trainer in the town even started paying me a retainer to have a table for six booked every Saturday of the year, except when they were away in Barbados in
January. "Much easier to cancel than to book," she'd said.
But she rarely canceled, and often needed the table expanded to eight or ten.

My phone rang in my pocket.

"Hello," I said.

"Max, you had better come down to the restaurant." It
was Carl. "Public Health has turned up."

"She said she'd meet me at the racetrack," I said.

"These two are men," he replied.

"Tell them to come down here," I said.

"I don't think they will," he said. "Apparently, someone
has died, and these two are sealing the kitchen."

# 2

Sealing the kitchen literally was what they were doing. By the time I arrived, there was tape over every window, and two men were fitting large hasps and padlocks to all the doors.

"You can't do that," I said.

"Just watch," one of them replied while clipping a large brass padlock in place. "I've instructions to ensure that no one enters these premises until they have been examined and decontaminated."

"Decontaminated?" I said. "From what?"

"No idea," he said. "Just doing what I'm told."

"When will this examination take place?" I asked him with a sinking feeling.

"Monday or Tuesday maybe," he said. "Or Wednesday. Depends on how busy they are."

"But this is a business," I said. "How can I run a restaurant with the kitchen closed? I've got reservations for this evening."

"Sorry, mate." He didn't sound very sorry. "Your business is now closed. You shouldn't have killed someone."

"Who died?" I asked him.

"No idea," he said, clipping another padlock in place. "Right, that's finished. Sign here, will you." He held out a clipboard with some papers on it.

"What does it say?" I asked.

"It says that you agree to the closing of your kitchen, that you won't attempt to gain entry—which, by the way, would be a criminal offense—that you agree to pay for my services and for the equipment used and that you will be responsible if anyone else gains entry or tries to do so without due authority from the county council or the Food Standards Agency."

"And what if I refuse to sign?" I asked.

"Then I have to get an enforcement order and have a policeman on-site at all times, and, in the end, you will have to pay for that too. Either way, your kitchen remains closed. If you sign, then the inspection might be tomorrow, or on Monday. If you don't, it won't."

"That's blackmail."

"Yup," he said. "Usually works." He smiled and offered me the clipboard again.

"Bastard," I said. "Enjoy your work, do you?"

"Makes a change from the usual."

"What is the usual?" I asked.

"Debt collecting," he said.

He was a big man, both tall and broad. He wore black trousers, a white shirt with a thin black tie and white running shoes. His accomplice was dressed in the same manner— uniform for the job. It crossed my mind that all that was missing was a baseball bat to back up his threats. I could tell that I wasn't going to be able to appeal to his better nature. He clearly didn't have one.

I signed the paper.

During this exchange, the second man had been placing sticky-backed plastic signs on the windows and doors. They were white, approximately eighteen inches square, with CLOSED FOR DECONTAMINATION and KEEP OUT printed in large red lettering.

"Are those really necessary?" I asked.

He didn't answer. I knew. He was just doing his job, just doing what he'd been told.

I don't know whether it was out of spite that they stuck one on the restaurant's sign at the gate on their way out. There would be little doubt to passing traffic that the Hay Net was empty and limp, unable to feed a Shetland pony, let alone the hundred or so we had booked for dinner.

Carl appeared from the dining-room end of the building.

"It's the same inside," he said. "The kitchen doors have been padlocked."

"What do you suggest?" I asked.

"Well," he said, "I've just phoned most of those booked for tonight and told them we won't be serving."

"Well done," I said, impressed.

"Some said they weren't coming anyway. Some said they had been at the racetrack last night and had suffered like the rest of us. And many others had heard about it."

"Does anyone know who it is who died?" I asked.

"No idea," said Carl. "I didn't exactly ask our customers."

"We'd also better tell the staff not to come in tonight," I said.

"Done that too," he said. "At least, I've left messages for most. And I've stuck a notice on the kitchen door, telling everyone to take the weekend off and report for work on Monday morning."

"Did you tell them why?" I asked.

"Nope," he said. "Thought it best not to just yet. Until we know for sure what the damage is." He wiped his forehead with his palm. "God, I feel awful. All sweaty and yet cold."

"Me too," I said. "But I suppose we can now take the afternoon off. The tractor makers from Wisconsin are going to have to get their grub elsewhere."

"Why so?" said Carl.

"Because their pie filling is in the cold-room behind padlocked doors, silly."

"No it's not," he said. "I'd already loaded the van before those men arrived." He waved a hand at the Ford van we used for outside catering that was parked up near the back

door to the kitchen. "The summer puddings are in there too."
He smiled. "The only thing I haven't got is the asparagus
and the new potatoes, but we can get some more of those
from Cambridge."

"You are bloody marvelous," I said.

"So we're going to do it, then?"

"Dead right we are. We need a successful service now
more than ever." Silly thing to say, really, but of course I had
no idea then of what was to follow.

CARL DROVE THE van to the racetrack while I took my
car, a beat-up VW Golf that had been my pride and joy. I had
bought it brand-new when I was twenty, using the prize
money from a televised cooking competition I had won. After eleven years, and with well over a hundred thousand miles
on the odometer, it was beginning to show its age. But it remained a special car for me, and I was loath to change it. And
it could still outaccelerate most others off the traffic lights.

I parked in the staff parking lot, on the grass beyond the
weighing room, and I walked back to the far end of the
grandstand, where Carl was already unloading the van. I was
met there by two middle-aged women, one in a green tweed
suit, woolly hat and sensible brown boots, the other in a
scarlet frill-fronted chiffon blouse, black skirt and pointed
black patent high-heeled shoes, with a mass of curly dark
hair falling in tendrils around her ears. I looked at them both
and thought about appropriate dress.

The tweed suit beat the scarlet-and-black ensemble by a
short head.

"Mr. Moreton?" she asked in her headmistressly manner
as I approached.

"Ms. Milne, I presume?" I replied.

"Indeed," she said.

"And I am MaryLou Fordham," stated the scarlet-and-
black loudly in an American accent.

I had suspected as much.

"Aren't you cold?" I asked her. Chiffon blouses and
early-May mornings in Newmarket didn't quite seem to go

together. Even on still days, a cutting wind seemed to blow across the Heath, and Guineas Saturday was no exception.

"No," she replied. "If you want to know what cold is, come to Wisconsin in the winter." She spoke with every word receiving its share of emphasis, with little harmonic quality to the tone. Each word was clipped and clearly separate; there was no Southern drawl here, no running of the words together.

"And what do you want to see Mr. Moreton about when he should be working for me?" she said rather haughtily, turning towards Angela Milne.

I could tell from her body language that Angela Milne did not take very kindly to being addressed in that manner. I wouldn't have either.

"It is a private matter," said Angela. Good old Ms. Milne, I thought. My friend.

"Well, be quick," said MaryLou bossily. She turned to me. "I have been up to the suites, and there seems to be no work going on. The tables aren't laid, and there's no staff to be found."

"It's OK," I said. "It's only half past nine. The guests don't arrive for more than two hours. Everything will be ready." I hoped I was right. "You go back upstairs, and I will be there shortly."

Reluctantly, she headed off, with a couple of backwards glances. Nice legs, I thought, as she trotted off towards the grandstand, her high heels clicking on the tarmac.

Just when I thought she had gone, she came back. "Oh yes," she said, "there's something else I was going to tell you. I've had three calls this morning from people who now say they aren't coming to the track today. They say they are ill." She didn't try to disguise the disbelief in her voice. "So there will be five less for lunch."

I decided, under the circumstances, not to inquire too closely if she knew what it was that had made them ill.

"It's such a shame," she said. "Two of them are horse trainers from Newmarket who have runners in our race." She placed the emphasis on the *market* while almost swallowing the *New*. To my ears, it sounded strange.

She turned abruptly and marched off towards the elevators, giving me another sight of the lovely legs. The mass of black curls bounced on her shoulders as she walked. I watched her go, and wondered if she slept in curlers.

"Sorry about that," I said to Ms. Milne.

"Not your fault," she said

I hoped nothing was my fault.

She gave me her card. I read it: ANGELA MILNE, ENVIRONMENTAL HEALTH OFFICER, CAMBRIDGESHIRE COUNTY COUNCIL. Just as she had said.

"Why have you sealed my kitchen and closed my restaurant?" I asked her.

"I didn't know we had," she said. "Where, exactly, is this restaurant?"

"On Ashley Road, near the Cheveley crossroads," I said. "It's called the Hay Net." She nodded slightly, obviously recognizing the name. "It is in Cambridgeshire, I assure you. I've just come from there. The kitchen has been padlocked, and I have been told that I would be breaking the law to go in."

"Oh," she said.

"Two men said they were acting for the Food Standards Agency."

"How odd," she said. "Enforcement is normally the responsibility of the local authority. That's me. Unless, of course, the incident is termed *serious*."

"How serious is *serious*?" I asked.

"If it involves *E. coli* or salmonella"—she paused slightly—"or botulism or typhus, that sort of thing. Or if someone dies as a result."

"The men said that someone has died," I said.

"Oh," she said again. "I haven't heard. Perhaps the police, or the hospital, contacted the Food Standards Agency directly. I'm surprised they managed to get through on a Saturday. The decision must have been made somewhere. Sorry about that."

"Not your fault," I echoed.

She pursed her lips together in a smile. "I had better go and find out what's happening. My cell phone battery is dead, and it's amazing how much we all now rely on the damn things. I'm lost without it."

She turned to go but then turned back.

"I asked the racetrack office about your kitchen tent last night," she said. "You were right. It's now full of beer crates. Are you still planning to do a lunch service for Miss America up there?" She nodded her head towards the grandstand.

"Is that an official inquiry?" I asked.

"Umm." She pursed her lips again. "Perhaps I don't want to know. Forget I asked."

I smiled. "Asked what?"

"I'll get back to you later if and when I find out what's going on."

"Fine," I said. "Can you let me know who it is that's died as soon as you find out?" I gave her my cell number. "I'll be here until about six-thirty. After that, I'll be asleep."

TWO OF MY regular staff had arrived to help Carl and me with the lunch and neither of them had been ill overnight. Both had eaten the vegetarian pasta bake on the previous evening, so, by process of elimination, the chicken became the prime suspect.

For more than an hour, they worked in the glass-fronted boxes while Carl and I set to work in the tiny kitchen across the passageway preparing the pies for the oven. Carl rolled out the pastry while I filled and covered the individual pie dishes. Our Cambridge greengrocer had successfully replaced the asparagus and the new potatoes, both of which were held captive in the restaurant's cold-room. The potatoes now sat ready in saucepans on the stove, and I began to relax. But tiredness creeps up on those who relax.

I left Carl to finish the pies while I went to check on the others.

They had successfully retracted the divider wall between the two boxes, making a single room about twenty feet square. Four five-foot-diameter tables and forty gold ladderback chairs had been waiting for us in the boxes, delivered by a rental company contacted by the racetrack, and they had been arranged to allow for easy access around them for serving.

I had originally planned for five staff, other than me and Carl, to work the event, one waiter for each pair of tables, two to provide the drink and wine service and one to help out in the kitchen, but the other three had failed to show. The idea was for one waiter to provide drinks or coffee to the guests as they arrived while the other helped with steaming the asparagus and heating the rolls. In the end, the rolls had been caught by the padlocks, so we had bought some French loaves at the local supermarket in their place. If MaryLou objected to this continental influence, that was too bad.

Only half my dining-room manpower had actually turned up, so they, and I, were still busy setting up the tables when the first of the lunch guests was due to arrive. We had nearly made it, with only the wineglasses on a couple of the tables still to be put out.

MaryLou had just stood back and watched us as we worked.

We had laid starched white tablecloths over the stained and chipped plywood tables, and it had instantly improved the look of the room. I liked using Stress-Free Catering, since their equipment was of a higher quality than other catering services. Kings-pattern cutlery and decent water glasses and wineglasses soon transformed the bare tables into settings fit maybe not for a king but certainly fit for tractor and harvester manufacturers from across the pond.

Carl had even managed to rescue the pink-and-white carnation table centerpieces from the cold-room before it was sealed, and they, together with the alternating pink and white napkins, gave the final touch to the room.

I stood back and admired our handiwork. I was sure the guests would be impressed. Even MaryLou seemed to be pleased. She smiled. "Just in time," she said as she placed seating name cards around the tables.

I looked at my watch. Twenty-five to twelve. Only the daylight outside told me it was a.m. and not p.m. My body clock had stopped hours ago and needed rewinding with a decent sleep before it would start again.

"No problem," I said.

I felt clammy all over and longed to put my head down on a nice feather pillow. Instead, I retreated to the kitchen and doused my aching crown under cold water at the sink. I hoped that Angela Milne couldn't see me through the window. The Food Standards Agency wouldn't approve of a chef wetting his hair under the kitchen tap. I emerged slightly more refreshed, but, overall, it wasn't a great improvement. I yawned loudly, with my mouth wide-open, leaned on the sink and looked out across the parade ring towards the town center.

Newmarket on 2000 Guineas day. The town was abuzz with excitement for the first Classic race of the year, with every hotel room for miles occupied with the hopeful and the expectant.

Newmarket was nicknamed "Headquarters" by racing people, although it had long since relinquished its role as the official power base of the Sport of Kings. The Jockey Club headquarters had been established at Newmarket in the 1750s to regulate the already-thriving local racing scene, and it had soon expanded its authority over all Thoroughbred racing in the land. Indeed, the Jockey Club had wielded such power that in October 1791 the Prince Regent, the future King George IV, was investigated for "irregularities in the running of his horse Escape." The irregularities in question were that the horse pulled up on one day at short odds only to win the next day at long. The prince sold his horses and his stud and never returned to Newmarket, and it is much rumored that he was, in fact, privately "warned off" by the stewards, although officially he was just "censured."

Nowadays, the Jockey Club was still a huge influence in Newmarket itself as it owned not only the two racetracks, but also some twenty-four hundred acres of training paddocks around the town. But the role it once had in running and controlling British racing has faded away to almost nothing with the establishment first of the British Horseracing Board and then, more recently, the creation of the British Horseracing Authority, which has taken over the inquiries and disciplinary matters within the sport. The Jockey Club has returned to what it was at its original meetings in a London tavern, a social gathering for like-minded individuals who enjoy their racing. That is, of course, unless they happened to be professional jockeys. There are no actual jockeys in the Jockey Club. In the eyes of the members, jockeys are servants and have no place socializing among their betters.

Carl roused me from my daydreaming.

"We can only get half the pies in these ovens," he said, "so we're borrowing the space in the ovens down the passage. They're serving a cold buffet, so there's plenty of room."

"Great," I said. I was so tired I hadn't even realized there was a problem. "What time do they go in?" I tried hard to do the mental arithmetic. First race at five past two, so sit down to lunch at half past twelve. Each pie takes thirty-five minutes. If there are forty pies, minus the five people who aren't coming, that makes . . . forty minus five pies . . . if one pie takes thirty-five minutes for the filling to cook and the pastry to go golden brown, how long does it take forty minus five pies . . . ? The cogs in my brain turned ever so slowly and then ground to a halt. If five men can build five houses in five months, how long will it take six men to build six houses? Did I care? I was beginning to think that the pies should have gone into the ovens the day before yesterday, when Carl saved me.

"Twelve-fifteen sharp," he said. "Sit-down time is twelve-thirty, pies on the table at one o'clock."

"Great," I said again. And my head on the pillow by one-thirty. Fat chance.

"And potatoes on in five minutes," Carl said. "All under control."

I looked at my watch. It took me quite a time to register where the hands were pointing. Ten to twelve. What is wrong with me? I thought. I'd stayed awake for longer than this before. My stomach rumbled to remind me that nothing had been put in it for a while. I wasn't sure that it was such a good idea to eat at all, in case it came up again in a replay of the night before, and I wasn't at all keen on that. But perhaps hunger was contributing to my lethargy.

I tried a dry piece of French bread. It seemed to provoke no immediate reaction from my guts, so I had another, larger piece. The rumblings abated.

The guests would be arriving in the boxes and I was hardly dressed to greet them, so I went down to my Golf, stood between the cars and changed into my work clothes, a pair of black-and-white, large-check trousers and a starched white cotton smock. The top had been loosely modeled on a hussar's tunic, with two rows of buttons in a sort of open V down the front. MAX MORETON was embroidered in red on the left breast, below a representation of a Michelin star. I had discovered that to look like a chef was half the battle in convincing customers and critics alike that I really did care about the food they ate and that I wasn't simply trying to fleece them.

I made my way back up to the boxes only to find Mary-Lou stomping around outside the elevator, looking for me.

"Ah, there you are," she said in a tone that implied I should have been there long before. "You must come and meet Mr. Schumann. He's our company chairman."

She almost dragged me by the arm down the corridor to the boxes, which now had large notices stuck to the doors: DELAFIELD INDUSTRIES, INC. — MAIN EVENT SPONSOR.

There were about twenty people already there, some standing around the tables while others had made their way out onto the balcony outside to enjoy the watery May sunshine and the magnificent view down the racetrack.

My role was as guest chef for the event rather than just the caterer. The usual racetrack hospitality company and I had a fine working relationship that was beneficial to both parties. They had no objection to me having "special" access to the track, and I would try to help them out if they were short staffed or stretched with a big function. Their managing director, Suzanne Miller, was a frequent client at the Hay Net, and she always claimed that it was a benefit for her company to have an association with, as she put it, "a local gourmet restaurant." The arrangement had worked well for more than five years, but time would tell whether it would survive Suzanne's approaching retirement. To be honest, I wouldn't mind if it didn't. The growing success of the Hay Net meant that I was finding it increasingly difficult to devote the time and energy needed to my track events, and I was not good at saying no to long-standing clients. If the new boss of the caterers didn't want me on his patch, then I could always blame him to get me off the hook.

MaryLou guided me across the room to the door to the balcony and then hovered next to a tall, broad-shouldered man of about sixty wearing a charcoal gray suit, white shirt and a bright pink-and-blue striped tie. He was deep in conversation with a younger woman who was much shorter than he. He leaned over her, supporting himself on the doorframe, and spoke quietly in her ear. I couldn't hear what was being said, but he certainly was amused by it, and he stood up, laughing. She smiled at him, but I had the impression that she didn't quite share in his pleasure.

He turned to MaryLou with what I thought was a degree of irritation.

"Mr. Schumann," said MaryLou in her clipped manner, "can I introduce Mr. Max Moreton, our chef for today."

He looked at me in my chef's garb, and I had the feeling that he thought I should be back in the kitchen and out of sight of his guests.

MaryLou, it appeared, must have read the same thing in his expression.

"Mr. Moreton," she went on, "is a chef of some reputation, and has often been seen on TV."

Some reputation indeed, I thought: the mass poisoner of Newmarket Town.

Mr. Schumann didn't seem impressed.

MaryLou hadn't finished. "We are very lucky to have Mr. Moreton cooking for us today," she said. "He is much in demand."

This wasn't altogether true, but I wasn't going to correct her.

Mr. Schumann reluctantly stretched out a hand. "Glad you could help," he said. "Young MaryLou here usually gets her man." He spoke with more of a drawl than his marketing executive, but his voice lacked warmth and sincerity.

I shook the offered hand, and we looked each other directly in the eyes. I found him somewhat intimidating and decided that retreat to my rightful place would be a wise option. However, I was prevented from going by a hand on my arm from the lady to my left.

"Max," she said. "How lovely. Are you cooking for us today?"

Elizabeth Jennings was a regular customer at the Hay Net along with her husband, Neil, who was one of the most successful trainers in town. Elizabeth herself was a tireless worker for charity and organizer of great dinner parties, some of which I had attended and others that I had cooked.

"Rolf," she said to Mr. Schumann, "you are so clever to have got Max to cook for you today. He's the absolute best chef in England."

Good old Mrs. Jennings, I thought.

"I wouldn't say that," I said, although I might privately think it.

"Only the best for you, my dear," said Mr. Schumann, turning on the charm and laying a hand on the sleeve of her blue-and-yellow floral dress.

She smiled at him. "Oh, Rolf, you are such a tease."

Rolf decided that he was needed by someone else outside on the balcony and, with a slight nod to me and an "Excuse me" to Elizabeth, he moved away.

"Is Neil here with you?" I asked her.

"No," Elizabeth said. "He should have been, but he wasn't too well last night. Something he ate, I expect. Probably the ham he had for lunch. I told him that it was past its sell-by date, but he ate it anyway. He always says that those dates are just to make you throw away perfectly good food all the time and get you to buy new stuff. Maybe now he'll change his mind."

"What did he have for dinner?" I asked as innocently as possible.

"We went to that big do here last night, you know. I saw you," she said. "Now, what did we have? You should know. I always forget what we eat at these things." She stopped and laughed. "Sorry, I suppose I shouldn't say that to a chef."

"Most people had chicken," I said.

"That's right. We did. And it was very good. And I loved the crème brûlée."

"So you definitely had the chicken?" I asked. "Not the vegetarian pasta?"

"Of course I had the chicken," she said. "Never have that vegetarian stuff. Vegetables should accompany meat, I say, not replace it. I always have a steak at your place, don't I?"

That's true, I thought. Maybe the chicken was not guilty after all. She was beginning to look puzzled at my questions. Time for me to depart to the kitchen.

"Sorry, Elizabeth, I must dash or you'll get no lunch."

THE LUNCH SERVICE went well in spite of the poor state of the chef. Louisa, one of my staff, came into the kitchen carrying empty plates and said how pleased MaryLou was with the steak-and-kidney pies. Apparently, everyone had loved them.

I had learned early on from Marguerite, my mother's cousin's fiery cook, that the real trick to cooking any meat was to not cook away the taste and texture. "What makes roast beef roast beef is not only its smell and its taste but its appearance and the feel of it on your tongue," she had said. "Food involves all the senses," she maintained, and she reveled in the chance to make food noisy to prove her point: sizzling steaks, and even whistling toads in the hole. "If you want to add flavor," she would say, "get it into the meat before you cook it, so that the natural taste of the meat still comes through."

And so I had. The pie filling had been well marinated in my special concoction of spices and herbs, with a little citrus fruit to add zest. Add a good dose or two of Scotch whisky and allow to soak for forty-eight hours or so to absorb the liquid and the flavors. Then cook slowly, at first in a moderate oven, before briefly placing it in a hot one to golden the pastry, and the results were delicious. Piece of cake—or pie.

Carl and I sat on stools in the kitchen and dozed. The summer puddings had been served, with whipped cream and the strawberry garnish, and, thankfully, the coffee was the regular caterer's responsibility. I leaned on the countertop, rested my weary head on my arms and went to sleep.

"CHEF. CHEF. Mr. Moreton," said a female voice. Someone shook my shoulder.

"Mr. Moreton," said the voice again. "Wake up, Chef."

I raised my head and opened an eye. It was Louisa.

"They want you in the dining room," she said.

"OK," I said with a sigh, "I'm coming."

I dragged myself up, pulled my fingers through my hair to straighten it and went across the corridor.

They applauded. I smiled. Being a chef was being a showman, an entertainer. Taking one's bow was what made it worthwhile. The heat of the kitchen is forgotten in the glow of appreciation from others.

Even Rolf Schumann smiled broadly. Elizabeth Jennings sat on his right and positively beamed. Reflected glory, I thought rather disingenuously. She stroked his arm and whispered in his ear in a manner that made me think that it was she who was the tease, not he.

Having milked the applause for all I could, I retreated to the kitchen to find Carl had stirred and was starting to clear up and load the wire cages for returning to Stress-Free. I really didn't feel like I had the energy to help him, so I went back across the corridor to find myself some strong coffee.

The lunch party was breaking up, with some of the guests going to place their wagers on the first race, which was due off any minute. Many decided to sit out the race at the tables, drinking their coffee and watching the action on the television sets placed high in each corner of the room. Others drifted out onto the balcony to watch it live.

Louisa poured me some coffee, and I stood, drinking the hot black liquid, and hoped that it would wake me up a bit.

MaryLou came over. "That food sure was terrific," she said.

"Thanks," I said. "Glad you enjoyed it."

"Certainly did," she said. "Mr. Schumann really liked it too."

I could tell that his approval was the most important thing. Mr. Schumann clearly intimidated her too. A successful lunch might mean her job was safe for a while longer.

The first race was over, and the guests drifted back from the balcony and many sat down again at the tables. I realized it would be some time before we could clear everything away and have a decent rest. Louisa and Robert, my other waiter, were busy refilling coffee cups and passing out chocolate mints. Everyone was in good humor and enjoying themselves.

THE 2OOO GUINEAS was the third race on the card, due off at three-fifteen. The excitement of the afternoon built towards the big event, with jazz bands and street entertainers helping to raise the pulse of the crowd. I could have done with a jazz band in the kitchen just to keep me awake.

As the time of the big race arrived, I went back to the boxes where Louisa and Robert were clearing the tables. Finally, all the guests had left their chairs and were crowding onto the balcony, or standing inside up against the windows, trying to get a good view of the horses as they approached along Newmarket's famous Rowley straight mile.

I picked up some dirty coffee cups and glanced up at the television set on the wall. The horses were running down into the dip, and the jockeys were jostling for position, ready for their final effort up the rise to the finish. So tired was I that I decided not to stay and watch. I could always see it later on the replay. I turned to take the cups out to the kitchen.

That decision unquestionably saved my life.

# 3

The bomb went off while I was crossing the corridor. I didn't understand immediately what had happened. There was a great blast of heat on my neck, and it felt like someone had hit me in the back with a sledgehammer.

I crashed into the kitchen door upright and fell, half in and half out of the room.

I still couldn't understand what was going on. Everything seemed to be in silence. I couldn't hear. I tried to speak, but I couldn't hear myself either. I shouted. Nothing. All I could hear was a high-pitched hissing that seemed to be in my head; it had no direction, and was unchanged when I turned my head from side to side.

I looked down at my hands, and they seemed to be all right. I moved them. No problem. I clapped. I could feel my hands coming together, but I couldn't hear the sound. It was very frightening.

My left knee hurt. I looked down and noticed that my black-and-white checked trousers had been torn where they had hit the doorframe. The white checks were turning red

with my blood. What's black and white and red all over . . . ?
My brain was drifting.

When I felt with my hands, my knee appeared to be in the
right place, and I could move my foot without any increase
in pain. It seemed that the blood was from superficial damage only.

My hearing came back with a rush, and suddenly there
was a mass of sound. Someone close by was screaming. A
female, high-pitched scream that went on and on, breaking
only occasionally for a moment as the screamer drew a
breath. An alarm bell was ringing incessantly somewhere
down the corridor, and there were shouts from some male
voices, mostly pleading for help.

I lay back, and rested my head on the floor. It seemed that
I was like that for ages, but, I suppose, it was only for a
minute or two at most. The screaming went on; otherwise, I
might have gone to sleep.

I became aware that I wasn't very comfortable. As well as
the pain in my left knee, my right leg was aching. I was lying
on my foot, which was tangled up underneath my rear end. I
straightened the leg and was rewarded with pins and needles.
That's a good sign, I thought.

I looked up and could see daylight between the walls and
the ceiling where a large crack had opened up. That was not
such a good sign. Water was pouring through the crack, I
thought lazily, probably from some burst pipe above. It was
running down the wall and spreading across the concrete
floor towards me. I turned my head and watched it approach.

I decided that, lovely as it was to lie there and let the
world get on without me, I didn't fancy lying in a puddle.
The floor was cold enough without being wet as well. Reluctantly, I rolled over and drew my knees up under me so that
I was kneeling. Not a good idea, I thought. My left knee
complained bitterly, and the calf muscle below it began to
cramp. I pulled myself up to a standing position using the
doorframe and surveyed the kitchen.

Not much seemed to have changed, except everything
was covered in a fine white dust that also still hung in the air.

I was wondering what had happened to Carl when he appeared next to me.

"Bloody hell," he said, "what happened?"

"Don't know," I replied. "Where were you?"

"Having a pee in the gents'." He pointed down the corridor. "Nearly shit myself when that bang went off."

I clung on to the kitchen door and felt unwell. I didn't particularly relish going to see what had become of my other two staff and the guests in the boxes, but I knew I must. I couldn't just stand here all day while others might need help. The screaming had lessened to a whimper, as I gingerly made my way across the corridor and looked in.

I hadn't expected there to be so much blood.

Bright, fresh, scarlet red blood. Masses of the stuff. It was not only on the floor but on the walls, and there were even great splashes of it on the ceiling. The tables had been thrown up against the back wall by the explosion, and I had to pick my way over broken chairs to get through the door and into the room that I had so recently vacated with ease.

When I had been a child, my father had regularly complained that my bedroom looked like a bomb had gone off in it. Like every other little boy, I had tended to dump all my stuff on the floor and happily had lived around it.

However, my bedroom had never looked like the inside of the two glass-fronted boxes at Newmarket that day. Not that the boxes had remained glass-fronted. The glass in the windows and doors had now completely vanished, and, along with it, large chunks of the balconies and about a third of the end wall from the side of box number 1.

I thought that if the blast could do such damage to concrete and steel, the occupants must have stood no chance.

*Carnage* was not too strong a word for the scene.

There had been thirty-three guests at lunch, two others having unexpectedly failed to appear, much to MaryLou's frustration and displeasure. Then there were my two staff. So there must have been at least thirty-five people either in that room or on the balconies when the bomb exploded, not counting any people who may have been invited in to watch the race after lunch.

Most of them seemed to have disappeared altogether.

A whimper to my left had me scampering under the up-turned tables to find the source.

MaryLou Fordham lay on her back close to the rear wall. I could only see her from the waist up, since she was half covered with a torn and rapidly reddening tablecloth. The blood that was soaking into the white starched cotton was an exact color match with her bright scarlet chiffon blouse that had fared rather badly and now hung as a tattered mass around her neck.

I knelt down beside her on my right knee and touched her forehead. Her eyes swiveled round in my direction. Big, wide, frightened brown eyes in a deathly pale face, a face cut and bleeding from numerous shards of flying glass.

"Help will be on the way," I said to her, somewhat inadequately given the circumstances. "Just hang on."

There was a lot of blood below her waist, so I lifted the tablecloth a little to see what damage had been done. It was not easy to see. There was not much light under the blood-soaked cloth, and there was a tangle of broken chairs and tables in the way. I shuffled down to get a better look and only then did my confused brain take in the true horror. Both of MaryLou's lovely legs were gone. Blown away.

Oh my God, what do I do now?

I stupidly looked around me, as if I could find her missing legs and snap them back into place. Only then did I see the other victims. Those who had lost not only their legs and feet but arms and hands too, and their lives. I began to shake. I simply didn't know what to do.

Suddenly, the room filled with voices and bustling people in black-and-yellow coats and big yellow helmets. The fire brigade had arrived. None too soon, I thought. I started to cry. It was unlike me to cry. My father had been one of the old school who believed that men shouldn't. "Stop blubbing," he would say to me when I was about ten. "Grow up, boy. Be a man. Men don't cry." And so I had been taught. I hadn't cried when my father had been killed by the brick truck. I hadn't even cried at his funeral. I knew that he wouldn't have wanted me to.

But now the shock, the tiredness, the feeling of inadequacy and the relief that the cavalry had arrived was just too much, and so the tears streamed down my face.

"Come on, sir," said one of the firemen into my ear as he held my shoulders, "let's get you out of here. Are you in any pain?"

My tongue felt enormous in my mouth, stifling me. "No," I croaked. "Well, my knee hurts a bit. But I'm fine . . . But she . . ." I pointed at MaryLou, unable to say anything further.

"Don't worry, sir," he said to me, "we'll look after her."

He helped me to my feet and turned my shoulders away. My gaze remained on where MaryLou's legs should have been until the fireman turned me so far that my head just had to follow. He held me firmly and pushed me towards the door, where a second fireman put a bright red blanket over my shoulders and led me out. I wondered if they used red blankets so that the blood didn't show.

The fireman guided me down the corridor towards the stairwell. I looked into the kitchen as we passed by. Carl was leaning over the sink, throwing up. I knew how he felt.

A man in a green jacket with DOCTOR written large across the back pushed past me. "Is he all right?" he asked my escort.

"Seems so," was the reply.

I wanted to say that no, I wasn't all right. I wanted to tell him that I had glimpsed an image of hell and that it would surely live with me forever. I wanted to shout out that I was far from all right and that I might never be all right again.

Instead, I allowed myself to be led to the stairwell, where I obeyed instructions to go down. I was assured that others would be waiting at the bottom to help me. But can they erase the memory? Can they give me back my innocence? Can they prevent the nightmares?

HAVING BEEN INSTRUCTED by the fireman, I obediently descended to ground level and, as promised, was met by helping hands and soothing voices. A brief assessment of my physical injuries left me, still wrapped in my red blanket, sitting on a row of white plastic chairs for what seemed like a very, very long time. Several times a young man in a bright green outfit with PARAMEDIC emblazoned in white letters across his shoulders came over to ask if I was OK. He said that they were sorry about the delay, but there were others in greater need. I nodded. I knew. I could still see them in my mind's eye.

"I'm fine," I said. But I didn't really mean it.

Ambulances came and went, their sirens wailing, and a line of black body bags, laid out close to the back of the grandstand, grew longer as the afternoon sunlight slowly faded towards evening.

I was finally taken to the hospital about seven o'clock. After so long sitting in the plastic chair, I was unable to stand properly on my left leg since my knee had swollen up and stiffened badly. My young paramedic friend helped me to an ambulance that then sedately drove off with no siren or flashing lights. It was as if the urgency of the crisis was passed. Those seriously injured and dying had been whisked away at speed. Those already dead were beyond help. We, the almost-walking wounded, could now be cared for with composure and calm.

The ambulance took me all the way to Bedford, as the hospitals more local to Newmarket had been overwhelmed by the seriously injured. At Bedford, an X-ray revealed no fractures in my swollen left knee. A doctor speculated that the collision with the door may have caused a temporary dislocation of my patella—my kneecap—which had resulted in some internal bleeding. A hematoma had formed in the joint, causing both the swelling and the pain. The blood loss that had stained my trousers was found to be due to a tear of the soft tissue of my lower thigh, also probably a consequence of the collision with the door. Although the flow had all but stopped, the doctor insisted on applying some adhesive strips to close the edges of the wound, which he then covered with a large white rectangular bandage. No such care was afforded to my trousers, which were unceremoniously cut off short on the left side. The hospital provided me with a tight blue rubberized sleeve for my knee to both provide support for the joint and to apply pressure to the hematoma to reduce the bruising. They also thoughtfully equipped me with a long white, closely woven cotton sock to wear on my left foot to reduce swelling in the lower leg and a supply of large white painkillers. I would be fine, they said, after a few days' rest. Fine in body, I thought, although it would take longer to heal the emotional injury.

A taxi was ordered to take me home. So I sat waiting in the hospital reception, somewhat embarrassed at having caused such a fuss and feeling guilty that I had escaped so lightly while others had not. I was utterly drained. I thought about Robert and Louisa, my staff. Had they survived? What should I do to find out? Who should I ask?

"Taxi for Mr. Moreton," said a voice, bringing me back to the present.

"That's me," I replied.

I realized I had no money in my pockets.

"That's all right, the National Health Service is paying," said the driver. "But they don't tip," he added. He's going to be unlucky, I thought, if he thinks he's going to get a tip from me.

He looked me up and down. I must have been quite a sight. I still wore my chef's tunic, but my black-and-white checked trousers now had one leg long and one short, with a blue knee brace and white stocking below.

"Are you some sort of clown?" asked the driver.

"No," I said, "I'm a chef."

He lost interest.

"Where to?" he asked.

"Newmarket."

THE TAXI ARRIVED at my cottage on the southern edge of Newmarket at about eleven o'clock. I had slept the whole way from Bedford Hospital, and the driver had real difficulty waking me up to get me out of the vehicle. Eventually, I was roused sufficiently for him to help me hop across the small stretch of grass between the road and my front door.

"Will you be OK?" he asked as I put the key in the lock.

"Fine," I said, and he drove away.

I hopped into the kitchen and took a couple of the painkillers with some water from the sink tap. The stairs were too much, I decided, so I lay down on the sofa in my tiny sitting room and went eagerly back to my slumbers.

I was lying on a hospital gurney that was moving slowly along a gray-colored, windowless corridor. I could see the ceiling lights passing overhead. They were bright rectangular panels set into the gray ceiling. The corridor seemed to go on forever, and the lights were all the same one after the other, one after the other. I looked up and back to see that I was being pushed by a lady in a red chiffon blouse with a mass of curly hair bouncing on her shoulders. It was Mary-Lou Fordham, and she was smiling at me. I looked down at her lovely legs, but she didn't have any legs and seemed to be floating across the gray floor. I sat up with a jerk and looked at my own legs. The bedding was flat where my legs should have been, and there was blood, lots of blood, bright red pools of blood. I screamed and rolled off the gurney. I was falling, falling, falling . . .

I woke up with a start, my heart pounding, my face cold, clammy, sweaty. So vivid had been the dream that I had to feel with my hands to be sure that my legs were actually there. I lay in the dark, breathing hard, while my pulse returned to something near normal.

It was the first of a repeating pattern.

Two disturbed nights in a row left me totally exhausted.


I SPENT MOST of Sunday morning lying down, first on the sofa and then on the floor, which was more comfortable. I watched the twenty-four-hour news channels to find out more about what was being dubbed "Terror at the Guineas." There had been dozens of television cameras covering the races, but only one had, peripherally, captured the scene on the balcony Head On Grandstand box numbers 1 and 2 at the moment the bomb went off. The fleeting footage was played over and over again with every news bulletin. It showed a bright flash, with bits of glass, steel and concrete being flung outwards, along with bodies. Many of the Delafield Industries guests had been literally blown from the balcony, falling, rag doll like, onto the flat roof below and then onto the unsuspecting racegoers in the viewing areas below that. They, apparently, had been the lucky ones, injured but alive. It had been those inside the rooms, like MaryLou, who had suffered the worst.

I thought again about Robert and Louisa. I knew I should call someone to ask what had happened to them. I also knew that I didn't want to make the call because I was afraid of the answer. I went on lying on the floor.

I discovered from the television that while I had been sitting obediently on my white plastic chair wrapped in my red blanket, there had been much activity at the racetrack. The police had moved in, en masse, and had taken the names and addresses of all the thousands in the crowd. I had somehow been missed.

The racing had been abandoned and the 2000 Guineas had been declared void, as half the horses had stopped during the final furlong while others had been driven hard for the line, their jockeys concentrating so intently on the race that they were unaware of the explosion until they pulled up after the finish. The television pictures clearly showed how one young rider's joy at winning his first Classic had quickly turned to despair as realization struck that he had won a race that wouldn't be.

Speculation was rife as to who had caused such murder and why.

One television channel had a reporter situated near the Devil's Dyke, with the racetrack clearly visible in the background, the front of boxes 1 and 2 now covered by a large blue tarpaulin. He claimed that a police source had indicated to him that the bomb may have struck the wrong target. The track manager, who was unavailable for comment due to ill health, had apparently confirmed to police that the occupants of box number 1 had been switched at the last minute. The reporter, who I thought was rather inappropriately dressed in an open-neck striped shirt with no jacket, went on to speculate that the real targets had been an Arab prince and his entourage who originally had been expected to be in box 1. The Middle East conflict has once again been brought to our shores, the reporter stated with confidence.

I wondered if MaryLou would feel better in the knowledge that she had lost her legs by mistake. I doubted it.

I called my mother, in case she was worrying about me.

She wasn't.

"Hello, darling," she trilled down the wire. "What an awful thing to have happened."

"I was there," I said.

"What, at the races?"

"No, I mean right there when the bomb exploded."

"Really. How exciting," she said. She didn't seem the least bit concerned that I might have been killed.

"I am very lucky to be alive," I said, hoping for some compassionate words from my parent.

"Of course you are, dear."

Since my father died, my mother had become somewhat blasé about death. I think she really believed that whether one lived or died was preordained and out of one's control. Recently, I thought that the collision with the brick truck had been, in my mother's eyes, a neat way out of what was becoming a loveless marriage. Some time after his death, I had discovered that he had been having several minor affairs. Perhaps my mother believed that the accident was some sort of divine retribution.

"Well," I said, "I thought I would let you know that I was OK."

"Thank you, dear," she said.

She didn't ask me what had happened, and I decided not to share the horror. She enjoyed her quiet world of coffee mornings, church flower arranging and outings to visit well-tended gardens. Missing limbs and mutilated torsos didn't have a place.

"Speak to you soon, Mum," I said.

"Lovely, darling," she said. "Bye." She hung up.

We had never been very close.

As a child, it had always been to my father that I had gone

for advice and affection. We had laughed together at my mother's little foibles and joked about her political naivety. We had smiled and rolled our eyes when she had committed another faux pas, an all-too-regular occurrence.

I may not have actually cried when my father died, but I was devastated nevertheless. I worshipped him as my hero, and the loss was almost too much to bear. I remember clearly the feeling of despair when, a few weeks after his death, I could no longer smell him in the house. I had come home from boarding school for the weekend, and, suddenly, he wasn't there anymore. The lack of his smell brought his demise into sharp reality—he wasn't just out getting a newspaper, he was gone forever. I had rushed upstairs to his dressing room to smell his clothes. I had opened his wardrobes and drawers, and I had held his favorite sweaters to my nose. But he had gone. I had sat on the floor in that room for a very long time, just staring into space, totally bereft but unable to shed the tears, unable to properly grieve for his passing. Even now, I ached to be able to tell him about my life and my job, my joys and my sadnesses. I cursed him out loud for being dead and not being around when I needed him. I longed for him to be there to talk to, to soothe my hurting knee, to ease my troubled brain and to take away the horrors in my memory. But, still, I couldn't cry for him.

THE ONE O'CLOCK news program started on the television, and I realized that I was hungry. Apart from a couple of pieces of French bread at the racetrack and a chocolate bar at the hospital, I hadn't eaten since Friday night, and that meal hadn't got past my stomach. Now that I thought about it, hunger was a nagging pain in my abdomen. It was one pain that I could do something about.

I limped gingerly into the kitchen and made myself a Spanish omelette. Food is often said to be a great comforter; indeed, most people under stress eat sugary foods like chocolate not only because it gives them energy but because it makes them feel better. I had done just the same at Bedford

Hospital. However, for me, food gave me comfort when I cooked it.

I took some spring onions from my vegetable rack, diced them into small rounds, then fried them in a pan with a little extra-virgin olive oil. I found some cooked new potatoes hiding in the rear recesses of my fridge, so I sliced and added them to the onions with a splash of soy sauce to season and flavor. Three eggs, I thought, and broke them one-handed into a glass bowl. I really loved to cook, and I felt much better, in both mind and body, long before I sat down on my sofa to complete the experience by actually eating my creation.

Carl called sometime during the afternoon.

"Thank God you're there," he said.

"Been here all night," I said.

"Sorry, should have called you earlier."

"It's all right," I said. "I didn't call you either." I knew why. No news was better news than we feared.

"What happened to you?" he asked.

"Hurt my knee," I said. "I was taken to Bedford Hospital, and then home by taxi late last night. And you?"

"I'm fine," he said. "I helped people to get down at the far end of the stand. Police took my name and address, then they sent me home."

"Did you see Louisa or Robert?" I dreaded the answer.

"I haven't seen either of them," he said, "but Robert called me this morning. He's all right, although quite badly shaken up. He was asking if I knew what had happened to Louisa."

"Wasn't Robert in the box when the bomb went off?"

"He said that the bomb was definitely in box 1, and he was behind the folded back dividing wall in box 2 when it exploded and that protected him. But it seems to have left him somewhat deaf. I had to shout down the telephone."

I knew how he felt.

"How about Louisa?" I asked.

"No idea," said Carl. "I tried the emergency number the police gave out, but it's permanently busy."

"Any news on anyone else?" I asked.

"Nothing, except what's on the TV. How about you? Heard anything?"

"No, nothing. I saw the American woman organizer, you know, MaryLou Fordham, just after the bomb went off." I could see the image in my head. "She'd lost her legs."

"Oh God."

"I felt so bloody helpless," I said.

"Was she still alive?" he asked.

"When I saw her she was, but I don't know if they got her out. She had lost so much blood. I was finally led away by a fireman, who told me to go down."

There was a pause, as if both of us were reliving the events at the racetrack.

"What shall we do about the restaurant?" Carl asked at length.

"I haven't even thought about it," I said. "I suppose the kitchen's still sealed. I'll start sorting it out tomorrow. I'm too tired now."

"Yeah, me too. Didn't get much sleep last night. Call me in the morning."

"OK," I said. "Call me tonight if you hear anything."

"Will do," he said, and hung up.

I spent the afternoon in an armchair with my left leg supported by a cushion on the coffee table. I seemed unable to turn the television away from the news channels, so I watched the same not-new news repeated time and time again. The Arab prince theory gained more credence throughout the day, mostly, it appeared to me, because there was nothing new to report and they had to fill the time somehow. Middle East experts were wheeled in to the studio to make endless, meaningless comments about a speculative theory about which they had no facts or evidence. It occurred to me that the TV networks were simply allowing several of these so-called "experts" the opportunity to postulate their own extremist positions, something that would do nothing to calm the turmoil that existed in their lands. Violent death and destruction were clearly nothing out of the ordinary to many of them, and some even appeared to justify the carnage, saying that the prince may have been seen as a legitimate target by rebel forces in his homeland, and the fact that innocents had died by mistake was merely unfortunate . . . you know, casualties of war and all that. It all made me very angry, but I still couldn't switch it off, just in case I missed some new item.

At some point around five o'clock, I drifted off to sleep.

I woke suddenly with the now-familiar thumping heart and clammy face. Another encounter with the hospital gurney, the windowless corridor, the legless MaryLou and the blood.

Oh God, I said to myself, not another night of this.

But, indeed, it was.

# 4

MaryLou didn't make it.

On Monday morning, *The Times* was delivered, as usual, to my cottage door at seven o'clock. Mary-Lou's name was clearly there, in black and white, along with six of the others known to have died. The remaining victims had yet to be identified or their next of kin informed. The current police estimate was that fifteen people had perished in the bombing, but they still weren't absolutely sure. They were still trying to piece together the bodies.

I was amazed that anyone near those boxes could have survived, but apparently half of them had, although, according to the paper, many of the survivors had been badly injured and more deaths were expected.

As for me, my knee was definitely getting better, and I had managed to hop upstairs to bed on Sunday evening, not that being more comfortable had been any more restful for my unconscious brain. I was beginning to expect the return of the windowless corridor like the proverbial bad penny. Perhaps now the sure knowledge that MaryLou was dead would get through to wherever gray-matter dreams originate.

I sat on my sofa in my dressing gown and read the reports through from start to finish. They ran to six pages, but the information contained in them was sketchy and thin. The police had obviously not been willing to give journalists too many hard facts until they themselves were sure of the details. Sources close to the police were quoted without names, a sure sign of a reporter fishing in the dark for information.

I made myself a coffee and flicked on the BBC breakfast news. More names had been released overnight by the police, and a press conference was expected at any time. We were assured that it would be covered in full, but, meantime, "here is the sports news."

Somehow, the weekend's sports results seemed somewhat inappropriate, sandwiched as they were between graphic reports of death and maiming at Newmarket racetrack. Karl Marx stated in 1844 that religion was the opium of the people, but nowadays sport in general, and soccer in particular, had taken over that mantle. And so I waited through an analysis of how City had defeated United and Rovers had trounced Albion, before a return to more serious matters. Apparently, a minute's silence had been observed before each of Sunday's games. This was not unexpected. A minute's silence might be observed at a soccer match over the death of the manager's dog. In fact, any excuse will be good enough for a bit of head bowing around the center circle.

Did people really care about unknown victims? I suppose they cared that it was not them or their families who had been blown up. It is difficult to care about people one hasn't met and never knew. Outrage, yes, that such an act had been perpetrated on anyone. But care? Maybe just enough for a minute's silence ahead of ninety further minutes' shouting and singing at the match.

My wandering thoughts were brought back to the television, as the Chief Constable of Suffolk police was introduced at the televised press conference. He sat, in uniform, in front of a blue board bearing the large star and crown crest of Suffolk Constabulary.

"Our investigations," he began, "are continuing into the explosion at Newmarket races on Saturday. I can confirm that, as of now, eighteen people are known to have lost their lives. Whereas next of kin have been informed where possible, there are still some victims whose families have as yet been impossible to contact. I cannot therefore give a full list of victims. However, I have the names of fourteen of those known to have died."

He read them out slowly, pausing dramatically after each name.

Some I didn't recognize, but others I knew all too well.

MaryLou Fordham, as expected, was on the list. So was Elizabeth Jennings, the tease. There was no mention of Rolf Schumann. And just when I was beginning to hope that Louisa had survived, the Chief Constable said, "And, finally, Louisa Whitworth."

I sat there, stunned. I suppose I should not have been greatly surprised. I had seen the devastation in that room for myself, and the surprise was that so many had lived, not that Louisa had died. But with Robert being alive, I had hoped against reason that Louisa was alive too.

The press conference continued, but I wasn't really listening. I could picture Louisa as I had last seen her, in a white blouse and black skirt, hurrying around the tables, doing her job. She had been a smart girl with, at nineteen years old, a great future. Having achieved better-than-expected results on her examinations, she had been toying with the idea of going to college. In the meantime, she had worked for me since September, and had been saving to go away to South America with her boyfriend. How bloody unfair, I thought. Cut down, with her whole life ahead of her. How could anyone have done such a thing?

Another policeman on the television was holding up a diagram, a map of the boxes in the Newmarket Head On Grandstand.

"The bomb was placed here," he said, pointing, "inside the air conditioner in box 1, just above the main window at the front of the room. Consequently, the bomb was between those people inside the room and those on the viewing balcony outside. We estimate that some five pounds of high explosive was used, and this was sufficient to cause considerable structural problems within the building. The majority of those killed or injured were subject to blast damage, although one person lost her life as a result of being hit by flying masonry."

In the wrong place at the wrong time, but so were we all.

The Chief Constable took over again.

"There has been some speculation in the media that the bomb was planted in an attempt to assassinate a foreign national." He paused. "Whereas it is too early for us to comment, I can confirm that the occupants of box number 1 were switched with box 6 down the corridor. This switch had been made at the request of the new occupants of box 1 since they would then be able to accommodate a larger party in boxes 1 and 2 with the dividing wall folded away between them instead of having two separate rooms as originally allocated. The switch was made early last week. It would appear that the explosive device was detonated by a timing mechanism. We have yet been unable to establish for how long the device had been in situ and therefore we have to consider the possibility that it was intended for a different target than that actually hit." He paused again before adding, "As part of the security check for the foreign national, the air conditioner in box 6 was opened and inspected early on Saturday morning and found to be clear."

Oh great, I thought.

The press conference went on for a while longer, but it was clear that the police had no idea who was responsible and seemingly no leads to act on.

My phone rang.

"Hello," I answered.

"Chef?" said a voice. "Gary here. Are you coming to work?"

Gary was my sous-chef, my underchef. My apprentice.

"Where are you?" I asked.

"At the Net," he said. He always referred to the restaurant as "the Net." "But I can't get into the kitchen."

"I know," I said. I looked at my watch: ten-fifteen. Our normal start time was ten. "Who else is there?"

"Ray, Julie and Jean are here, and the kitchen porters are somewhere around," he said. "Oh, and Martin's here too," he added.

Martin, my barman, must have recovered, I thought. It was he who had gone to the hospital on Friday night.

"How about Richard and Carl?" I asked.

"No sign of them," he said. "Nor of Robert and Louisa."

He obviously hadn't heard about Louisa.

"Tell everyone to go into the dining room and wait for me," I said. "Tell Martin to make some coffee using the bar machine." He could do that without going into the kitchen.

"How about milk?" he asked. It was in the cold-room.

"Drink it black. I'll be there in fifteen minutes."

IT ACTUALLY TOOK me twenty minutes to reach the restaurant, not least because my car was still at the racetrack and I had to phone for a taxi. By the time I arrived, Richard had made it there as well, and he had brought with him the bad news about Louisa. Julie and Jean were in tears and consoling each other, and Ray, Martin and Gary just sat in silence with their heads bowed. Louisa had been a very popular member of the team and was loved by us all.

Martin asked me about Robert, and I was able to assure them that he was all right. But it did little to lighten the mood. Richard was expressing his anger at the "bastards" who had done this. He kept banging his fist on the table, and, in the end, I suggested it might be best if he went outside to cool off. I could see him through the window kicking a tree near the parking lot. He was in his mid-forties, and was my maître d', meeting and greeting the customers and taking their dinner orders as they enjoyed a drink in the bar. Louisa had been his own teenage daughter's best friend at school, and I knew that he thought of her as an extension of his family. It had been because of Richard that Louisa had come to work at Hay Net, and he now probably felt in some way responsible. His anger was directed not just at the bastards who did this but at the whole situation that had led to her death.

Carl arrived to join this happy throng.

"Hi," he said to me. "How's the knee?"

"I'll survive."

"Pity." He forced a smile. I knew he slightly resented having a boss who was ten years his junior, especially one who took all the credit when Carl thought he had done the lion's share of the work. But I paid him well, so he stayed.

I convened a meeting in the dining room. Richard came in from the parking lot with red and tearful eyes, Julie and Jean still clung to each other, with Martin fussing over them both, and Ray and Gary sat close together facing me. I suddenly wondered if they were, in fact, a couple. Our two kitchen porters had wandered off somewhere, but I wasn't so concerned about them.

"It is absolutely dreadful news about Louisa, and I know that we are all angry and disturbed by her death." Richard nodded furiously. "This has been an appalling weekend for everyone in Newmarket, and especially for us who were involved with the event on Saturday."

"I feel so guilty," said Richard, interrupting.

"Why guilty?" I asked.

"Because I was meant to be there on Saturday," he said, "but I didn't go because I was so unwell on Friday night. Maybe I could have saved her if I'd been there." He started crying again.

"Richard," I said, "you mustn't blame yourself. If you were there, you might have been killed too."

He looked at me in a manner that suggested he knew that and still would have preferred to have been there just the same.

"Martin and I were ill on Friday night as well," said Jean. "I called an ambulance because he was so bad."

"I was also meant to be at the racetrack on Saturday," said Martin, "but they didn't let me out of the hospital until about one and it was too late by then." He looked at me for reassurance.

"It's fine, Martin," I said. "I wouldn't have expected anyone to come to work after being so ill." He looked relieved.

"I was ill as well," added Julie in her high-pitched manner.

"And us," said Gary, indicating him and Ray. Perhaps I was right about them. Gary went on. "I should also have been there on Saturday, but I was too sick to make it. Sorry, Chef."

"It's all right." I said, looking at him. "I think we were all food poisoned on Friday evening, along with most of the guests who attended the function at the racetrack."

The enormity of what I had said slowly sank in.

"Is that why the kitchen is padlocked?" said Gary.

"Yes." I explained to them all I knew about the situation. I told them that someone had apparently died from food poisoning but that I didn't yet know who it was. I told them that I would try to get the kitchen inspected quickly and that we would try to be back in business as soon as possible. "Louisa would have wanted that," I said. I thought it was true, and they all nodded in agreement.

"So," I said, "you can all go home now and come in again at ten tomorrow. I can't promise that we will be back in business by then, but I will try. When we find out when Louisa's funeral is, we will close so we can all attend. How about if we offer the restaurant to her parents and ask them if they want to invite everyone back here after the funeral?"

They all nodded again.

"I'll do that if you like," said Richard.

"Yes, please," I said. "Tell them it's also fine if they don't want to have it here, but we will do the catering for them wherever, free of charge."

Richard smiled. "Thanks, I will."

The phone rang, and Carl went and picked it up from the desk in the corner. He listened for a bit and then said, "Thank you for letting us know." He hung up.

"A cancellation," he said. "For tonight."

"Just as well," I said.

"I'll call around to the other bookings," said Carl. "We should have their numbers."

"Good," I said, trying to sound upbeat and businesslike. "OK, everyone, the meeting's over. If anyone wants me, I'll be in my office, trying to get us back up and running."

I called it my office, but it was used by everyone. Martin

was in charge of the bar and was responsible for the ordering of all the drink, including for the restaurant, although it was me who decided which wines actually appeared on the list. Carl dealt with all the food and equipment ordering. The office had one wall with three rows of seven hooks each. On each hook was hanging a large bulldog clip. Each of the seven hooks in each row represented a day of the week, Monday to Sunday. The top row was for notes of things to be ordered. The middle row was for orders placed. And the bottom row for delivery notes of orders received.

On Thursdays and Fridays, my part-time bookkeeper, Enid, came in to check delivery notes against orders made, and invoices received against both. Checks were then written against invoices, receipts from sales were counted and banked and salaries and other costs were paid. The system was very low-tech, but it seemed to work well, and we rarely, if ever, ran out of ingredients, or napkins and the like, and, since the first year, receipts from sales had far exceeded both checks written and the cost of salaries and the rest, so we made a profit. A handsome profit, in fact.

I sat at my desk and shuffled the paperwork to make some space. I had been working on new menu items and there were notes and recipes strewn about. We kept basically the same menu each day, since my regular customers didn't like it if their favorite dish was unavailable, but we generally added a special or two. I didn't want the specials to be recited aloud by the waiters, as happens so often in American restaurants, so we printed new menus daily, with any specials highlighted in bold type.

I dug in my pocket and pulled out Angela Milne's card.

"Angela Milne," she answered on the first ring.

"Hello, Angela," I said, "Max Moreton here."

"Oh good," she said, "I was going to call you."

"Who died?" I asked.

"What, from the poisoning?" she said. I wish she wouldn't use that term.

"Of course," I said.

"Well, it appears now that the death in question may not be connected with the event on Friday."

"Explain," I said.

"As you might expect, everything is rather chaotic at the moment with the bombing at the racetrack. Dreadful, isn't it? I understand that the local coroner's department has been somewhat overwhelmed. There's a backlog of postmortems to be done. A refrigerated truck has been commandeered by the hospital to act as a temporary morgue."

It was more information than I really wanted.

"So," I said, "what about the death on Friday night?"

"It seems it may have been due to natural causes and not food poisoning."

"What do you mean?" I asked her rather irately, thinking about my sealed kitchen.

"A patient presented himself at the hospital emergency room on Friday night with abdominal pain, nausea and severe vomiting, consistent with having been poisoned." She paused. "He arrived at the hospital alone but at the same time as several other cases, and it was assumed that since he had the same symptoms he was suffering from the same problem. The patient died at seven-thirty on Saturday morning, and a young doctor from the hospital called the Food Standards Agency emergency number in London and an impetuous junior officer from there ordered the sealing of the kitchen." She paused again.

"Yes," I prompted, "go on."

"I'm not sure I should be telling you all this," she said.

"Why not?" I said. "It's my kitchen that was closed because of it."

"Yes, I know. I'm sorry about that."

"So what did he die of?" I asked.

"The postmortem has not been done yet, but it appears he may have died from a perforated bowel."

"What's that?" I asked.

"What it says. The bowel has a hole in it and empties itself into the abdominal cavity. It apparently causes peritonitis, and death, if not treated rapidly."

"So the person died of peritonitis?"

"I don't know," she said. "As I said, the postmortem hasn't been done. But his family now says that he had

Crohn's disease, which is an inflammation of the bowel, and that he had been complaining of abdominal pains for several days. Crohn's disease can lead to blockage of the bowel and then perforation."

"Why didn't he go to a doctor before Friday night?" I said.

"I don't know, but apparently it wasn't unusual for him to complain of abdominal pain. But I would have thought it was most unlikely that he would have gone to a dinner at the track if he was suffering from such discomfort that he needed hospital treatment."

"So my kitchen is in the clear?" I asked.

"Well, I wouldn't say that," she said. "There were definitely other cases of food poisoning, even if that death was not connected with them."

"But the food wasn't cooked in my restaurant kitchen and had never been in the building."

"Yes, I know that."

"Then please get someone to remove the padlocks."

"The kitchen will need to be inspected first," she said.

"Fine," I said. "You could eat off the floor in that kitchen, it's so clean. Get your inspectors out here today so I can get my business back on track. I hate to think how much damage has been done by having 'Closed for Decontamination' plastered all over the place."

"I'll do what I can," she said.

"Good," I said. "Otherwise, I might start making a fuss about a doctor who doesn't know the difference between food poisoning and peritonitis."

"I think that fuss is already being made by his family."

I bet it was.

"So when my kitchen is inspected, that will be the end of the matter?" I asked.

"Not entirely," she said. "From my point of view, as the Cambridgeshire environmental health officer, I will have no objection to your kitchen reopening once it has passed an inspection, but there will still be an investigation of what poisoned everyone on Friday evening and put people in the hospital."

"But the kitchen I used on Friday is no more, and also none of the food is left, so how will you do an investigation?" I asked. I decided not to tell her just yet that the only two of my regular staff who hadn't been ill had eaten the vegetarian option. It was not that I purposely wanted to hinder an investigation. It was merely that I didn't want to initiate one.

"Samples were taken of vomit and feces from those admitted to the hospital," she said. "They will be analyzed in due course."

What a lovely job, I thought, sifting through other people's sick and diarrhea. Rather them than me. "And when can I expect the results?" I asked.

"The results will be for me, not for you," she said, using her best headmistressly voice.

"But you will tell me, won't you?" I said.

"Maybe," she said with a hint of amusement in her voice. "As long as they are not grounds for a prosecution. Then the police will tell you the results after they arrest you."

"Oh thanks," I said.

We hung up on good terms. In my line of business, I needed Angela Milne as a friend, not a foe.

CARL DROVE ME to the racetrack to retrieve my car. My Golf wasn't the only vehicle in the staff parking lot. There was a battered old green Mini there too. It was Louisa's.

"Oh God," said Carl. "What do we do about that?"

"I'll inform the police," I said. "They can deal with it."

"Good idea," he said, obviously happy to leave it to me.

We sat for a moment and stared at Louisa's depressing little Mini. It had been her pride and joy. For some reason, it reminded me of a commuter rail crash in west London when the primary identification of some of the burned bodies was achieved by recording the registration numbers of the cars in the Reading station parking lot that remained uncollected at the end of the day.

I climbed out of Carl's car. "I'm going to go back to the restaurant this afternoon to continue working on the new menus," I said. "I'll see you in the morning."

"I might go back there too," he said. "Nothing else to do."

"OK, I'll see you in a bit, then, but I'm going home first."

"Right," he said again. I closed the car door and he drove off.

I stood there and looked over the hedge towards the grandstand. All was quiet, save for a policeman standing guard and the flapping of some blue-and-white tape stretched across behind the grandstands, presumably to prevent people straying in and contaminating what had to be seen as a crime scene. I suspected there was more activity taking place, out of sight, around the front, and also inside the building, where the forensic teams would probably be still searching for bomb fragments.

I limped my way over to the policeman and told him about the car in the parking lot and that it had belonged to one of the victims, Louisa Whitworth. "Thank you, sir," he said, and promised to tell the appropriate person to get it returned to her family. I suspected it was the last thing on their minds at the moment.

I thought of asking him if there was any more news about what had happened, but he wouldn't have known, and, even if he had, he wouldn't have told me. So I waved a good-bye to him, went back to my car and drove away, leaving the sad little green Mini alone on the grass.

I WENT HOME and swallowed a couple of the painkillers to dull the ache in my knee. I had been walking and standing on it for too long and it was protesting. I lay on the sofa for a while, to give the painkillers time to work, then I drove to the local garage to fill the car with gas and to buy the local newspaper. The roads were very quiet, and Barbara, the middle-aged woman in the garage who processed my credit card, assured me that the whole town was in shock. She told me at considerable length that she had been to the town supermarket and never seen it so empty. And those people who were there, she said, were talking in hushed tones, as if talking loudly would disturb the dead.

I entered my PIN in her machine and escaped back to my

car, where I sat and read the reports of the bombing in the *Cambridge Evening News,* whose front page carried a photo of the blue tarpaulin–covered grandstand under the headline MURDER AT THE RACES. Even though the police had named only fourteen of the eighteen dead, the paper listed them all, and also gave the names of many of those seriously injured. The paper obviously had good contacts at the local hospitals and with the police.

I looked through the lists. Eight of the dead were Americans from Delafield Industries, including MaryLou Fordham. Elizabeth Jennings was there among the local residents known to have died, along with Louisa and four others, including another couple who were regular customers at the Hay Net. The remaining four victims included three I knew. There was a racehorse trainer and his wife who had lived in Lambourn, as well as a successful Irish businessman who had invested much of his wealth in high-speed Thoroughbreds. The seriously injured but alive list included Rolf Schumann, the Delafield chairman, as well as half a dozen or so others I recognized from the racing world. Along with their names, the paper had printed photographs of some of the non-American dead and injured, especially those with local racing connections.

What a dreadful waste, I thought. These were nice people who worked hard and didn't deserve to be mutilated and killed by some unseen bomber who, it seemed, may have been motivated by political fervor far removed from and alien to the close-knit community involved in the Sport of Kings. Sure, there was rivalry in racing. Sometimes that rivalry, and the will to win, may spill over into skulduggery and a bending of the rules, and the law, but murder and maiming of innocents was what happened elsewhere in the world, not in our cozy Suffolk town on its biggest racing day of the year. Would it, I wondered, ever be the same again?

I glanced through the rest of the paper to see if there was any more information that I had missed. On page five, in inch-high bold type, another headline ran: RACING FOLK POISONED BY THE HAY NET — ONE DEAD.

Oh shit!

The story beneath was not totally accurate and had probably been pulled together with a considerable amount of guesswork, but it was close enough to the truth to be damaging. It claimed that two hundred and fifty racing guests at a dinner had been poisoned by the Hay Net kitchen, with celebrity chef Max Moreton at the controls. It further claimed that one person had died and fifteen others had been hospitalized. The Hay Net, it stated, had been closed for decontamination. The tone of the piece was distinctly unpleasant.

Alongside the article was a photograph of my roadside restaurant sign with its large KEEP OUT—CLOSED FOR DE-CONTAMINATION sticker prominently displayed at an angle across the all too clearly recognizable THE HAY NET RESTAU-RANT beneath.

Oh shit! I thought again. That really won't be great for business.

# 5

True to her word, Angela Milne moved mountains to get an inspection of my kitchen done late on Monday afternoon. The inspector, a small man in a suit with dark-rimmed glasses, arrived at about a quarter to five and stood in the parking lot, putting on a white coat and a white mesh trilby hat.

"Hello," he said as I went out to meet him, "my name is Ward. James Ward." He held out his hand and I shook it. I half expected him to inspect his palm to see if I had left some dirty scrap behind, but he didn't.

"Max Moreton," I said.

"Yes," he said, "I know. I've seen you on the telly."

He smiled. Things might be looking up.

"Now," he said, "where's this kitchen?"

I waved a hand, and we crunched across the gravel towards the back door.

"Have you got the keys?" I asked.

"What keys?" he said.

Things were not looking up that much.

"The keys for the padlocks," I said. "The two men who

came and put this lot on last Saturday said the inspector, when he came, would have the keys."

"Sorry," he said. "No one told me."

I bet my nonfriends, the bailiffs, didn't bother to tell anyone. They probably tossed the keys into the river Cam.

"What do you suggest we do?" asked Mr. Ward.

"Do you have a crowbar?" I asked.

"No, but I have a tire iron in the car."

It took several attempts, but the clasp finally parted from the doorframe with a splintering crack. No doubt it would be me that would have to pay for the damage as well as for the keyless lock.

The inspection was very thorough, with James Ward literally looking into every nook and cranny. He ran his fingers along the top of the exhaust hoods, looked for residue in the industrial dishwasher drains, and even poked a Q-Tip swab into the tiny gap between the built-in fryer and the worktop. It was clean. I knew it was clean. I left that gap there on purpose specifically for health inspectors to find and test. I had it cleaned out every day in case there was an unannounced visit.

"Fine," he said at length. "Nice and clean all round. Of course, I will have these swabs tested tomorrow for bacteria." He indicated the swabs he had placed in small plastic bags not just from the gap by the fryer, but also those wiped on the worktops, the chopping boards, the sinks and anywhere else he thought appropriate.

"But the kitchen is now open?" I asked.

"Oh yes," he said. "I spoke with Angela Milne, and she was happy that you be reopened as long as I was happy with the kitchen, and I am, provided I don't get any surprises from these." He held up the swabs. "And I don't think there will be. I've inspected lots of kitchens and this is one of the cleanest I've seen."

I was glad. I had always been insistent on having a clean kitchen and not just to pass inspections. There was a note printed on every menu that invited my clients to visit the kitchen, if they so wished. Many did, and all my regulars had been in there at some time or another, and one individual in particular always made a point of taking his guests in to see me, or Carl, and Gary. I had toyed with the idea of putting a chef's table in a corner of the kitchen to allow diners to watch us at work. But as my limited star had risen over the years, I did tend to be elsewhere for an increasing number of the service periods in any given week. Also, I knew that even now the customers were apt to complain and be disappointed if I wasn't actually there in the flesh, so I decided it was probably less troublesome overall to keep the clientele eating in the dining room only.

I thanked James Ward, and saw him to his car and off the premises. Even though he was pleasant and helpful, there is something about health inspectors that gives all chefs the willies, so I was glad to see him depart.

Carl and I spent the next hour removing all the CLOSED FOR DECONTAMINATION stickers, which seemed to be stuck on with Super Glue. Then we tried our best to remove the remaining padlocks without causing too much damage to the structure of the building. At last, it was done, and we sat together in the bar and pulled ourselves a pint each.

"We reopen tomorrow, then?" Carl asked.

"If we have any customers left," I said.

I showed him the newspaper.

"That's all right," he said. "No one who comes here reads that."

"They will have done so today," I said. "Like me, they'll have bought it to read about those killed on Saturday. They're all bound to have seen it."

"Nah, don't you worry, our regulars will trust us more than a newspaper." But he didn't sound very convincing.

"Most of our regulars were at the dinner on Friday and will know it's true," I said, "because they were throwing up all night."

"Ahh, I'd forgotten that."

"How about those you phoned earlier?" I asked him. "You know, to say we would be closed tonight."

"Well, most said they weren't going to be coming anyway."

"Did they give a reason?" I asked.

"If you mean did they say they weren't coming because

we were akin to a poison factory, then, no, they didn't. Only one person mentioned it, and she said that she and her husband wouldn't have come only because they hadn't fully recovered from a bout of food poisoning. Most simply said it would be inappropriate for them to enjoy an evening out while the bodies of those killed had hardly gone cold, or words to that effect."

We sat in silence and finished our beers. The thought of the bodies getting colder in the commandeered refrigerated truck had been drifting around the periphery of my consciousness for most of the day.

I CALLED MARK WINSOME. I thought it was time my silent business partner knew that we might have a spot of bother ahead. He listened carefully as I told him the whole story about Friday night and also about the bombing on Saturday. He knew, of course, about the bombing but hadn't realized how close his investment had been to biting the dust.

"I'm so sorry about your waitress," he said.

"Thank you," I said. "It's been very distressing for the other staff. I sent them all home this morning."

"But you say the restaurant will reopen again tomorrow?"

"Yes," I said. "But I don't expect there to be much business, and not only because of the food-poisoning incident but because the whole area is in shock and I don't think people will be eating out much."

"So you might have a bit of time this week?" he said.

"Well, I think I should be here for those who do come," I said. "Why?"

"I just thought it's time you came to London."

"What, to see you?"

"No. Well, yes, of course I would love to see you. But what I really meant was that it's time for you to come to London permanently."

"What about the restaurant?"

"That's what I mean," he said. "I think it's time you opened a restaurant in London. I've been waiting six years for you to be ready and now I think you are."

I sat in my office and stared at the wall. I had called Mark with considerable trepidation since I feared he might be angry that I had seemingly poisoned a sizable chunk of Newmarket society and damaged his investment. Instead, he was offering me . . . what? Fame and fortune, or maybe it would be humiliation and disaster. At the very least, Mark was offering me the chance to find out.

"Are you still there?" he said at length.

"Mmm," I replied.

"Good. Then come see me sometime later this week." He paused. "How about Friday? Lunch? At the Goring."

"Fine," I said.

"Good," he said again. "One o'clock, in the bar."

"Fine," I repeated, and he hung up.

I sat there for a while, thinking about what the future might bring. There was no doubt that the Hay Net was becoming very well known in the area and, at least until Friday night, had been generally well respected. Indeed, so popular had we become that securing a table for dinner was a challenge and needed considerable forward planning, especially weekends. In the past year, I had been featured in a few magazines, and the previous autumn we had entertained a TV crew from the BBC. The Hay Net was busy, comfortable and fun. Maybe it had become rather too easy, but I loved being part of the world of racing, the world in which I had been brought up. I liked racing people and they seemed to like me. I was enjoying life.

Was I ready to give up this provincial coziness to move to the cutthroat world of restaurants in the metropolis? Could I afford to walk away from this success and pit myself against the very best chefs in London? Could I afford not to?

THE NIGHT WAS slightly less disturbed than the previous one, and with a few new variations of the dream. It was mostly MaryLou pushing the gurney, and occasionally she became a legless skeleton as she pushed. More than once, it was Louisa doing the pushing, and she still had her legs. Thankfully, on these occasions the dream ended peacefully rather than with the endless fall and racing heart. Overall, I slept for more hours than I was awake, and I was reasonably refreshed by the time my alarm clock noisily roused me at a quarter to eight.

I lay in bed for a while, thinking about what Mark had said the previous afternoon. The prospect of joining the restaurant big boys was, at once, hugely exciting and incredibly frightening. But what an opportunity!

I was brought back to earth by the ringing of my telephone on the bedside table.

"Hello," I said.

"Max, is that you?" said a female voice. "It's Suzanne Miller here."

Suzanne Miller, the managing director of the racetrack catering company.

"Hi, Suzanne," I said. "What can I do for you so early?" I looked at my clock. It was twenty-five to nine.

"Yes, sorry to call you at home," she said, "but I think we might have a problem."

"How so?"

"It's to do with last Friday," she said. I wasn't surprised. "It seems that some people who were at the gala dinner were ill afterwards."

"Were they?" I said in a surprised tone. "How about you and Tony?" Tony was her husband, and they had both been at the event.

"No, we were fine," she said. "It was a lovely evening. But I always find these big evenings nerve-racking. I get so wound up, in case anything goes wrong."

And it wasn't even her firm doing the cooking, I thought, although they had been responsible for the guest list and all the other arrangements.

"So what's the problem?" I asked innocently.

"I've had a letter this morning. It says"—I heard paper being rustled—" 'Dear Madam, This letter is to give you advance warning of legal proceedings that will be initiated by our client against your company to recover damages for distress and loss of earnings as a result of the poisoning of our client at a dinner organized by your company at Newmarket racetrack on Friday, May 4.' "

"And who is their client?" I asked.

"It says 'Ref: Miss Caroline Aston,' at the top."

"Was she a guest on Friday?" I asked.

"She's not on the guest list, but so many of them weren't named. You know what it's like, Mr. So-and-So and guest. Could be anyone."

"You said people. Who else?"

"Apparently, quite a few," she said. "I mentioned this to my secretary just now when I opened it and she says that lots of people were ill on Friday night. Her husband is a doctor, and she says he had to see quite a few of his patients. And she said there was an article in the newspaper about it yesterday. What shall we do?"

"Nothing," I said. "At least, nothing yet. If anyone asks, tell them you're looking into it." I paused. "Out of interest, what did you and Tony have to eat on Friday night?"

"I can't remember," said Suzanne. "What with all this bomb business, I can't think."

"It is dreadful, isn't it?" I said.

"Dreadful," she agreed. "And I am so sorry to hear about your waitress."

"Thank you. Yes, it has been an awful blow to my staff. Louisa was much loved by them all."

"Seems that a bit of food poisoning is irrelevant, really," she said.

I agreed, and silently hoped that the episode would be soon forgotten. Who was it who tried to hide bad news behind a much bigger story? It had cost them their job.

"So what shall I do about this letter?" Suzanne asked.

"Could you make a copy and send it to me?" I said. "Then, if I were you, I'd just wait to hear from them again. Maybe they're just fishing for a reaction and will forget about it when they don't get one." Or maybe that was just my wishful thinking.

"I think I ought to consult higher," she said. The local racetrack catering company was just part of a national group, and I suspected that Suzanne was not sure enough of her position to simply sit on the letter. She would want the parent company's lawyers to see it. I couldn't blame her. I'd have done the same in her position.

"OK," I said, "but could you send me a copy of it first?"

"I will," she said slowly, as if thinking, "but I will send it to you with a covering note officially informing you of the letter, as the chef at the event. And I will also send a copy of that covering note to my head office."

Why did I suddenly get the feeling that I was being distanced here by Suzanne? Was I the one that the catering company was preparing to hang out to dry? Probably. After all, business is business.

"Fine," I said. "And if you can remember what you ate on Friday, let me know that too, will you?"

"Tony is a vegetarian," she said, "so he would have eaten whatever you had for them."

"And you?" I asked. "Would you have eaten the vegetarian dish?"

"What was it?" she asked.

"Broccoli, cheese and pasta bake."

"I can't stand broccoli, so I doubt it. Let me think." There was a short pause. "I think I had chicken. But I was so nervous about the evening, I hardly ate anything at all. In fact, I remember being so hungry when I got home I had to make myself a cheese sandwich before I went to bed."

Not really very helpful.

"Why do you want to know?" she asked.

"Just in case it was some of the food at the dinner that made people ill," I said. "Helps to eliminate things, that's all." Time, I thought, to change the subject. "Were all your staff all right on Saturday?"

"Oh yes, thank you," she said. "Some of them were pretty shocked, though, and one of my elderly ladies was admitted to the hospital with chest pains after having been told by a fireman to run down four flights of stairs. But she was all right after a while. How about you? How did you get out?"

We spent some time telling our respective war stories.

Suzanne had been in her office on the far side of the weighing room and she hadn't even realized there had been a bomb until she heard the fire engines arrive with their sirens, but it didn't seem to stop her from having a lengthy account of her actions thereafter.

"I'm sorry, Suzanne," I said during a pause in the flow, "I must get on."

"Oh sorry," she said. "Once I start, I never stop, do I?"

No, I thought. But at least we had moved away from talking about food poisoning.

"Speak with you soon," I said. "Bye, now." I hung up.

I laid my head back on the pillow and wondered who Miss Caroline Aston was, and where she was. I could wring her bloody neck. Distress and loss of earnings indeed. How about me? I'd suffered distress and loss of earnings too. Who should I sue?

THERE WAS ANOTHER letter from Miss Aston's lawyers waiting for me when I arrived at the Hay Net. It confirmed that she was suing me personally as well as the racetrack catering company. Great. I could wring her neck twice, if only I knew who and where she was. What did she think? That I had poisoned people on purpose?

I sat in my office reading and rereading the letter. I supposed I ought to find a lawyer to give it to. Instead, I called Mark again.

"Send it to me," he said. "My lawyers will look at it for you and they will give you a call."

"Thanks."

I faxed it to the number he gave me, and his lawyer called me back within fifteen minutes. I explained the problem to him.

"Don't worry," he said, "we'll deal with this."

"Thanks," I replied. "But please let me know who this woman is so I can make a voodoo doll of her and stick pins in it."

The lawyer laughed. "Why don't you just poison her?"

"Not funny," I said.

"No. Sorry," he said. "I'll be able to do a search and find her within the day. I'll get back to you."

"I could wring her neck," I said.

"I wouldn't advise it," said the lawyer, laughing. "Suing is done in civil court and you can only lose your money, not your liberty."

"Thanks, I'll try and remember that when you find her."

He laughed again and hung up.

I wondered what I would do if he did find her. Probably nothing. It just annoyed me that she wanted to claim damages from me for a minor bit of accidental food poisoning when the lovely Louisa had lost her life due to some deranged madman bringing his grudges two thousand miles from the Middle East to Newmarket.

Carl arrived and I shared the good news with him.

"Will they lock you up?" he asked hopefully.

"Sod off," I said.

"Charming," he said, smiling. "So the boss has returned in both body and mind. Shall we get this show on the road?"

"Indeed, we shall," I replied, returning the smile.

There is a lot more to running a restaurant than cooking a few meals. For a start, the customers want a choice of dishes, and they want them without having to wait too long. At the Hay Net, we usually offered between eight and ten starters and about the same number of main courses. Some of the starters were hot and some were cold, but everything was prepared fresh to order, and our aim was to have a dish ready for the table within fifteen minutes of the order being taken. Ideally, main courses should be ready ten minutes after the starters have been cleared from the table, or, if no starters are ordered, within twenty-eight minutes of the order arriving in the kitchen. I knew all too well that if a customer was kept waiting for longer than he or she thought reasonable, it didn't matter how good the food tasted when it arrived, only the wait would be remembered and not the flavors.

There were three of us who worked in the heat of the kitchen, Carl, Gary and me, while Julie dealt with the cold dishes, including the salads and desserts. It was not a big operation compared to the large London restaurants, but, at the height of the service, it was an energetic kitchen, with everyone working hard. The plan was that the bookings were taken to stagger our busy dinner period over at least a couple of hours, but our customers were notorious for not being on time for their reservations so sometimes we were madly rushed to get everything out on time.

Food is fickle stuff. The difference between vegetables that are just right and vegetables that are overcooked can be a matter of a minute or two. For a steak, or a tuna fillet, it can be much less time than that. Our clients, understandably, want their food delivered to the table when it is perfect. They also want all the servings for the table delivered at once—who wouldn't? They expect their food to be attractive, to be hot and to have an appetizing aroma. And, in particular, they want the food delivered in the same sequence as the orders were taken. Nothing, I had learned, upsets the customers more than to see a party that ordered after they did being served ahead of them.

To the casual observer, the kitchen might appear as a chaotic scramble, but, in reality, it was only as chaotic as a juggler's hands keeping four balls in the air at once. Appearances, in either case, are deceptive.

Needless to say, we didn't always get everything right, but, overall, the number of compliments far exceeded the few complaints, and that was good enough for me. Occasionally, someone would say that they weren't coming back, but, usually, it would be someone I didn't want back anyway. I would just smile and politely show them the way to the parking lot. Thankfully, those were few and far between. Most of my customers were friends, and it was just like having them to my house for dinner except, of course, they paid.

My thoughts were interrupted by the arrival of a delivery from my butcher. I used a man from Bury St. Edmonds who slaughtered all his own meat. He had told me that he knew all his farm suppliers personally, and he claimed that he could vouch for the well-being and comfortable life of every one of the animals. That is, of course, until he killed and butchered them. I had no reason to doubt his claims, since his meat and poultry were excellent. A fine restaurant obviously needs a good chef, but even the best chefs need good ingredients to work with and so the choice of supplier is paramount.

The driver had almost finished stacking the delivery in the cold-room by the time the rest of my staff arrived at ten o'clock. Gary was all excited that the padlocks had been removed and went around the kitchen like a little boy allowed to roam freely in a toy store. He was having one of his good days, I thought. He had the energy and the enthusiasm to be a good chef, even a great one, but I felt that he had to learn to be slightly less adventurous in his combinations of flavors. He was, like me, a great believer in using fruit with meat. Everyone was familiar with pork with apple, turkey with cranberries, duck with orange, gammon with pineapple and even venison with quince. The flavors complement one another, the fruit bringing out the best in the meat, and satisfying the palate. Gary was apt to choose exotic, strong-tasting fruits and, to my mind, serve them inappropriately with meats of a delicate flavor, such as veal or chicken. It was a matter that we had discussed at length and with passion.

Ever since he had arrived a couple of years previously, I had attempted to have at least one dish on our menu of his design, and, at the moment, it was an herb-crusted red snapper, topped with a roasted caramelized pear, over a lightly garlic mashed-potato base, with a pear reduction. It was a tasty and popular dish, and it usually kept Gary busy throughout the service.

However, the bookings for lunch on that particular Tuesday were not spectacular, and, during the morning, several calls to cancel left us looking very bare. More calls canceling dinner reservations made the day look bleak indeed.

I called a short meeting of the staff in the dining room at noon.

"It seems that a combination of the bombing on Saturday and the problems we had on Friday evening may result in a bit of a lean time this week," I said. "But I am sure that things will pick up soon. We will continue as normal and do our best for those that do come. OK?" I tried to sound upbeat.

"How about Louisa's job?" said Jean. "And when is Robert coming back? Ray and I can't do the whole dining room on our own."

"Let's wait and see how many covers we will be doing," I said. "Richard can help out in the dining room, as he usually does anyway when we're busy." I looked at him and he nodded in agreement. "I will call Robert and find out when he will be coming back. Anything else?"

"I spoke to the Whitworths," said Richard. "They said to thank you for the offer, but they wanted to have the wake at home. And Beryl, that's Louisa's mum, said that she will do the food, if that's all right."

"Of course," I said, and wondered if the Whitworths blamed Louisa's death on her job. I decided that I had better go visit them. It would be the proper thing to do anyway.

"Do you know yet when her funeral will be?" I asked.

"Friday, at two-thirty, at the crematorium in Cambridge."

Damn, I thought, I'd have to rearrange my lunch with Mark.

"OK," I said. "We will be closed all day on Friday. You can all have the day off to go to the funeral, if you wish. I will be there." I paused. "Is there anything else?" No one said anything. "OK, let's get to work."

In the end, we did just four lunches, two separate couples who stopped while passing. None of the six still booked actually turned up, and there were three more calls during lunch to cancel for the evening. That left us just twenty-four from what had been a full dining room, and I seriously doubted whether even those twenty-four would show.

I spent some time during the afternoon calling the clients who had made reservations on Friday to tell them that we would be closed and why. Most said they probably wouldn't have come anyway, but only two said rather tactlessly that it was because they had heard that you could get poisoned at the Hay Net. At one point, I had dialed a number and it was ringing before I realized that it was the Jennings number I was calling. I was about to put the phone down when Neil answered.

"Hello," he said slowly. "Neil Jennings here."

"Hello, Neil," I said. "It's Max Moreton from the Hay Net."

"Ah yes," he said, "Hello, Max."

"Neil," I said slightly awkwardly, "I'm so very sorry about Elizabeth. Such a dreadful thing."

"Yes," he said.

There was an uncomfortable pause. I didn't know quite what to say.

"I saw her at the races on Saturday," I said, "at lunchtime."

"Really," he replied, seemingly rather absentmindedly.

"Yes," I went on. "I cooked the lunch she attended."

"Didn't poison her, did you?" I wasn't sure if he was making a joke or not.

"No, Neil," I said, "I didn't."

"No," he said, "I suppose not."

"Do you have a date for the funeral?" I asked. "I would like to come and pay my respects."

"Friday," he said, "at eleven, at Our Lady and St. Etheldreda."

I hadn't realized that they were Roman Catholics, but, then, why would I?

"I'll try and be there," I said.

"Fine," he said. There was another difficult little pause, and I was about to say good-bye when he said, "I suppose I should thank you for saving my life."

"Sorry?" I said.

"If you hadn't made me so ill on Friday night," he went on, "I would have been in the box with my Elizabeth on Saturday."

I couldn't tell whether he was pleased or not.

# 6

Wednesday dawned bright and sunny. As a general rule, I slept with my curtains open and tended to wake with the rising sun. However, for a few weeks each side of midsummer I tried to remember to pull them across my east-facing bedroom window to prevent the early brightness from rousing me too soon from my slumbers. I cursed myself for forgetting, as the sun peeped over the horizon at a quarter past five and forced its rays past my closed eyelids and into my sleeping brain. For the first time in nearly a week, I had slept soundly and uninterrupted. That is, until five-fifteen.

As I had feared, Tuesday evening had been a dismal affair at the restaurant. Just five tables had finally appeared, and one of those was from passing street traffic who couldn't believe their luck that we had space for them. In fact, we had so much space that they had twenty tables to choose from. It felt like the kitchen was working in slow motion. Perhaps I should have been happy to have had a less tiring time after what had happened over the preceding days, but it seemed all wrong, and I could also feel the tension among my staff. They weren't happy either. They were worried about the security of their jobs and the future. As I was.

Refreshed by a decent sleep and a vigorous shower, I resolved to do something to rectify the position the restaurant found itself in. I decided that it was no good sitting around just waiting for the business to pick up while the Hay Net slowly died. What was needed was positive action. I thought about walking along Newmarket High Street with sandwich boards on my shoulders, stating that Socrates would be safe at the Hay Net, there being no hemlock on the menu. Instead, I looked up the telephone number of the *Cambridge Evening News*. Use a thief to catch a thief.

I reckoned that an evening paper would start work early, so I sat on the edge of my bed in a bathrobe and called the news desk at a quarter to eight. I waited for some time until Ms. Harding, the paper's news editor, finally came on the line.

"Yes?" she said. "Can I help you?"

"Would you be interested in an exclusive interview with Max Moreton?" I asked, deciding not to reveal my identity at this stage in case she wanted to do the interview over the telephone. "About both the food-poisoning episode of last week and the bombing of the racetrack on Saturday?"

"What has Max Moreton to do with the bombing?" asked Ms. Harding.

I told her that he was the chef for the lunch in the bombed boxes and that he had been first on the scene immediately after the bomb went off, well before the fire brigade had arrived. She took the bait.

"Wow!" she said. "Then, yes, please, we would love to have an interview with Mr. Moreton." An exclusive with a witness to the biggest national news stories of the hour was like manna from heaven for a local newspaper.

"Good," I said. "How about at the Hay Net restaurant, at ten-thirty this morning?"

"Hasn't that restaurant been closed down?" she said.

"No," I replied, "it hasn't."

"Right." She sounded a little unsure. "Will it be safe?"

I stifled my irritation and assured her it would.

"And one more thing," I said. "Don't forget to bring a photographer."

"Why do I need a photographer?" she asked.

I thought about saying to her: so she could rephotograph the restaurant sign, this time with OPEN FOR WONDERFUL FOOD stuck across it. Instead, I said, "I am sure that Mr. Moreton would be happy for you to photograph his injuries from the bombing."

"Oh," she said. "OK. Tell him someone will be at his restaurant at ten-thirty."

"But won't it be you?" I asked.

"No, I doubt it," she said. "I'll send one of the reporting staff."

"I do think that Mr. Moreton would only be interested in speaking with the news editor," I said. "In fact, I'm pretty sure that he would only speak to the most important person in the newsroom."

"Oh," she said again, "do you think so? Well, I might just be able to do this one myself." Flattery, I thought, could get you everywhere. "OK," she said decisively. "Tell Mr. Moreton I will be there myself at ten-thirty."

I promised her that I would do just that, and hung up, smiling.

Next, I called Mark. I knew he was always at his desk by seven-thirty each morning, and sometimes he was still there at eleven at night. To my knowledge, he survived on a maximum of six hours' sleep a night. All his waking hours he devoted to making money, and I was under no illusions that his plan to bring me to London would include him getting even richer. I was not saying that I wouldn't get richer too, just that I knew that Mark wouldn't be contemplating the move out of feelings of altruism or philanthropy. He had pound and dollar signs in his eyes, and he would have already calculated the potential profit in his head.

"No problem," he said. "Come to dinner instead. You choose where. I'll pay."

"OK," I said. "How about the OXO Tower?" I had always liked their food.

"Fine. I'll make the reservation. Eight o'clock suit you?"

I mentally calculated train times. "Make it eight-thirty."

"Fine," he said again. "Eight-thirty on Friday at the OXO."

He hung up, and I lay back on the bed, thinking about what the future might bring. How ambitious was I? What did I want from my life?

I would be thirty-two in November. Seven years ago I had been the youngest chef ever to be awarded a Michelin star. But, by now, there were two younger than me, each with two stars. I was no longer seen by the media as the bright young thing of whom much was expected, I was more the established chef who was now thought to be making his fortune. The truth was that I was doing all right, but the Hay Net was both too small and too provincial to be a serious cash generator. Whereas nationally I was only a minor celebrity chef, at the local level I was well known and admired, at least I was before last Friday, and I enjoyed it. Did I want to give that up to seek fame and fortune in London? What else in my life was important?

I had always wanted a family, to have children of my own. In that respect, so far I had been a singular failure, literally. A few relationships with girls had come and gone. Mostly gone. Restaurant work is never very conducive to interactions of a sexual nature. The hours are antisocial by their very design: having dinners out is other people's social activity. Exhausting evenings and late nights are not ideal preparations for lovemaking, and I could remember more than a few occasions when I had been so tired that I had simply gone to sleep in the middle of the act, something not greatly appreciated by the other party.

But being alone was not something that kept me awake nights, worrying. I was not actively searching for a partner. I never had. But if the opportunity arose, I would take it. If not, then I would go on living alone, working hard and keeping my eyes open so as not to miss the chance if it came along. London, I thought, might well increase the probability of such a chance.

The telephone rang on the bedside table. I sat up and picked up the receiver.

"Hello," I said.

"Morning, Mr. Moreton," said Angela Milne. "Lovely day."

"Yes, lovely," I said. My heart rate rose a notch. "Do you have any news for me?"

"Yes, indeed I have," she said. "I'm afraid I have some good news and some bad news. Which do you want first?"

"The good news, I suppose," I said.

"The swabs taken by James Ward in your kitchen are all clear."

"Good," I said. I hadn't expected otherwise. "So what's the bad news?"

"You poisoned everyone with phytohemagglutinin."

"Phyto . . . What?" I said.

"Phytohemagglutinin," she repeated. "And, yes, I did need to look up how to pronounce it."

"But what is it?" I asked.

"Kidney bean lectin."

"And what's that when it's at home?"

"It's the stuff in red kidney beans that makes them poisonous," she said. "You gave your guests kidney beans that hadn't been properly cooked."

I thought back hard to last Friday's dinner. "But I didn't serve any kidney beans."

"You must have," she said. "Maybe in a salad or something?"

"No," I said confidently, "there were definitely no kidney beans in that dinner. I made everything from scratch, and I swear to you there were no kidney beans, red or otherwise, in any of it. The tests must be mistaken."

"Samples were taken from sixteen different individuals at the hospital and all of them contained phyto what's-its-name." She didn't actually say that it was me that must be mistaken and not the tests, but the tone of her voice implied it.

"Oh." I was confused. I knew there were no kidney beans

in that dinner. At least, I hadn't knowingly put any in it. "I'll have to check the ingredients on the supplier's invoice."

"Perhaps you should," she said. She paused briefly. "In the meantime, I will have to write an official report stating that the poisoning was due to an ingestion of incorrectly prepared kidney beans. The report will be sent to the Food Standards Agency."

I would have preferred to have been given a criminal record.

"I'm sorry, Max," she went on, "but I have to warn you that the Forest Heath District Council, that's the district council for Newmarket racetrack, may choose to send the report to the Crown Prosecution Service for them to consider whether proceedings should be mounted against you under section 7 of the Food Safety Act." She paused, as if thinking. "I don't suppose I should really be calling you at all."

Perhaps I was going to get the criminal record as well.

"Well, thank you for warning me," I said. "What are the penalties?"

"Maximum penalty is an unlimited fine and two years' imprisonment, but it won't come to that. That would be for a deliberate act. At worst, you would get an official caution."

Even an official caution counted as a criminal record. Maybe enough to put an end to any London aspirations. It also might be the death knell of the Hay Net.

"I'll write just the facts," she said. "I will emphasize that no one was really seriously ill, not life-threatening or anything. All those who went to the hospital were either discharged immediately or went home the following day. Maybe they will just give you a written warning for the future."

"Thanks," I said.

She hung up, and I sat and stared at the telephone in my hand.

Kidney beans! Every chef, every cook, every housewife, even every schoolboy, knows that kidney beans have to be boiled to make them safe to eat. It was inconceivable that I would have included kidney beans in any recipe without boiling them vigorously first to destroy the poisons in them.

It just didn't make sense. But there was no escaping the fact that I had been ill, and so had nearly everyone else, and that tests on sixteen people had shown that kidney bean lectin was present in them. The situation was crazy. There had to be another explanation. And I intended to find it.

I SAT IN my office at the restaurant and searched the Internet for information on kidney beans. Sure enough, phytohemagglutinin was the stuff in them that made people ill. I discovered that it was a protein that was broken down and rendered harmless by boiling. Interestingly—or not—I also found out that the same stuff was used to stimulate mitotic division of lymphocytes maintained in a cell culture and facilitate cytogenetic studies of chromosomes, whatever that all meant.

I dug around on my paper-strewn desk to find the delivery note and invoice from Leigh Foods Ltd, the supplier I had used for all of last Friday's ingredients. Everything I had used was listed: the Norwegian cold smoked salmon; the smoked trout and the mackerel fillets; the herbs, wine, cream, olive oil, shallots, garlic cloves, lemon juice and mustard I had used in the dill sauce; the chicken breasts, the cherries, the pancetta and the fresh truffles, wild chanterelle mushrooms, shallots, wine and the cream I had used to make the sauce; all the butter, eggs, sugar, vanilla pods and so on for the brûlées—everything, including the salt and pepper— and not a hint of a kidney bean to be seen. The only ingredient I could think of that I had used and which wasn't listed was some brandy I had added to the truffle and chanterelle sauce, to give it a bit of zing, and I was damn sure there were no kidney beans floating in that.

So where did the toxin come from? I had brought in rolls for the occasion, but surely they weren't stuffed full of beans? The wine? But wouldn't it affect the taste? And how would it get in the bottles?

I was completely baffled. I called Angela Milne. She didn't answer and so I left a message on her voice mail.

"Angela, it's Max Moreton," I said. "I have checked the

ingredients list for last Friday's dinner and there are no kidney beans anywhere. Everything, other than the rolls, was made by me from basic ingredients. I cannot see how any kidney bean toxin could have been present. Are you sure the test results are accurate? Could you please ask whoever did them to have another look? They simply cannot be right."

I put the phone down and it rang immediately before I had even removed my hand.

"Angela?" I answered.

"No," said a male voice. "Bernard."

"Bernard?" I said.

"Yes, Bernard Sims," said the voice. "She's a musician. Plays the viola."

"Sorry," I said. "I'm afraid you've lost me."

"The lady is a musician."

"Who, Bernard Sims?"

"No, Caroline Aston," he said. "I'm Bernard Sims, Mr. Winsome's lawyer."

The penny dropped at last.

"Oh, I see," I said. "Sorry about that, I was thinking about something else." I sorted my thoughts. "So whose guest was Miss Aston at the dinner?"

"No one's. She was a member of the string quartet that played during the evening," said Bernard. "She obviously had the same dinner as all the others who were ill."

I remembered the players, four tall, elegant, black-dressed girls in their twenties. I also remembered being slightly fed up that night that I was working so hard that I hadn't had a chance to chat them up between their rehearsal and the start of the reception. Odd, I thought, how emotions worked. Far from still wanting to wring her neck, I was sorry now that she had been ill in the first place. I told myself to stop being such a softie, that I was probably perfectly justified in sticking pins in the voodoo doll, and that, anyway, she would almost certainly have a six-foot-six bodybuilding boyfriend who would eat me for breakfast if I went near her.

"Where does she work?" I asked.

"Not entirely sure of all the details just yet. I'm still working on it," he said. "She seems to play for the RPO, but

I can't work out why she was in Newmarket in a string quartet last Friday."

"RPO?" I asked.

"Sorry. Royal Philharmonic Orchestra. Real professional stuff. She must be good." I remembered that, to my untrained ear, they had all sounded good, as well as being pleasing on the eye. "Do you want her address?"

"Sure," I said, not knowing quite what I would do with it.

"She lives in Fulham," he said, "on Tamworth Street." He gave me the full address, and her telephone number too. I wrote them down.

"How did you get it?" I asked.

He laughed. "Trade secret."

I assumed that what he had done to get the information wasn't entirely legal, so I didn't push it.

"What should I do?" I asked.

"Don't ask me," he said. "And don't tell me either. I don't want to know." He laughed again. I'd never come across a lawyer like him before. All the others I had met had been so serious. "Perhaps you should ask her out to dinner but taste all her food before she eats it." He guffawed at his little joke. He was clearly enjoying himself hugely, and was still chuckling as he hung up the phone.

I wished I felt like laughing with him.

Gary came into the office. "There's a bird here to see you. Says you would be expecting her."

"Did this bird give you her name?" I asked.

"Harding, I think she said. From some newspaper."

The news editor of the *Cambridge Evening News*. Since having received the information from Angela Milne, I was not sure if this was now such a good idea. Perhaps a low profile would have been the best approach. If I made too much of how clean and hygienic my kitchen was, would I be setting myself up for an even bigger fall if and when the papers reported that I had been cautioned, fined or imprisoned for "rendering food injurious to health," as section 7 of the Food Safety Act of 1990 so concisely defined it? Well, it was too late now. If I didn't see her after making the arrangements, then she would probably write something nasty about me or the restaurant and even more damage would be done.

She was waiting for me in the bar, thirtyish, with shoulder-length dark hair tied back in a ponytail. She was seriously dressed in a dark skirt down to her knees, with a white blouse, and she carried a black, businesslike briefcase. I bet she would have just loved to have been referred to by Gary as "a bird."

"Ms. Harding," I said, holding out my hand, "I'm Max Moreton."

She looked at my hand for a moment, then shook it gingerly. Clearly, she believed that her health was in danger anywhere near me or my restaurant.

"Would you care for a cup of coffee?" I asked.

"Oh no, no thank you," she said with just a touch of panic in her voice.

"Ms. Harding," I said with a smile, "my coffee is quite safe, I assure you. Perhaps you would like to see the kitchen to satisfy yourself that it's clean. I assure you, it is. But don't take my word for it. Ask the local authority. They inspected it on Monday, and the inspector told me it was the cleanest and most hygienic kitchen he had ever visited." It was a little bit of an exaggeration, but so what?

She didn't seem totally reassured, but she did reluctantly agree to come with me into the kitchen.

"Did you bring a photographer?" I said over my shoulder as I led her through the swinging door from the dining room.

"No," she said. "There wasn't one available on such short notice, but I brought a camera. These days, all our reporters carry their own digital cameras. If they take enough shots, then one of them usually turns out to be good enough to print." She looked from side to side as we went past the serving station, where the plated meals were kept under infrared lamps to keep warm before being collected by the waiters and waitresses and taken out into the dining room. She walked with her free hand up near her face, as if she might touch something and be contaminated if she let it down.

Oh dear, I thought, this is going to take more persuasion than I had imagined.

"This is the point at which the kitchen and dining room meet," I said. "Kitchen staff on one side, waiters on the other."

She nodded.

"Perhaps you might want to take a picture," I prompted.

"No," she said. "It's fine. But what I really want to do is talk to you about the bombing."

"OK," I said, "we will. But I want that coffee first." I could have made the coffee in the bar, but I was determined to take her through to my kitchen even if she wouldn't take a picture.

We went on right to the back, where I had purposely placed the coffee machine that usually sat on the sideboard in the dining room. "Are you sure you won't have a cup?" I said. "It's freshly brewed."

She spent a moment or two looking around her at all the shining stainless steel. The work surfaces were so bright she could have fixed her makeup in them, and the cooktops around the gas burners positively gleamed. I noticed her relax a fraction.

I held out a mug of steaming coffee. "Would you like milk and sugar?" I asked.

"Just a little milk," she said. "Thank you." I smiled. Round one to Moreton.

"Is all this stuff new?" she asked, putting her briefcase on the floor and taking the mug of coffee.

"No," I said. "Most of it is six years old, although that stove"—I pointed to the one at the end—"was added a couple of years ago, to make life a little easier."

"But it's all so shiny," she said.

"It has to be to pass the health inspection. Most domestic kitchens wouldn't be allowed to cook food for a restaurant. There would be far too much dirt and grease. When did you last clean the floor under your refrigerator?" I pointed at the kitchen fridge we used exclusively for raw poultry.

She shrugged her shoulders. "No idea." Round two to Moreton.

"Well, the floor under that fridge was cleaned yesterday. And it will be cleaned again today. In fact, it is cleaned every day except Sundays."

"Why not on Sundays?" she asked.

"My cleaner's night off," I said. What I didn't tell her was that I was the cleaner and I never worked on Sunday evenings. Carl ran the kitchen then, as I went home and rested after the busy Sunday lunch service.

She relaxed a little more and even rested her left hand on the work top. "So how come," she said in an accusing tone, "if everything is so clean, you managed to poison so many people and had this place shut down for decontamination?" Round three to Harding.

"The food wasn't cooked here, for a start," I said. "The event was at the racetrack, and a temporary kitchen was set up there. But it was still as clean as this."

"But it couldn't have been," she said. I didn't respond. She pressed the point. "So why did all the guests get food poisoning?"

I decided not to mention anything about the elusive kidney beans, so I said nothing at all and simply shrugged my shoulders.

"Don't you know?" she said in apparent amazement. "You poisoned upwards of two hundred people and you don't know how?" She rolled her eyes. Round four to Harding. But we still were all square.

"I prepared that meal from basic ingredients," I said, "and everything was fresh, clean and thoroughly cooked. I made everything myself, except the rolls and the wine."

"Are you saying it was the bread that made people ill?"

"No, I'm not," I said. "What I am saying is that I don't understand how the people were made ill, and I stake my reputation on the fact that I would do exactly the same if I was preparing that dinner again tonight." First knockdown to Moreton.

She came up punching "But there's no doubt that people were ill. Fifteen were admitted to the hospital and one person died. Don't you feel responsible for that?" It was a body blow, but I countered.

"There is no doubt that people were ill. But your paper was wrong to report that someone died as a result of the dinner. They didn't. And what's more, only seven people were admitted to the hospital, not fifteen."

"Fifteen, seven—it doesn't matter exactly how many. It doesn't change the fact that some people were made so ill they needed hospital treatment."

"Only as a result of dehydration." I knew as I said it that it was a mistake.

"Dehydration can kill very quickly," she said, pouncing. "My great-uncle died from kidney failure brought on by dehydration." Second knockdown, this one to Harding.

"I'm sorry," I said, recovering. "But I assure you, no one died from being ill due to my dinner. Perhaps I could sue you for writing that." Moreton lands a right hook.

"Then why did a source at the hospital say that someone had?"

"It seems that a man did die on Friday night from something that was originally thought to be the food poisoning but turned out not to be. He hadn't been at the dinner. He died from something else."

"Are you sure?" she said suspiciously.

"Absolutely," I said. "You should check with the hospital."

"They wouldn't tell me," she said, "due to their damn privacy policy."

"Then you'd better ask your unofficial source," I said. "It was because of that same incorrect and damaging information that the Food Standards Agency shut down this kitchen, in spite of it not being where the dinner was even cooked. You can see for yourself how clean it is."

"Mmm," she mused. "I have to admit that it doesn't seem very fair." Another round to Moreton.

I pressed home my advantage. "And I was ill too. Do you really think I would have eaten the food myself if I had any thoughts that it might contain toxins?"

"How about if you were ill before you cooked it. It may have been that it was you that contaminated everything and not the ingredients."

"No, I've thought of that," I said. "I wasn't ill beforehand,

and my symptoms were exactly the same as everyone else's. I was poisoned in the same way by the same thing. I just don't know what." I poured myself another cup of coffee and held out the pot to her. She shook her head. "So will you write a piece for your paper that exonerates my restaurant?" I asked.

"Maybe," she said. "It depends. Will you give me any interesting new angles on the racetrack bomb blast?"

"Maybe," I echoed. "If you promise to print it all."

"I can't promise anything without it going through the editor," she said, and smiled. "But since he's my husband, I ought to be able to swing it."

Damn, I thought, another possible romantic opportunity had just slid past me. I quite liked the feisty Ms. Harding. What a shame she was a Mrs.

Carl and Gary needed to get into the kitchen to start preparing for lunch, so Mrs. Harding and I went back to the bar for the rest of the interview, but not until I had insisted on having my photograph taken in the kitchen with as much gleaming stainless steel in the background as I could manage.

I gave her the new angles on the bombing that she had hoped for without fully recounting the graphic details of the blood and the gore. I told her a little about MaryLou, and how horrible it was to have discovered afterwards that she had died. I tried to describe the frustration of not knowing how to cope with the situation without actually admitting to having been a sobbing, shaking wreck.

Finally, she looked at her watch, closed her notebook and said she had to dash, since she had things to finish before the newspaper went to press.

"This will not make it into today's," she said. "Look for it tomorrow."

"Fine," I said. We shook hands, this time without even the slightest hesitation on her part. "Have you ever been here to eat?" I asked her.

"No, never."

"Then come as my guest. Bring your husband. Anytime you like."

"Thank you," she said, smiling, "I'd love to."

Moreton wins by a knockout.

# 7

Angela Milne called first thing on Thursday morning, and I could tell at once that she was more than slightly irritated at having received my message. She told me in no uncertain terms that the testing at the hospital was not wrong or mistaken, and that I should look at myself carefully in the mirror and ask who is fooling who here.

"You served kidney beans that hadn't been properly cooked," she said. "Why don't you just admit it?"

Was I going mad? I knew there were no kidney beans in that dinner. Or did I? What I was absolutely sure of was that I hadn't put any kidney beans in it myself, cooked or otherwise. Could I be so sure that no one else had? But surely, I thought, I would have seen them. Red kidney beans are pretty obvious, as anyone who has eaten chili con carne can testify. Perhaps they had been chopped up and added by someone. But why? And by whom?

There had been plenty of us in the kitchen tent that night, not just my usual team. There had been at least five or six temporary assistants plating the meals, and all the waitstaff had had access as well. Most of these had been from a catering agency, but some were friends of my crew, and one or two had been late recruits from the racetrack caterers when others had dropped out. Did someone purposely poison the dinner due to some catering war? Was it jealousy? Surely not. It just didn't make sense. But I was increasingly steadfast in the knowledge that since I hadn't put the beans in that dinner, someone else must have.

It might be difficult, however, to convince anyone else that I was right. They, like Angela Milne, would simply believe that I had made a basic culinary mistake and was not prepared to admit it.

Wednesday evening had been depressing, with the dining room far less than a quarter full, although one couple who did come had also been at the racetrack event the previous Friday and they had both been ill afterwards.

"Just one of those things," the wife had said. "I'm sure it wasn't your fault." I wished all my customers were like them. I had asked them what they had eaten, but they couldn't remember. I had asked them if they were vegetarians. No, they'd assured me, they were not, and they had ordered a steak each to prove the point.

Thursday proved to be slightly more encouraging with the arrival on my desk of the *Cambridge Evening News,* courtesy of Richard, who went into town to get it. As he said, he had plenty of time on his hands since we had just three tables in the restaurant for lunch, just eight covers in all.

The article in the paper centered mostly around my answers to Ms. Harding's questions concerning the bombing, which I suppose was fair. It did mention, lower down, that further to the article in Monday's edition the Hay Net restaurant was now open for business, having been inspected by the local food inspectors and found clear of any contamination. Ms. Harding also had written that she herself had visited the kitchen of the Hay Net and had been impressed by the standard of hygiene. Good girl. The picture of me with all that gleaming stainless steel had been included next to the article, and I suppose I should be happy even if it was on page seven rather than on the front page as I would have liked.

I thought it would be too soon for the paper to have had any real effect, but Thursday night showed a little improvement, with the numbers up into the mid-thirties. This was far below our usual Thursday-night complement, and still not enough to cover our costs, but, nevertheless, the place felt better, with a slightly livelier atmosphere in the dining room. Perhaps things were looking up. We were going to be closed all day on Friday, for Louisa's funeral, so maybe Saturday evening would tell.

FRIDAY WAS A busy day for funerals in and around Newmarket, at least for people I knew.

Elizabeth Jennings was first up at Our Lady and St. Etheldreda Catholic Church on Exeter Road, near the town center, a modern building constructed in the 1970s but in a traditional style, with rows of Norman arches and columns set either side of the nave and a rose window high above the west door. It was a big church, designed for a town where many of the residents, or their parents, came from Ireland, that most Catholic of countries. Needless to say, for the funeral of the wife of one of the country's most successful and popular trainers the building was packed, standing room only.

I squeezed in to the end of an already-crowded pew. If we had realized that the service would last for well over an hour, with a full Eucharist, I might have found somewhere more comfortable, and my neighbor may not have been so keen to move up to accommodate me.

Bravely, Neil Jennings delivered the eulogy for his wife, and he reduced most of us to tears. He himself managed to hold everything together and get through it with a firm voice, but he looked much older and more vulnerable than his sixty years warranted. He and Elizabeth had never had any children, and I wondered if that was because they were unable to. Consequently, they had always conferred on their horses the love that others might have showered on their offspring. Now, with the untimely and violent passing of his partner, I worried that Neil might go into decline, both personally and in his business.

He stood at the door to the church for at least half an hour and shook the hand of everyone who had been at the service. It is one of those occasions when words are not really enough to transmit one's sorrow, one person for another. Inadequately, I smiled the tight-lipped smile with sad eyes that tries to say "I am so very sorry about your loss," and also "I know that it must be dreadful for you at the moment," without the words actually coming out and sounding so awfully cheesy. He smiled back with the same tight lips but with a furrowed brow and raised eyebrows that said "Thank you for coming," and also "You can have no idea how lonely I am feeling at home." I suppose I should be thankful that he hadn't lowered his brow over his eyes and used them to say "It is all your fault that I am not with her right now."

I stood and chatted with some of the other mourners, most of whom I knew well enough to be on nodding terms with if we passed on the High Street. One of them was George Kealy, the top Newmarket trainer whose wife kept a table on retainer at my restaurant each Saturday night.

"Hello, George," I said to him. "This is a rum do, isn't it?"

"Dreadful." We stood together in silence.

Emma Kealy, George's wife, stood alongside Neil Jennings and held his hand as he finished saying his good-byes at the door. I remembered that Emma was Neil's sister. I watched them both walk slowly over and climb into the back of a black limousine that then pulled away from the curb behind the hearse for Elizabeth's last journey to the cemetery.

George, beside me, shook his head and pursed his lips. I wondered why he hadn't gone with Emma and Neil to the cemetery, but it was no secret in the town that there was no love lost between the two great rival trainers, even if they were brothers-in-law. George suddenly turned back to me. "Sorry about Saturday night," he said. "After all that happened, Emma and I didn't make it to your place for dinner."

"We didn't open anyway," I said. I decided not to add anything about the padlocks.

"No," he said, "I thought you might not." He paused.

"Better cancel us for tomorrow as well. In fact, better leave it for a while. Emma will give you a call. OK?"

"OK," I said, nodding. He turned to leave. "George?" I called. He turned back. "Is your decision anything to do with the event at the racetrack last Friday evening?"

"No," he said unconvincingly. "I don't know. Both Emma and I were dreadfully ill, up all night. Look, I said we'll give you a call, OK?" He didn't wait for an answer but strode off purposefully. I decided that persistence at this time would not be to my advantage in the future.

NEXT, AT TWO-THIRTY, it was Louisa's funeral at the West Chapel at Cambridge Crematorium.

I had been to visit the Whitworths on Wednesday afternoon and I had almost been able to touch the sorrow and anguish present in their house. I had been much mistaken in thinking that Louisa's parents might have blamed her death on her job at the restaurant. In fact, they couldn't have been more effusive about how it had done so much to give her confidence in her own self, as well as the financial independence that she had cherished.

"Not that we didn't help her out, of course," her father had said, choking back the tears. Beryl, Louisa's mother, had clung so tightly to my hand, as if doing so might have brought her daughter back to life. So grief-stricken was she that she had been unable to speak a single word to me throughout my half-hour visit. What cruelty, I thought, had been visited on these dear, simple people whose great pleasure in life was to have had a beautiful, clever and fun-loving daughter, only to have had her snatched away from them forever in such a brutal manner.

I had left their house more disturbed than I had expected and had sat in my car for quite some time before I was able to drive myself back to the restaurant. And her funeral became the biggest ordeal of the day.

I pride myself on being a fairly emotionally stable character, not easily moved either to tears or to anger. However, I suffered dearly in that chapel with both tears and anger very close to the surface. I clenched my teeth together so hard to control myself that my jaw ached for hours afterwards.

As one would imagine, at least two-thirds of those present were young people in their teens, school friends of Louisa. I guessed that for many of them, this was the first funeral they had ever attended. If the grief displayed was a measure of the love and affection that existed for the deceased, then Louisa had been large in the hearts of so many. If grief is the price we pay for love, then overwhelming grief is the price for adoration, and Louisa had been adored by her friends. Before the service finished, several of them needed to be helped outside to sit in the fresh air to recover from near hysteria. By the time I returned to my car in the crematorium parking lot, I was totally exhausted.

And, still, the day had more sorrow to come.

Brian and June Walters had been one of my first-ever customers when I had opened the restaurant. Brian had once been a fellow steeplechase jockey of my father's, and for years they had been close friends, as well as fierce competitors. I think they had come to have dinner at the Hay Net that first time only to support me, as the son of his dead friend, but they had quickly become regular customers, which said a lot for how much they had enjoyed the food, both then and since.

Almost thirty years before, Brian had retired from the dangers of race riding and had joined Tattersalls, the company that owned and ran the world-famous Newmarket horse sales. He had worked hard and had risen steadily up the ladder to be Sales Manager. While he hadn't been the overall decision-making boss, he had been the person whose job it was to make sure that everything ran smoothly on a day-to-day basis, and run smoothly it had. He had recently retired from this lofty position and had been settling down to what he had hoped would be a long and happy retirement, choosing to continue living in the town where his standing was quite high. High enough for him to have been included in the Delafield Industries guest list of local dignitaries at the 2000 Guineas; high enough for him to have been standing with his wife right next to where the bomb had exploded on Saturday. His long and happy retirement had lasted precisely six weeks and one day.

Brian and June had produced four grown-up children between them, but none were actually theirs together, both having been previously married and divorced. As June had often told me over an after-dinner port in my dining room, they were not very close to any of their children since both the divorces had been acrimonious and the children had tended to side with the other partner in each case. Consequently, their joint funeral, late in the afternoon at All Saints', was more unemotional and functional than those I had attended earlier. Many of the same people, including George Kealy, gathered in the Anglican church for the Walterses that had earlier been across the High Street in the Catholic church for Elizabeth Jennings. Was it ungracious of me, I thought, to wonder how many had passed the intervening hours in the bar of the Rutland Arms Hotel, which sat halfway between the two places of worship?

After the service, I decided not to join the cortege of other mourners for the trip to the cemetery for the interment. Instead, I drove the fifteen or so miles from the church in Newmarket to the railway station in Cambridge. Yea, it seemed to me, that I had walked all day through the valley of the shadow of death by the time I wearily boarded the six-fifty train to London. I applied a gin and tonic to comfort me, as I lay down beside the still waters in the green pastures of a first-class seat. I had had my fill of ashes to ashes, dust to dust, and the Twenty-third Psalm for one day.

I sat back, sipped my drink and reflected back on the events of the last week. It seemed much longer than that since I had been preparing the gala dinner in a tent at the racetrack the previous Friday evening.

How seven days can change one's life. Then I had been a confident businessman; diligent, respected, profitable and sleeping like a baby. And I had been happy with my lot. Now, in a mere week, I had become a self-doubting shambles; inactive, accused of being a mass poisoner and a liar, on my way to probable bankruptcy and the victim of regular nightmares about a legless woman. Yet here I was contemplating giving up this easy life for even more stress and anxiety in London. Perhaps I really was going mad.

The train pulled into King's Cross station just before a quarter to eight. I should have been looking forward to my evening with Mark. But I wasn't.

"RISE ABOVE IT," Mark said over dinner. "Have faith in yourself, and bugger what people think."

"But you have to attract the customers," I said. "Surely it matters what they think?"

"Gordon Ramsay just swears at everyone, and they love him for it."

"Trust me, they wouldn't in Newmarket," I said. "For all the earthiness of racing and its reputation for bad language, those within it value being given their due respect. Trainers may swear at their stable lads, but they wouldn't dream of swearing at their owners. The horses would disappear quicker than you could say abracadabra."

"But I'm not talking about Newmarket," said Mark, getting us around to the real reason for our dinner. "It's time you came to London to run a place like this. Time you made your name."

We were in the restaurant of the OXO Tower, on the eighth floor overlooking the City of London skyline. It was one of my favorite venues, and, indeed, if I was to run a restaurant in the metropolis then this would be the sort of establishment I would create, a combination of sophistication and fun. It helps, of course, to have an interesting and unusual venue, and this was it. According to the brief history printed on the menus, the restaurant sat atop what had been a 1920s warehouse built by the Liebig Extract of Meat Company, who made OXO beef stock cubes. When the company was refused planning permission to put up the name OXO in lights on the front of the building to shine across the Thames, an architect incorporated the word in the window shapes on all four sides of a tower built above the warehouse. The meat extract company has long gone from the site, which now contains design shops, residential accommodation, as well as four different cafés and restaurants, but the tower remains, with its OXO windows. Hence, the name.

"Well?" said Mark. "Lost your tongue?"

"I was thinking," I said. "It's quite a change."

"You do want to make your name, don't you?" he said earnestly.

"Yes, absolutely," I replied. "But I'm more worried at the moment of making it in the tabloids as a mass poisoner."

"In a week it will be forgotten about. All anyone will remember will be your name, and that's an advantage."

I hoped he was right. "What about the girl that's suing me?" I asked.

"Don't worry about her," he said. "Settle out of court and it won't be reported. Give her a hundred quid for her trouble and move on. Stupid idea anyway, suing over a bit of food poisoning. What does she hope to get? Not much loss of earnings through the night anyway, not unless she was on the game!" He laughed at his own joke, and I relaxed a little.

We were sat in the round-backed, blue leather chairs of the restaurant at the OXO, and I was enjoying allowing someone else to do the cooking for a change. I chose the foie gras galantine, with a fig chutney and brioche, to start, and then the rack of lamb with sweetbreads for my main course, while Mark went for the lobster to start and the organic Shetland cod for his main. In spite of his choice of fish, Mark was a red wine man, so we sat and took pleasure from an outstanding bottle of 1990 Château Latour.

"Now, then," he said once the first courses were served, "where shall we have this restaurant and what style do you fancy?"

Why did those questions ring alarm bells in my head? Mark had stuck absolutely to his deal over the Hay Net. He had provided the finance but given me a free hand in everything else: venue, style, menus, wines, staff—the lot. I had asked him at the time to give me an indication of an overall budget for the setting up and for the first year of operation. "More than half a million, less than a million," is all he said. "And what security?" I had asked him. "The deeds to the property and a gentlemen's agreement that you will work at the venture for a minimum of ten years unless we both agree otherwise." In the end, I had used nearly all his million, but his fifty percent of the profits for the past five years had paid back far more than half of it, and he still held the deeds. Over ten years, at the prepoisoning turnover rate, the Hay Net would provide for a very healthy return on his investment. I, of course, was delighted and proud that my little Newmarket establishment had proved to be such a success, both financially and in terms of "standing" in the town. However, what had been more important to me than anything was my independence. It may have been Mark's money that I had used to set it up, and he ultimately owned the building in which it was housed, but it was my restaurant and I had made all the decisions, every one.

Did I detect in Mark's questions his intent to have a more hands-on role in any new London venture? Or was I jumping to conclusions? Did he not mean where shall *you* have the restaurant? Not where shall *we*? I decided it was not the time to press the point.

"I would have a place like this," I said. "Traditional yet modern."

"It can't be both," said Mark.

"Of course it can," I said. "This restaurant has traditional values, with white tablecloths, good service, fine food and wine, and a degree of personal privacy for the diners. Yet the décor is modern in appearance, and the food has an innovative nature, with Mediterranean and Asian influences. In Newmarket, my dining room is purposely more like one you might find in a private house, and my food is very good but less imaginative than I would attempt here. It is not that my clients are less sophisticated than London folk. They're not. It's just that their choice of restaurant is fewer, and many come to eat at the Hay Net often, some every week. On that regular basis, they need to be comfortable rather than challenged, and they want their food predictable rather than experimental."

"Doesn't everyone?" he said. "I'm having cod. Surely that's predictable."

"Wait and see," I replied, laughing. "I bet you look at it

twice and ask yourself if it's what you ordered. It won't be a slab of fish in batter with chips that you would get wrapped in newspaper at the local chippie. It comes with a cassoulet, which is a rich bean stew, usually with white haricots, and a purée of Jerusalem artichoke. Would you know what a Jerusalem artichoke looks like? And what it tastes of?"

"Hasn't it got spiky leaves?" he said. "That you suck?"

"That's a *globe* artichoke," I said. "A Jerusalem artichoke is a type of sunflower, and you eat the roots, which are tubers, like potatoes."

"From Jerusalem, I assume."

"Actually, no." I laughed again. "Don't ask why it's called the Jerusalem artichoke. I don't know. But it definitely has nothing to do with Jerusalem the city."

"Like the hymn," said Mark. "You know, 'did those feet' and all that. Nothing to do with the city. Jerusalem there means 'heaven.' Perhaps the artichokes taste like heaven too."

"More like a radish," I said. "And they tend to make you fart."

"Good," said Mark, laughing. "I might need my own train carriage home."

Now, I decided, was the moment.

"Mark," I said seriously, "I will have absolute discretion in any new restaurant, won't I? Just like at the Hay Net?"

He sat and looked at me. I feared for a moment that I had misjudged things.

"Max," he said, finally, "how often have I asked you how to sell a mobile phone?"

"Never."

"Exactly. Then why would you ask me how to run a restaurant?"

"But you do eat in restaurants," I said.

"And you use a cell phone," he countered.

"Fine," I said. "I promise I won't discuss cell phones with you if you promise not to discuss restaurants with me."

He sat in silence and smiled at me. Had I really outflanked the great Mark Winsome?

"Can I have a veto?" he asked at length.

"On what?" I asked rather belligerently.

"Venue."

What could I say? If he didn't like the venue, he wouldn't sign a contract for a lease. He had a veto on the venue anyway.

"If you provide the finance, then you get a veto," I said. "If you don't, then you don't."

"OK," he said. "Then I want to provide the finance. Same terms as before?"

"No," I said. "I want more than fifty percent of the profit."

"Isn't that a bit greedy?" he said.

"I want to be able to empower my staff with participation in profit."

"How much?"

"That's up to me," I said. "You get forty percent and I get sixty percent and then I decide, at my sole discretion, to give as much or as little of that as I want as bonuses to my staff."

"Do you get a salary?"

"No," I said. "Same as now. But I get sixty instead of fifty percent of the profit."

"How about during setting up? Last time, you took a salary from my investment for the first eighteen months."

"But I paid it back," I pointed out. "This time, I won't need it. I have savings, and I intend to back myself with it as far as my salary is concerned."

"Anything else?" Mark asked.

"Yes," I said. "Ten years is too long. Five years. Then I get the chance to buy you out at a fair price."

"How do you define 'fair price'?"

"I can match the best offer, public or private, made by an independent third party."

"On what terms?"

"The cost of the lease plus forty percent of their valuation of the business."

"Fifty," he said.

"No, forty of the business value and one hundred percent of the lease."

"How about if I want to buy you out?" he asked.

"It would cost you sixty percent of the business value,

and I could walk away." I wondered how much the value of the business might change if the chef walked away. But, then again, I could think of no circumstances in which he would buy me out.

Mark sat back in his chair and looked at me. "You drive a damn hard bargain."

"Why not?" I said. "I have to do all the work. All you have to do is sign a big check and then sit on your arse and wait for the money to flood in." At least, I hoped it would flood in.

"Do you know how many restaurants in London close within a year with huge losses?" he said. "I'm taking quite a risk with my money."

"So?" I said. "You've got plenty of it. I'm gambling with my reputation."

"For what it's *now* worth," he said, and laughed.

"You said to rise above it and have faith in myself. Well, I have. We won't close in a year, not even in two."

He looked at me with his head to one side, as if thinking. He suddenly leaned forward in his chair. "OK, you're on," he said, and stretched out his hand.

"Just like that?" I said. "We haven't even found a place and we haven't started to draw up a budget."

"I thought you said that was your job. I just write the check, remember?"

"How big a check?" I asked him.

"As big as you need," he said, again offering his hand.

"Fine," I said. "You're on too."

I shook his hand warmly, and we smiled at each other. I liked Mark a lot. Even though his lawyers would have to draw up the contract, his word was his bond and mine was mine. The deal was done.

I COULD HARDLY sit still for the rest of our dinner, such was my excitement. Mark laughed when his cod arrived. I had been absolutely right.

The chef came out of the kitchen and joined the two of us for a glass of port at the end of the evening. The previous year, he and I had been the judges of a cooking contest on afternoon daytime television and we now enjoyed catching up on our friendship.

"How's that place of yours doing out in the sticks?" he asked.

"Very well," I said, hoping he didn't have copies of the *Cambridge Evening News* delivered daily to his door. I also wondered if he would be quite so friendly if he knew that Mark and I had been sitting in his restaurant planning our move into his territory. "How's business here?" I asked by way of conversation.

"Oh, the same," he said without actually explaining what "the same" meant.

The conversation progressed for a while in a similar, noncommittal and vague manner, neither of us wanting to pass on our professional judgment to the other. The world of haute cuisine could be as secret as any government intelligence service.

The need to catch the last train home finally broke up the dinner at eleven o'clock, and Mark and I walked in easy companionship along the Thames embankment towards Waterloo station. We strolled past some of the lively pubs, bistros and pizza parlors that had transformed the south bank. Late on this Friday evening, loud music and raucous laughter spilled out across the cobblestones towards the river.

"Where and when will you start looking for a venue?" asked Mark.

"I don't know, and as soon as possible," I said, smiling in the dark. "I suppose I will contact some commercial real estate agents to see what's available."

"You will keep me informed?" he said.

"Of course." We walked past an advertising board. A poster read RPO AT THE RFH in big bold black letters on a white background. Thanks to Bernard Sims, I knew what RPO stood for—the Royal Philharmonic Orchestra. "What's the RFH?" I asked Mark.

"What?" he said.

"What's the RFH?" I repeated, pointing at the poster.

"Royal Festival Hall," he said. "Why?"

"No reason. Just wondered." I looked closely at the poster. The RPO, with, I presumed, Caroline Aston playing the viola, was due to appear next month at the Royal Festival Hall. Perhaps I would go and listen.

Mark and I said our good-byes outside the National Theatre, and he rushed off to get his lonely ride home while I decided to walk across the Golden Jubilee footbridge to the Embankment tube station, north of the river. Halfway across, I briefly leaned on the bridge rail and looked eastwards towards the tall city buildings, many of them with all their windows bright in the night sky.

Among the high-rises, and dimly lit by comparison, I could see the majestic dome of St. Paul's. My history master at school had loved that building with a passion, and he had drummed some of its facts into the heads of his pupils. I recalled that it had been built to replace the previous cathedral that had been destroyed by the Great Fire of London in 1666. Constructed in just thirty-five years, it had, amazingly, remained the tallest building in London for more than a quarter of a millennium, right up until the glass-and-concrete towers of the nineteen sixties.

As I stood there, I wondered whether Sir Christopher Wren had ever believed that he had embarked on a project that was beyond him. Was I now embarking on a project that was beyond me?

I raised an imaginary glass towards his great achievement and made a silent toast: Sir Christopher, you managed it. And I can too.

# 8

K idney beans!"

"Yes, kidney beans, probably red kidney beans. According to the tests done on those customers taken to the hospital, there was something called phytohemagglutinin in the dinner and that's what made everyone ill. It's also known as 'kidney bean lectin.'"

It was late Saturday afternoon, and I was having a meeting with Carl and Gary in my office prior to us opening for dinner. We didn't do lunches on Saturday. Too many of my clientele were away at the races.

"But there weren't any kidney beans in that dinner," said Carl.

"That's what I thought," I said. "But, apparently, there were samples taken from sixteen different individuals, and this stuff was in all of them."

Gary and Carl looked at each other. "Beats me," said Gary.

"Where in the dinner could they have been?" asked Carl.

"That," I said, "is what I intend to find out. And then I'll find out who put them there."

"Surely you're not saying that someone poisoned everyone on purpose?" said Carl.

"What else can I think?" I replied. "Consider the facts. Loads of those who ate the dinner were ill, including me. Tests on sixteen of them show this phyto stuff in them. The stuff made them ill, and it only comes from kidney beans. Doesn't take a genius to conclude that there must have been kidney beans in the dinner. I know I didn't put any in the dinner. So, QED, someone else must have, and it must have been done on purpose to make people ill."

"But why?" said Gary.

"I don't know." I was exasperated. "But it had to be done by someone who had access to the kitchen."

"Loads of people had access to the kitchen," said Carl. "We didn't exactly have a guard on duty. There were all the kitchen staff from the agency, and all the waiters too."

"And there were others from the racetrack caterers there as well," I said. "But, believe me, I intend to find out who it was."

"But wouldn't you see red kidney beans in anything?" said Gary.

"I thought that myself," I said. "But you wouldn't if they were chopped up very finely."

"How many beans would you need to poison over two hundred people?" said Carl. "Surely there would be so many it would affect the taste?"

"I looked it up on the U.S. Food and Drug Administration Web site on the Internet," I said. "It says there that four or five raw beans are enough to make people quite ill. It also says that if the beans are heated to not more than eighty degrees centigrade, they are five times as poisonous as the raw ones. That means just a single bean per person could be enough. And it also says that the attack rate is one hundred percent—that means everyone who ate the beans would be ill."

"But where were they?" said Gary.

"I think they must have been put in the sauce," I said. No one, I thought, would taste a single partially cooked kidney bean, especially if it was finely chopped up and mixed with the chanterelle mushrooms, the truffles and the shallots, not to mention the white wine, the brandy, the garlic and the cream.

"But you have to reduce the wine in that sauce," said Carl. What he meant by "reduce" was that the sauce was boiled to remove some of the excess liquid by evaporation. "Surely that would render the beans harmless even if they were in there?"

"They had to have been added after the reduction," I said. "That sauce had cream in it to add richness. It wasn't boiled after the cream was added." To prevent it curdling in the acidity of the wine.

I remembered back to the dinner. In order to produce enough, I had used four large aluminum cooking pots to produce the sauce, similar to domestic kitchen saucepans only bigger, with handles on each side. The ones that Stress-Free Catering had provided would each hold about six liters of liquid, if full. I had estimated that we would require fifty milliliters of sauce per person. So for two hundred and fifty servings, I had needed twelve and a half liters of sauce. I had made it in four separate batches, just in case a batch curdled. In the end, all four batches had been fine, and there had been plenty left over. I remembered it well, as I loved the sauce and had poured extra on my own dinner. Just my bad luck.

The four half-full pots had stood in the serving area, where we had made up the dinners on the plates with the sliced stuffed chicken breasts, the roasted new potatoes, the snow peas and the sauce, with a sprig of parsley on the potatoes to garnish. The pots hadn't been directly heated on a range for some minutes, as I had judged that they were hot enough and would maintain their temperature throughout the serving if simply placed on top of the hot stainless steel servers. I had told one of the temporary kitchen staff to stir the sauce to prevent it from separating. He had been of little use for anything else, and I remembered him because it had taken me some time to explain what was required because he didn't understand English very well. I had assumed at the time that he was Polish or Czech, or from some other eastern European country, as so many staff in the catering business seem to be these days.

I reckoned there had been about a ten-minute window when the beans could have been added to the sauce between being moved from the kitchen and the service. At that time, I mostly had been around the corner in the kitchen or out in the dining area. Either way, I had been out of sight of the pots during that vital time. Due to the positioning between the kitchen and the dining room, almost any of the staff that night could have had the chance to add something to the pots. But it had to have been someone who knew the place, and surely my stirrer or someone else would have seen them. It still made little sense to me.

"So what do you suggest we do?" said Gary.

"Nothing we can do," I said, "except carry on as before. We have sixty-five booked for dinner, and, so far, no one has called today to cancel."

The telephone on my desk rang. Why didn't I keep my stupid mouth shut, I thought, as I lifted the receiver.

"Hello," I said. "Hay Net restaurant."

"Max? Is that you?" said a female voice.

"Certainly is," I said.

"Good. This is Emma Kealy. I understand you saw George at Elizabeth's funeral yesterday."

"Yes," I said, "I did. I'm so sorry about Elizabeth."

"Yes," she said. "Thank you. A dreadful thing, especially for poor Neil." She paused for a moment. "But life has to go on for the rest of us."

"How can I help?" I asked her.

"Well, George tells me that he canceled our booking for tonight."

"Yes, he did. He said to leave it for a while."

"Stupid old fool," she said. "We still have people staying tonight, and there's no food in the house. What does he think I'm going to do? Go to the Raj of India?" The Raj of India was a seedy take-out curry place on Palace Street. It would never have crossed my mind that Emma Kealy would have even known about it, let alone thought of going there. "Can you fit four of us in for tonight at eight-thirty?" she said imploringly. "I will perfectly understand if we can't have our usual table."

"Of course we can fit you in," I said. "Look forward to seeing you."

"Great. See you later, then." I could hear the relief in her voice. I wondered how much of a row had gone on between her and George.

I put the phone down and looked at Gary and Carl. "Four more bookings for tonight," I said, smiling. Thank goodness for the Kealys.

The other two went into the kitchen to start preparing for dinner while I sat at my desk to complete some paperwork. I shuffled the stack of already-tidy papers, checking that there were no outstanding bills that had to be paid immediately. I came across the delivery note from Leigh Foods, the supplier I had used for the gala dinner. I looked through the ingredients again, as if I could have missed the kidney beans before. They weren't there. Of course they weren't there. I would swear on my father's grave that I had not put any damn kidney beans in that dinner.

I called Suzanne Miller on her cell.

"Hi, Suzanne," I said, "Max Moreton here. Sorry to disturb you on a Saturday afternoon. Do you have a minute?"

"Fire away," she said. "I'm in my office anyway. We've had a wedding here today, so I'm still working."

"I didn't know you had weddings at the racetrack," I said.

"Oh yes," she said. "Most Saturdays during the summer, when there's no racing, of course. We use the Hong Kong Suite for the ceremony and then, often, the Champions Gallery restaurant for the reception. It works quite well."

"You live and learn," I said.

"How can I help you?" she asked.

"I wonder if I could have a copy of the guest list from last Friday night?"

"Sure," she said, "no problem. I have it on my computer. I'll e-mail it to you now."

"Thanks," I said. "There is another thing. Do you have a list of the names of all the temporary staff that you found through the agency?"

"Not their names," she said. "The agency just gave me the number that would be there, not their names."

"But, you remember, some of them failed to turn up, and we had to draft in a few of your own staff at the last minute," I said. "Do you, by chance, have the names of those that didn't come, and also the names of your staff that we drafted in?"

"I'll e-mail the agency's phone number and you can ask them directly," she said. "Why do you need to know the names of my staff?"

How much should I tell her? She had been quick to hang me out to dry when the letter from Caroline Aston had first appeared on her desk. Would she now simply think I was looking for a scapegoat?

"I have reason to believe that something may have been put into the dinner that shouldn't have been there," I said, "and I am trying to determine the names of everyone who was there and had access to the food so I can find out who was responsible."

There was a long pause at the other end of the line.

"Are you saying that you think my staff are to blame for making people ill?" Suzanne said rather frostily.

"No," I replied hastily. "I'm not saying that, and I don't think it. Your staff were all last-minute replacements, so it is impossible for them to be the ones." I thought it most unlikely that anyone could buy and prepare a large number of kidney beans on such short notice. "I would just like their names so that I can eliminate them from my inquiry." I was beginning to sound like a policeman.

"I will look it up," she said. "But I will have to ask them first if they are happy for you to have their names."

"That's fine by me," I said.

"Do you really think that the food was poisoned on purpose?"

"Suzanne," I said, "I know it sounds crazy, but I have absolutely no other explanation. Hospital tests have shown beyond doubt that there was stuff in that dinner that I didn't put in there, so what am I to think?"

"What stuff?" she asked.

"I'd rather not say," I said. I don't know why I thought it might be useful to keep some of the facts secret. Perhaps I had hopes of catching out the culprit by him saying "kidney beans" when I hadn't mentioned it. I was sure that I had once read a detective novel where that sort of thing had happened and the policeman had instantly solved the case.

"All sounds very cloak-and-dagger to me," she said. "And a bit far-fetched as well, if you ask me. Why would anyone want to poison so many people anyway?"

"I don't know why," I said. "Why do so many people have the urge to break things? Perhaps it was just done for kicks. There's no logic to many things."

"Are the police looking for whoever did it?" she asked.

"Not that I'm aware of," I said. "I think the police are preoccupied looking for last Saturday's bomber."

"You're probably right," she said. "They're certainly still here at the racetrack, and we nearly had to cancel today's wedding because of them, but, thankfully, we don't use the Head On Grandstand. That's now going to be closed for months. But surely you should inform the police if you have suspicions about the dinner?"

"Maybe I will," I said, although privately I thought they would believe the same as Angela Milne, that I had simply served undercooked kidney beans and was not prepared to admit it.

"What else do you intend to do?" she asked.

"Probably nothing," I said. "A bit of food poisoning that didn't do any permanent harm to anyone is not really important compared to the bombing." And, I thought, it might be better for my reputation, and for the restaurant, if I were to let the incident slowly fade from people's memory rather than keep stirring it up.

"Let me know if I can be of any help," said Suzanne.

"Thanks, I will," I said. "And don't forget the guest list and the agency information."

"On their way to you right now." I could hear her tapping away on a keyboard. "Gone," she said. "Should be with you any moment."

"Brilliant. Thanks." We hung up, and I turned to my computer.

YOU'VE GOT MAIL, it told me, and, sure enough, with a

couple of clicks, the guest list from the gala dinner appeared before my eyes. How did we function before e-mail?

I scanned through the list of names, but I didn't actually know what I was looking for, or why, so I printed it out and left it lying on my pile of stuff to be dealt with. I logged on to the Internet instead.

I made a search for RPO and soon I was delving into the details of concerts and operas of the Royal Philharmonic. Sure enough, the concert program at the Royal Festival Hall was widely advertised, and, if I wished, I could purchase a ticket with just a couple of clicks of my computer mouse. I noticed that tonight, and for most of the next week, the orchestra was performing the works of Sibelius and Elgar at Carnegie Hall in New York City. Lucky Caroline Aston, I thought. I had been to New York in the springtime the previous year and had loved every moment.

I looked at Ms. Aston's telephone number on the notepad where I had written it on Wednesday morning when Bernard Sims had called. If she was in New York, she wouldn't be at home now. Three times I punched her number into my phone without actually pushing the button for the final digit. I wondered if there might be a voice message, so I could hear what she sounded like. The fourth time, I completed the number and let it ring twice before I lost my nerve and hung up. Maybe she didn't live alone and someone would be there to answer after all.

I played with the phone for a while longer and then called the number again. Someone answered after a single ring.

"Hello," said a female voice.

Oops, I thought, no recorded voice message. A real live speaking person.

"Is this Caroline Aston?" I asked, confident in the knowledge that she was, in fact, three thousand miles away.

"Yes," she replied. "Can I help you?"

"Er," I said, sounding like an idiot, "would you like to buy some double glazing?"

"No thank you," she said. "Good-bye!" She hung up.

Stupid, I thought, as I sat there with my heart thumping in

my chest. Really stupid. I put the phone down and it rang immediately.

"Hello," I said.

"Would *you* like to buy some double glazing?"

"Excuse me?" I said.

"See. Why do you think I would want to buy double glazing from someone I don't know who rings me up out of the blue? You don't like it and neither do I."

I didn't know what to say. "I'm sorry." It sounded ridiculous even to me.

"Who are you anyway?" she said. "You're not very good at selling."

"How did you get my number?" I asked.

"Caller ID," she said. "I didn't think you people would have a number that was visible. More important, how did you get *my* number?"

I could hardly tell her the truth, but whatever else I said now was going to get me into deeper trouble. I decided to retreat gracefully.

"Look, I'm sorry, but I have to go now. Good-bye." I hung up quickly. My hands were sweating. Really, really stupid!

I went out into the kitchen and found Carl trying to explain rather sarcastically to one of the kitchen porters that it was indeed necessary for him to get all the old food off the frying pans when washing up.

In spite of the name, kitchen porters rarely carry things. They mostly spend their lives up to their elbows in hot water washing up the pots and pans. We had two of them at the Hay Net. At least, that was the plan. But all too often a kitchen porter would be there one minute and gone the next. No explanation, no good-bye, just gone, never to return. The current incumbents of the posts included a man in his fifties whose father had come to England from Poland in 1940 to fight with the RAF against the Nazis. He had unpronounceable Polish names, with lots of *p*s and *z*s, but he spoke with a broad Essex accent, and was always "tinking." "I tink I'll go hame na," he'd say. Or, "I tink I'll 'ave a cap o' tea." He'd been with us for nearly a year, much longer than the norm, but he mostly kept himself to himself and communicated rarely with the other staff.

The other porter was called Jacek (pronounced *Ya*-check), and he was now in his fourth week and seemingly not very good at scrubbing the frying pans. He was more typical of those now sent to us by the local job center, in his mid to late twenties, and from one of the newer member countries of the European Union. He knew very little English, but he did manage to ask for my help sending money every week to his wife and baby daughter, who were still in the homeland. He seemed quite happy with life, always smiling and singing to himself, and he had been a positive influence on kitchen morale over the previous week. Now he stood in front of Carl and bowed his head, as if asking for forgiveness. Jacek nodded a lot, and I wondered how much of Carl's tirade he was actually understanding. I was certain that he was not appreciating the sarcasm. I felt quite sorry for him, so far from home, in a strange environment and separated from his family.

I caught Carl's attention. That's enough, I mouthed to him. Jacek was hardworking, and I didn't really want to lose him at the moment, not least because the current pair appeared to get on quite well together and neither of them was a heavy drinker, generally the bane of all kitchen porters.

Carl stopped almost in midsentence and dismissed the miscreant with a brief wave of his hand. Jacek passed me on the way back to his duties at the scullery sinks, and I smiled at him. He winked at me and smiled back. There was more to this kitchen porter, I thought, than meets the eye.


SATURDAY NIGHT HAD the feel of the Hay Net back in business. Sure, we were only serving at about two-thirds capacity, but the bar and the dining room were humming with excitement, and the horrors of the previous week were forgotten, albeit temporarily.

George and Emma Kealy and their two guests arrived promptly at eight-thirty, sat at their usual table and seemed to enjoy themselves, though quietly. Nothing was mentioned about my discussion with George at the funeral, but, as they were leaving, Emma turned to me and said, "See you next week, then, as usual."

"For six?" I asked.

"Book for six," she said. "I'll let you know on Friday."

"Fine," I said, smiling at her.

"Have you found out yet what made everyone ill last week?" she asked. George looked horrified that his wife had been so tactless as to mention it.

"Not quite," I said. "It appears that the dinner may have been contaminated."

"What with?" asked Emma.

"I'm not quite sure yet," I said. I wondered if it was simply embarrassment that was preventing me from mentioning anything about undercooked kidney beans. "I'm still trying to work out how something was put into the food."

"You are surely not saying it was done on purpose," she said.

"That is my inescapable conclusion," I said.

"Sounds a bit fanciful to me," said George.

"Maybe to you," I said, "but what else can I think? Just suppose, George, you had a horse that ran like the wind on the gallops and then was more like a cart horse when you sent it out to run in a race, and it subsequently tested positive for dope. If you absolutely knew you hadn't personally given it any substance to slow it down, then you would conclude that someone else must have done so. The same here. I absolutely know I didn't put anything in that dinner to make people ill, but tests have shown that there was a food-poisoning agent present. So someone else must have put it there. And that, I believe, only could have been done on purpose. And, I can assure you, I intend to find out who was responsible."

I thought that I probably shouldn't be telling them quite so much, but they were supporting me when others were deserting, so maybe I owed them.

"Well, it did us a big favor anyway," said Emma.

"How so?" I asked.

"We were invited to that lunch where the bomb went off," she said. "We didn't go only because we had both had such a bad night. How lucky was that! Although, I must admit, on the Saturday morning I was bloody angry with you." She poked me in the chest with her finger. "I had been so looking forward to that day at the Guineas. Anyway, it turned out to be a blessing in the end." She smiled at me. "So I forgive you."

I smiled back and put a hand on her arm. "That's all right, then," I said. I always responded positively when flirted with by female customers who were old enough to be my mother. It was good for business.

"Come on, Emma," said George impatiently, "we must go. Peter and Tanya are waiting." He waved his hand towards their guests, who were standing patiently by the front door.

"All right, George," she replied, irritated. "I'm coming." She stretched up her five-foot-three frame to my six feet for a kiss, and, leaning forward, I duly obliged. "Night-night," she said. "It's been a lovely evening."

"Thank you for coming," I said, meaning it.

"And you can poison us anytime you like if it saves our lives." She smiled.

"Thanks," I said, trying to think of an appropriate response.

George was hopping from one foot to the other. "Come on, my darling," he said with exasperation. Emma complied with a sigh. I watched through the window as the four of them got into and drove away in a new, top-of-the-line Mercedes.

That made three people that I now knew of who should have been in the bombed box but weren't because they had been made ill by the dinner. Poor old Neil Jennings had wished he had been there with Elizabeth, but the Kealys certainly didn't. They were perversely grateful for having been poisoned. Perhaps this particular dark cloud had a silver lining after all.

THE FEWER NUMBER in the restaurant had tended to make the service somewhat quicker than usual, and the last few diners departed just before eleven. On some Saturday nights, we could be still pouring ports and brandies after midnight, and, once or twice, it had been after one in the morning before I had cajoled the stragglers out through the front door and into the night.

I sat at my desk in the office and silently hoped that the worst was over. If I could nip the lawsuit in the bud, and plead ignorance and forgiveness over the poison kidney beans, then maybe normality would return to the Hay Net, at least for a few months, until I was ready to announce a move to the big city. How wrong I could be.

I looked at my watch. Eleven-fifteen. Time to go home, I thought. A nice early night for a change.

The telephone rang at my elbow.

"Hello," I said into the receiver. "Hay Net restaurant."

There was just silence at the other end.

"Hello," I said again. "The Hay Net restaurant. Can I help you?"

"Why did you tell me you were selling double glazing?"

"Er." I sat there, not knowing quite what to say.

"Well?" she said. "I'm waiting."

"I don't know why," I mumbled.

"Are you a bloody idiot or something?"

Yes, I probably was. "No," I said. "Can I please explain?"

"I'm waiting," she said again.

"Not here, not now, not on the telephone," I said. "Perhaps we could meet?"

"How did you get my number?" she demanded.

"Directory inquiries," I said.

"I'm ex-directory."

"Oh. I don't remember," I said. "Maybe it was through the orchestra."

"They only have my cell number."

I was getting into deeper water, and quickly.

"Look," I said, "if we can meet I will be able to explain everything. Perhaps I can give you dinner?"

"I'm not coming to Newmarket," she said. "I'm not giving you another bloody chance to poison me."

"You choose the venue and I'll pay for the dinner. Anywhere you like."

There was a short pause as she thought.

"Gordon Ramsay," she said.

"At Claridge's?" I asked.

"No, of course not," she said. "The Restaurant Gordon Ramsay, in Royal Hospital Road. I'm free every night this week until Friday."

The Restaurant Gordon Ramsay, quite apart from being one of the most expensive restaurants in the world, was notoriously difficult to get into. Bookings were taken from nine A.M., two calendar months in advance, and were often completely filled each day by ten-thirty. I would have to try to pull strings of a fellow-professional sort if I was to have any chance of getting a table in the coming week.

"I'll call you," I said.

"Right, you do that." Was it me or did her tone imply that I wouldn't be able to fix it?

"Why, aren't you in New York?" I asked somewhat foolishly.

"Your bloody dinner took care of that," she said angrily. "I couldn't make it to the airport last Saturday and was replaced."

"Oh," I said.

"Oh indeed. I'd been looking forward to the New York trip for months, and you bloody ruined it."

"I'm sorry," I said.

"Is that an admission of guilt?"

I could imagine Bernard Sims going crazy with me. "No, of course not," I said.

"My agent says I should take you to the bloody cleaners," she said. "He says that I should get ten thousand at least."

I thought back to Mark's advice and reckoned that it might need more than a hundred quid to buy her off. "I think that your agent is exaggerating," I said.

"You think so?" she said. "I've not just lost out on my pay for the tour, you know. There's no guarantee that I will be invited back into the orchestra when they get home. The directors can be very fickle. I've only just been promoted to principal viola, and now this bloody happens." She clearly liked to say "bloody" a lot.

"Tell me," I asked, trying to change the subject, "what's the difference between a violin and a viola?"

"What?" she screamed over the phone. "Didn't you hear me? I said that you might have cost me my bloody career."

"I'm sure that's not really true," I said. "You should calm down. It's not good for your blood pressure."

There was a pause. "You're very annoying," she said.

"So my brother always used to say," I said.

"He was absolutely right." She paused. "Well?"

"Well what?" I asked.

"What are you going to do about it?"

"Nothing," I said.

"Nothing! In that case, I'll see you in court."

"OK," I said. "But do tell me, what is the difference?"

"Difference?"

"Between a violin and a viola?" I said.

"It's not a viola," she said, pronouncing it like I had done with the *i* as "eye." "It's a viola." She said it with the *i* short, as in "tin" or "sin."

"So what is the difference?"

"A viola burns longer than a violin."

"What?" I said.

"Oh, I'm sorry," she said, and laughed. "It's an old joke among musicians. We viola players tend to be the butt of all the worst orchestra jokes. We get used to it, and we don't really care. I think everyone else is jealous."

"So what is the difference between them?"

"They're different instruments."

"I know that," I said. "But they look the same."

"No they don't," she said. "A viola is much bigger than a violin. That's like saying a guitar looks like a cello."

"No it's not. That's silly," I retorted. "A cello is played upright and a guitar is played horizontally, for a start."

"Ha!" she said smugly. "Jimi Hendrix played his guitar upright most of the time."

"Don't be pedantic," I said, laughing. "You know what I mean. Violins and violas are both played with a bow, under the chin."

"Or with the fingers," she said. "*Pizzicato*. And it's not so much under the chin as on the shoulder."

"Does that mean you have your chin in the air?"

"It might," she said. I could tell from the tone of her voice that she was smiling. I decided that it might be a good time to get out of this call before she started asking again how I knew her home telephone number and her occupation.

"I'll call you about dinner," I said. "It will be probably be Tuesday." It tended to be one of our least busy nights at the Hay Net, and often the night I would be away, either cooking elsewhere or at some other event.

"You really think you can get a table?" she said.

"Of course I can," I replied. "No problem."

I hoped I was right. It might just save me ten grand.

# 9

W e were seated at a table for two against the wall near the door. Let's face it, it wasn't the best table in the place. But Caroline was impressed nevertheless.

"I never thought you would manage to get a table," she said when she arrived. "To be honest, if I had thought you actually could I wouldn't have suggested it in the first place. I'm not at all certain that I really want to be here." And she had a scowl on her face to prove it.

I wasn't sure how to take that comment, but she had come, and that was all that was important to me at the time. Over the past couple of days, I had tried hard to recall the string quartet at the gala dinner. I could recall that they had all worn long black dresses with their hair tied back in pony-tails, but, try as I might, I had failed to remember their faces. However, when Caroline had walked through the front door of the Restaurant Gordon Ramsay I had known her straight-away.

Securing a table had been harder, and very many favors had been cashed in and more still promised. "Sorry," they had said on the telephone with a degree of amusement at my folly, "tables are usually booked two months in advance." They hadn't needed to add that less than two days was in "absolutely no chance" territory.

However, I was not a celebrity chef for nothing, albeit a very minor one. The world of cordon bleu cookery may be as competitive as any, with chefs happily dreaming of using their cook's knives on the throats of their rivals, but, deep down, we knew that we needed them alive and well, not only to maintain the public interest in all things kitchen but also to be the guests on each other's television shows.

Having sold my soul, if not exactly to the devil then to the keeper of his kitchen, and having made such promises that may be difficult, if not impossible, to honor, I was rewarded with an offer of "a small extra table fitted in to the already-full dining room at nine o'clock. But it might be close to the door."

"That's great," I had said. On the pavement outside would have been fine by me.

"You must know Gordon Ramsay very well to have got this," she said.

"Professional courtesy," I said, smiling. "We chefs stick together." What a load of rubbish, but better that than to tell the truth. Better than telling her that I had needed to beg for this table. Perhaps the ten-grand lawsuit would have been cheaper?

"Is he nice?" she asked. "He always seems so rude on his program."

"Very nice," I said. "He just puts on an act for television." In truth, I had never actually met Gordon Ramsay, but I wasn't going to tell Caroline that, not yet anyway.

"So," I said, changing the subject, "tell me about what you do."

"I make music," she replied. "And you make food. So you sustain, and I entertain." She smiled at her joke. It transformed her face. It was like opening the curtains in the morning and allowing in the sunlight.

"Isn't music described as food for the soul?" I said.

"The quote is actually about passion," she said. " 'There's sure no passion in the human soul, but finds its food in music.' I can't remember who said it, or even what it means, but it was carved on a wooden plaque in the hallway at my music school."

"Which school?" I asked.

"RCM," she said. "Royal College of Music."

"Ah," I said. "And why the viola?"

"That stems from when I was in elementary school. The music teacher was a viola player, and I wanted to be like her. She was great." Caroline smiled. "She taught me to enjoy performance. It was a gift I will always be grateful for. So many of my colleagues in the orchestra love music, but they don't really enjoy the performance of it. It seems such a shame. For me, music is the performance. It's why I say that I make music, not play it."

I sat and watched her. My memory had not been wrong. She was tall and elegant, not dressed tonight in black but in a cream skirt with a shiny silver wraparound blouse that raised my heart rate each time she leaned forward. Her hair was very light brown, not quite blond, and was tied as before in a ponytail.

A waiter came over and asked if we had decided. We looked at the menus.

"What is pied de cochon?" Caroline asked.

"Literally," I said, "it means 'foot of pig.' Pig's trotter. It's very tasty."

She turned up her lovely nose. "I'll have the lobster ravioli, and then the lamb, I think. What's a morel?"

"A morel," I said, "is an edible fungi, like a mushroom."

"Fine, I'll have the lamb with the morel sauce." I was reminded of that previous mushroom sauce, the one that had probably made her ill. I decided not to mention it.

"And I'll have the pied de cochon and the sea bass."

"Thank you, sir," said the waiter.

"What would you like to drink?" I asked.

"I'd prefer red," she said, "but you're having fish."

"Red is fine by me." I ordered a moderately priced Médoc—at least it was moderate for this wine list, but, at this price, would have been by far the most expensive bottle available at the Hay Net. I would have to get used to London prices.

"So what made me ill?" she asked, getting sharply to the point. "And how did you get my phone number? And how come you know so much about me?"

"Tell me," I said, ignoring her questions, "how come you were playing in a string quartet at Newmarket racetrack when you normally play for the RPO?"

"I play *with* the RPO, not for them," she corrected swiftly. "It's a very important distinction."

It reminded me of my father, who always hated people saying that he had fallen off when he maintained that the horse had fallen and he had simply gone down with it. That distinction had been very important to him too.

"So why the string quartet?"

"Friends from college," she said. "The four of us paid our tuition by playing together in the evenings and on weekends. We did all sorts of functions, from weddings to funerals, and it was good training. Two of us are now pros while one of the others teaches. Jane, that's the fourth, is now a full-time mum in Newmarket. It was her idea to get us all together last week. We still do it when we can, but, sadly, it's less and less these days, as we all have other commitments. But it's fun. Except last week, of course. That wasn't fun. Not afterwards anyway."

"Yes," I said, "I'm really sorry about that. But if it makes you feel any better, I was dreadfully ill as well."

"Good," she said. "Serves you right."

"That's not very sympathetic."

She laughed. "Why should I be sympathetic to the infamous Newmarket poisoner?"

"Ah, but I'm not," I said.

"Then who is?"

"That," I said seriously, "is the million-dollar question."

I am sure that Bernard Sims would not have approved, but I told her everything I knew about the poisoning, which, after all, wasn't that much.

Our starters arrived halfway through my description of

the dire effects of phytohemagglutinin on the human digestive system, and I was sure that Caroline looked closely at her ravioli as if to spot any misplaced kidney beans.

Thankfully, my pig's trotter didn't actually look like it would walk around my plate, and it was absolutely delicious. I did so love my food, but, because it was also my business, there was a degree of eccentricity about my appreciation of other chefs' creations. Call it professional arrogance, or whatever, but I perversely enjoyed eating food that I knew I could have prepared better myself. Conversely, I felt somewhat inferior when I tasted something that I knew was beyond me, and this meal was. The pied de cochon, with its poached quail's egg, ham knuckle and hollandaise sauce, would send me back to my kitchen with increased determination to do better in the future.

"So who do you think did it?" asked Caroline at last, laying down her fork.

"I think the more important question is, why did they do it?" I said.

"And?"

"I don't know," I said. "That's what I have spent most of the past week trying to figure out. At first I thought it must have been someone who was trying to ruin me and my restaurant, but I can't think who. There aren't that many restaurants near Newmarket, and none that seem to be going bust because of me."

"How about your own staff ?" she asked.

"I've thought of that," I said. "But what would they hope to gain?"

"Maybe they want your job."

"But I own the restaurant," I said. "If they put me out of business, there won't be any jobs to have, mine or theirs."

"Maybe someone is jealous of your success," said Caroline.

"I've thought of that too, but I can't think who. It just doesn't make any sense." I took a sip of my wine. "I have another wild theory, but it sounds so daft."

"Try me," she said, leaning forward and giving my heart another lurch. Keep your eyes up, I told myself.

"I have begun to wonder if the poisoning at the dinner and the bombing of the racetrack are in some way linked," I said. "I know it sounds stupid, but I am simply searching for anything that might explain why anyone would purposely poison the food of more than two hundred and fifty people."

"How do you mean they are linked?" she asked.

"Well," I said, "and I may be crazy, but suppose the dinner was poisoned so that someone wouldn't be at the races on the Saturday afternoon so they wouldn't get blown up by the bomb."

"Why does that make you crazy?" she said. "Sounds eminently sensible to me."

"But it would mean that, contrary to all accepted opinion, the bomb hit the target it was meant to. It would mean it was not aimed at the Arab prince, and all the newspapers are wrong."

"Why does it mean that?" she said.

"Because if someone was prepared to poison the food the night before the bombing, they surely would know by then that the occupants of the box to be bombed had been changed several days earlier. Also, I don't think that anyone who was at the dinner would have been scheduled to be in the prince's box, since the newspapers say that his entire entourage flew in on the morning of the race. However, seven people who were meant to be in the bombed box for lunch didn't turn up on the day, and I know for a fact that at least three of those were missing due to being poisoned the night before."

"Wow!" she said. "Who else have you told this to?"

"No one," I said. "I wouldn't know who to tell. Anyway, I would be afraid they would laugh at me."

"But why would they?"

"Haven't you read the papers?" I said. "The reports all week have been about the Middle East connection. Even the television reports assume that the prince was the real target."

"Perhaps they have some information you don't," she said. "The security services must have something."

"Maybe," I said. "But according to the Sunday *Times*, no group had yet claimed responsibility."

"But would they if the attempt failed?"

"I don't know," I said.

Our main courses arrived, and we chatted for a while about more mundane subjects, such as our families, our schools and our favorite films and music. Without actually asking her outright, I deduced that she didn't have a current boyfriend, let alone the six-foot-six bodybuilder I had feared would eat me for breakfast. It seemed that, just like being a chef, playing the viola every evening did not assist in the search for romance.

"I'm sorry to say it," she said, "but most of the orchestral musicians I've met are pretty boring, not really my type."

"What is your type?" I asked her.

"Aha," she said. "Now, that is a good question."

Indeed, it may have been, but, as she failed to give me an answer, I changed the subject. "Is the lamb good?" I asked her.

"Delicious," she said. "Would you like a taste?"

We swapped mouthfuls on forks, her lamb and my fish. As we did, I looked closely at her face. She had bright blue eyes, high cheekbones and a longish, thin nose above a broad mouth and square-shaped jaw. Maybe she wasn't a classic beauty, but she looked pretty good to me.

"What are you staring at?" she said. "Have I got morel sauce down my chin?" She wiped her face with her napkin.

"No," I said, laughing. "I was just taking a close look at this person who is suing me so that I will recognize her in court." I smiled at her, but she didn't really smile back.

"Yes, that now seems rather a shame."

"You could just drop the suit," I suggested.

"It's my agent who's insisting on suing you. He doesn't like not getting his commission."

"Does he get a share of everything you earn?"

"Absolutely," she said. "He gets fifteen percent."

"Wow," I said. "Money for old rope."

"Oh no, he deserves it," she said. "He negotiated my contract with the RPO, for a start, and he got me much more money than many agents would have managed. Also, I do solo work when I'm not playing with the orchestra, and he handles all my bookings and contracts. All I have to do is turn up and play."

"He keeps you busy, then?"

"He certainly does," she said. "I'm only free this week because I was meant to be in New York. To tell the truth, it's been fantastic having evenings at home to veg on the sofa, watching the telly."

"Sorry I disturbed your vegging by asking you out."

"Don't be silly, I'm loving this."

"Good," I said. "So am I."

We ate for a while in contented silence. I really was loving this. A pretty, intelligent and talented female companion, a wonderful dinner and a passable bottle of Bordeaux. What could be better?

"So who are you going to tell of your crazy theory?" Caroline asked over coffee.

"Who do you suggest?" I said.

"The police, of course," she said. "But you need to get your facts straight first."

"How so?" I asked.

"Do you have the guest list from the gala dinner?"

"I do," I said. "But it's not really very helpful since it doesn't list everyone individually. Quite a few tables were groups of ten, and only the host is named on the guest list, the others as guests of so-and-so. I obtained a copy of the seating plan too, but it's the same thing. Only about half of the guests are actually named."

"How about the guest list where the bomb went off?" she asked.

"I haven't managed to get that," I said. "I think the only person who probably knew the full guest list was the marketing executive of the sponsor company and she was killed in the explosion. It's pretty easy to find out who was actually there, because they either are on the list of the dead or on the list of the injured. But I am more interested in the names of the seven people who should have been there but weren't."

"Surely someone must have the names of those who were invited," she said.

"I have tried," I said, "but no luck." I had spent much of Monday morning trying to acquire the list. Suzanne Miller, at the racetrack catering company, only had "guests of Delafield

Industries" in her paperwork, and William Preston, the track manager, had been even less helpful, with simply "sponsor and guests" on his.

"How about the sponsor company?" she asked. "Have you tried them?"

"No," I said. "I don't think that they would be very likely to know who was invited, other than their own staff flown over from America. I think that MaryLou Fordham—that's the marketing woman who was killed—I think she added the UK guests to the list after she was here, and after she knew who would be suitable. I remember that she was very cross beforehand when a couple of trainers from the town pulled out at the last minute. And I think I know who those two were anyway."

"Can't you ask them?" she said.

"I did ask one of them yesterday," I said. I had called George Kealy. "But, as he said, it is difficult to know who else was invited to a party that you didn't go to."

"That's true, I suppose," she said. "How about the injured people from the sponsor company? One of them might know who was meant to be there."

"I've thought of that too," I said. "According to yesterday's local newspaper, two of them are still in intensive care, and the others have already been flown home to America."

I asked a passing waiter for the bill and winced only a little when it arrived. The same amount would have fed a good-sized family at the Hay Net, and a small army at a burger joint, but neither would have given as much pleasure as that dinner with Caroline had given me.

When I suggested that I should see her home to Fulham, she insisted that she would be fine if I simply put her in a taxi. Reluctantly, I hailed a cab and she climbed in alone.

"Can I see you again?" I asked through the open door.

"Sure," she replied. "You'll see me in court."

"That's not exactly what I meant," I said.

"Well, what do you mean, then?"

"I don't know," I said. "Another dinner? A trip to the races?" I felt like asking her to make a trip to my bed.

"What are you doing two weeks from Thursday?" she asked.

"Nothing," I replied. Nothing, that is, except cooking sixty lunches and a hundred dinners at the Hay Net.

"I'm due to play a viola concerto with the orchestra at Cadogan Hall. Come and listen."

"I'd love to," I said. "Dinner after?"

"Lovely," she said. She gave me a full-toothed smile with her broad mouth as the door closed and the taxi moved away. Suddenly, she was gone, and I was left on the pavement, feeling somewhat wretched and alone. Was I that desperate, I asked myself, that I would jump at the first girl that came along? Caroline was suing me for ten thousand pounds in damages, and maybe I should have been more careful not to have told her so much. Perhaps she would use what I told her against me. But there had been a certain rapport between us, of that I was certain. Even on Friday evening, on the telephone, I was pretty sure that we would get along, and I think we had. I wasn't being desperate, I told myself. I was being sensible. But why, then, did I feel such an ache from not still being with her?

I hailed another taxi and reluctantly told the driver to take me to King's Cross station, rather than to Tamworth Street in Fulham.

I CAUGHT THE last train to Cambridge with less than a minute to spare. I sat and pondered what I had discussed with Caroline, as the train pulled out of the station on the hour-and-ten-minute journey northeastwards.

Somehow, putting my thoughts into words had made them sound rather more plausible. However, I still felt that the authorities would dismiss my theories as highly fanciful. But were they any more fanciful, I wondered, than thinking that a Middle East terror group had attempted an assassination of a foreign royal prince on Newmarket Heath?

I didn't really believe it. But if I was right in thinking that the dinner had been poisoned to prevent someone being blown up, then I could safely assume that the bomb had in fact hit its intended target. So what made Delafield Industries so special that someone wanted to blow them up on their big day out in England? Who would want to kill Elizabeth Jennings or Brian and June Walters, and why? Or was it the likes of Rolf Schumann and MaryLou Fordham who were the real targets?

I knew Delafield Industries made tractors and combine harvesters, but what else did they do? I resolved to look them up on the Internet in the morning, along with Mr. Schumann.

I lay back against the headrest and thought about more pleasant things like the evening two weeks from now, on Thursday, at the Cadogan Hall. In truth, I wasn't a great lover of classical music. But I would listen to anything with huge pleasure if I was able to have dinner with Caroline afterwards. Even the thought of it made me smile, although it was more than fifteen whole days away and that seemed a very long time to have to wait to see her again. Maybe I could entice her to Newmarket somewhat sooner than that, like tomorrow.

The train pulled into Cambridge station at twenty-five minutes past one in the morning. As always on the late-night stopping service, I had to force myself to stay awake in order that I didn't end up with the train at King's Lynn, or wherever.

I had left my car in the Cambridge station parking lot, as was usual when I went to London for the evening. At five in the afternoon, nearly all the spaces had been full with commuters' cars, but now my little Golf stood alone at the far end of the lot awaiting my return. I had drunk no more than half a bottle of wine throughout the evening, as well as having had a full meal with coffee. It had been nearly three hours since Caroline and I had finished the wine, and I reckoned that I was fine to drive, and well under the drink-drive limit.

I was slightly surprised to find my car wasn't locked. The driver's door was not fully shut, only half latched. I couldn't actually remember leaving it like that, but, then, it wouldn't have been the first time, not by a long shot. After so many years of misuse, the door needed a good slam to get it shut properly. The manager of my garage had often tried, at great expense, to sell me a new door seal, but I had always declined his offers on the grounds that the cost of the seal was only a fraction less than what the whole car was worth.

I had a good look around the car. I checked the tires, but they seemed all right. I got down on my hands and knees and looked underneath. Nothing. I even opened the hood and looked at the engine. I didn't really know what a bomb would look like, so the chances of me spotting something amiss were slight, but nonetheless there were no suspicious packages I could see attached to the car's electrical system or anything else. Perhaps I was becoming paranoid. It must be all this talk of conspiracy to poison and to bomb. However, my heart was thumping in my chest a little louder than normal when I turned the ignition key to start the engine.

It sprang to life, just as it should. I revved it up for a few seconds, but all sounded fine to me, with no clunks or clangs. I wiggled the steering wheel, but nothing untoward occurred. I drove forward a bit in the parking lot and then braked hard. The car stopped with a jolt, as was normal. I drove around in circles, a couple of times in both directions, pulling hard on the wheel. The vehicle behaved in exactly the manner expected. I was indeed paranoid, I told myself, and I drove home, uneventfully, although I checked the brakes often, and with some vigor, on all the straight bits of road.

MARYLOU FORDHAM'S LEGS, or rather the lack of her legs, made further unwelcome visits to my subconscious during another disturbed night. Surely, I thought, my brain should be able to control these episodes. Surely, it should realize, as soon as the dream started was the right moment to wake me and put a stop to the misery. But, every time, the whole episode would play out, and, every time, I would wake with terror in my heart and panic in my head. My dimming memory of MaryLou's face did nothing to lessen the horror evoked by her legless torso.

I tried to ignore the interruptions to my rest by simply

turning over and trying to go back to sleep, telling myself to dream of happier things, like cuddling up with Caroline, but I would remain annoyingly awake for ages before the adrenaline level in my bloodstream dropped low enough to allow me to drift off, seemingly only for the dream to start again immediately. It was all very exhausting.

WEDNESDAY, when it finally arrived, was one of those May mornings to savor, especially in the flatlands of East Anglia: cloudless blue skies and unparalleled visibility. From my bedroom window, I could see the white-arched, cantilevered roof of the Millennium Grandstand at the racetrack, and, in the clear air and the sunshine, it appeared much larger and nearer than normal.

If only my life was as clear, I thought.

My cell phone rang.

"Hello," I said, hoping it might be Caroline, which was stupid, really, since I hadn't even given her the number.

"Max. It's Suzanne Miller. I'm afraid I have some rather bad news. I've received a letter this morning from Forest Heath District Council indicating their intent to prosecute under section 7 of the Food Safety Act of 1990."

Oh bugger, I thought. If they were prosecuting the racetrack catering company, who had been only the overseer of the event, they were sure to prosecute the chef as well, i.e., me.

"Do they say exactly who they intend to prosecute?" I asked.

"Everyone," she said somewhat forlornly. "There's letters for me individually and for the company. There's even a letter for you here at the racetrack addressed to 'Mr. Max Moreton,' care of us."

Oh double bugger. There was probably another letter at the Hay Net.

"What does your letter actually say?" I asked her.

She read it out to me. Not a single bit of good news to be found.

"My letter is probably identical to yours," I said. "I'll come and collect it, if you like."

"Yes, please do. Look, Max, all the food was your responsibility, and I will have to say that. All I did was organize the venue. I'm not being convicted of serving food that was hazardous to health, not with my retirement coming up later this year. I'm not losing my pension over this." She was in tears.

"Suzanne," I said as calmingly as I could, "I know that, you know that, Angela Milne from Cambridgeshire County Council knows that. If anyone is taking the fall for this, it will be me, OK?"

"Yes, thanks," she sniffed.

"But, Suzanne, I need more help from you. I need a fuller list of who was at the dinner, and the names of as many of the staff as you can manage. I also need the names of those invited to the Delafield box on Guineas day. If you can get me all that, then I will happily say that you had nothing to do with the food at the dinner."

"But I didn't have anything to do with it," she wailed.

"I know that," I said. "And I will say so. But get me the lists."

"I'll try," she said.

"Try hard," I said, and hung up.

I called the newsroom of the *Cambridge Evening News* and asked for Ms. Harding.

"Hello," she said. "Are you checking to see if I'll still be coming to dinner at your restaurant?"

"Partly," I said. "But also to tell you some news before you hear it from somewhere else."

"What news?" she said, her journalistic instincts coming firmly to the fore.

"I am to be prosecuted by the local authority for serving food likely to be hazardous to health," I said in as deadpan a manner as I could manage.

"Are you indeed?" she said. "And do you have a quote for me?"

"Not one you could print without including a warning for young children," I replied.

"Why are you telling me this?" she asked.

"I assume that you would find out eventually, and I thought it better to come clean," I said.

"Like your kitchen," she said.

"Thank you," I said. "I'll take that as a compliment and put you down as on my side."

"I wouldn't necessarily say that. My business is selling newspapers, and I don't know whose side I am on until I see the way the wind is blowing."

"That's outrageous," I said. "Don't you have any morals?"

"Personally? Yes," she said. "In my job? Maybe. But not at the expense of circulation. I can't afford that luxury."

"I'll do a deal with you," I said.

"What deal?" she replied quickly. "I don't do deals."

"I will keep you up-to-date on all the news I have about the prosecution of the poisoning, and you give me the right of reply to anything anyone says or does to me or the restaurant, including you."

"That's not much of a deal for me," she said.

"I'll throw in a guaranteed exclusive interview at the end of the proceedings," I said. "Take it or leave it."

"OK," she said, "I'll take it."

I told her about the letters that had arrived at the racetrack catering offices. I also told her that I intended to mount a determined defense to the allegation.

"But people were made ill," she said. "You can't deny that."

"No," I said, "I don't deny that people were ill. I was one of them. But I vehemently deny that I was responsible for making them ill."

"Then who was?" she asked.

"I don't know," I said. "But it wasn't me." I decided not to mention the kidney bean lectin. Not yet. Was that breaking my deal? No, I thought. It was just bending it a little. "If I do find out who was responsible, I promise you I'll definitely tell you who it was." I'd tell everyone.

"What am I meant to write in the meantime?" she pleaded.

"I would prefer it if you wrote nothing," I said. "But if you must, then write what you like. But I get the chance to reply."

"OK," she said, sounding a little unsure. Time, I thought, to change direction.

"Do you have any further news about the people injured in the bombing?" I asked. "I read in your paper that most of the Americans have gone home, but two of them are still here in intensive care."

"Only one now," she said. "The other one died yesterday. From her burns."

"Oh," I said. "How many is that now?"

"Nineteen," she said.

"You don't happen to know what became of a Mr. Rolf Schumann, do you? He's the chairman of Delafield Industries."

"Hold on a minute," she said. I could hear her asking someone else. "Apparently, he was air-ambulanced home to America over the weekend, out of Stansted." And I hadn't yet been paid for the Guineas lunch.

"Do you know what his injuries were?" I asked.

I could hear her again relaying the question. "Head injuries," she said. "Seems he's lost his marbles."

"I hope you don't write that in your paper," I said.

"Good God no," she said. "He's suffering from mental distress."

"How about the others who were injured, the non-Americans?" I asked.

She relayed the question again. "There's a couple from the north who are still in the hospital with spinal injuries or something. The others have all been discharged from Addenbrooke's. But we know of at least one who has been transferred to Roehampton."

"Roehampton?" I said.

"Rehab center," she said. "Artificial limbs."

"Oh." The images of missing arms and legs made another unwelcome visit to my consciousness.

"Look, I must go now," said Ms. Harding. "I've got work to do."

She hung up, and I sat on the end of my bed wishing that she hadn't stirred my memories of the carnage, memories that had started to fade but which all too easily rose to the surface like a cork in a bucket of water.

I decided to cheer myself up by calling Caroline.

"Hello," she said. "You've still got my number, then."

"You bet," I said with a smile. "I called to thank you for last night."

"It should be me thanking you," she said. "I had a great time."

"So did I. Any chance I could entice you up to Newmarket for dinner tonight or tomorrow?"

"Why don't you beat around the bush a little?" she said. "Why don't you talk about the weather or something?"

"Why?" I asked.

"It might make you sound rather less eager," she said.

"Do I sound too eager?" I said. "I'm sorry."

"Don't apologize," she said, laughing. "In fact, I think I rather like it."

"So will you come?" I asked.

"To dinner?"

"Yes," I said.

"Where?"

"At my restaurant."

"I'm not eating on my own while you do the cooking."

"No, of course not," I said. "Come and watch me cook, and then we'll have dinner together afterwards."

"Won't that be rather late?" she said. "How will I get home?"

I wanted to ask her to stay with me, in my bed, in my arms, but I thought it might not be prudent. "I will get you on the last train to King's Cross or I will treat you to a night in the Bedford Lodge Hotel."

"On my own?" she asked.

I paused for a long while. "That's up to you," I said finally.

There was an equally long pause at her end. "No promises and no strings?"

"No promises and no strings," I agreed.

"OK." She sounded excited. "What time and where?"

"Come as early as you like, and I'll pick you up from Cambridge station."

"Isn't there a station at Newmarket?" she asked.

"There is, but you have to change at Cambridge anyway and it's not great service."

"OK," she said again. "I'll look up the train times and call you back. At this number?"

"Yes," I said. I was elated at the thought of seeing her again so soon.

"What do I wear?" she said.

"Anything," I said.

Even the prospect of being prosecuted under the 1990 Act couldn't dampen my spirits as I skipped down the stairs. I laughed out loud and punched the air, as I collected my coat and went out to the car. Caroline was coming to dinner! At my restaurant! And she was staying the night! Pity it wasn't going to be at my cottage.

The brakes of my Golf failed at the bottom of Woodditton Road.

I was feeling good, and my speed, probably like my expectation, was rather too high. I put my foot on the brake pedal and nothing happened. I pushed harder. Nothing. The car actually increased in speed down the hill, towards the T junction with Dullingham Road at the bottom. I suppose I could have been quicker in my thinking. I suppose I could have tried the handbrake, or maybe downshifted the gears to slow me down. I suppose, as a last resort, I could have turned the car through the hedge on the left and into the field beyond. Instead, I gripped the steering wheel tightly in panic and kept pushing the useless brake pedal harder and harder into the floor.

In a way, I was lucky. I didn't hit a truck carrying bricks head-on like my father. My dear little car was struck by a fifty-three-seat, fully air-conditioned passenger coach, with individual video screens built in. I knew this because the Golf ended up on its side around the back of the bus, and I could read the details of their service, as advertised, in large white letters painted on a red background. Funny how the mind works. I remembered the words as my consciousness slowly drained away: fifty-three seats.

# 10

I was being wheeled on a hospital gurney along a gray corridor. I could see the lights in the ceiling. But they weren't the usual bright rectangular panels; they were different. They were round glass globes. And there were windows, lots of bright, sunlit windows. And voices too, lots of voices, both male and female.

"I think he's come round again," said one male voice above me.

"Hello," called a female voice on my left. "Mr. Moreton, can you hear me?"

A face came into view. The face smiled at me.

"Mr. Moreton," said the face again. "You've had a bit of an accident, but you are going to be just fine."

That was a relief, I thought.

Nothing seemed to hurt much, but my body, strangely, didn't feel attached to my head. I felt like I was looking down on somebody else's corpse. Oh no, I thought, surely I haven't broken my back?

I began to panic and I tried to sit up.

"Just lie back and rest," said the female voice, a restraining hand placed firmly on my shoulder. She looked into my face. "You've had a nasty bang on the head."

Oh God, I must have broken my neck.

I tried to wiggle my toes and was rewarded with the sight of the blanket moving. Waves of relief flowed over me. I lifted my hand to my face and wiped the cold sweat from my forehead. All was well, I thought, even if the sensations were a bit unusual.

"You're probably concussed," she said. "You're on your way now to have a brain scan."

I hoped they'd find one.

I wondered where I was. I knew that I was in the hospital, but where? And why was I in the hospital? The questions were too difficult for my befuddled brain, so I decided to take the easy option and do as I was told. I laid my head back on the pillow and closed my eyes again.

FOR THE NEXT few hours, I was dimly aware of being lifted and poked, of being talked about but not talked to. I just let the world get on without me.

I couldn't remember why I was here. Rather worryingly, I couldn't remember very much at all. Who am I? I wondered, and was comforted by at least knowing that it mattered. I decided that I probably wasn't crazy. Surely, I thought, if I was crazy I wouldn't know to ask myself the question in the first place. But what was the answer?

Thoughts drifted in and out of my consciousness without any threads of connection. Come on, I said to myself, sort it out. There were clearly some priorities to set. Who am I? Why am I here? And where is here?

"Mr. Moreton? Mr. Moreton?" a woman called from my left, and someone stroked my arm. Was Mr. Moreton me? I supposed it must be. Did I really want to come back into the land of the living just yet? I supposed I should.

I opened my eyes.

"He's back again," said the woman. "Hello, Mr. Moreton, how are you feeling?"

I tried to say that I was fine, but it came out as a croak.

The woman obviously thought it was a good sign that I had reacted at all. She leaned over me and smiled into my face. "Well done," she said. "You are going to be all right."

Why did I think that she was trying to convince herself as much as she was trying to convince me?

I tried again to speak. "Where am I?" I croaked.

"Addenbrooke's hospital," she said. "In Cambridge."

I knew I knew something about Addenbrooke's hospital, I thought. What was it? Memory circuits in my head flipped and flopped and came up with an answer: Addenbrooke's hospital was where the food-poisoning victims went.

Why did I think that? Who were the poison victims? Would they be OK? I decided not to worry about them. They would be all right, I said to myself. The woman had said so, and I believed her. I closed my eyes again. I wasn't yet ready to participate in the world any further.


WHEN I WOKE next, it was dark. There was a window to my right and it was black, with the exception of a couple of yellow streetlights visible in the distance. I lay there, looking out. I remembered I was in the hospital. Addenbrooke's hospital, in Cambridge. But I couldn't remember why. Then I wondered what was happening at the restaurant.

"Hello, Max," said a voice on my left.

I rolled my head over. It was Caroline. I smiled at her.

"Hello, Caroline," I said. "How lovely."

"You know who I am, then," she said.

"Of course I do," I said. "I may be in the hospital, but I'm not stupid."

"The doctor warned me that you might not remember who I was. He said that earlier you appeared not to remember who you were either. Seems you have been drifting in and out all day. How do you feel?"

"Better, for seeing you," I said. "But why am I here?"

"You had an accident," she said. "You were hit by a bus and you banged your head. They think it must have been on the side window of your car. They say that you are just a bit concussed, but you should be fine in a few days."

I couldn't remember an accident or a bus. "How did you know I was here?" I asked her.

"I called your cell to tell you the time of the train I was coming on and a nurse answered it. She told me you were in the hospital, so I came straightaway." Caroline smiled.

That's nice, I thought.

"What time is it?" I said.

"About two o'clock," she said.

"In the morning?"

"Yes."

"I'm sorry about dinner," I said. "Where are you staying?"

"Right here," she said. That was nice too. "It took a bit of persuasion, but, in the end, they let me stay."

"But you must have somewhere to sleep," I said.

"I'm happy right here." She smiled at me. I was so glad. "I'll find somewhere to sleep in the morning."

Wow, I thought.

"Are you still suing me?" I asked.

"Absolutely," she said, and she laughed. Her laughter turned to tears that streamed down her face. She was laughing and crying at the same time. "Oh God, I'm so relieved you are all right. Don't you ever do that to me again."

"Do what?" I said.

"Don't you ever frighten me like that again. When I called your phone, they told me you were having a brain scan to check for any pressure buildup. They told me that they didn't yet know of the extent of any permanent brain damage." She was crying from the memory. "I don't want to lose you, not when I've only just found you."

"I thought it was me who found you."

"Yes," she said, choking back the sobs. "So it was. How was that, exactly? Perhaps it's better I don't know." She leaned forward and kissed me on the forehead. Then she kissed me gently on the lips. I could get used to that, I thought.

"I'm sorry," I said. "It's not a convenient time, but I really need to go to the bathroom."

"I'll get a nurse," she said, and disappeared. She came back with a large, middle-aged woman wearing a blue nurse's tunic.

"Ah, you're back with us again, Mr. Moreton," said the nurse. "How are you feeling now?"

"Not too bad," I said. "I've got a bit of a headache, and I need to go to the bathroom."

"Bottle or bedpan?" she said. It took me quite a few seconds to understand what she meant.

"Oh," I said. "Bedpan. But can't I go to the bathroom?"

"I'll see if I can find a wheelchair," she said. "I don't want you walking yet after such a bang. You have a concussion, and your balance may be affected."

She returned with the wheelchair and helped me out of bed and into it. I was wearing what could only be described as a nightshirt with an opening down the back. It did nothing for my modesty, since my rear end was exposed for all to see as the nurse lowered me gently into the chair. My balance indeed wasn't very good, and the maneuver could hardly be described as elegant. I hoped very much that Caroline hadn't been watching.

The nurse pushed me down the corridor to the bathroom. I was getting rather urgent and I started to get myself out of the chair and onto the toilet.

"Just a minute," said the nurse. "Let me put the brakes on first."

The brakes? Wasn't there something else about brakes? I tried to remember what it was.

As if wearing a gap-backed nightshirt wasn't bad enough, the nurse insisted on standing next to me and holding my shoulders throughout the procedure in case I toppled off the toilet and onto the floor. Being in the hospital, I concluded, did nothing for one's dignity.

Feeling much better but still embarrassed by the process, I was wheeled back to my bed by the nurse. She applied the brakes of the wheelchair. I sat there. Why was it that I hoped the brakes wouldn't fail again?

"Caroline?" I called out loudly.

"Shhh," said the nurse. "You'll wake everyone up."

"I'm here," said Caroline, coming and crouching down to my level.

"The brakes on my car failed," I whispered.

"I know," she said. "A policeman told the doctors they thought it was the brakes failing that caused the accident."

"It wasn't an accident," I said.

"What do you mean?"

"I think someone tried to kill me."

"YOU'RE REALLY SERIOUS, aren't you?" Caroline said.

"Never more so," I said.

I had told her all about my car not being locked at Cambridge station, and about my concerns that the brakes or the steering may not have been all right on Tuesday night.

"But you don't know for sure that someone had tampered with the brakes," she said. "You said that they seemed OK when you drove home."

"True," I said. "But there's no escaping the fact that they did fail on Wednesday morning."

"It might have been a coincidence," she said.

I looked at her and raised my eyebrows.

"OK, OK," she said. "But coincidences do happen, you know." She held my hand. I liked that. "So what are we going to do about it?"

"I wonder if the police have someone who would look at the brakes on my car to see if they have been interfered with?"

"Don't they have accident investigators?" Caroline asked. She yawned. "Sorry."

"You need to go to sleep," I said.

"I'm fine," she said, yawning again.

I wanted to ask her to get into the bed and sleep next to me, but I thought the nurse wouldn't like it.

"You can't stay here all night," I said.

"Nowhere else to go."

"Go to my cottage," I said. "The key must be somewhere."

She looked through my things, which someone had thoughtfully placed in a white plastic bag in the bedside locker. There was no key.

"I remember now," I said. "It's on the same ring as the car keys." Probably still with the car, I thought.

"I don't want to go to your cottage on my own anyway," said Caroline. "Especially not if someone really is trying to kill you. I'll stay here, thanks."

In the end, she slept in the chair next to my bed. It was one of those chairs that reclined, so that bedridden patients could be lifted into it to have a change of posture. Caroline reclined in it, covered herself with a blanket from the bed and was asleep in seconds.

I looked at her for a while, thinking that it had been a strange recipe for romance: first poison your intended, next irritate her with fatuous telephone calls, then stir thoroughly at dinner before frightening badly with a life-threatening car crash, finally serve up a conspiracy theory of intended murder.

It seemed to have worked like a charm.


THEY LET ME go home the following day. Caroline had convinced the doctors that I would be fine at home if she was looking after me. And who was I to object to that?

A black-and-yellow NewTax taxi delivered us to my cottage about one o'clock. I had called my occasional house-cleaner to arrange for her to meet us with her key so we could get in. Lunch presented us with another problem. I rarely had much food in the house, other than for breakfast, since I usually ate lunch and dinner at the restaurant. Caroline briefly inspected the premises, and then she searched the kitchen for food.

"I'm starving," she said. "At least they gave you some breakfast at the hospital, I've had nothing since yesterday morning."

She found some sugarcoated cornflakes in the cupboard and some milk in the fridge, so we sat at my tiny kitchen table and had bowls of cereal for lunch.

Carl had phoned the hospital first thing to find out how I was, and, as I expected, he had given the appearance of being mildly disappointed to find that I was not only alive but my brains were unscrambled and functioning properly. The hospital operator had put him through to my bedside telephone.

"So, you're still with us, then?" he had said with a slightly frustrated tone.

"Yeah, sorry about that," I'd said. "How are things at the Hay Net?"

"Doing well without you," he had said. "As always," he had added rather unnecessarily, I thought. Cheeky bastard.

For all his seemingly bad grace about my well-being, I couldn't really imagine that Carl would have had anything to do with a conspiracy to kill me. Surely it was just his warped sense of humor. Tiresome as his little irritating comments could be at times, I didn't think there was anything truly sinister behind them.

In fact, the more I thought about it, the less likely it seemed that anyone would seriously want me dead. Perhaps the brake failure had been coincidence after all. Anyway, tampering with brakes didn't seem to me to be a particularly good way of trying to kill someone, not unless they were driving down a steep mountain road full of hairpin bends, and steep mountain roads were somewhat conspicuous by their absence in Newmarket.

After our cereal lunch, I lay on my sofa and called the restaurant, while Caroline explored upstairs.

"Had a relapse?" Carl asked hopefully when I said I wasn't coming in.

"No," I said. "I've been told by the doctors to take it easy for a few days. I'll see how I get on."

"Don't hurry back," said Carl in a dismissive manner.

"Look," I said, "what's eating you at the moment? Why are you being so damn unpleasant?"

There was a longish pause at the other end.

"It's just my way," he said. "I'm sorry." There was another pause. "I will be delighted when you get back, I promise."

"Now, don't go too far the other way," I said with a laugh. "I won't know if I'm coming or going."

"Sorry," he said again.

"Apology accepted," I said. "How was lunch?"

"So-so," he said. "But we had a good one last night. About eighty percent full."

"Great."

"Everyone asked where you were. Richard told them all about your accident, which was then the talk of the place," he said. "Lots of people sent their best wishes. And the staff are concerned about you too."

"Thanks." I wasn't sure that the overfriendly Carl wasn't more annoying than the surly one, but I decided not to raise the subject again. "Tell everyone I'm fine and I'll be back at work as soon as I can, probably by the middle of next week."

"OK," said Carl. "I've booked a temporary chef from that agency in Norwich to help over the weekend. I hope that's OK."

"Good," I said. "Well done, Carl." All this mutual admiration was too much. "Now, sod off and get back to work." I could hear him laughing as I hung up. Carl was one of the good guys, I was sure of it. Or was I?

Next I telephoned the Suffolk police to discover what had happened to my car.

"It was towed by Brady Rescue and Recovery of Kentford," they said. "They'll have it there."

"Has anyone inspected it?" I asked.

"The attending officer at the accident would have briefly inspected the vehicle before it was removed."

"Apparently," I said, "someone from the police told a doctor at the hospital that the accident was due to brake failure."

"I don't know anything about that, sir."

"Is there any way I could speak to the policeman who attended the accident?" I asked.

"Can you hold, please?" I didn't have a chance to say either yes or no, before I found myself listening to a recorded message telling me of the services offered by Suffolk Constabulary. I listened to the whole thing through at least three times before a live voice came back on the line.

"I'm sorry, sir," it said. "The officer is not available to speak to you."

"When will he be available?" I asked. "Can I leave a message for him to call me?" I gave my cell number, but I didn't hold out much hope that the message would get through. They were very busy, they said, but they would see what they could do.

I called the towing company. Yes, they said, they had my Golf. But it was not in great shape. Could I come and visit? I asked. Yes, they said, anytime.

Caroline returned to the sitting room after her investigation of my property.

"Nice place," she said. "Better than my hovel in Fulham."

"Do you want to move in?" I asked.

"Don't push your luck, Mr. Moreton," she said, smiling. "I've been looking for where I would be sleeping tonight."

"But you are staying?" I said, perhaps a touch too eagerly for her liking.

"Yes," she said, "but not in your bedroom. If that's not OK by you, then I will go back to London now."

"It's OK," I said. Not brilliant, I thought, but OK.

I took some painkillers for my throbbing head, and then Caroline and I went by taxi to Kentford to see my car.

As the man from the towing company had said on the telephone, it wasn't in great shape. In fact, I had to be told which one of the wrecks was mine since I didn't recognize it. The roof was missing completely, for a start.

"What on earth happened to it?" I asked one of their men. My pride and joy for so long was now just a mangled heap.

"The fire brigade cut the roof off to get the occupant out," he said. "The car was on its side when I got there with my truck and the roof was already gone. Maybe it's still in the ditch, next to where the car was."

It didn't matter. Even to my eyes, the car was a complete write-off. Not only had the roof disappeared, the front fender was completely ripped away and the wheel beneath was sitting at a strange angle. That must have happened, I thought, when I hit the bus.

"Has anyone been to inspect it?" I asked him.

"Not that I'm aware of. But it's been sitting here since yesterday morning, and I don't exactly keep guard."

"Here" was down the side of the workshop, behind a pair of tow trucks.

"I was the driver," I said to him.

"Blimey, you were lucky, then. I thought it was a fatal when I first arrived."

"Why?" I asked.

"Fire brigade and ambulance spent ages getting you out. That's never a good sign. Had you in one of those neck-brace things. You didn't look too good, I can tell you. Not moving, like. I thought you were probably dead."

"Thanks," I said sarcastically.

"No," he said. "I'm glad you're not, like. Easier for me too."

"Why?" I said.

"If it had been a fatal," he said, "I would have to keep this pile of garbage here for the police inspectors, and they take bloody ages to do their stuff. Since you're OK, I can get rid of it, off the premises, just as soon as your insurance bloke looks at it. Also," he added with a smile, "since you're alive I now can send you a bill for recovering it from the roadside."

I made a mental note to phone the insurance company, not that they would give me much. I suspected that the car was worth little more than the policy's deductible, but it just might pay the wretched man's bill for getting rid of the wreck.

"I think the accident occurred because my brakes failed," I said. "Is there any way of checking that by looking?"

"Help yourself, it's your car." He turned away. "I've got work to do."

"No," I said quickly. "I wouldn't know what to look for. Could you have a look for me?"

"It'll cost you," he said.

"All right," I said. "How much?"

"Usual labor rates," he replied.

"Can you look at it now?" I said. "While I'm here?"

"Suppose so," he said.

"OK," I said. "Usual rates."

He spent about twenty minutes examining what was left of my car, but the results were inconclusive.

"Could have been the brakes, I suppose," he said finally. "Difficult to tell."

I assured him that it definitely was the brakes that had failed and caused the accident.

"If you were bloody certain it was the brakes, what did you want me to check it for?"

"I want to know if the brakes had been tampered with," I said.

"What, on purpose?" He stared at me.

"I don't know," I said. "That's what I want you to tell me."

"Blimey," he said again. He leaned back over the car.

"Look here," he said. I joined him in leaning over what had been the front bumper. He pointed at a jumbled mass of metal pipes and levers. "The brake system on this old Golf was a simple hydraulic, non-power-assisted system." I nodded. I knew that. "What happens when you push the brake pedal is you force a piston along this cylinder." He pointed at what looked like a metal pipe about an inch in diameter and about an inch and a half long. "The piston inside pushes brake fluid through the pipes to the wheels, and the pressure causes the brake pads to squeeze the brake discs. That's what slows the car down."

"Like a bicycle brake?" I asked.

"Well, not exactly. On a bike, there is a cable going from the brake lever to the brake pads. In a car, the pressure is transmitted through the fluid-filled pipes."

"I see," I said. But I wasn't sure I did completely. "So what caused the brakes to fail?"

"Brakes will fail if air gets into the pipes instead of the brake fluid. Then, when you push the pedal, all you do is compress the air and the brakes don't work." He spotted my quizzical look. "You see, the brake fluid won't compress, but air will." I nodded. I knew that from my school chemistry.

"So all someone needed to do," I said, "was to put some air into the pipes and the brakes wouldn't work."

"Yes," he said. "But it's not that easy. For a start, there are two brake systems on this car, so if one failed the other should still work."

"There were no brakes at all when I pushed the pedal," I said.

"Air must have got into the master cylinder," he said. "That's very unusual, but I have come across it once before. That time was due to the pipe from the reservoir to the master cylinder coming loose." He had lost me.

"But can you tell if it was done on purpose?" I asked him.

"Difficult to tell," he said again. "Might have been. The joins are still tight, so someone would have had to split the metal pipe." He pointed. "It could have been done by flexing it up and down a few times until it cracked open due to fatigue. You know, like bending a wire coat hanger until it snaps."

"But wouldn't that make the brakes fail immediately?" I asked him.

"Not necessarily," he said. "It might take a while for the air to seep from the cracked pipe into the master cylinder."

"Can you tell if that is what happened here?" I asked.

He looked again at the jumble of broken pipes. "The accident seems to have smashed it all. It would be impossible to tell what had been done beforehand."

"Would the police accident investigators have any better idea?" I asked him.

He seemed a bit offended that I had questioned his ability. "No one could tell from that mess what it was like before the accident," he said with some indignation.

I wasn't sure that I totally agreed with him, but I didn't think it was time to say so. Instead, I paid him half an hour's labor cost in cash and used my cell phone to call a taxi.

"Do you have the keys of the car?" I asked the man.

"No, mate," he said. "Never seen them. Thought they were still in it."

They weren't. I'd looked. "Never mind," I said. "They wouldn't be much use now anyway." But they had been on a silver key fob. A twenty-first-birthday present from my mother.

"Can I send it off to the scrap, then?" he asked.

"Not yet," I said. "Wait until the insurance man has seen it."

"Will do," he said. "But don't forget, you're the one paying for the storage."

What a surprise.

"WELL, THAT WASN'T very conclusive," said Caroline as we sat in the taxi taking us back to Newmarket. "What do you want to do now?"

"Go home," I said. "I'm feeling lousy."

We did go home, but via the supermarket in Newmarket. I sat outside in the taxi as Caroline went to buy something to eat for supper, as well as a bottle of red wine. I was pretty sure that the painkillers I was taking didn't mix too well with alcohol, but who cared.

I lay on the sofa and rested my aching head while Caroline fussed around in the kitchen. Once or twice, she came and sat down next to me, but soon she was up and about again.

"Relax," I said to her. "I won't eat you alive."

She sighed. "It's not that. I'm restless because I haven't got my viola here to play. I usually practice for at least two hours every day, even if I'm performing in the evening. I haven't played a note since the day before yesterday and I'm suffering from withdrawal symptoms. I need my fix."

"Like me and my cooking," I said. "Sometimes, I just get the urge to cook even if there is no one to eat it. The freezers at the restaurant are full of stuff I intend getting round to eating one day."

"Shame there's none of it here," she said.

"I could call and ask one of my staff to bring some over."

"No," she said, smiling. "I'll take my chances and cook for the cook. It also might be better not to mention anything about this to your staff."

"Why not?" I said.

"They might get the wrong idea."

"And what, exactly, is the 'wrong idea' they might get?" I asked.

"Oh, I don't know," she said. "If they knew I was staying here, they might jump to the wrong conclusions."

I wasn't sure I liked the way the conversation was going. Too much analysis of any situation was apt to make it appear somewhat stupid, whereas uninhibited and thought-free actions were more often an accurate reflection of true feelings. The raw and honest emotion of last night in the hospital was in danger of being consumed by too much good sense and the weighing up of consequences.

"What do you play when you practice?" I asked, changing the subject. "And don't say 'the viola.' "

"Finger exercises mostly," she said. "Very boring."

"Like scales?" I had been forced to do hours of scales on the piano when I was a child. I had hated it.

"Exactly," she said. "But I also play pieces as well. Scales alone would drive anyone crazy, even a pro musician."

"What is your favorite piece to play?" I asked.

"Bach's Violin Concerto in E Major," she said. "But, of course, I play it on the viola."

"Doesn't it sound all wrong?"

She laughed. "No, of course not. It sounds fine. Take the song 'Yesterday.' You know the one, by the Beatles. It can be played on the piano, the guitar, the violin or anything else. It still sounds like 'Yesterday,' doesn't it?"

"I suppose so," I said. I would take her word for it.

I looked at my watch. It was six o'clock. The sun, if not exactly over the yardarm, was well into its descent from the zenith, so I opened the wine, and we sat and drank it, content in each other's company.

Caroline fixed fresh salmon with a parsley sauce, new potatoes and salad, and it was delicious. We sat together on the sofa and ate it on our laps while watching a satirical news program on the television. Real domesticity.

As she had planned, Caroline didn't sleep in my bedroom.

But, then again, neither did I.

# 11

Caroline got up early and called herself a taxi.

"Was it something I said?" I asked.

"Oh no," she said, laughing. "It's just that I have to get back to London. I've got a meeting at the RPO offices in Clerkenwell Green. I want to convince them to let me fly out for the rest of the tour."

She sat on the end of the bed in my spare room, putting on some black socks. I sat up and pulled her back until she was again lying next to me, in my arms.

"I didn't mean for this to happen," she said. "But I'm glad it did."

I did mean for it to happen and I was also glad it did. I kissed her.

"Are you coming back here after your meeting?" I asked.

"I can't," she said. "The orchestra finishes the run in New York tonight and then moves on to Chicago for the second part of the U.S. tour. I am desperate to regain my chair for that. If all goes well today, I will be flying out to Chicago on Sunday."

It was now Friday. Sunday seemed much too soon for her to disappear from me across the wide Atlantic.

"But you haven't even seen my restaurant," I said. "How about tomorrow? For dinner?"

"Don't be so eager, Mr. Moreton. I have a life, you know. And I have things to do if I'm going to be away next week." She sat up and finished dressing.

"When will you be back from the States?" I asked.

"I don't know that I'll be going yet. The orchestra is due to return next weekend to spend time preparing for our Festival Hall season. It's during that time I'm playing my solo at the Cadogan Hall. Are you still coming?"

"If you'll still have dinner with me afterwards," I said.

"Deal." We sealed it with a kiss.

We went downstairs, and Caroline made us some breakfast.

"Watch that toaster," I said to her. "It's broken and doesn't pop up like it should, and I'm forever forgetting and setting off the smoke alarm."

She watched it, carefully and without incident. We sat at the kitchen table and munched our way through two slices each of toast and marmalade.

The taxi hooted from outside. Too soon, I thought, much too soon.

After Caroline left, I moped around the house all morning, wishing she were still there. I tidied the kitchen at least three times, and I even vacuumed the floor in the sitting room until the noise began to make my head ache. I had a bowl of cereal, with painkillers, for my lunch.

It was with mixed emotions that I took Caroline's telephone call around one o'clock. She was so excited at having been welcomed back into the orchestral fold and busy making plans for her trip to Chicago. I was pleased for her, but I would have been kidding myself if I didn't admit I was rather disappointed that she was going.


"YOU DIDN'T," said Bernard Sims incredulously. "I've heard of clients sleeping with their lawyers, and jury members sleeping with each other, and even the odd judge or two sleeping with a barrister, but I've never before heard of the defendant sleeping with the plaintiff, not even if they were married to each other." He laughed loudly. I wished I hadn't told him.

He had called during the early afternoon to say that he had received another letter from Miss Aston's lawyers giving the grounds for her complaint and inviting our side to make a reasonable offer to Miss Aston for the distress and loss of earnings she had suffered.

I had foolishly told him that I had taken his advice to ask her out to dinner and now a relationship had developed between us.

"But did you sleep with her?" he had asked persistently.

"Well," I'd said finally, "what if I did?"

Now he was enjoying the situation hugely.

"Did she drop the lawsuit at the same time as she dropped her knickers?" he asked, barely able to contain his mirth.

"Bernard," I said sharply. "That's enough. And, no, she hasn't dropped the suit. Her agent is insisting that she persevere with it. He wants his percentage."

"Perhaps he's sleeping with her too." He was out of control.

"Bernard, I said stop it, that's enough." I had raised my voice.

"You're serious about her, aren't you?" he said.

"Yes."

"Well, blow me down," he said. "What shall I tell her lawyers?"

"Don't you dare tell them anything," I said.

"Not about that," he said. "What shall I tell them about an offer?"

"Let me think about it over the weekend. I'll speak to you on Monday. She's away for a week now, so they won't be able to tell her anything anyway."

"Is she away with you?" he asked.

"No she isn't," I said. "And it would be none of your business if she was."

"Everything about you is my business," he said, laughing. "I'm your lawyer, remember?" He was still laughing when he hung up. I wondered if all his clients gave him so much pleasure.

At about half past two, I called Carl to ask him to come and fetch me.

"Thought you had to rest for a few days," he said.

"I do," I replied. "I'm not coming in to work. I need to use my computer to get on the Internet."

"Right," he said. "I'll be there in five minutes."

THERE WERE nearly a million hits when I typed "Rolf Schumann" into the search engine on my computer. Most of the hits were in German. Rolf and Schumann were obviously very common names in Germany, Austria, Switzerland, and in Holland, too.

I added "Wisconsin" to my search criteria and was still surprised that the number of hits still exceeded twenty-eight thousand. It seemed that Rolf and Schumann were quite common names in Wisconsin as well.

I discovered that more Germans had emigrated to the United States than from any other nation, including Ireland and England, and that many of them had settled in the state of Wisconsin since the climate and agriculture were similar to those at home. So great was the influx that, according to one Web site I visited, a third of the total population of the state in 1900 had been born in Germany. Milwaukee, the largest city in Wisconsin, and less than thirty miles from Delafield, had even been known as the German Athens during the nineteenth century.

Adding "Delafield" narrowed my search down to just a few hundred, and there he was: Rolf Schumann, president of Delafield Industries, Inc., with his date of birth, education details, family tree, the lot. Good old Internet.

I spent the next hour or so discovering not a great deal useful about Mr. Schumann. He was sixty-one years old, and had been president of Delafield Industries for seven years, having been their finance director before that. It appeared that he was a pillar of society in Delafield and was involved either as a donor to or an administrator of various local charities. I learned that he was a leading light in the Delafield Chamber of Commerce and an elder at one of the local Lutheran churches. There was absolutely nothing I found to suggest that he would be the target of a bomber six thousand miles from his home.

Back in the 1840s, Delafield Industries, Inc., had been established at a local blacksmith's forge, making hand tools for the new settlers of Wisconsin to work the land and grow their corn. With the coming of the internal combustion engine, the firm had diversified first into tractors and then into every type of agricultural machinery. According to their own Web site, the company was now the biggest supplier of combine harvesters to midwestern farmers, and even I knew there was an awful lot of corn in the American Midwest. Unless huge success and mammoth moneymaking were motives for murder from jealous competitors, I could glean no reason why Delafield Industries should be a target.

I didn't seem to be doing very well in my new career as an investigator.

Carl came into the office and handed me a letter. "This came for you the day before yesterday," he said.

It was the letter from Forest Heath District Council informing me that they intended to prosecute me. I remembered that I had been on my way to collect the other letter from Suzanne Miller when my brakes had failed. I called her office number.

"Hello, Suzanne," I said, "Max Moreton here."

"Hello, Max," she said in her trill manner. "Are you all right? I heard about your accident."

"I'm fine, Suzanne, thank you," I said. "Just a little concussion, although my car has had it completely."

"Oh dear," she said, "I'm sorry."

"And I'm sorry that I never made it to you to collect the letter from Forest Heath District Council."

"Don't worry about that," she said. "But it's still here, waiting for you."

"They sent another copy to the restaurant," I said.

"I thought they might have," she said.

"Have you had any luck with the lists I asked you to get?" I asked, coming to the real purpose of my call.

"I'm afraid I can't help you with the guest list from the dinner," she said. "The one you already have is the only one available. Short of calling all the people named on the list and asking them for the names of their guests, I can't think of anything else to do. But I've had a bit more luck with the Delafield Industries list. Apparently, the Special Branch asked for lists of the guests in all the boxes. Something to do with security for that Arab." She didn't sound too impressed by the Special Branch. "Fat lot of good it did."

She still thought, like everyone else apart from me, that the bomb had been aimed at the prince.

"Where are the lists?" I asked her.

"The Special Branch has them, I suppose," she said. "I only found out about the lists because another of the box holders told me. He was rather indignant at having to tell the police the names of his guests. If you ask me, it was because he had his mistress with him and he wanted to keep her name a secret."

"Are you sure?" I said.

"Oh yes," she said. "He told my staff she was his niece, but it was obvious she wasn't. We had a great time playing them along." She laughed over the phone.

I wouldn't have believed it of her. "Who was it?" I asked eagerly.

"I'd better not say," she said, but then she did. She couldn't resist it. I knew who it was. Everyone in racing would have known who it was. She then told me the name of his mistress too. How delicious. "But don't tell anyone," she said seriously.

I didn't need to. In time, Suzanne would see to that.

"So how do I get the list from Special Branch?" I asked.

"Why don't you ask them for it," she said.

So I did.

I typed "Special Branch UK" into my computer and found a Web site that told me that every police force has its own Special Branch. So I called the Suffolk Police, who told me that protection for VIPs was handled by Special Branch of the Met, the Metropolitan Police. They kindly gave me a number.

"We don't give out information to members of the public," I was told firmly by a Detective Inspector Turner when I called and asked for the lists.

"But I'm not just a member of the public; I was there," I said. "I was blown up by the bomb and I ended up in the hospital." I didn't tell him that it was only for a bit of a sore knee and a scratched leg.

"And what, exactly, is it you are after?" he said.

I explained to him that I had been the chef at the lunch that had been served in the bombed box and that one of my staff had been killed in the explosion. He was appropriately sympathetic. I told him that I believed the Special Branch had been given a list of all the guests invited to that box, and I was trying to obtain that list, so that I could invite the survivors to join a self-help therapy group being set up in the name of my dead waitress. To help them recover from the trauma of the bombing.

It was the best I could think of on the spur of the moment.

"I'll see what I can do, sir," he said.

I thanked him, and gave him my e-mail address as well as my telephone number.

I looked at my watch. It was nearly half past four. I called Caroline.

"Hello," she said over the line. "I was just thinking about you."

"Good thoughts, I hope," I said.

"Mostly." I wasn't sure about her tone.

"Not regretting last night, are you?" I said.

"Oh, you know. All a bit sudden."

"Yes," I agreed. As far as I was concerned, all the best things in life were a bit sudden, and she was no exception. But I wasn't going to push things. Who was it, I thought, who said, "Things may come to those who wait"?

"Have you had a good afternoon?" I asked.

"Wonderful," she said. "I've played my viola for three whole hours. My fingers are tired, but I feel so alive. Music is like oxygen—without it, I'd suffocate."

"I thought you would be packing," I said.

"I'm not going now until Monday," she said. "The first night in Chicago is not until Wednesday, and the rest of the orchestra are going off to see Niagara Falls for the weekend. I will join them in Chicago on Monday night."

"Will you come back to Newmarket, then?" I asked.

"I can't," she said. "I'm having my hair done tomorrow at four, and I have to get ready for the trip."

"Oh," I said rather glumly. "When will I see you, then?"

"Don't sound so miserable," she said. "I said I can't come to Newmarket, but you could come here if you want to."

I did want to. "When?"

"Whenever," she said. "Come tomorrow and stay until Monday morning. You can help me get to Heathrow with all my stuff and see me off to the States."

I hated the thought of seeing her off to anywhere. "OK," I said. "I'll be at your place tomorrow around lunchtime."

"No, later," she said. "I've got to go shopping before my hair appointment. Come at seven, and we'll go down the pub for dinner."

"That'll be lovely," I said. "I'll call you later."

We hung up, and I sat at my desk, smiling. I had never been so eager to see someone in my life. Was this *it*? I wondered. It was all a bit sudden, and a bit scary.

I asked my computer who had said the quote. It came back with the answer: Abraham Lincoln. But his full quote was: "Things may come to those who wait, but only the things left by those who hustle." In the future, I resolved to hustle.

I SPENT another hour at my computer, hunting for anything that would give me a direction in which to look. I dug out the copy of the *Cambridge Evening News* that had listed the dead and searched the Internet for any lead for each name. Nothing. I did discover that one of the Delafield men who had died, Gus Witney, had been connected with the equine world, being involved with a polo club. The Lake Country Polo Club, to be precise.

I looked it up. The club had a very expansive Web site for what was clearly an expanding enterprise. Sure enough, Gus Witney was there, named as their president, and there was even a photograph of him smiling. They clearly were not very quick at updating their site, as nearly two weeks had now passed since their president had died and there was still no mention of it. The club was sponsored, not unexpectedly, by Delafield Industries, Inc., and Rolf Schumann himself was named in the list of patrons and vice presidents.

There was a link to the United States Polo Association, and I was surprised to see that polo was such a big activity over there. Obviously, it wasn't in the same league as baseball or football, but there were more than four times as many polo clubs in the U.S. as there were Thoroughbred racetracks. And about ten times as many clubs as in England. Now, that was a surprise. I had always thought of polo as a minor sport, and a peculiarly British minor sport at that, played by British army cavalry officers on the plains of India to while away the boredom of a long posting far from home.

YOU'VE GOT MAIL, my computer said via a little blue box in the bottom right corner of the screen.

It was from Detective Inspector Turner. It was the Delafield guest list for 2000 Guineas day. Good old D.I. Turner. However, it didn't give me what I wanted. What he had sent was a scan of a piece of paper that had originally had the full invited list printed on it. However, someone had drawn a thick black line through the seven names of those who had failed to show up. Against sixteen of the remaining names, someone had placed a *d,* presumably for "deceased," since there were *d*'s next to Elizabeth Jennings, MaryLou Fordham and the Walterses. Also, someone had handwritten "Louisa Whitworth" and "Elaine Jones" at the bottom of the list. They too had a *d* next to their names. I remembered from the *Cambridge Evening News* report that Elaine Jones had been the unfortunate woman killed by flying masonry.

I suppose I shouldn't complain. I had asked for the list of survivors and D.I. Turner had given me exactly that, together with the names of those who had died. But what I still lacked was the names of the seven people who should have been there but weren't.

I called the number I had used earlier.

"Is D.I. Turner there?" I asked.

I had to wait a few minutes before he came on the line. I thanked him for sending me the list, but could he help just one more time? He listened patiently to my explanation, that I would like to have the names of those who had escaped death only by a fraction, in order that they too might share in the benefit of the therapy group, did he have the seven missing names?

He seemed to hesitate, but then he agreed to try to find the original list.

"Can't promise we still have it," he said. "Not so important for us to keep a list of people who weren't there, especially when they weren't even the intended target."

I thought about telling him my theory that, actually, they *were* the intended target, but it still seemed rather fanciful, and I had no hard facts to back it up. My afternoon's searching on the Internet had hardly turned up anything of note, and I was beginning to seriously doubt my original thoughts that my car crash had been deliberately arranged. I simply thanked him again and said that I would be waiting for the list.

"I go off duty in half an hour," he said. "I'll see what I can do."

I hung up. Was I right or were the police right? Perhaps I should have shared my ideas with the policeman and then at least he could have shown me the errors in my reasoning. Maybe, as Caroline had said, the police had more information than I did, information from MI5 and the other intelligence services. Or maybe they were just sticking to the Arab prince theory because they didn't have any other.

I thought about calling Neil Jennings, but it seemed too soon to intrude on his grief by asking questions about how and why he had been invited to the Delafield box. Instead, I called the Kealys.

"Hello, Max," said Emma. "Are you checking up whether we're coming tomorrow?"

I had to think about what she was talking about. "No," I said. "I just assumed you were."

"Oh yes," she said. "I think there will be six of us, as usual."

"Great," I said. I decided not to mention that I wouldn't be at the restaurant. I would be down the pub with Caroline. I couldn't remember when I was last "down the pub" on a Saturday night. I was looking forward to it. "No, the real reason I called was to ask if you knew why you had been invited to that lunch on Guineas day."

"Oh that," she said. "We had a runner in the race. I think that was the reason."

"But they couldn't have asked all the trainers," I said.

"I don't know about that," said Emma. "We were, and I know Neil and Elizabeth were invited as well. Elizabeth and I had discussed it." She paused briefly. "Poor Elizabeth."

"Yes," I said. I waited a few seconds. "Emma, I'm sorry to be a nuisance, but can you remember when you received the invitation?"

"Oh." There was a pause. "I can't, I'm afraid. It was some time ago, I know that."

"Was it a proper printed invitation, on stiff card?" I asked.

Another pause. "I don't think it was," she said. "I can't remember it being on the mantelpiece. That's where we put all our invitations." I suspected that their mantelpiece was kept pretty full.

"Well," I said, "thanks anyway."

"No problem," she said. "I'll ask George when he gets in. He's out at some damn committee meeting for the club he's chairman of. I'll call you if he thinks of anything more."

"Thanks. Bye, now." I hung up. Another dead end.

I looked again at the list that Detective Inspector Turner had sent. Of the seventeen names not crossed out and without a *d* next to them, I knew eleven. I suspected that the others, the ones I didn't recognize, were Delafield people, one of whom, according to Ms. Harding at the newspaper, had since died from her burns. The eleven that I did recognize included one couple who were regulars at the Hay Net, and at least four others lived locally and had been occasional customers. The remaining five were from farther afield, and included a trainer and his wife from Middleham in Yorkshire, the wife of the Irish businessman who had been killed and an ex-jockey from the West Country who now made a meager living giving tips to corporate guests at race meetings. I couldn't remember him giving a talk before the lunch, but I would have been in the kitchen by then anyway. None of them looked likely targets of a terrorist.

The last one was Rolf Schumann. Was he the target?

I checked my e-mails again. Nothing new.

I looked at my watch and the half hour was up. D.I. Turner would have gone off duty for the day, maybe for the weekend, so I would just have to be patient and wait.

It was seven-thirty and the restaurant dinner service was beginning to get into full swing, so I went into the kitchen to check if everything was going well and was promptly ordered out by Carl.

"You're sick," he said. "Go home, and let us get on with it."

"I'm not sick," I said. "I've just got a headache. You can't catch concussion, you know."

He grinned at me. "No matter. We are coping fine without you. This is Oscar." Carl pointed at a new face in the kitchen. "He's doing fine." Oscar smiled. Gary didn't. He was clearly not having one of his good days. I left them and returned to my office. I would have loved to go home, but I still wanted to search a little more on the Internet and I had no computer at home.

I checked my e-mails yet again but still nothing more. I was beginning to give up on D.I. Turner when my phone rang. It was him.

"Sorry," he said. "I have found a copy of the original list, but I can't seem to work this damn scanner, now the secretary's gone home. And I've got to go home now as well. I'm meant to be taking the missus out to the cinema for her birthday, and I'm going to be late as it is. I'll send it to you next week."

"Couldn't you just read it out?" I said. "I'll write them down."

"Oh all right. But quickly."

I grabbed a pen and wrote down the names on the back of an old menu card. Neil Jennings was there as expected, as were George and Emma Kealy, and I knew of two of the other four, Patrick and Margaret Jacobs, who together ran a successful saddlery business in the town. The other couple I'd never heard of. Their names were Pyotr and Tatiana Komarov.

I thanked him and wished him a pleasant evening with his wife and to blame me for his lateness. He said he intended to, and hung up.

I looked at the names I had written on the menu. Why had I thought that the key to everything would be the names of those invited to but not present in the bombed box? Patrick and Margaret Jacobs were nice people who, I knew, looked after their customers with efficiency and charm. They seemed well respected, even liked, by most of the local Newmarket trainers, some of whom had even brought them to dinner at the Hay Net. I searched through the copy of the guest list for the Friday-night dinner and, sure enough, "Mr. & Mrs. Patrick Jacobs" were listed as having been present.

There was no such luck with the Komarovs, who were absent from the Friday-night list. That didn't necessarily mean they hadn't been at the dinner, just that they were not named.

I typed "Komarov" into my computer. My Google search engine threw up over a million hits. I tried "Pyotr Komarov" and cut it down to about thirty-eight thousand. The one I wanted could be any of them, most of whom were Russians. I asked my machine to look for "Tatiana Komarov." "Do you mean Tatiana *Komarova*?" it asked me. I remembered that in Russian and other Slavic languages the female version of a surname ends in *a*. I tried "Tatiana Komarova." Another eighteen thousand hits. Pyotr and Tatiana Komarov together produced sixteen thousand. It was like searching for the correct needle in a needle stack when you didn't even know what the correct one looked like.

One of the hits caught my eye. A certain Pyotr Komarov was listed as the president of the St. Petersburg Polo Club.

He must be the one, I thought. Pyotr Komarov and Rolf Schumann must be acquainted through polo.

I searched further, bringing up the Web site for the St. Petersburg Polo Club. I hadn't expected there to be so many until I realized that most of the results were for St. Petersburg in Florida. The one club I was after was in the burg founded by Tsar Peter the Great in 1703, the original St. Petersburg, the city on Russia's Baltic coast.

According to the club site, polo in post-Soviet Russia was clearly on the rise. Clubs were apparently springing up like a rash and the new middle class was seemingly keen to emulate its American counterpart by making a trip to a polo match one of *the* social events of the week. In Russia, they even played polo on snow during the long winter, using an inflatable, football-sized orange ball instead of the traditional white solid-wood one. It was reported that the Snow Polo Cup, sponsored by a major Swiss watchmaker, was the premier event of the St. Petersburg winter season, the place to see and be seen among the most chic of society.

So what? What could polo possibly have to do with the bombing of Newmarket racetrack? I didn't know for sure that it did, but polo was undeniably a connection between some of the victims of the bomb and someone else who hadn't been, although they had been expected to be.

# 12

I had a restless night, again. However, rather than the all-too-familiar nightmare of MaryLou and her missing legs I instead lay awake, trying to get my mind to think of Caroline but always returning to the burning questions: Who poisoned the dinner? And why? Was it really done to try to stop someone being at the races the following day? And, if so, who? Did someone, in fact, try to kill me by fixing the brakes of my car? And, if so, who? And why? And, finally, was it anything to do with the polo connection? Lots of questions but precious few answers.

I had spent most of the previous evening on the Internet. I had learned all sorts of things about polo I hadn't known, and would probably have been happy never to know. It had been an Olympic sport five times, but not since 1936, when Argentina had won the gold medal. It seemed they were still the major force in world polo, and most of the ponies used still came from South America.

The Hurlingham Polo Association was the governing body of the game in the United Kingdom, even though no matches have, in fact, been played at Hurlingham Club since the polo fields were dug up to provide food for war-torn Londoners in 1939.

I had looked up the rules on their Web site. They ran to fifty pages of closely printed text and were so complicated that it was a surprise to me that anyone understood them at all. I was amused to discover that if the three-and-a-half-inch wooden ball were to split into two unequal parts after being hit by a mallet or trodden on by a pony, a goal could still be scored if the larger part were deemed to have passed between the posts. I could just imagine what a defender might have said if defending the wrong part of the ball. The rules even went so far as to state in writing that the mounted umpires were not allowed to use their cell telephones during play, while the nonmounted referee should avoid distractions like talking to his neighbors or using his phone while watching from the sidelines.

I had also discovered that polo ponies were not actually ponies at all. They were horses. Many were Argentinean Criollo horses, and others were ex–Thoroughbred racehorses that had proved to be not fast enough to be winners on the track. In America, Thoroughbreds were often crossed with quarter horses to produce fast, sure-footed animals capable of quick acceleration and deceleration, and able to make the sharp turns essential for success. But ponies, they certainly were not, averaging over fifteen hands, or five feet, at the withers, rather than the maximum fourteen and a half hands of a true pony.

In spite of a head full of fairly useless information, I came up with no answers to my questions. However, I did find out the final of a tournament was scheduled for that coming Sunday at the Guards Polo Club, near Windsor. Perhaps I would go. Even better, perhaps I would take Caroline.

"ARE YOU CRAZY?" said Caroline when I phoned her. "I haven't got time to go to a bloody polo match. And you're meant to be resting. You're still concussed, remember?"

"It's only for the afternoon," I said. "And concussion affects memory."

"You're really serious about going, aren't you?"

"Absolutely," I said.

"But I know nothing about polo," she complained.

"So what?" I said. "Neither do I."

"Then what on earth do you want to go for?" she said.

"Well, you know my mad theory about the bombing and the poisoned dinner?" I said. "I have an itching feeling that it might have something to do with polo. I know it sounds daft and I might be barking up the wrong tree, but I want to go to a polo match and ask a few questions."

"Why didn't you say so?" she said. "Of course I'll come. Shall I wear my deerstalker and bring a magnifying glass?"

"Do I detect a degree of skepticism?" I asked, laughing. "To tell the truth, I'm very doubtful as well. But I have nowhere else to look."

"So what do I wear?" Caroline asked.

"Tweed suit and green wellies," I said.

"I don't have a tweed suit," she said.

"Good," I said. "Something fairly smart and warm. The forecast is not great for Sunday."

"Do I need a hat?" she said.

"I don't know," I replied.

"You're no bloody good," she said. "I thought you knew about the horsy world."

"Racing," I said, "not polo."

"Same thing. Both messing about on horses."

She had lots to learn.

I SPENT most of Saturday kicking my heels around the cottage and studying the hands of my watch as they swept ever so slowly around and around, wishing they would hurry up so I could be on my way to Fulham. On my way to Caroline.

But the day wasn't a complete waste. During the morning, I called Margaret Jacobs at the saddlery shop. She wasn't very friendly.

"What do you want?" she demanded in a rather cross tone.

"What's wrong, Margaret?" I said.

"You made Patrick and me so ill after that dinner," she said. "I thought we were dying."

"I'm sorry," I said. "If it is any consolation, I was desperately ill as well. And I didn't make everyone ill on purpose."

"No, I suppose not." She mellowed, but only a bit. "But it said in the paper that your restaurant was closed for decontamination. There must have been something wrong for them to do that. And we'd been eating there only the week before too."

"There's nothing wrong with the restaurant," I told her. "We have been inspected by the Food Standards Agency and given a clean bill of health. There never was anything wrong with it."

"There must have been," she said. "Otherwise, why were we so ill?"

I decided not to tell her about the kidney beans and my belief that someone had poisoned the dinner on purpose. Instead, I changed direction.

"Margaret," I said, "I know that you and Patrick were invited to the lunch given by Delafield Industries on 2000 Guineas day. Was your illness the reason why you didn't go?"

"Yes," she said firmly. "I was really looking forward to that day, but we had both been up all night."

"I suppose, in the end, it was good that you didn't go," I said.

"Why?" she asked.

"Don't you know?" I said. "The box where the bomb went off at the races was the box where that lunch was held. All those people who died were the Delafield staff and their guests."

There was a long silence on the other end of the line.

"Margaret," I said, "are you still there?"

"I didn't realize it had been that box that had been bombed," she said, sounding very shocked. "My God. We could have been killed."

"But you weren't," I said, trying to be reassuring.

"I was so cross we couldn't go," she said. "In fact, I still wanted to in spite of feeling so lousy. It was Patrick who insisted we shouldn't and we had a huge row about it." She paused. "Those poor people."

"Yes," I said. "I was there. I cooked the lunch."

"Did you?" she said, somewhat surprised. "If I'd known that, I might not have been so keen."

"Oh thanks," I said.

"Sorry," she said. But she didn't add that she didn't mean it.

"Margaret," I said, "the Hay Net restaurant is perfectly safe, I promise you."

"Mmm," she replied, not sounding as if she believed it.

"Come to dinner as my guest, and bring Patrick."

"Maybe," she said. And maybe not, I thought. The saddlery business run by Patrick and Margaret Jacobs supplied equine equipment to the majority of the stables in the town, and I needed them not to spread their suspicions about my food. It was very easy to get a bad reputation, whether deserved or not, and a bad reputation was very hard to get rid of.

"Think about it," I said. "And feel free to bring a couple of guests with you." How much would I have to offer, I wondered, before she agreed?

"When?" she asked. I had her hooked.

"Anytime you like," I said, reeling her in. "How about next weekend?"

"Saturday?" she said.

"No problem," I said. "I'll book you in for four. At eight o'clock?"

"OK," she said with a little trepidation in her voice. "Thank you." The catch was landed. But it didn't move me any further along in my search for answers.

LIFE WITHOUT a car was becoming a real bore. The invention of the internal combustion engine has proved to be the greatest provider of personal freedom that man has ever known, but it has become a freedom we tend to take for granted. The most recent provider of my own personal freedom was still sitting in a mangled heap at the back of the towing garage, and I severely missed its convenience for quick simple journeys, journeys that were now neither quick nor simple.

I called the NewTax taxi number, which I now knew by heart, and booked myself a ride to Cambridge station to catch the five o'clock train to London. I threw a few things into an overnight bag and waited impatiently for the taxi to arrive. Why, I wondered, did I feel like a naughty schoolboy skipping lessons?

Almost as an afterthought, I put my passport in my bag just in case. I told myself I was being foolish, but so what? Hadn't Shakespeare said in *As You Like It* something about not having loved unless one could remember having run off on some folly or other? Was I falling in love? Yes, I think I probably was.

KING'S CROSS station was full of disappointed soccer supporters waiting for the train back north after their team's defeat in the Cup Final. The mood was somber, and not a little aggressive. Hard as I tried, it was impossible for me not to be smiling broadly with excitement at the prospect of spending two nights with Caroline. Consequently, I received some unwelcome attention from a group of half a dozen red-soccer-shirted young men who were all rather the worse for drink.

"What are you smiling at?" demanded one of them, pushing his face close to mine and giving me a generous sample of his alcoholic breath.

"Nothing," I said rather timidly.

"You can bloody well sod off, then," he said, slightly slurring his words. I could read in his eyes the thought processes going on behind them in his intoxicated brain. He was obviously the leader of the troupe, and I could see that the others were watching his every move. I sensed that he was weighing his options, and the simple choice of moving away and leaving me be would mean, in his eyes, a loss of face among his followers. It might have been funny if it hadn't been so frightening. His eyes widened, as I saw his irrational reasoning come to the conclusion that physical violence was his only viable course of action.

So slow were his reactions that I saw his haymaker of a right hook coming from a very long way back and I was simply able to sway backwards out of his reach. There was a slight expression of surprise on his face as his fist sailed harmlessly past the end of my nose with an inch or two to spare. The momentum of his plump, flailing arm proceeded to throw him off balance and he went down heavily onto the station concourse. Time, I thought, to make a swift exit. I turned and ran.

A very scary few minutes ensued, with me haring through the station with the remaining pack in pursuit. Fortunately, most of them were not only carrying an excess of beer in their bellies but also some substantial extra pounds around their waists and they were no match for my adrenaline-fueled flight. However, two of them were remarkably nimble in spite of these handicaps, and more than once I felt their fingers on my coat. On one occasion, I swung my overnight bag at one of them and was rewarded with an audible grunt.

I tore out of the station and leaped over the pedestrian barrier into the traffic on the Euston Road, dodging buses, cars and taxis as I sprinted for my life. Fortunately for me, a combination of good sense and the timely intervention of a passing police car meant that the chasing pair did not follow me as I weaved across the four lanes and jogged rapidly westwards along the pavement, breathing heavily.

I slowed down and laughed out loud in relief. I received a few strange looks from people I passed, but, thankfully, this time there was nothing more sinister than amusement in their eyes. I felt on top of the world, and I literally skipped along the pavement as I searched the oncoming vehicles for a vacant cab to take me to Fulham.

CAROLINE LIVED in what she described as a lower-ground-floor apartment. Tamworth Street, like many residential streets in west London, was bordered on each side by rows of stucco-fronted terraced town houses built in the 1920s and '30s to house an increasing urban population. Whereas they had originally all been single-family homes, many had since been subdivided into flats as the pressure for accommodation increased further in the latter part of the twentieth century. All along the road the lower-ground-floor flats had been created out of the original "below stairs" areas, where the servants had once tended to the family living above. Access to Caroline's abode was not through the house's front door but by way of the old staff entrance, via a gate in the iron railing and down eight or so steps to a small concrete yard below street level.

She opened her door with what appeared to be a squeal of delight and threw her arms round my neck, planting a long, welcoming kiss on my lips. If she was having any second thoughts about our relationship, she had a funny way of showing it.

Her flat ran through the house from front to back and had access to a small exterior space at the rear, just big enough for a table and a few chairs.

"I get the morning sun during the summer," she said. "It's a lovely little garden. It was the reason I had to have the flat."

How was it, I thought, that human beings were happy to live so close together in this urban jungle that a table and chair on a six-foot-square concrete slab constituted a garden to delight in? I was happier with the wide-open spaces of Newmarket Heath, but I knew that I would soon have to move and join the throng in this conurbation if I was to fulfill Mark's ambition.

The flat itself was modern and minimalist in style, with plenty of bare wooden floors, and chrome barstools in the white-fronted kitchen. She had two bedrooms, but the smaller of them had been converted into a practice room, with a chair and music stand in the center and piles of sheet music around the walls.

"Don't the neighbors object?" I asked.

"No," she replied rather firmly. "I don't play late at night or before nine in the morning, and no one has complained.

In fact, the lady upstairs has said how much she loves to listen."

"Will you play for me?" I asked.

"What, now?"

"Yes."

"No," she said. "I'm not playing for you until you've cooked for me."

"That's not fair. I would have cooked for you during the week if my car hadn't crashed."

"Excuses, excuses," she said, laughing.

"What's in your fridge?" I asked her. "I'll cook for you now."

"No you won't," she said. "We're going down the pub. I've had to bribe the barman to hold us a table."

Going down the pub with Caroline on a Saturday night was everything I had hoped it would be. The pub in question was The Atlas, around the corner in Seagrave Road, and it was packed. Even though she had somehow managed to make a reservation, this was unquestionably a pub and not a restaurant like the Hay Net, our bleached wooden table being underneath the window of the bar. Caroline sat on an upright wooden chair that reminded me of those at my school, while I fought my way through the crowd at the bar to choose a bottle of Chianti Classico from the blackboard and chalk wine lists that were proudly displayed above the mirror-backed serving area.

The food was good and also imaginative. Caroline chose grilled whole sea bass with couscous salad, while I plumped for the Cumberland sausages and garlic mashed potatoes. I wondered about the garlic, and so, obviously, did Caroline. She used her fork to pinch some of my potato. I caught her eye as she was putting it in her mouth. For a moment, we glanced deeper, into the inner soul, and then laughed as we both understood, unspoken, the reason why.

Caroline was excited about the Chicago trip, and we talked about her job and especially about her music.

"I feel so alive when I'm playing," she said. "I exist only in my head, and, I know this sounds stupid, but my hands on the bow and the strings seem somehow disconnected from my body. They have a mind of their own and they just do it."

I just sat there, looking at her, not wanting to interrupt.

"Even if I have a new piece that I haven't played before, I don't really have to consciously tell my fingers where to go. I just look at the notes on the paper and my fingers seem to do it by themselves. I can feel the result. It's wonderful."

"Can you hear what you yourself are playing with all the others instruments around you?" I asked.

"Oh yes," she said. "But I actually feel the sound I make. I feel it through my bones. If I press hard on my viola with my chin, my whole head becomes full of my music. In fact, I have to be careful not to press too hard, as then I can't hear any of the rest of the orchestra. Playing in a great orchestra is so exhilarating. Apart, that is, from all the damn people."

"What people?" I asked.

"The other members," she said. "They can be so catty, so prima donna-ish. We are all meant to be one team, but there are so many petty rivalries. Everyone is trying to be one better than everyone else, especially in their own section. All the violinists want to end up being leader, and most of the other instruments hate the fact that the leader is always a violinist. It's like a bloody school playground. There are the bullies and the bullied. Some of the older members hate the younger ones coming along and getting the solo parts that they think they should have. Hell hath no fury like a passed-over would-be soloist, I can tell you. Once, I even saw a senior member of an orchestra try to sabotage the instrument of a younger soloist. I just hope I never get to be like that."

"Chefs can be pretty devious too, you know," I said, and I wondered again if jealousy of my success had been the real reason for someone adding poisonous kidney beans to the dinner.

"But I bet you've never had to work with eighty or so of them at once, all trying to show that they're better than their neighbors while at the same time having to come together to bring a score to life."

"Maybe not," I said. "But it feels like it sometimes."

She smiled. "Now, don't get me wrong," she said. "I adore being in a really good professional orchestra. It can be so moving and so wonderfully fulfilling. The climax to a work can be fantastic. You know, like Tchaikovsky's 1812 Overture, with all the cannon blasts and everything, in the Royal Albert Hall with seven thousand people there, it's unbelievably exciting." She laughed. "Better than an orgasm."

I wasn't sure how to take that comment. Practice, I thought. I just needed more practice. "Wait and see," I said.

"Is that a promise?" she said, laughing.

"Absolutely," I replied, stroking her hand across the table.

We sat and finished our meals in contented silence, perhaps not wanting to break the spell, until a waiter came over to collect our empty plates. We ordered two coffees, and I poured the last of the Chianti into our glasses. Neither of us gave the outward impression that we wanted to rush back to her flat and put my promise to the test. So much for outward impressions. Inside, I was desperate.

"So what are you playing in Chicago?" I asked her, putting my desperation back in its box.

Her face lit up. "Mostly Elgar. We do his first symphony, and also the variations, which I love. There is also some Sibelius in the program. His fourth symphony, to be precise, but I'm not as keen on it, I find it too heavy. Very dark." She screwed up her face.

"Who chooses what is played?" I asked.

"The directors and the conductor, I suppose," she said. "I don't really know. I expect the Americans had something to do with it too. I suppose the Elgar is there, as it is quintessentially English. And, of course, there's the anniversary of his birth."

Of course, I thought.

"Surely Sibelius wasn't English," I said.

"No," she said. "Finnish, I think, but I'm not sure. But the Americans seem to like his stuff. Must be something to do with all that hardship and living in log cabins." She laughed. "Far too dark and gloomy for me."

"Like treacle," I said.

"Exactly, but less sticky." She laughed again. An uninhibited, happy laugh.

"But it will be worth going just for the Elgar," she said.

" 'Nimrod' was one of the pieces I had to play for my audition to the Royal College. I adore it, and I play it every time I need some comfort in my life, which I have to tell you, has been quite often. My music, and especially my viola, has been a huge support to me at times." She stared somewhere over my head, but she wasn't really looking. "I love my viola so much that I couldn't possibly live without it."

I was jealous. It seemed silly. Of course Caroline loved her music. After all, I loved my cooking. Could I live without that? No I couldn't. Well, then, I told myself, stop being jealous of a viola. It was an inanimate object. I tried hard not to be, but with limited success.

In time, we walked back arm in arm to her flat and both went eagerly to her bed, where I strived to make good on my promise.

She didn't exactly say that it was better than Tchaikovsky's 1812, but she didn't say it wasn't. Viola, eat your heart out.

# 13

We woke early and lay dozing side by side in the bed, just touching occasionally. I rolled over and cuddled her, but she didn't respond, and I sensed that she was troubled.

"What's the matter?" I asked her.

"Oh nothing," she said. "I was just thinking."

"About what?" I asked.

"Nothing important," she said. But it clearly was.

I started to explore her body with my hands, but she sat up. "Not now," she said. "I want some tea." And she proceeded to get up, put on her dressing gown and go down the corridor to the kitchen. I lay back on the pillow and wondered if I had said or done something wrong.

She returned with two steaming mugs of tea and got back into bed, but she did not remove the dressing gown.

"Was I that much of a disappointment?" I said, propping myself up on an elbow and sipping my tea.

"Oh no," she said. "In fact, quite the reverse. That's part of the problem."

"So what is the problem?" I said. "Tell me."

She leaned her head back against the wall with a sigh. "I can't come and live in Newmarket," she said. "I need to live in London for my job."

I laughed with relief. "I'm not asking you to live in Newmarket," I said.

"Oh," she said rather gloomily. "I had thought you might."

"Well, I might," I said. "But I will probably be coming to live in London."

"That's all right, then," she said with a big smile. "But when? What about your restaurant?"

"It's not certain when," I said, "and I don't want my staff to know yet, but the plan is to open a new restaurant in London sometime later in the year."

"Oh goodie," she said with excitement.

"Am I right, therefore, in thinking that you are throwing yourself into my life on a permanent basis?" I asked.

"Maybe." She shrugged off her dressing gown and snuggled down next to me in the bed.

"That is definitely all right, then," I said.

AT LUNCHTIME, we caught the train to Virginia Water and took a taxi from there to Smith's Lawn, the home of the Guards Polo Club. Neither of us had the faintest idea of what to expect, but we had chosen to dress for all eventualities. Caroline selected a black-and-white floral-print dress that seemed to me to touch her in all the right places, show off her considerable natural attributes and turn many an eye on the train. Over the dress, she wore a fitted tweed coat, with brown fur around the collar and the cuffs. If she had brought a deerstalker and magnifying glass with her, I couldn't see where she'd hidden them. Meanwhile, I had decided on a blue blazer, gray flannel trousers, with a white shirt and a striped tie. Uniform, I reckoned, for any self-respecting off-duty Guards officer.

We both opted not to wear green wellies, not least because we would have had to buy them first. The weather forecast for the day had improved as the weekend had progressed and the promised rain was not now due to arrive from the west until the following day, so I wore my usual slip-on black brogues while Caroline picked a pair of sensible knee-length black patent leather boots with low heels.

Having been brought up in the world of horse racing, where any physical contact between the competitors was frowned upon and where even the slightest bump between participants could result in the loss of a race in the stewards' room, I was unprepared for the roughness, almost violence, perpetrated on the polo field.

Players were permitted to "ride off" an opponent even when he was not in possession of the ball. Riding off involved crashing one's pony into the flank of an opponent's mount and pushing with the knee and the elbow to change the direction of travel. The players all wore big thick kneepads for that very purpose, along with spurs, which, I was reliably informed, were not actually permitted to be dug into an opponent's leg, although, it appeared to me, that they were.

I knew that the aim of the game was to hit the little white ball with the mallet between the goalposts to score. But that is to simplify what seemed to me to be a hybrid cross between hockey, croquet and American football, all played at high speed on horseback.

It was clearly hugely exhilarating both for the players and for the spectators. There was lots of shouting between the team members, and appeals to the umpire for some penalty or other to be awarded. I knew from my brush with the fifty-page rule book that the game would be more complicated than just riding down the field and slotting the ball between the goalposts. However, in play, it had a simplicity I had not expected, and both Caroline and I were soon caught up in the excitement on the members' grandstand.

We had arrived at the grounds, as they were referred to, to find that there was a members' area for those who are, and the remaining space for those who aren't. The "members" was where I wanted to be. There was no point in being there at all unless I was able to ask my questions of those in the know.

We had hung around a bit in the members' parking lot until a group of five others had arrived in a Range Rover. Caroline and I had simply attached ourselves to the rear of the party as they were waved through past the gateman. I decided not to push my luck by trying to bluff my way into the holy of holies, the two-story Royal Box, with its colonial-style verandas and red tile roof, together with neatly tended window boxes and a white-picket-fenced lawn in front.

Since I had no idea of what to expect, I didn't know whether the "crowd" of just two or three hundred was considered a good turnout or not. Many of the spectators had parked their vehicles on the far side of the field and simply sat on the roofs to watch the action. A chorus of car horns rather than applause tended to greet each goal.

Fortunately, the day was fine, with even some watery sunshine helping to warm us as Caroline and I sat in the open, on green plastic seats, along with about a hundred or so others, most of whom appeared to either know or be related to the players, exchanging waves and shouts, as the teams milled around in front of us before the start.

Polo matches are divided into periods known as chukkas, each chukka lasting about seven minutes. Matches can be four, five or six chukkas long, with gaps in between. In this particular event, each match was four chukkas, with approximately a five-minute gap between each, and a little longer at halftime.

Caroline asked a middle-aged man who was sitting close to her what the score was. Now, this was not as stupid as it may have sounded, since the game can be very confusing. For a start, it was not always clear if a goal had been scored because, unlike soccer, there was no net for the ball to end up in. Second, the teams changed the direction of play after each goal, and, for a beginner's eye, it was not always easy to decide which team was playing in which direction.

"That depends," said the man. "Do you mean with or without handicap goals?"

"What are 'handicap goals'?" Caroline asked him.

The man resisted the temptation to roll his eyes, not least because they were firmly fixed on the alluring crossover at the front of Caroline's dress. "Each player is assigned a handicap at the beginning of the season," he said. "In matches, you have to add the handicaps of each player in the team, and subtract one team's handicap from the other's. That gives you how many goals' start the lower-handicapped team gets." He smiled, but he wasn't finished. "But, of course, in this match, which is only four chukkas, you only get two-thirds of those goals."

"So what is the score?" asked Caroline again rather desperately.

"The Mad Dogs are beating Ocho Rios by three and a half goals to two." He pointed to the scoreboard at the left-hand end of the field, where the score was clearly displayed in large white numbers on a blue background for all to see.

We wished we had never asked. We didn't even know which team were the Mad Dogs and which weren't, but it didn't matter. We were having fun, and we giggled to prove it.

At halftime, many of those in the stands went forward to meet the players as they dismounted from and changed their ponies. There were about thirty animals tied to the pony lines alongside the field, and some players had all their spare mounts saddled and bridled, ready for quick changes during a chukka if a pony tired, the game not being stopped for such a substitution. They each appeared to have a groom or two to look after their mounts and to assist with the quick transfer of rider and equipment from one pony to another. Playing polo was clearly not a poor man's sport.

During the halftime break, I asked our friend on the stands if he had ever come across Rolf Schumann or Gus Witney from a polo club in Wisconsin, in the United States. He thought for a bit but shook his head.

"Sorry," he said. "But it's unlikely. U.S. polo is somewhat different than this. They mostly play arena polo." I must have looked somewhat quizzical as he went on. "It's played indoors or on small board-bounded areas, like a ménage. You know, like they use for dressage." I nodded. "They play just three players to a team, and . . ." He tailed off. "Well, let's just say it's different to what we enjoy." He didn't actually say that he thought it was inferior, but he meant it.

"How about someone called Pyotr Komarov?" I asked.

"Oh yes," he said. "Everyone's heard of Peter Komarov."

"Peter?" I said.

"Peter, Pyotr, it's the same thing. Pyotr is Peter in Russian."

"How come everyone knows him?" I asked.

"I didn't say everyone knows him. I said everyone's *heard* of him," he corrected. "He is the biggest importer of polo ponies in Britain. Probably in the world."

"Where does he import them from?" I asked, trying to sound nonchalant.

"Anywhere," he said. "But mostly from South America. Flies them in by the jumbo jet full. I should think at least half the ponies here were bought from Peter Komarov."

"Is he based in England?" I asked.

"No, I don't think so," he said. "I know he spends quite a lot of time here, but I think he lives in Russia. He runs a polo club over there, and apparently he's done wonderful things for Russian polo. He's often brought teams over to play here."

"How do you know how much time he spends here?" I asked him.

"My son knows him," he replied. "That's my son over there. He's number three for the Mad Dogs." He pointed at some players, but I wasn't sure which one he meant. "He buys his ponies from Mr. Komarov."

"Thanks," I said. "You've been most helpful."

"How?" he said with a hint of annoyance. "How have I been helpful? You're not a damn journalist, are you?"

"No." I laughed. "I'm just someone who knows little or nothing about the game, but I want to learn. I've inherited pots of money from my grandmother, and I thought I might spend some of it having fun playing polo with the nobs."

He quickly lost interest in us, no doubt believing that we were ignorant proles who should go spend our money elsewhere, just as I intended. I don't exactly know why, but I didn't really want either Peter or Pyotr Komarov to hear that I had been asking after him at the Guards Polo Club.


THERE WERE two matches played, each lasting a little over an hour total, and we stayed for them both. We watched the second from the tables and chairs placed in front of the clubhouse. The sun shone more strongly through the high cloud, and it became a delightful spring afternoon, ruined only slightly by the continuous stream of noisy jetliners overhead in their climb away from Heathrow airport. I didn't want to think about the one that would take Caroline so far away from me the following day.

We chatted to half a dozen more people, and all of them had heard of Peter Komarov, although not all of them were as positive about him as our man in the grandstand.

"He's not a good influence," said one man. "I think he has too much power in the game."

"How come?" I asked him.

"He not only sells horses, he leases them too, especially to the top players," he said. "That means that some of the best international players are beholden to him. Doesn't take an Einstein to work out the potential for corruption."

"But surely there's not a lot of prize money in polo?" I said.

"Maybe not, but it's getting bigger all the time," said the man. "And there's been an increase in gambling on the matches. You can now wager on polo with some of the betting Web sites. And who knows how much is gambled overseas on our matches, especially in Russia. I think we would be much better off without his money."

"Does he put money into the game, then?" I asked.

"Not half as much as he takes out," he said.

No one had heard of either Rolf Schumann or Gus Witney, but I didn't mind, I had reaped a wonderful amount of information about the elusive Mr. Komarov, including a gem from the clubhouse caterer, who also provided the food for the Royal Box. She was certain of it. Both Pyotr Komarov and his wife, Tatiana, were vegetarians.


"WHY ARE you so excited?" asked Caroline as we stood on the platform waiting for the train back to London. "Apart, of course, from the fact that you are with me again tonight."

"Did you hear what that catering woman said?" I asked.

"Something about the Komarovs being vegetarians," she said. "So what's exciting about that?"

It means that even if they were at the gala dinner at the racetrack, they couldn't have been food-poisoned, because I'm pretty certain the poison was in the sauce that was on the chicken."

"So?" she said.

"They didn't turn up at the Delafield box on the Saturday when they were expected to," I said. "And they couldn't have missed that lunch because they had been ill the night before, at least not like everyone else, because they hadn't eaten the right stuff. So why didn't they turn up? Was it because they knew there would be a bomb going off?"

"Hold on a minute," she said. "That's a hell of a conclusion to suddenly jump to, especially when you've claimed in the past that the poisoning was to stop someone being at the lunch and now you're saying that maybe the bomber wasn't poisoned at all but still didn't turn up."

She was right, of course. It was confusing.

"But suppose there was someone else the bomber didn't want to be at the lunch," I said. "Then both could be true."

"You need more than 'suppose,'" she said. "Suppose the bomb was aimed at the Arab prince after all. You can make anything you like sound sensible with 'suppose.'"

Our train arrived, and we sat in a carriage surrounded by a party of children on their way home from a theme park. It had been a birthday outing, and they were all so high on the experience, describing with screams and laughter how frightening the rides were and how much fun it had been to survive them.

Caroline leaned on my shoulder. "I want lots of kids," she said.

"That's a bit sudden," I said. "We're not even living together yet and you want kids?"

For an answer, she just snuggled down closer to me and hummed. I don't think it was "Nimrod," by Edward Elgar.

I COOKED dinner in Caroline's white-and-chrome kitchen, and she played her viola for me as I did. We had stopped at the supermarket in Waterloo station and bought some ingredients and a bottle of wine. I prepared a beef stroganoff while Caroline played the first movement of Bach's Violin Concerto in E Major, her favorite piece. She was right. It sounded great on the viola.

"Is that the piece you're playing at Cadogan Hall?" I asked.

"No, sadly not," she said. "I would have to play the violin to ever play this at a concert."

"But surely you could play a violin too?" I said.

"Oh yes, I could," she said. "But I don't want to. I'm a violist, not a violinist, and it's out of choice. Violins are so tinny compared to the mellow tones of a viola. Most of the orchestra think that we violists are failed violinists, but it's not true. That's like saying trombonists are failed trumpeters or flautists are failed oboists. It's ridiculous."

"Like saying waiters are failed chefs," I said, although I knew quite a few waiters who were just that.

"Exactly," she said. It was clear to me that this wasn't the first time she had built up a head of steam over the issue.

"Caroline," I said seriously, "you don't have to prove your worth, certainly not to me. Be confident in your role as a violist. You don't have to apologize for not being something else."

She stood next to me and leaned back against the worktop.

"You are so right," she said in a determined tone. "I'm a violist and pleased to be so."

We laughed and drank a toast to Miss Caroline Aston, violist and proud of it.

"So what are you playing at the Cadogan Hall?" I asked.

"Concerto for Violin and Viola by Benjamin Britten," she said.

"Can you play it for me?" I asked.

"No," she said. "It would sound silly."

"Why?"

"Because it needs to be played by two people, one with a violin and one with a viola. It would be like listening to only one person while they were having a conversation with someone else that you couldn't hear, like they were on the telephone. You wouldn't get the full meaning."

"Does music always have a meaning?" I asked.

"Definitely," she said. "Playing a musical score is like telling a story, using notes and harmonies instead of letters and words. Music can invoke huge passion, and a symphony should carry the listener through the full range of emotions, from anticipation and sadness and melancholy in the early movements to delight and joy at the climax."

I couldn't claim that my dinner would tell a story, but I hoped that it might provide a share of delight and joy, albeit briefly, on the taste buds.

I trimmed the beef and cut it into strips before seasoning and then searing it in a hot frying pan. Then I fried a sliced onion and some mushrooms until they were tender and added them to the beef with some plain flour. I poured a generous measure of cognac over the mixture and, much to Caroline's horror, flamed off the alcohol.

"You'll set the whole bloody building on fire," Caroline shouted as the flames leaped towards her ceiling, and I laughed.

Next, I carefully poured in some sour cream and a small amount of lemon juice, and sprinkled some paprika over the top. I had previously taken a large potato and, since Caroline didn't have a kitchen mandolin, I had grated it on the large-hole side of her box cheese grater to produce long thin strips of potato that I now fried briefly in a deep fryer to produce crisp brown potato straws, while my beef mixture warmed on a low heat.

"I thought beef stroganoff was served with rice," she said, watching me. "And I didn't expect a chef to use my deep-fat fryer."

"I use one all the time," I said. "I know that fried food is not considered very healthy, but it tastes so good, and it's fine if you eat it only in moderation and use the right oil for the frying. I certainly wouldn't use lard like they used to." I lifted the basket of potato straws out of the oil. "It's traditional in Russia to serve beef stroganoff with potato straws, although lots of people like serving it with rice."

We sat together on the sofa in her sitting room and ate off trays on our laps.

"Not bad," she said. "Why is it called stroganoff?"

"After the Russian who invented it, I think."

"Another Russian," she said. "Is that why you chose it for tonight?"

"Not consciously," I said.

"It's nice." She took another forkful. "What gives it such a distinctive flavor?" she asked with her mouth full.

"The sour cream and the paprika," I said, laughing. "This dish used to be on lots of restaurant menus, but, unfortunately, these days it tends to be made without the beef, is called mushroom stroganoff and is served up for vegetarians."

"Like the Komarovs," she said.

"Indeed," I said. "Just like the Komarovs."

MONDAY MORNING was full of contradictions and wildly different from the evening before.

Caroline was eager to leave for the airport and could hardly contain her excitement at the prospect of jetting to Chicago to join the orchestra. She kept complaining at how slowly the time was passing as we waited for the taxi she had ordered to take us to Heathrow.

I, meanwhile, was dismayed at how quickly the hours were rushing by. I was sickened by the thought of her being so far away from me, while, at the same time, I was trying to share her pleasure in going.

We arrived at the terminal more than two hours before her plane was due to leave, and she checked in with no problems.

"I've been upgraded to business," she exclaimed with a squeal, clutching her viola case to her chest.

"The check-in man must have fancied you," I said.

"It was a woman," she said, poking me in the ribs with her finger.

We sat on high stools and had coffee. There was an uneasiness between us. I wanted to spend every last moment with her, while she was desperate to get through to departures, as if in doing so her plane would leave more quickly. Neither of us wanted to express our eagerness to the other, as we both understood the situation.

"Do you want another coffee?" Caroline asked.

"No thanks," I said. "I think you ought to go on through now, in case the lines for security are long." I didn't want her to. I wanted her to stay with me forever.

"I'll stay a little longer," she said. But I don't think she really wanted to. She was trying to please me.

"No," I said. "You go now, and I'll get the train back to London, then on to Newmarket."

"Perhaps you're right," she said, clearly relieved.

I waved to her until the very last second, until she and Viola finally disappeared into the security area and the departure lounge beyond. I then stood there for a while, waiting just in case they came back, just in case they needed something. But, of course, they didn't.

How was it, I thought, that she could be so close to me, just through a door or two, and yet so far away? I even spoke to my overnight bag. "How could she go without me?" I asked it. It didn't reply. I thought of my passport, sitting in the side pocket. Why didn't I just fly to Chicago? Would Caroline be pleased or embarrassed by my arrival? What would Carl say if I didn't go back to the Hay Net for another week?

"Stop being so silly," I said to the bag, and received some strange looks from people around me.

I caught the Heathrow express train to Paddington and felt very lonely. It wasn't so much that I was not with her; it was also the fact that I couldn't even call her on the telephone if I wanted to, and wouldn't be able to do so for at least the next nine hours. I couldn't tell her how much I was missing her already, how much I was hurting. Perhaps it was just as well, I thought.

By the time I got to King's Cross station, I reckoned that her flight must have surely departed. She would be sitting comfortably in her business-class seat, sipping business-class champagne and deciding which movie to watch. She was cocooned in an aluminum tube, rushing away from me at six hundred miles an hour, and I felt dreadful.

CARL COLLECTED me from Newmarket station at three o'clock and drove me to the Hay Net. I didn't want to go home and sit alone in my cottage.

"We did sixty-five lunches yesterday," said Carl.

"Good," I said. "Perhaps we can now say we're back to normal."

"Still down a bit on dinners," he said. "We only had twenty last night, and that's low, even for a Sunday."

"Perhaps we should close on Sunday evenings," I said. "What do you think?"

"It would give us all Sunday evening off," he said. Fixing the weekly staff rotation to provide for time off was always a headache.

"How many lunches did we do today?" I asked him.

"It was quite good," he said. "At least thirty-five. But we're the only place that does lunches on Mondays."

We arrived at the Hay Net to find that Gary was busy with the kitchen porters cleaning in the kitchen. They had moved all the stainless steel worktop units and were scrubbing the floors beneath.

"What's all that about?" I asked Carl as we went into the office. "Gary seems very industrious all of a sudden."

"I think he's trying to impress," said Carl with a laugh. "He's had his nose put out of joint a bit by Oscar."

"Oscar?" I said.

"You know, the temporary chef from the agency." I nodded remembering. "Seems that Gary thinks that Oscar is muscling in on his life and he doesn't like it."

"But that's ridiculous," I said. "Oscar will only be here for a few more days."

"Ah, but it's not just in the kitchen," said Carl. "Seems that Oscar has designs on Ray as well." Ray and Gary, the couple. "Gary is jealous."

"I'm keeping out of it," I said. "As long as it doesn't affect the running of the kitchen."

"Are you working tonight?" Carl asked. "I could let Oscar go now if you're going to be back full-time."

"No," I said. "Keep him here for a while longer. I don't feel fully back to normal yet." Also, I thought, I might need to be away more for the next few weeks as I looked for a London site. And I had been thinking of having another chef in the kitchen anyway to help with the workload. Having Oscar around for a bit longer might help me decide if it was really necessary. Staff salaries were the biggest of my overheads, and I certainly didn't want to employ more chefs than I needed.

IN THE END, I did work in the kitchen that evening, although it wasn't because I was needed. It was more to take my mind off Caroline's flight. We did more than fifty dinners, which, while not quite at prepoisoning levels, was a huge improvement over last week.

I immersed myself in my cooking, panfrying fillets of Scotch beef and roasting sea bass, glazing racks of lamb and braising pork medallions. It felt good to be back in the groove even if the numbers were still down.

Twice I found Jacek standing, watching me work. His job involved coming into the kitchen to collect the used pots and pans for washing in the scullery and then returning them to the chefs for reuse. The first time, I thought he was just waiting for me to finish with the pan I was using, but on the second occasion I was sure he was observing me cook. I dismissed him back to the scullery with a wave.

"You want to mind that one," said Gary, who had witnessed the exchange. "I don't trust him."

I think I agreed with him, and I resolved that in the morning I would try to find out more about our new kitchen porter.

Two of the evening's customers were Ms. Harding, the news editor from the *Cambridge Evening News,* together with, I presumed, Mr. Harding, the paper's overall editor. I hadn't seen them arrive, and I didn't even realize they were in the dining room until Richard came to see me about their bill.

"She says you invited them to come for free," he said somewhat accusingly. Richard was never one to allow anyone to get away with something for nothing. That was one of the reasons I employed him.

"That's right," I said, taking their bill from the plate he was carrying. I looked at it. They had ordered a bottle of wine, but it was one of the cheaper ones on our list, and I decided to allow that too. Richard wouldn't have approved.

I went over to the Hardings' table with a bottle of port and three glasses.

"Do you fancy a nightcap?" I asked.

"Hello," said Ms. Harding warmly. "This is my husband, Alistair. Max Moreton." I saw him read the embroidered name on my tunic.

Alistair stood up, and we shook hands.

"Thank you for the dinner," he said. "We've really enjoyed the evening."

"Good," I said. "Can I join you for a port?" I held up the bottle.

In the end, only Ms. Harding had one with me since her husband was driving.

"I can't go on thinking of you as Ms. Harding," I said to her. "But I don't know your first name."

"Clare," she said.

"Well, Clare," I said, "I hope you don't suffer any ill effects after eating here."

She looked rather startled and then smiled broadly as she realized I was only joking. At least, I hoped I was only joking.

"I am sure I will be fine," she said. "I had the snapper with the pear, and it was absolutely delicious." Gary would be pleased.

"And I had the medallions of pork," said Alistair. "They were wonderful."

"Thank you," I said. "I am so glad you enjoyed it."

We chatted for a while longer, and then they departed, promising to be back again, and next time at their expense.

And they hadn't mentioned anything about the intended prosecution. Perhaps things were indeed getting back to normal.

My cell phone rang in my pocket.

"Hello," I said.

"Hello, my darling," said Caroline excitedly. "I've arrived, and it's beautiful. I have a lovely room overlooking the river. I wish you were here."

I wished it too. "Did you have a good flight?" I asked.

"Lovely," she said. "I slept for about three hours, so I'm doing pretty well."

"Well done," I said. "It's eleven-thirty here, and I'm going home to bed."

"Where are you?" she asked.

"At the restaurant," I said. "I've been helping with the dinner service."

"You're a naughty boy," she said. "You should be resting."

"What, like yesterday?" I said, laughing.

"I've got to go," she said. "I'm meeting everyone else downstairs in five minutes. We're going out on a boat. I'm going to be exhausted." She sounded excited.

"Have a great time," I said. We hung up, and I positively ached to be there with her.

I yawned. I was exhausted too, both emotionally and physically.

I changed, and then Carl gave me a lift home, and it was not until after he had driven away that I realized that I had left my overnight bag in the office at the restaurant.

"Oh well," I said to myself, "I'll have to go to bed without brushing my teeth."

And I did.


I DREAMED that I could smell toast. But someone had left it in my broken toaster for too long and it was beginning to burn. Burned toast. My father had always rather liked his toast burned black. He had joked that it wasn't burned, it was just well-done.

I was awake and I could still smell the burned toast.

I got up and opened my bedroom door.

My cottage was on fire, with giant flames roaring up the stairway and great billowing black smoke filling the air.

# 14

Oh shit! I thought. How am I going to get out of this? I closed my bedroom door. Perhaps it was all a dream. But I knew it wasn't. I could smell the smoke coming through the cracks around the door, and I could feel the heat, even on the other side of the wood. It wouldn't be long before the fire had eaten its way through.

I went to the window.

My cottage had been built more than two hundred years before, and the windows were the original leaded lights, small panes of glass held in place by a lattice of lead strips. The windows were themselves small, with only a tiny hinged opening for ventilation that definitely wasn't large enough for me to get through.

I opened the ventilator and shouted at the top of my voice.

"Fire! Fire! Help! Help! Somebody help me!"

I couldn't hear if there was a response. The noise of the fire below my feet was becoming louder with every second.

I shouted again: "Fire! Fire! Help! Help!"

There were no sirens, no hoses, no yellow-helmeted men on ladders.

The air in my bedroom was getting thicker with smoke and it made me cough. I stood up near the ventilator to get some fresh air from outside but, even here, smoke billowed up from the window below. And it was getting very hot.

I knew that people who died in fires usually did so from smoke inhalation rather than from the flames themselves. I wasn't sure whether this was comforting or not. I didn't want to die, and I especially didn't want to die like this, trapped in my burning house. Instead, I got angry—bloody mad, in fact—and my anger gave me strength.

The air in the room had almost completely filled with smoke. I dropped to my knees and found that it was quite clear near the floor. But I could feel the heat from below, and I noticed that my carpet was beginning to smolder close to the wall near the door. If I was to get out of this alive, it had to be soon.

I took a deep breath of the clear air, stood up, picked up my bedside table and ran with it towards where I knew the window to be. I couldn't see anything, as the smoke stung my eyes. At the last second, I caught a glimpse through the glass of the light from the fire beneath and made a slight adjustment to my path.

I crashed the bedside table into the window. The window bent and buckled but didn't move. I repeated the process and the window bent more, and some of the small panes dropped out, but still the damn lead framework held.

I again dropped to my knees for a breath. The space beneath the smoke had diminished to just a few inches, and I knew this was it. Either I broke out now or I would die.

This time, the table went right through the window and fell out of sight into the smoke and flames below, taking the remains of the window with it. There was no time to think or worry about what I was jumping into. I clambered through the opening and leaped, trying to jump away from the building, away from the fire.

One of the advantages of having such an old property is that the ceilings were very low, and, consequently, the fall from my bedroom window to the lawn below was only about ten feet. Quite far enough, I thought. I landed with my feet together and my body moving forward, so I kept on rolling like a parachutist over the grass and into the road beyond. I got to my feet and moved to the far side of the road and looked back.

Flames were clearly visible through what was left of my bedroom window. I had literally jumped in the nick of time.

I gasped fresh air into my lungs, coughing wildly. I was cold. I stood shivering on the grass verge, and only then did I realize that I was completely naked.

My neighbor, roused perhaps by my shouts, was outside watching and now walked towards me. She was a small, elderly lady, and I could see by the light of the flames that she was wearing a fluffy pink dressing gown with matching pink slippers, and her white hair was held neatly in place with a hairnet.

I looked for something to cover my embarrassment and ended up just using my hands.

"That's all right, dear," she said. "I've seen it all before. Three husbands, and a nurse for forty years." She smiled. "I'm glad you got out all right. I'll fetch you a coat." She turned to go. "I've called the fire brigade," she said over her shoulder. She seemed totally unperturbed at finding a naked man on the side of the road in the middle of the night next to a raging inferno no more than fifteen feet from her own bedroom window.

The fire brigade arrived with flashing lights and sirens, but there was little they could do. My cottage was totally engulfed in flames, and the firemen spent most of their time and energy hosing down my neighbor's house to ensure the searing heat didn't set that alight as well.

I sat out the rest of the night at my neighbor's kitchen table wearing one of her ex-husband's coats and a pair of his slippers. I didn't ask her if he was ex- by death or ex- by divorce. It didn't matter. I was grateful anyhow, and also for the cups of tea that she produced for me and the fire brigade at regular intervals until dawn.

"Just like the Blitz," she said with a broad smile. "I used

to help my mother provide refreshments for the police and firemen. You know, WRVS."

I nodded. I did know. Women's Royal Volunteer Service.

THE MORNING brought an end to the flames but little other comfort. My home was a shell, with no floors, no windows, no doors and nothing left within, save for ash and the smoldering remains of my life.

"You were lucky to get out alive," said the chief fireman. I knew. "These old buildings can be death traps. Timber stairs and thin wooden doors and floors. Even the interior walls are flammable, plaster over wooden slats. Death traps," he repeated while shaking his head.

We watched from the road as his men sprayed more water over the ruin. The stonework of the exterior walls had survived pretty well, but it was no longer whitewashed as it had been yesterday. Great black scars extended upwards above every windowless void, and the remainder was browned by the intense heat and the smoke.

"Can you tell what caused it?" I asked him.

"Not yet," he said. "Still far too hot to get in there. But electrical, I expect. Most fires are electrical, or else due to cigarettes not being properly put out. Do you smoke?"

"No," I said.

"Did you leave anything switched on?" he asked.

"Not that I can think of," I said. "I suppose the TV would have been on standby."

"Could be that," he said. "Could be anything. Have to get the investigation team to have a look later. Thankfully, no one was hurt. That's what really matters."

"I've lost everything," I said, looking at the black and steaming mess.

"You haven't lost your life," he said.

But it had been close.

AT EIGHT O'CLOCK, I used my neighbor's phone to call Carl.

"It has not been your week," he said after I told him.

"I wouldn't say that," I said. In the past seven days, I had been informed of an intended prosecution, written off my car in a collision with a bus, spent a night in the hospital with a concussion, lost my house and all my personal possessions in a fire and now stood wearing nothing but my neighbor's ex-husband's coat and slippers. But look on the bright side, I thought. It was only seven days since I had taken Caroline out to dinner at the Restaurant Gordon Ramsay. I may have lost plenty, but I had gained more.

"Can you come and collect me?" I asked him.

"Where do you want to go?" he said.

"Do you have a shower I could use?" I said. "I smell like a garden bonfire."

"I'll be there in five minutes," he said.

"Oh, Carl," I said. "Can you bring some clothes?"

"What for?" he asked.

"I escaped with my life," I said. "But with absolutely nothing else."

He laughed. "I'll see what I can find."

I STOOD for a good ten minutes in Carl's shower and let the stream of hot water wash the smoke from my hair and the tiredness from my eyes.

The fire brigade had arrived on the scene at three thirty-two a.m. I knew that because the chief had asked me, as the property owner, to sign an agreement that the fire service investigation team had my permission to access the property later that day, when the building had cooled.

"What would you have done if I'd died in the fire?" I'd asked him.

"We wouldn't need your permission, then," he'd said. "We have automatic right of entry if there has been serious injury or a death."

Convenient, I had thought.

"And we can always get a warrant to enter if you won't sign and we believe that arson is involved."

"Do you believe it was arson?" I'd asked him, somewhat alarmed.

"That's for the investigation team to find out," he'd said. "Looks just like a normal domestic to me, but then they all do."

I had signed his paper.

After my shower, and dressed in Carl's tracksuit, I sat at his kitchen table and took stock. I did, in fact, have some personal possessions left to my name, since my overnight bag had been sitting safely all night under my desk at the Hay Net. Carl had fetched it while I showered, and I was able to shave and brush my teeth with my own tools.

Carl lived in a modern, three-bedroom semidetached house in a development in Kentford, just down the road from where my mangled wreck of a car still waited for the insurance assessor to inspect it.

Carl and I had worked side by side in the same kitchen for five years, and, I realized with surprise, this was the first time I had ever been in his house. We were not actually friends, and while we might share a beer together often at the Hay Net bar, we had never socialized together elsewhere. I had felt uneasy about calling to ask for his help, but who else could I ask? My mother would have been useless and would have left me with the lady in the pink slippers for most of the day as she went through her normal morning rituals of bathing at leisure, applying her copious makeup and then dressing, a task that in itself could take a couple of hours as she continuously changed her mind over what went with what. Carl had been my only realistic choice. But I hadn't really liked it.

"So what are you going to do now?" he asked.

"First, I need to hire a car," I said. "Then I'm going to book myself into a hotel."

"You can stay here, if you like," he said. "I've plenty of room."

"What about Jenny and the kids?" I said, noticing for the first time how quiet it was.

"Jenny went back to her mother nearly a year ago now," he said. "Took the girls with her."

"Carl," I said, "I'm so sorry. Why didn't you say something to me?"

"Didn't seem to matter," he said. "To tell the truth, I was relieved when she went. I couldn't stand the rows. I'm much happier on my own. We're not divorced or anything, and she and the girls come over for the weekends and it's sometimes pretty good."

What could I say? Restaurant work, with its odd hours, never was highly recommended for happy marriages.

"Could I stay for a couple of nights, then?" I asked. "I will be gone by the weekend."

"Stay as long as you like," he said. "I'll tell Jenny that she and the girls can't stay over this weekend."

"No," I said quickly. "Don't do that. I'll find myself a more permanent place by then. Much better all around."

"You might be right," he said. "Are you coming in to work today?"

"Oh yes," I said. "I think so. But maybe not until later. I want to hire the car first."

Carl dropped me at the car-rental offices on his way into work.

"Certainly, sir," they said. "What sort of car would you like?"

"What have you got?" I asked.

I decided on a Ford Mondeo. I wanted a fairly nondescript vehicle that wouldn't attract attention if, for example, I went again to the members' parking lot at Smith's Lawn and the Guards Polo Club.

One of the car-rental company staff insisted on coming with me to my bank to make the payment arrangements before he would give me the keys of the Mondeo. It often seemed to me that the restaurant business was one of the few that allowed its customers to consume the goods before asking for any payment, or even a guarantee of payment. The old joke about washing dishes had worn a bit thin over the years, and I had never known anyone who actually did it, although I had come across many a customer who didn't have the wherewithal to pay for his dinner after he had eaten it. What could I do? Reach down his throat and pull it out again? In truth, there wasn't anything one could do except send him on his way, accepting his promise to return with the money in the morning. In most cases, a check quickly appeared, with profuse apologies. Only twice in the six years that I had been open had I simply not heard anything afterwards, and one of those times was because the person in question had died the day after, but, thankfully, not from eating my food. On the other occasion, two couples that I didn't know, and who had enjoyed the full dining experience we offered, including three courses with coffee and two bottles of my best wine, had both then claimed that they thought the other couple was paying. They had given me just their assurances and their addresses, both of which turned out to be false, and I had carelessly failed to record the license plate number of their car. I bet they had thought it was funny. I hadn't. I would recognize any one of them instantly, if they ever tried it again.

While I was at the bank, I drew out a large wad of cash and also arranged for a replacement credit card to be sent to me at the Hay Net at the earliest opportunity. Tomorrow, they said. How about this afternoon? I asked. We would try, they said, but I would have to pay for the messenger. Fine, I said, get on with it. Without my credit card, I felt as naked as I had been in the road last night.

I sat in my new wheels and took stock of my situation. I was alive, I had a change of clothes in my overnight bag, my passport in my pocket, somewhere to sleep for the next two nights, and I could always put up a bed in the office of the restaurant if I had to. But I had no watch, and my cell phone was, I was sure, totally beyond repair, having been alongside my wallet in the pocket of my blazer, which had been hanging over the back of the sofa when I went to bed last night.

I parked the car and went into the cell phone shop in the High Street. I explained to the young woman behind the counter that my house had burned down with my phone still in it and I needed a replacement, preferably with the same number as before. Now, this didn't seem like an unreasonable request to me, but it took me more than an hour to achieve it and involved me having to raise my voice on several occasions, something I was not used to doing.

For a start, she kept asking if I had the SIM card from the phone, and I tried to explain to her that my phone, along with the damn SIM card, was no more. I told her that it had been melted away into a puddle of silicon, solder and plastic. "You shouldn't have put the phone battery in a fire," she said. "It's not good for the environment." Only a semblance of remaining decency prevented me from strangling her at this point. Finally, we neared the end of our tortuous affair. I had the phone in my hand, as yet uncharged, and I had my stack of money ready and available for payment. "Do you have any form of identification?" she asked, somewhat belatedly to my mind. I proudly flourished my passport. "That won't do," she said. "I need something with your address on it. Do you have a utility bill?"

I stared at her. "Have you listened to anything I have told you?"

"Yes," she replied.

"Then how would I have a utility bill if my house has been completely burned to a crisp?" I said. "At the time, I hadn't exactly thought that a utility bill was something I needed to save from the inferno along with my life." My voice rose to a crescendo. But I somehow managed not to boil over completely. "Sorry," I said more calmly. "No, I don't have a utility bill."

"Then I'm sorry, sir, I must have something to confirm your address."

We were getting nowhere.

"Can you please produce a duplicate of my last month's phone bill?" I asked her, now back to my usual calm tone.

"Certainly, sir," she said. I gave her my cell phone number, and, unbelievably, she also wanted the first line of my address, for security reasons. I told her. A printer under the counter whirred, and she handed over a copy of my bill, complete with my full address printed in the top right-hand corner.

"There," I said, handing it back to her. "One utility bill."

She didn't bat her thickly mascaraed eyelashes.

"Thank you, sir," she said, and processed my order. Hallelujah!

"Can I leave the phone here to charge for an hour?" I asked her.

"Sorry," she said. "You will have to do that at home."

I sighed. Never mind, I thought, I'll try elsewhere.

In the end, I bought an in-car charger from her and again sat in the Mondeo with my new phone connected to the cigarette lighter socket. Progress had been slow. I looked at my wrist. No watch. It had been on my bedside table. The car clock told me it was half past eleven. Half past five in the morning in Chicago. Still too early to call Caroline, even if I knew the number. I was sure she would call me when she woke. I hoped my phone would be sufficiently charged by then.

I left it charging while I went for a coffee. I sat in the window of a café with the car parked right outside. I had needed to leave the car unlocked with the keys in the ignition in order for the charger to work, so I kept a close eye on it. I didn't fancy the prospect of having to go back to the young woman to explain that my new phone had been stolen before I had even had a chance to use it.

I next went into a luggage shop and bought myself a suitcase, which, during the following hour and a half, I proceeded to fill with new pants and socks, five new shirts, three new pairs of chinos, a navy blue blazer, two tweed jackets and a tie. Fortunately, my work clothes, the sets of specially designed Max Moreton embroidered tunics and the large-check trousers, were safe at the restaurant. I never wore them home, since they went every morning with the tablecloths to a commercial laundry. But, I thought, I would look a bit stupid wearing a chef's tunic to the Cadogan Hall next week.

Caroline called around two o'clock and was appropriately horrified to hear my news about the cottage.

"But are you all right?" she asked for the umpteenth time.

I assured her that I was fine. I told her that I was staying with Carl for a couple of days, and I would find myself some temporary accommodation while I decided what to do long-term.

"You can come and live with me," she said.

"I would love to," I said, smiling. "But I need to be nearer to the restaurant, at least for a bit. I'll think of something. It's all a bit hectic in my mind at the moment."

"You look after yourself," she ordered.

I promised I would.

"I'll call you at seven your time, after rehearsal," she said, and hung up.

I looked again at my empty wrist. It seemed a long time until seven my time.

Using the rest of my cash, I bought myself a new watch in one of the Newmarket High Street jewelers. That was better, I thought, as I checked to see if it was running properly. My existence was regaining some semblance of normalcy.

I returned to my bank and drew out another sheaf of banknotes and used some of them to buy a box of chocolates and a bouquet of spring flowers for my neighbor.

I parked the Mondeo on the road outside my cottage, the same road I had rolled across the previous night. I took a brief look at the sorry remains of my abode. It was not a pretty sight, with its blackened walls standing pitifully alone and roofless, pointing upwards at the gray sky above. I turned away gloomily and went and knocked on my neighbor's door. She answered, not in her pink ensemble of last night but in a green tweed skirt with a long-sleeved cream sweater and sensible brown shoes. Her hair was as neat as before, but this time without the hairnet.

"Oh hello, dear," she said, smiling. She looked at the bouquet. "Oh, are those for me? They're lovely. Come on in."

I gave her the flowers, and she headed back towards the kitchen. I closed her front door and followed, sitting again at the now-familiar kitchen table.

"Would you like some tea, dear?" she said as she placed the flowers in a vase by the sink.

"I'd love some," I said.

She set the kettle to boil and fussed around with her flowers until she was happy with the arrangement.

"There," she said at length. "So beautiful. Thank you."

"Thank *you*," I said. "I'm not sure what I would have done without you last night."

"Nonsense, dear," she said. "I was just glad to be able to help."

We sat and drank tea, just as we had done some twelve hours ago.

"Do you know yet what caused it?" she asked.

"No," I said. "The fire brigade say they will send their investigation team to have a look. It's pretty well burned everything. You can just about tell the difference between what was the fridge and what was the washing machine, but even those are badly melted by the heat. The oven is recognizable, but the rest has seemingly gone completely."

"I'm so sorry, dear," said my kindly neighbor.

"Well, at least it didn't get me," I said with a smile.

"No, dear," she said, patting my arm. "I'm glad about that."

So was I.

"Do you know what you will do?" she asked.

"I'm staying with a work colleague for the next couple of days," I said. "Then I'll try to find somewhere more permanent."

"I really meant with the house, dear," she said. "Are you going to rebuild?"

"Oh, I expect so," I said. "I'll have to wait and see what the insurance company says."

I stayed with her for over an hour, and by that time, dear, she had showed me photos of all her many children and her very many grandchildren. Most of them lived in Australia, and she was obviously quite lonely and thankful for having someone to talk to. We opened the chocolates, and I had a second cup of tea.

I finally extricated myself from her life story and went back next door for a closer look at the remnants of my castle. I was not alone. A man in a dark blue jersey and royal blue trousers was picking his way through the ash.

"Hello," I said. "Can I help you?"

"I'm fire brigade," he said. "From the investigation team."

"Oh right," I said. "I own this heap of garbage."

"Sorry," he said.

"Ah well." I smiled. "At least my ashes aren't here for you to find."

"Are anyone's?" he asked seriously.

"No," I said. "There was no one else in the house. Well, not unless they broke in after I had gone to bed and then died in the fire."

"It wouldn't be the first time," he said, not amused.

He went on poking the ash with a stick. At one point, he stopped and bent down, placing some of the ash into a plastic bag that he produced from his pocket.

"What have you found?" I asked him.

"Nothing special," he said. "It's just for an accelerant test."

"What's that?" I asked.

"Test to see if an accelerant had been present," he said. "An accelerant like petrol, paint thinners or paraffin, that sort of thing."

"I thought it was electrical," I said.

"Probably was," he said. "Most fires are electrical, but we need to do the test anyway. I don't expect it to show much. This place is so badly burned out that it will be damn near impossible to determine how it started."

He went back to his poking of the ash. After a while, he lifted something up on his stick, as if landing a salmon.

"Aha," he said. "What have we got here?"

It looked like a black molten lump to me. I didn't recognize it as anything I had once owned.

"What is it?" I asked.

"Your smoke detector," he said.

I couldn't remember having heard its alarm go off.

"You should have had a battery in it," he said. "It's not much use without a battery. You might have got the brigade here sooner and saved something if your detector had had a battery."

"But it did have a battery," I said.

"No, sir," he said with conviction. "It did not. See how the heat has caused it to seal up completely?" He showed the lump to me. I would have to take his word for it. "If there had been a battery, then it would still be there, or at least the remains of it would. I still can see the clip, but there are no battery terminals attached to it. It definitely did not have a battery in it." He paused, as if for effect. "It's not the first time I've seen this. Loads of people forget to replace a detector battery, or, like you, they take out the old one and then forget to put a new one back in."

But I hadn't forgotten. There had to have been a battery in the detector. I had replaced it, as I always did, when the clocks went forward for summertime in March. It had gone off just last week when I had again burned some toast. It definitely had a battery. I was sure of it, just as sure as my investigator friend was that it had been batteryless.

I went cold and clammy. Someone had obviously removed my smoke detector battery before setting my house alight with me in it. With or without an accelerant, an established fire at the bottom of the stairs would have given me little chance of escaping. I had simply been lucky to wake up when I had.

I suddenly was certain that the fire had been the second time someone had tried to kill me.

# 15

I was frightened. Very frightened. Twice I had cheated an assassin. I didn't like to think "third time lucky" or "if at first you don't succeed—try, try again."

"Who could it be?" I asked myself yet again. "Who on earth could want me dead, and why?"

It was six o'clock in the evening, and I sat in the rented Mondeo in the empty parking lot of the Newmarket racetrack. I didn't know why I chose there, particularly. I just wanted to be somewhere away from anyone else, and with enough space to see someone coming. The lot was deserted, save for my Mondeo in the center of it. I looked all around. There was no one about.

Who could I trust? Could I, in fact, trust anyone?

Caroline, I thought. I would trust her with my life. I suddenly realized that indeed it was my life I would lose if I made a mistake and trusted the wrong person.

The safest course was to trust no one. Not even my kindly neighbor, dear.

But I couldn't stay sitting here in this parking lot forever.

Could I trust Carl? Was I safe to sleep in his house? Was

he safe if I was sleeping in his house? I had witnessed only too clearly what a fire could do and how close I had come to joining my smoke detector as its victim. I really didn't want to take that risk again.

Should I now go to the police? But would they believe me? It all seemed so unreal, even to me. Would they take me seriously enough to give me protection? It was not worth going to the police if they simply took a statement and then sent me away to my death. It wouldn't help if they only believed me after I was dead.

I used my new cell phone to call the Hay Net. Martin, my barman, answered, and I asked him to get Carl for me.

"He's in the kitchen, Chef," said Martin. "I'll get him."

I waited.

"Hello," Carl said finally. "Everything OK?"

"No, not exactly," I said. "I've got to go away for a few days."

"Where to?" he said.

Where to indeed? I thought. "Er, I'm not sure."

"Are you all right?" he asked.

"Yes, I'm fine," I said. "My mother is unwell, and I need to be with her. Can you cope without me for the rest of the week?"

"Sure," he said rather uncertainly. "Is there anything I can do to help?"

"No," I said. "I'll be fine. But has anything arrived for me, by messenger?"

"Yes," he replied, "about half an hour ago. Do you want me to bring it somewhere?"

"No, it's all right. I'll come and collect it."

"How about your stuff at my place?" he said. I had left my overnight bag and shaving kit at his house.

"Don't worry about them," I said. "I'll buy myself a new toothbrush and razor."

"I can fetch them, if you like," he said, still sounding a little unsure.

"No, it's fine," I said. "I have to go right now. Leave the package by the front door, will you?"

"All right, if you say so." He clearly thought I was crazy.

I drove down the familiar road to the restaurant, looking left and right for any danger. There was none, at least none that I could see. I left the engine running as I jumped out and dashed inside the restaurant. The package was where I had asked Carl to leave it, and I grabbed it and went straight back out to the car.

"Max," called Carl, following me outside. "Max, wait."

I stood by the open door of the car.

"I'm sorry, Carl, I've got to go."

"Call me, then," he said.

"Later," I said. "I'll try to call you later."

I climbed in and drove off, checking my rearview mirror every few seconds to see if I was being followed. I wasn't. I was running away, and even I wasn't sure where I was going.

THE FOLLOWING morning, I ran farther away. I caught the ten-fifty a.m. flight to Chicago.

After leaving the restaurant the previous evening, I had driven aimlessly down the A14 to Huntingdon and had stopped in the deserted parking lot of a closed carpet store.

Someone once told me that it was possible to trace the location from which a cell phone call was made. I had taken the risk, and first called my mother. Second, I called Caroline.

"Have you told the police?" she'd asked after I had told her everything.

"Not yet," I'd said. "I'm worried they won't take me seriously."

"But someone has tried to kill you twice. Surely they will take that seriously."

"Both attempts were designed to look like accidents. Maybe the police will think I'm irrational or something." I was beginning to suspect as much myself.

"How could someone have got into your house to tamper with the smoke alarm?" she'd asked.

"I'm not sure," I'd said. "But I'm absolutely certain that someone did. My front door key was on the fob with my car keys that went missing after the crash. Whoever removed the battery and set light to my cottage must have it."

As I had told her the full story, it had all seemed less and less plausible. I had no firm idea who the "someone" could be who was trying to kill me, or even why. Would the police believe me or dismiss it all as some crazed, circumstantial conspiracy theory? I would have had to tell them I believed that the someone may be a Russian polo pony importer that I suspected only because he hadn't turned up at a lunch to which he had been invited. If that was a crime, then half the population would be in court.

"You can go and stay at my flat, if you like," Caroline had said. "My upstairs neighbor has a key, and I can call her to let you in."

"I'm not sure that's safe either. Suppose someone has been following me. They would have seen me go there last weekend. I'm not taking that chance."

"You really are frightened, aren't you?" she'd said.

"Very," I'd said.

"Then come here. Come to Chicago. We can discuss everything through. Then we'll decide what to do and who to tell."

I had driven to one of the hotels on the northern edge of Heathrow and had booked myself in for the night under a false name, using cash to pay in advance for my room. The staff raised a questioning eyebrow, but they accepted my fictional explanation that I had stupidly left my passport and credit cards at home and that my wife was bringing them to me at the airport in the morning. Maybe I was being rather overdramatic, but I was taking no chances that I could be traced through my credit card. If someone really had been in my house at three in the morning to start a fire at the bottom of my stairs, then it didn't stretch the imagination much further to realize they might have taken my old phone and credit cards, with all the access that the numbers could bring to my accounts, and maybe my whereabouts if I used them. I had turned off my new phone just in case.

On Wednesday morning, I had left the rented Mondeo in the hotel parking lot, where, according to the hotel reception staff, it would be quite safe but would incur charges. Fine, I'd said, and I had paid them up front for one week's parking with the remains of my cash. I then had taken the hotel shuttle bus to the airport and had reluctantly used my new credit card to purchase the airline ticket. If someone could then find out I was at Heathrow buying a ticket, that was too bad. I just hoped that they wouldn't be able to get to the airport before my flight departed. If they could further discover that the ticket was to Chicago, well . . . it's a big city. I planned to stay hidden.

I had decided not to sit in some dark corner of the departure lounge while I waited for the flight. Instead, I'd sat in the open next to an American family with three small children who played around my feet with *brmmm-brmmm* noises and miniature London black taxis, souvenir toys of their trip. It had felt safer.

Departure had been uneventful, and I now dozed at forty thousand feet above the Atlantic. I had not slept particularly well in the hotel, and three times during the night had checked that the chair I had propped under the door handle was still there. So as the airplane rushed westwards, I lay back and caught up on my lack of sleep from the previous two nights, and had to be woken by one of the cabin staff as we made our final approach to O'Hare airport in Chicago.

I KNEW that Caroline would not be waiting for me at the airport. She had told me that she had a rehearsal all afternoon, ready for that evening's first night, and I had told her not to try to come anyway. I had somehow thought it might be safer. However, I still looked for her when I emerged from immigration and customs.

She wasn't there. Of course she wasn't there. I hadn't really expected her to be there, but I felt a little disappointed nevertheless. There were several couples greeting each other with hugs and kisses, with I LOVE YOU or WELCOME HOME printed helium-filled balloons attached to their wrists or to the handles of strollers full of smiling babies. Airport arrival concourses are joyful places, good for the soul.

However, the source of my particular joy was not there. I knew that she would be deep into Elgar and Sibelius, and I was jealous of them, jealous of long-dead composers. Was that another example of irrational behavior?

I took a yellow cab from the airport to downtown, specifically to the Hyatt Hotel, where I knew the orchestra was staying, and sank into a deep leather armchair in the lobby that faced the entrance. I sat and waited for Caroline to return, and promptly went straight back to sleep.

She woke me by stroking my head and running her hands through my hair.

"Hello, my sleeping beauty," she said.

"You're the beautiful one," I said, slowly opening my eyes.

"I see you're keeping a good lookout for potential murderers," she said.

"Don't even joke about it," I said. But she was right. Going to sleep in plain view of the hotel entrance and the street beyond was not the most clever thing I had done in the last twenty-four hours if I wanted to stay alive.

"Where are the rest of the orchestra?" I asked.

"Some are upstairs. Others—boring, boring—are still hanging around at the concert hall. And a few have gone shopping."

I looked at my new watch. It read eleven-thirty. Six-hour time difference, so it was five-thirty in the afternoon. "What time is the performance?" I asked.

"Seven-thirty," she said. "But I have to be back, changed and ready by six forty-five, and the hall is a five-minute taxi ride away."

We had an hour and ten minutes. Was she thinking what I was thinking?

"Let's go to bed for an hour," she said.

Obviously, she was.


I MANAGED to stay awake for the whole concert. I remembered my father having seriously advised me, when I was aged about eight or nine, that you never, ever clap at a concert unless others did so first. He didn't tell me, but there must have been an embarrassing moment in his life when he had burst into applause, isolated and alone, during the silent pause between orchestral movements. I sat on my hands to prevent a repeat.

Caroline had worked a miracle to find me a seat. A single house seat in the center of the eighth row. It was an excellent position, ruined only by the fact that the conductor, a big man with annoyingly broad shoulders, stood between me and Caroline, and I couldn't see her.

Even though I wouldn't have admitted so to Caroline, I wouldn't have known which piece was by whom without the program telling me that it was all Elgar before the intermission and Sibelius after. But I did recognize some of it, especially "Nimrod" from the *Enigma Variations*. Listening to it reminded me so much of my father's funeral. My mother had chosen "Nimrod" to be played at the conclusion of the service, as my father, in his simple oak coffin, had been solemnly carried out of East Hendred Church to the graveyard for burial, an image that was so sharp and vivid in my memory that it could have happened yesterday. Caroline had told me how powerful music could be, and, now, I felt its force.

For the first time, I cried for my dead father. I sat in Chicago's Orchestra Hall surrounded by more than two thousand others and wept in my personal, private grief for a man who had been dead for thirteen years, a condition unexpectedly brought on in me by the music of a man who had been dead for more than seventy. I cried for my own loss, and my mother's loss too, and I cried because I so longed to tell him about my Caroline and my happiness. What would we give to spend just one hour more with our much-loved and departed parents?

By the time the intermission came, I felt completely drained. I was sure that those alongside me had no idea of what had taken place right next to them. And that was as it should be, I thought. Grief is a solitary experience, and the presence of others can lead to discomfiture and embarrassment for all parties.

Caroline had told me that she wouldn't be able to get out to see me during the intermission, as the directors frowned upon such behavior and she wasn't in the mood for crossing them at the moment, not after missing the original flight. It was probably a good thing, I thought. Even though we had met only last week, Caroline knew me all too well already, and I didn't yet feel comfortable with every one of my innermost thoughts and emotions being open to her scrutiny. So I remained in my seat and decided against buying a cardboard cup of ice cream to eat with a miniature plastic shovel, as everyone around me seemed to be doing.

The second half of the concert was the Sibelius symphony, and I didn't find it so dark and gloomy as Caroline had warned me to expect. In fact, I loved it. Somehow, as I sat there absorbing the music, I felt released from the past and fully alive for the future. I had no house, no car and precious few belongings to worry about. I was about to embark on two new and exciting journeys, one with a new London restaurant and the other with a new companion whom I adored. And someone was trying to kill me, either for what I knew or for what I had said, neither of which seemed that important to me. I had run away to America and was now enjoying the heady excitement of having left my troubles behind. The troubles in question may not have been resolved, but they were out of sight and, for an hour or so, out of mind too.

The audience stood and cheered. They even whooped with delight and put fingers in their mouths and whistled. Anything, it seemed, to make a noise. There was no decorum or restraint here. Unlike we British, who sit and politely applaud, the Americans' way of expressing their approval is to holler and shout and dance on their feet.

The orchestra smiled and the conductor bowed, repeatedly. The ovation lasted for at least five minutes, with the conductor leaving the stage and reappearing six or seven times. Some in the audience even bellowed for more, for an encore, as if this were a pop concert. Eventually, the conductor shook the hand of the orchestra leader, and they left the stage together, putting an end to the acclaim and allowing the players to retire gracefully for the night.

I met Caroline outside the stage door, and she was as high as a kite.

"Did you hear them?" she said breathlessly. "Did you hear the noise?"

"Hear it?" I said, laughing. "I was making it."

She threw her arms around my neck. "I love you," she said.

"You're just saying that," I said, mocking her slightly.

"I've never said that to anyone in my life before," she said rather seriously. "And yet it seems so simple and obvious to say it to you."

I kissed her. I loved her too.

"It made such a difference," she said, "to have you in the audience. But I spent the whole concert trying to find you in the sea of faces."

"I was behind the conductor," I said. "I couldn't see you either."

"I thought you must have gone back to the hotel."

"Never," I said. "I really enjoyed it."

"Now, you're just saying that," she said, mocking me a little too.

"I'm not," I said. "I loved it, and . . . I love you."

"Oh goodie," she squealed, and hugged me. I hugged her back.

I STAYED the night in Caroline's room without telling the hotel or giving them my name. Even though it was very unlikely that anyone would have traced me, I took no chances and propped the chair from the desk under the door handle when we went to bed.

No one tried to get in, at least I didn't hear anyone trying. But, then again, by the time we finally went to sleep at midnight I was so tired that I don't think I would have heard if someone had tried blasting their way through the wall with a hand grenade.

In the morning, we lay in bed and watched breakfast television, which wasn't very good and full of far too many commercial breaks for my liking.

"What do you have to do today?" I asked Caroline while running my finger down her spine.

"Nothing until four o'clock," she said. "We will have a run-through of a couple of movements. Then tonight's performance is at seven-thirty, like last night."

"Can I come again?" I asked.

"Oh, I hope so." She giggled.

"I meant to the concert," I said.

"You can if you want to," she said. "Are you sure? It'll be just the same as last night."

"You could surely eat the same dinner two nights running?" I said.

"Only if you cooked it."

"Well, then," I said, "I want to come and hear you play again tonight."

"I'll see if I can find you a ticket."

"So what do you want to do until four o'clock?" I asked.

She grinned. "We could stay in bed."

But we didn't. We decided to get up and go have some breakfast at the restaurant on the ninety-fifth floor of the John Hancock Building, which, according to the tourist guide in the room, was the second-highest building in the Midwest, after the Sears Tower.

I took the elevator down to the lobby while Caroline went to put a note under the door of a fellow violist with whom she had agreed to go shopping, explaining that her plans had changed. As I waited for her, I asked the concierge for a map of the area and found the John Hancock Building clearly marked. I also found O'Hare airport to the northwest of the city center. And something else on the map caught my eye.

Caroline arrived, having delivered her note.

"Are you aware," I asked, "that the state of Wisconsin starts only a few miles north of Chicago?"

"So?" she said.

"Wisconsin is where Delafield is, and that's where Delafield Industries, Inc., is based."

"But how far away?" she said. "Some of the states are huge."

I found out. The hotel concierge was most helpful. Delafield, Wisconsin, he said, was under two hours' drive away. Yes, of course, he could arrange for a rental car, all he needed was a credit card. Caroline lent me hers. Better safe than dead.

INTERSTATE HIGHWAY 94 conveniently ran directly from Chicago to Delafield, and, as the hotel concierge had said, it took us less than two hours in our rented Buick.

We turned off the Interstate at the Delafield exit and found ourselves in an urban environment repeated thousands of times across the United States. The junction was surrounded on all sides by flat-roofed commercial and retail development, including gas stations, drugstores, supermarkets and the ubiquitous fast-food outlets, each with an over-tall sign designed to be visible for miles along the highway in each direction. I thought back to when I had opened the Hay Net and the flurry of objections that had been raised by the local planners over the modest sign I had wanted to erect next to the road. In the end, I had been given my permission, on the condition that the top of the sign be not more than two meters from the ground. I smiled to myself. The Cambridgeshire County Council planning officer would have had palpitations in this neck of the woods.

Beyond the retail areas, with their acres of tarmac parking lot, and sitting on a small hill, I could see some substantial industrial buildings with DELAFIELD INDUSTRIES, INC. in big bold black letters on a yellow sign sticking up from the roof. Below the sign, painted large on the wall of the factory in fading paint, was THE FINEST AGRICULTURAL MACHINERY IN AMERICA.

I wasn't really sure what I hoped to achieve by coming all the way up to Delafield from Chicago. It just seemed to me to be an obvious thing to do, having discovered that it was so close. I had no idea what I would find. Indeed, I had no idea what I was even looking for. But if I was right and Delafield Industries was indeed the intended target, then if anyone knew the motive for the bombing it would surely be Rolf Schumann. Whether he would tell me or not was another matter.

We drove up to the main gate, where a sturdy-looking barrier blocked our path.

"Can I help you, sir?" asked a security guard who appeared from the glass-fronted gray booth on my left. He wore a dark blue uniform, complete with flat-topped cap and a belt around his waist with more gadgets hung from it than I thought was prudent. Surely, I thought, a belt with all that weight would pull his trousers down rather than hold them up.

"I was passing and wondered if Mr. Rolf Schumann was in," I said.

"And your name, sir?" the guard asked. He himself wore a plastic name badge with BAKER embossed on it.

"Butcher," I said, deciding against "candlestick maker." "Max and Caroline Butcher." I had no idea why I didn't tell him my real name. If Mr. Schumann was in fact in, then he might just remember me from Newmarket racetrack and wonder why I had given a false name to his security guard. But it didn't matter.

"Do you have an appointment, Mr. Butcher?" asked the guard politely.

"No, I'm afraid we don't," I replied equally politely.

"Then I'm sorry," he said. "We don't accept visitors without an appointment."

"OK," I said. "But is Mr. Schumann actually here?"

"I couldn't say," he said.

"Couldn't or won't?" I asked.

"Couldn't." He had lost the politeness from his voice.

"Why not?" I asked him.

"Please, sir," he said, not amused and not wanting to play the game any longer, "turn your vehicle around and leave the premises." He pronounced "vehicle" as if it were two words, "veer-*hickle,*" with the emphasis on the "hickle." "Otherwise, I shall have you forcibly removed."

He didn't appear to be joking. I resisted the temptation to say that I was still owed some money by his company for having cooked a lunch at which his boss had been blown up. Instead, I did as he asked, turned my veer-hickle around and pulled away. I could see him large in the rearview mirror. He was standing in the road with his hands on his hips, and he watched us all the way down the hill until we disappeared around the bend at the bottom.

"That didn't seem to go too well," said Caroline some-what sarcastically. "What do you suggest we do now? Climb their fence?"

"Let's go get that breakfast we've been promising our-selves."

We parked the Buick on Main Street and sat in the window of Mary's Café, drinking coffee and eating blueberry muffins.

Delafield was somewhat topsy-turvy. What was known as Delafield Town was all the new development near the interstate highway, including the shopping malls and the agricultural machinery factory, while the city of Delafield was a delightful old-world village set alongside Lake Nagawicka. Nagawicka, we were reliably informed by the café owner, meant "there is sand," in the language of the local Native Americans, the Ojibwe Indians, although we couldn't actually see any sand on the lakeshore.

"More coffee?" asked Mary, coming out from behind her counter and holding up a black thermos pot.

"Thank you," said Caroline, pushing our mugs towards her.

"Have you heard of someone called Rolf Schumann?" I asked Mary as she poured the steaming liquid.

"Oh yes," she said. "Everyone around here knows the Schumanns."

"I understand he's president of Delafield Industries," I said.

"That's right," she said. "At least, he was. It's such a shame."

"What's a shame?" asked Caroline.

"About his condition," Mary said.

"What about his condition?" I asked.

Mary looked around, as if checking that no one else was listening. There were only the three of us in the café. "You know," she said, shaking her head from side to side, "he's not all there."

"How do you mean?" I said. Mary was embarrassed. I was surprised, and I helped her out. "Is the problem to do with his injuries?" I asked.

"Yes," she said quickly. "That's right. Due to his injuries."

"Do you know if he's still in the hospital?" I asked her.

"Yes," she said. "I believe so." She looked around again and then continued in a hushed tone. "He's in Shingo."

"Shingo?" I said.

"Yes," she said. "Shingo. You know, the mental hospital." She said the last two words in little more than a whisper.

"Where exactly is Shingo?" I asked her, in the same manner.

"In Milwaukee, on Masterton Avenue."

"Do the Schumanns live in Milwaukee?" I asked more normally.

"No, of course not," she said. "They live here. Up on Lake Drive."

We took our leave of Mary and her muffins, not because I had gained enough information—I hadn't—but because I felt that she was just as likely to tell the Schumanns about us, and our questions, as she was willing to tell us about them. Discretion, I thought, was not one of her strong points.

The city of Delafield, the village, had numerous shops full of stuff that one has no good use for but just has to have anyway. We visited each in turn and marveled at the decorative glass and china, the novelty sculptures, the storage boxes of every size, shape and decoration, the homemade greeting cards and the rest. There was a lovely shop with racks of old-fashioned-looking signs, one with fancy notebooks and another with legend-embroidered cushions for every conceivable occasion, and more. There were toys for boys and toys for girls, and lots of toys for their parents too. Delafield was a stocking-stuffer's paradise. Not that it was cheap. Caroline's credit card took quite a battering, as she bought far too much to easily get into her suitcase for the flight home. Presents, she explained, for her family, although we both knew that she wanted it all for herself.

Everywhere we went, I managed to bring the Schumanns into the conversation. In the embroidered-cushion store, the lady appeared to be almost in tears over them.

"Such nice people," she said. "Very generous. They have

done so much for the local community. Mrs. Schumann is always coming in here. She's bought no end of my cushions. It's so sad."

"About Mr. Schumann's injuries?" I prompted.

"Yes," she said. "And all those other people killed in England. They all lived around here, you know. We used to see them all the time."

"Terrible," I said, sympathizing.

"And we're all dreadfully worried about the future," she went on.

"About what, exactly?" I asked her.

"About the factory," she said.

"What about it?" I prompted again.

"It's not doing so well," she said. "They laid off a third of the workers last November. Devastating, it was, just before the holidays and all. Something about the Chinese selling tractors for half the price that we could make them for here. There's talk in the town of the whole plant closing. My husband works there, and my son. I don't know what we'll do in these parts if they close down." She wiped a tear from her eye. "And then that disaster happens in England, and poor Mr. Schumann and the others . . ." She tailed off, unable to continue.

The 2000 Guineas excursion had obviously been a last-ditch effort to try to find a new market for the ailing giant. The resulting carnage, with the loss of key personnel, might prove to be the final nail in the company's coffin.

"Is there much unemployment around here?" I asked her.

"No, not at the moment," she said. "But three thousand still work at the tractor factory. No small community can absorb that number laid off at once. Many of them will have to leave and go to Milwaukee to make beer or motorcycles."

"Beer or motorcycles?" I asked. It seemed a strange combination.

"Miller beer and Harley-Davidsons," she said. "Both are made in Milwaukee."

"And how far away is that?" I said.

"About thirty miles."

"Maybe they will be able to continue living here and commute," I said, trying to cheer her up. "It won't be so bad."

"I hope you're right," she said, clearly not believing it.

"I wonder what will happen to the Schumanns," I said during a pause.

"Don't you worry about them," she said. "They've got lots of money. Just built themselves a new house. More like a mansion. It's never the bosses who end up broke. They'll make sure they get their bonuses and pensions sorted before the plant closes. You watch."

She obviously wasn't as keen on the Schumanns as she had originally implied. After her husband and son are laid off, I thought, she probably won't have a good word left for anyone to do with Delafield Industries, Inc.

Only one person we spoke to knew of MaryLou Fordham. It was the man in the novelty sculpture shop.

"Nice legs," he'd said with a knowing smile. I had smiled back at him, but it was not her legs that I remembered. It was the lack of them.


WE DROVE slowly along Lake Drive, staring at each of the impressive residences. This was millionaires' row for Delafield. Each house sat in the center of its own large garden, with impressive fences, walls and gates to keep out the unwanted. From the road, it wasn't very easy to see the buildings due to the many pine trees and the bountiful rhododendrons, but Caroline and I had previously driven over to the far side of the lake and had looked back to identify the Schumann home. As the cushion lady had said, it was quite a mansion: a modern, three-story house in gray stone with a red roof, set above a sweeping, well-tended lawn that ran down to the water and a dock, complete with boat.

Was this the home of the true target of the Newmarket bombing? Was this the home of a victim, or a villain? Was this the home of a friend, or a foe?

Only one way to find out, I thought, and I pushed the button on the intercom beside the eight-foot-high wrought-iron security gates.

# 16

Dorothy Schumann was a slight woman. Although she was not more than five foot eight, she looked taller due to her slender shape. She had long, thin hands that were ghostly white, seemingly almost transparent, and they shook slightly as she rested them in her lap. Caroline and I and Mrs. Schumann sat on green-and-white sofas in her drawing room, the view down to the lake as spectacular as I had imagined.

"So you met my Rolf in England," said Mrs. Schumann.

"Yes," I said. "At Newmarket racetrack."

"On the day of the bomb?" she asked.

"Yes," I said. "I was at the lunch."

She looked at me closely. "You were very lucky, then."

"Yes," I agreed. I explained to her that I was staying in Chicago on business and had decided to come and see how Rolf was doing, now that he was home.

"How kind," she said somewhat despondently. "But Rolf is not home here. He's still in the hospital in Milwaukee having treatment."

"Oh," I said. "I'm so sorry. I thought I had heard that he was well enough to go home."

"He was well enough to be flown back last week," she said. "But I'm afraid he's not very well at all." She was having difficulty holding herself together. "He has some kind of brain damage." She swallowed. "He just sits there, staring into space. He doesn't even seem to recognize me. The doctors don't seem to know if he will ever recover." She shook with sobs. "What am I going to do?"

Caroline went across to the sofa where Mrs. Schumann was and sat next to her and put an arm around her shoulder.

"I'm sorry," Dorothy said. She took a tissue from her sleeve and dabbed at her eyes, smearing her makeup and causing her to cry even more.

"Come on," said Caroline. "Let's go and sort you out."

Caroline almost pulled Mrs. Schumann to her feet and guided her gently into the master bedroom suite, which, like in many modern American homes, was on the ground floor.

I looked around the drawing room. There were masses of family photographs in silver frames sitting on a table near the window. I looked at the pictures of Rolf Schumann in happier times, many with a much-healthier-looking Dorothy at his side. There were also images of him at dinners in black tie, and at a building site in a bright yellow hard hat and muddy steel-tipped boots. There were two of him dressed for polo, one of him mounted, smiling broadly, with his mallet in the air, and another dismounted, receiving a silver trophy from a man who even I recognized as a senior American politician with presidential aspirations.

But there was little else in the room that could give me much insight into the man that Rolf Schumann used to be.

I opened a door on the far side of the room from where the women had disappeared and found myself in Rolf's study. In contrast to the brightness of the white-decorated drawing room, his study was dark, with heavy wood paneling, and a great oak desk in the center. On one wall was a "map" of Africa in which each of the countries was depicted by a different animal hide. Above and behind the desk, a huge stag's head leaned out from the wall, its magnificent multipointed antlers almost reaching up to the impressively high ceiling. There were more photographs here too: Rolf Schumann, in a safari suit and wide-brimmed hat, in the African bush with rifle in hand and his left foot resting on a huge, downed elephant; Rolf Schumann, in waist-high waders, with fishing rod in one hand and a salmon held high in the other; Rolf Schumann, in hunting pink jacket and hard hat and on horseback, sipping a stirrup cup before the chase. Rolf Schumann was clearly a man of many sports, many blood sports. I felt slightly uneasy, and it wasn't solely due to the lifeless stag's glass eyes that I illogically sensed were somehow following me as I moved around the room.

I went back to the drawing room, and just in time. Mrs. Schumann and Caroline came back from makeup repairs, as I sat down again on a green-and-white sofa.

"I'm so sorry," Dorothy said to me. "I don't seem to be myself at the moment."

"That's quite all right," I said. "We shouldn't have disturbed you. I'm sorry to have caused you so much distress. We should go." I stood up.

"No, no," she said. "It's nice to have some company. Please, stay a little longer. You've come such a long way. And I would really like to hear more about what happened at the racetrack."

I sat down again. I explained to her as much as I thought was prudent about the bombing at Newmarket, leaving out the gory details, and the blood. She sat bolt upright on the sofa, listening intently to every word. Once or twice, the tears welled up in her eyes, but this time she was able to maintain her composure.

"Thank you for telling me," she said. "It has been very hard not knowing anything."

"I'm so sorry," I said. She smiled wanly at me and nodded.

"Will you have something to drink?" she said. "I have some ice tea in the kitchen."

I looked at my watch. It was just after twelve. "We'd love some," I said.

All three of us went through to her kitchen, and Dorothy poured three tall glasses of golden liquid over slices of lemon. I had always preferred my tea hot, but I had to admit that the iced version was tasty and very thirst quenching. Caroline and I sat on stools at what Dorothy called "the bar." The kitchen was spectacular, with a great view down to the lake and the "city" beyond. The bar, in fact, was one side of a large island in the center of the huge room.

"Dorothy," I said. "Can you think of any reason why Rolf would be a target for a bomber?"

She stopped in the middle of pouring more tea and looked at me. "The local police told me that Rolf wasn't the target. They said he was bombed by mistake."

"I know," I said. "But how about if they were wrong?"

Dorothy Schumann sat down heavily on one of the stools. "Are you saying that someone may have tried to kill Rolf?"

"Yes," I said. There was a long silence. "Can you think of anyone who might want him dead?"

She laughed, just a single titter. "Only about a thousand of the locals," she said. "They all got fired last winter. And they all seem to blame Rolf."

"But surely . . ." I said.

"No, no," she said. "I'm not really serious."

"But is there anyone else you could think of who might want to hurt him or damage his company?" I said.

She pursed her lips and gently shook her head.

"Do you know a man called Komarov?" I asked her.

"Of course," she replied. "I know Peter very well. He imports polo ponies. But you're not telling me that he has something to do with what happened to Rolf?"

"I don't know," I said. "I just wondered if you had heard of him."

"He and his wife come and stay with us," she said in a tone that implied her houseguests were beyond reproach. "They are friends of ours."

"Lots of people have been murdered by their friends," I said.

*Et tu, Brute?*

"When exactly do they stay with you?" I asked her.

"For the polo," she said.

"At the Lake Country Polo Club?" I asked.

"Yes," she said. "Rolf is a vice president."

"Does Rolf have any polo ponies himself?" I asked her.

"Hundreds," she said. "I wish he would devote as much time to me as he does to his damn polo." She stopped suddenly and looked blankly out of the window. Life was going to be very different for her from now on.

"Is Peter Komarov anything to do with the polo club?" I asked her.

She turned back to face me. "I don't think so," she said. "But I do know that all his horses go there for a few days when they first arrive in the country."

"Where do the horses originally come from?" I asked.

"South America," she said. "Argentina, Uruguay and Colombia, mostly, I think."

"And where do they go after they leave the polo club?" I asked.

"All over the country," she said. "I have occasionally been to some of the sales with Rolf. You know, at Keeneland, in Kentucky, and at Saratoga."

I had heard of both of them. They were major bloodstock sales for Thoroughbreds. "So they're not all polo ponies, then?"

"Oh no," she said. "I think that most are, but there are definitely some racehorses as well."

"Why do they all come here first, then," I said, "to the polo club?"

"I don't really know," she said. "But I do know they arrive by plane at O'Hare, or at Milwaukee airport, and then they go to the club by horse van. I've seen them being unloaded. Perhaps they need to get over the journey, like jet lag or something. I think they stay for up to a week before being shipped. Except the ones that Rolf keeps himself, of course." She sighed, and again the tears welled up in her eyes.

"Seems strange to me not to send the racehorses directly to where they'll be sold," I said.

"Rolf says they have to be inspected by the vet," she said. "And he has to do something with the balls."

"The balls?" I asked.

"Yes," she said. "The metal balls. They're something to do with the journey. I don't really know what, but Rolf always has a big box full of them here a few days after the arrival of each planeload."

"Do you have any of these balls here at the moment?" I asked.

"I think there are a few in Rolf's desk," she said.

She went out of the kitchen and soon returned with a shiny metal ball about the size of a golf ball. She placed it on the counter in front of me and I picked it up. I was expecting it to be heavy, like a large ball bearing, but it was surprisingly light, and hollow.

"What are they for?" I asked her.

"I have no idea," she said. "But I think they might be also something to do with breeding the ponies."

"Can I have this one?" I said.

"I don't think Rolf would be very pleased with me if I let it go," she replied. "He's always extremely careful to check he has the right number. He counts them over and over."

"But it might help me find out why he was injured," I said.

"Do you really think so?" said Dorothy, again looking so frail and forlorn.

"I don't know, but it may."

"Well, I suppose just one will be all right," she said. "But you must promise to give it back after you have finished with it."

I promised, and Caroline smiled at her.


WE LEFT the Schumann residence at five to two, having been cajoled by Dorothy into staying for a ham-and-cheese-sandwich lunch. We were late. I swung the Buick back onto I-94 and put its engine to the test. It was a hundred miles to Chicago and Caroline's rehearsal with the orchestra at four o'clock. And she had to get to the hotel first, to collect her dress for the evening and her beloved viola. It was going to be tight.

"So what do you think this is?" Caroline asked. She sat in the car's passenger's seat and tossed the shiny metal ball from hand to hand.

"I have no idea what it's for," I said. "But if it has anything to do with Komarov, then I'm interested in finding out." I accelerated past a huge eighteen-wheeler truck that was thundering along in the center lane.

"Don't get a speeding ticket," Caroline instructed.

"But you said . . ." I tailed off. She had said that her ass would get roasted if she was late.

"I know what I said." She laughed. "But don't get stopped or we really will be late." I eased off the accelerator slightly and the speedometer came back within the limit. Well, it almost did.

"Something to do with polo ponies," I said. "That's what Mrs. Schumann said."

"Perhaps it's for *table* polo." She laughed out loud at her joke. It did look a bit like a metal table-tennis ball, but perhaps it was a fraction bigger than that. "Does it open, I wonder?" she said.

The ball had a slight seam around its equator, and Caroline took the ball in both hands and tried to separate the two halves. She tried to prize it open by pushing her thumbnail in the seam, but without success. She tried to twist one half off the other. In fact, it wasn't difficult at all, when you knew how. The two halves screwed together with a counterclockwise movement.

I briefly looked at the two hemispheres sitting in Caroline's hands.

"I'm none the wiser," I said. "But I do know that it's not a toy. It's not easy to make those screw threads on a spherical object as thin as that. Especially one that fits so tightly together. Quite a piece of precision engineering is involved. If Mrs. Schumann is right about Rolf having a big box full of them, then they must have cost a packet to produce."

"But what are they for?" said Caroline.

"Perhaps they are for putting something in that mustn't leak out," I said. "But I don't know what."


WE MADE it back to the hotel with five minutes to spare. Caroline grabbed her dress and viola and rushed away with a kiss. "See you later," she said. "I'll leave a ticket at the box office." She skipped out of the hotel and into the waiting bus taking the orchestra to the hall. The door closed behind her and off they went.

I stood in the lobby and felt lonely. Would I ever get used to saying good-bye to her even for just a few hours? While she had rushed off with such excitement at the prospect of rehearsal and then performance, I was left feeling abandoned and jealous. How could I be so green-eyed about a musical instrument? But I shivered at the thought of her wonderful long fingers caressing Viola's neck and plucking her strings when I wanted Caroline to do it to me. It was irrational, I knew, but it was real nevertheless.

"Pull yourself together," I said to myself, and went in search of the concierge.

"Lake Country Polo Club?" he repeated, as a question.

"Yes," I said. "I think it's near Delafield, in Wisconsin."

He tapped away on his computer for a while. "Ah," he said finally, "here it is."

His printer whirred, and he handed me a sheet of paper with the directions. The club was about five miles nearer to Chicago than Delafield. In fact, we had driven right past it twice today, since according to the directions it sat just off the interstate highway on Silvernail Road. I thanked him, and arranged to keep the rental car for another day.

I thought the Thursday concert was even better than the previous evening. For a start, I could see Caroline, and she knew it. The hall had been sold out completely, with not so much as a spare stool for me to be found in the auditorium. When I arrived at the box office at seven o'clock, there wasn't a ticket for me, but there was a note.

"Come to the stage door and ask for Reggie," it had said in Caroline's handwriting. So I had done just that.

"Right," Reggie had said. "So you're the English guy she's been yappin' about all week." He was a big, burly black man, and he spoke with a rhythmic lilt that made me want to boogie.

"You got it, man," I replied, mimicking him.

He guffawed expansively, giving me a glimpse of a mouth full of gold-capped teeth. "You're a dude," he said. I wasn't sure whether it was a compliment or not, but he smiled broadly. "I've got just the place for you. Come along with me."

His place turned out to be a couple of metal chairs set out of sight of the audience behind black curtains in the wing of the stage. One of the chairs had a particularly fine view of the first desk of the viola section, a view of my Caroline. As I sat there, I could see her through the gap between the second violins and the French horns. In truth, I could only see the back of her shoulders and part of her right side, but it was enough.

On this occasion, I quietly hummed my way through "Nimrod" with hardly a tear. It still reminded me vividly of my father's funeral, but I was now at peace with the mental image of that day, not that it didn't remain a poignant and emotional memory.

Caroline came over and sat with me during the intermission while the rest of the orchestra disappeared down some concrete steps at the back of the stage.

"What do they all do during the intermission?" I asked as we watched them go.

"Same as the audience, I expect," she said. "Some have a cup of tea. There's usually some waiting for us in the dressing room. Others have something a little stronger, although they're not supposed to. One or two go outside for a smoke. Believe it or not, some sit and go to sleep for fifteen minutes."

"What do you normally do?" I asked her, taking her hand.

"All of the above." She laughed.

"Do you want to go and have your tea, then?" I asked her.

"No. I want to stay here. I share a dressing room with twelve other women and I'd much rather be here with you."

Good. I would much rather it too.

"I'm going back to Delafield tomorrow," I said. "I'm going to have a snoop around the Lake Country Polo Club. Rolf Schumann was a vice president of the club, and one of those killed by the bomb at Newmarket was the president."

"But I can't come with you," she said miserably. "There are some changes to the program for tomorrow night, and I have rehearsals at eleven and at three."

"How about on Saturday?" I asked.

"We have a matinee on Saturday at two-thirty, as well as the evening performance," she said. "You go tomorrow without me, but be careful. Remember, someone tried to kill Rolf Schumann, and that same person may have tried to kill you twice already."

"You don't need to remind me," I said.

THE LAKE COUNTRY POLO CLUB was a very grand affair, with rows and rows of white-painted stables with brown roofs alongside four or five polo fields and a mass of club facilities. There were also dozens of horses in white-railed paddocks, their heads down as they chewed the spring grass. This was clearly a busy place, but also one where everything oozed money, and lots of it.

I pulled the Buick nose first into the visitors parking lot next to the club offices and walked in where it said RECEPTION on the door. There was a woman in a white crewneck sweatshirt and jeans sitting at a desk, typing on a computer. She looked up.

"Can I help you?" she said.

"I wondered if Mr. Komarov is anywhere about," I said.

"No," she said. "I'm afraid he won't be back here now until next month at the earliest. For the Delafield Cup, I expect. He's usually here for that."

So they knew Mr. Komarov. In fact, they seemed to know him quite well.

"So he doesn't own this club, then?" I asked her, feigning surprise.

"Oh no," she said. "But he does own most of the ponies.

His pony man is here, if you'd like to see him?" I wasn't sure whether I did, but, before I could stop her, she lifted a phone and pushed some buttons. "What did you say your name was?" she asked me.

I hadn't, in fact, said anything about my name. "Mr. Buck," I said, looking out at my car. I very nearly said Buick.

Someone answered at the other end. "Kurt," said the woman. "I have a Mr. Buck here asking after Mr. Komarov. He wants to know when he will be coming back to the club. Can you help?" She listened for a moment and then said, "Hold on, I'll ask him." She looked up at me. "Kurt says to ask you how you know Mr. Komarov."

"I don't," I said. "But I want to ask him about something that happened in England."

She relayed the message and then listened briefly. "Where in England?" she asked me.

"Newmarket," I said loudly.

She didn't say anything but listened a while longer. "Fine, I'll tell him." She hung up. "Kurt is coming over to see you," she said to me. "Kurt's in charge of all Mr. Komarov's ponies."

"Thank you," I said. "I'll wait for him outside."

Why were the hairs on the back of my neck standing on end and signaling danger, danger? Perhaps it would be safer to get back in the car and leave immediately. Instead, I went for a stroll and walked through a horse passageway beneath the empty grandstand and out onto the polo pitch beyond.

It put the Guards Polo Club in the shade. While it was true that there wasn't a Royal Box, the rest of the facilities for watching were outstanding, with covered stands and hundreds of padded armchairlike seats for maximum comfort. The playing area had been set up for what the man at the Guards Club had called arena polo, but it could obviously be converted into a larger field for the real thing by removal of the boundary boards. There was plenty enough of the well-tended grass for even the biggest polo pitch.

I was standing, looking at the grandstand, when a man called out to me.

"Mr. Buck?" he shouted as he came through the passageway. Kurt, I presumed, and he wasn't alone. A second man was with him, and he made me feel decidedly uncomfortable. Whereas Kurt was small and jockeylike in stature, his sidekick was tall and wide. And he carried a five-foot-long polo mallet across his chest like a soldier might carry a gun. I was left in no doubt that it was there to intimidate. It worked. I was very intimidated. Why hadn't I got in the car and gone away when I had had the opportunity?

I stood in the middle of the grass polo arena and my exit route was on the other side of the grandstand. I had no choice but to brazen it out.

"What do you want?" Kurt asked brusquely. No word of welcome. But there wouldn't be. His body language said it all. I wasn't welcome one little bit.

I smiled, tying to relax. "I understand," I said cheerfully, "that you know Mr. Komarov. Is that right?"

"It might be," he said. "Depends on who wants to know."

"I was hoping Mr. Komarov might be able to help me identify something," I said.

"What?" he said.

"It's in my car," I said. I set off quickly past him towards the passageway.

"What is it?" he asked again.

"I'll show you," I said over my shoulder without breaking step. He wasn't to know that the item was, in fact, in my trouser pocket, but I had no intention of getting it out here. I thought I would be safer at the car, but that might only be illusory.

Kurt didn't seem happy and snorted through his nose, but he followed, and, sadly, so did his shadow. I walked ahead of them, and while I didn't actually run they would have had to in order to overtake me. The larger man was unfit, and by the time I reached my car he was some way back and blowing hard.

But I hadn't driven all this way for nothing. I still wanted to find out what I had come here for in the first place. I opened the car door and reached inside as if I was finding something, but I was actually getting it out of my pocket. I turned around and held the shiny steel ball out to Kurt in my open palm, like giving a piece of sugar to a horse.

He was dumbstruck. He stared at the ball and then at my face, as if searching for words.

"Where the fuck did you get that?" he said. He made a grab for it, but I closed my hand and easily beat his grasp.

"Tell me what is it and I'll tell you where I found it," I said.

"You give me that back right now," he said, winding himself into a rage.

"You can have it back if you tell me what it is," I said, sounding like a teacher who has confiscated some type of electronic gadget from a miscreant schoolboy but doesn't know what it is.

Without warning, the big guy swung the polo mallet and struck me on the forearm. He was partially behind me, and I didn't see the mallet coming until the very last millisecond. I had no time to avoid it, but, thankfully, I had time to relax as he hit me. Otherwise, I think he would have broken my arm completely in two. As it was, it wasn't great. The mallet caught me just above my right wrist. There was a sharp crack, and my arm went instantly numb. I dropped the shiny metal ball. It rolled away towards Kurt. As he stooped to pick it up, I dived into the car, slammed the door and pushed the central locking button.

My right arm wouldn't work. I couldn't get the key in the ignition, which was on the right side of the steering column. I spent valuable seconds trying and failing before leaning completely over to my right and getting the key into the slot using my left hand. I turned the key, started the car and threw the automatic gearshift into reverse with my left hand. The rear window of the Buick disintegrated behind me. I ignored it. I looked through the space where the glass had been and gunned the engine. The car leaped backwards towards the mallet-wielding maniac behind me. Surprisingly, he deftly sidestepped the car and swung the mallet again in my direction. The passenger's door window shattered, showering me with tiny squares of glass. Kurt was at the driver's door, banging on the window and hauling on the door handle, but he had no mallet and his fist was no match for the toughened glass.

I braked hard to a stop and shoved the gearshift back into drive with my elbow. But the mallet maniac hadn't finished. As the car accelerated forward towards the gate and the highway, he took one last swing. The business end of the mallet came right through the laminated windshield in front of the passenger's seat, and stuck there. I didn't stop. I caught a glimpse of the look of panic on the man's face as I shot off with the mallet head stuck firmly through the glass. He had his hand equally firmly stuck in the twisted leather loop on the handle end.

In the rearview mirror, I saw the loop pluck him off his feet. I heard him strike the side of the vehicle somewhere low down on the nearside rear door, but I wasn't going to stop, not even if I had to drag him all the way back to Chicago. As it was, he somehow disentangled his hand and dropped away before I turned out onto Silvernail Road and sped away towards the relative safety of the thundering eighteen-wheelers on I-94, the polo mallet still sticking out sideways from the windshield.

After a mile or so, I pulled over to the shoulder and managed to extricate the mallet. The leather loop on the handle had broken. I hoped that the wrist that had so recently been in it would be broken as well. I threw it on the backseat and set off again, glad that I wouldn't now have to explain to any highway patrol why I had a polo mallet stuck out of my windshield. The Buick was missing two windows completely, and had a two-inch-diameter hole plus multiple cracks in the windshield, but I could live with that. The fact that I was alive at all was what really mattered to me.

"Damn," I shouted out loud. Not only had I got my arm injured, and I was pretty sure that a bone had been broken by that blow, but I had also lost the shiny metal ball.

I'll have to go and get another, I thought, and turned the car around at the next junction. I just hoped that Dorothy Schumann hadn't had second thoughts about lending me one of the balls since Caroline and I had been at her house the previous day.

My trip to the Lake Country Polo Club had taught me two useful pieces of information. First, the balls were significant.

How exactly they were significant, I hadn't yet worked out. And second, if some of his staff were anything to go by, Mr. Komarov was definitely not on the side of the angels.

BY THE TIME I got back to the Hyatt Hotel, my arm was hurting like hell. I pulled up at the valet parking booth and received some very strange looks from the staff. I ignored them, picked up the polo mallet from the backseat and went into the lobby. I tossed the car keys to the concierge and explained to him that some of the glass had got damaged and would he deal with it with the rental company.

"Certainly, sir," he said. He looked briefly at the polo mallet. "Right away, sir." Absolutely nothing fazes a good concierge.

I went up in the elevator and lay on Caroline's bed. The bedside clock showed me that it was three o'clock. The orchestra were just starting their second rehearsal. I realized that I wasn't very comfortable, so I removed everything from my pockets and put it all on the bedside table: wallet, money, room key, handkerchief and a shiny metal ball about the size of a golf ball and made in two halves that was somehow crucial to the bombing of Newmarket racetrack some four thousand miles away.

Mrs. Schumann hadn't been at all pleased to hear that I had already lost the ball that she had been so insistent that I should keep safe. However, I eventually managed to coax her into handing over another ball, but only after I had convinced her that it would be decisive in finding out why her Rolf had been so injured.

Maybe I had been convincing myself too.

# 17

Caroline returned between the final rehearsal and the evening performance to find me still lying on her bed, and in a bad way. In spite of me swallowing copious painkillers, my arm was so sore that every movement caused me to wince.

"You need a doctor," Caroline said. She was very concerned, and not a little frightened.

"I know, but I don't want to use my credit card to pay for it," I said.

"Do you really think someone can trace you from your credit card?" she said.

"I'm not taking the chance," I said. "Especially after today. Who knows what Komarov is capable of? I think he's somehow responsible for killing nineteen people at the Newmarket races. He won't worry about killing one more." Or two, I thought, and I didn't like it. "How long have you got before the performance?"

"About an hour before I have to go," she said.

"It will have to be enough," I said. "Come on, let's go, and bring your credit card with you."

"How do you know they can't trace mine as well?" she asked, suddenly alarmed.

"I don't," I said. "But I think it's less likely that they will search for Miss Aston when trying to find Max Moreton."

We went by taxi to the Northwestern Memorial Hospital emergency room on Erie Street, with me biting back a scream with every bump, with every pothole.

As at any accident-and-emergency department in England, there were endless forms to fill out and lots of waiting time. Here, though, as well as the appointments with the medical staff there was also the all-important one with the hospital cashier.

"Do you have insurance, Mr. Moreton?" asked the casually dressed young woman behind the counter.

"I believe I do have some travel insurance, but I can't find the details," I said.

"Then I'll put 'no' down on the form," she said, and checkmarked it accordingly. "Do you therefore intend to self-pay for your treatment?"

"Yes," I said. "At least for the time being."

She worked away for a while. "As you are a non–U.S. citizen, I will need full prepayment of this estimate before you can be treated," she said.

"How much is it?" I asked her. She pushed a piece of paper towards me with her final figure at the bottom. "I only want my arm seen to," I said, reading it. "I don't want to buy the whole damn hospital."

She wasn't amused. "Full prepayment of this estimate will be needed before any treatment is given," she repeated.

"What would happen if I couldn't pay it?" I asked.

"Then you would be asked to go someplace else," she said.

"How about if I was dying?" I said.

"You're not dying," she replied. But I got the impression that if I had been and couldn't have paid, I might still be expected to go and die someplace else, preferably another hospital.

Caroline gave the woman her credit card and flinched only slightly when she saw the amount on the slip she was asked to sign. We went back and sat down in the waiting area, with an assurance that I would be called soon. I kissed her gently, and promised to repay her as soon as I got home.

"What if someone kills you first?" she whispered. "Then what would I do?" She grinned. It made me feel better.

"I'll leave it to you in my will," I said, grinning back. Laugh in the face of adversity, for laughter is the best medicine.

We sat for a while together. The clock on the wall crept around to six-forty.

"I hate to say it," she said, "but I've got to go now or I'll miss the performance, and then I really will get fired. Are you sure you'll be all right?"

"I'll be fine," I said. "I'll see you later."

"They won't keep you in here all night, will they?" she asked.

"Not without more money," I said with a hollow laugh. "No, I don't think so. I'll see you later at the hotel." She was reluctant to go. "Go on, go," I said, "or you'll be late."

She waved as she went through the automatic doors. I didn't really want her to go. I needed her here, mopping my brow and easing my pain, not caressing that damn Viola.

"Mr. Moreton," shouted a nurse, bringing me back to my reality.

I BEAT Caroline back to the hotel room, but only by about ten minutes. As before, she was high on the applause-induced adrenaline rush, while I was high on a mix of nitrous oxide and painkillers. And I was sporting a fiberglass cast on my wrist that stretched from the palm of my hand, around the thumb, to the elbow.

An X-ray had clearly shown that I had a broken wrist, my ulna having been well and truly cracked right through, about an inch above the joint. Fortunately, it hadn't been displaced much, and the fracture had been reduced by a doctor simply pulling on my hand until the ends of the bone had returned to their rightful positions. I hadn't enjoyed the experience, in spite of the partial anesthetic effects of the nitrous oxide.

Laughing gas it may be, but the procedure had not been a laughing matter.

The cast was designed to immobilize the joint, and the doctor had told me it would have to stay on for at least six weeks. I remembered the stories my father used to tell about his injuries when he was a jump jockey. He always claimed that he was a quick healer, and he often told of how he would start trying to remove a plaster with scissors only about a week after breaking a bone. But jump jockeys are mad, everyone knows that.

As instructed, I kept my right arm raised on a pillow throughout the night to reduce swelling under the cast. It wasn't great for romance, but it did keep the pain to a minimum.

SATURDAY CAME and went, with me spending most of the time horizontal on the bed in Caroline's hotel room. I watched some televised baseball, which was not very exciting, and then some motor racing that was more so.

I ordered some room-service Caesar salad, for a midafternoon, left-handed lunch, and then called Carl using the hotel phone.

"Where are you?" he said. "I've had three phone calls from people saying they need to contact you urgently."

"Who are they?" I asked.

"One was your mother," he said. "One said they were from the Inland Revenue, and the third wouldn't say."

"Did you get their numbers?" I asked.

"You must know your mother's number, surely," he said. "The others didn't leave one. They said they would call back. Where shall I tell them you are?"

I wondered again if I could trust Carl.

"Just tell them that I'm away," I said. "And I will be for at least another week."

"And will you?" he asked.

"Will I what?" I said.

"Will you be away for at least another week?"

"I don't know," I said. "Could you cope if I was?"

"I could cope even if you stayed away forever," he said, and I wasn't quite sure if he was expressing confidence in his own ability or contempt for mine.

"I'll take that to mean that everything's all right at the restaurant, then," I said.

"Absolutely."

"Then I'll call you again on Monday," I said.

"OK," he said. "But where are you, exactly? You told me you were going to your mother, so how come she called for you?"

"Better if you don't know," I said rather theatrically, which must have added to his suspicion.

"If you say so," he said, sounding somewhat miffed. "But don't forget to go and see your mother—she seemed very insistent that you should."

"OK, I will," I said, and hung up.

My mother wasn't at home. I knew that because the night before I left for Chicago I had told her to go stay with another cousin in Devon, and she never needed telling twice to go down there because she loved it. I also told her not to call me since I would be away. But she almost never called me anyway. It was always me who called her.

I called my mother's cousin's house in Torquay, again using the hotel phone. She answered on the second ring.

"Hello, Max," she said in her usual deep voice. "I expect you want to talk to Diane." Diane was my mother.

"Yes, please," I said.

"Hold on a minute." She put the phone down, and I could hear her calling for my mother.

"Hello, darling," my mother said over the line. "I'm having a wonderful time. It's so beautiful down here." She had always wanted to move to Torquay but had never actually got around to it. My mother didn't actually get around to much, really.

"Hello, Mum," I said. "Have you been trying to call me at the restaurant?"

"No," she said. I knew she wouldn't have. "Should I have?"

"No, of course not," I said. "I'm just calling to make sure you're fine."

"Oh yes, darling," she said. "Everything is fine here. Janet has asked me to stay for another week." Good old Janet, I thought. Janet was my mother's cousin.

"Fine, Mum," I said. "Have a nice time. I'll call you in a few days."

"Bye, darling," she trilled, and hung up.

I lay back on the bed and wondered who it was who had told Carl she was my mother.

I used my cell phone to call my brother. Toby and I hardly ever spoke, but it was not due to any animosity, just a result of us never having been close as children and less so as adults.

"Hello," he said. "Long time no see."

"Yes," I said. "How are Sally and the children?"

"Fine, thanks," he said. "The kids are growing up fast." I don't think he said it as a criticism of me for neglecting my two nephews and niece. We both knew that for some unknown reason his wife, Sally, and I didn't really get on very well. He and I were both content with the fact that we saw each other only very occasionally, and usually at Newmarket, when he was there alone for the bloodstock sales.

"Mum's in Torquay," I told him.

"So I've heard," he said.

"She'll be there for another week at least," I said.

"Thanks for letting me know," he said. I knew that he popped in to see her fairly often. He lived in my father's old house, next to the training stables, while our mother now lived in a cottage down the road.

"Toby," I said, "can I see you sometime this coming week?"

"Sure," he said. "When?"

"I'm not certain," I said. "Monday, probably. Maybe Tuesday."

"Fine," he said.

"Can I stay the night?" I asked him.

There was a pause before he answered. "Is everything all right?"

"My house burned down," I said.

"Oh my God, Max," he said. "I'm so sorry."

"I don't think it was an accident," I said.

There was another pause, longer this time. "Are you asking for my help?" he said.

"Yes I am, but it's not financial help I need."

"Good." He sounded relieved. "Come when you like," he said. "And stay as long as you want. I'll fix it with Sally."

"Thanks," I said. "Can I bring someone with me?"

"A girl?" he asked. He knew me better than I imagined.

"Yes."

"One room or two?"

"One," I said.

"OK," he said, amused. "Give me a call when you know when you're coming."

"Thanks," I said again, and I meant it. "I will."

CAROLINE AND I both flew back to London on Sunday night, but, annoyingly, on different airplanes. I couldn't get a seat on the same flight as the orchestra in spite of being number one on the standby list, so I followed them into the Illinois evening blue sky some fifty minutes later. The airline had shown pity on my injured wrist and had provided me with an empty seat on my right so that I could rest the cast on a pile of aircraft pillows and blankets. Even so, I slept only in fits and starts, and was thankful when we touched down gently at Heathrow on time, at seven o'clock on Monday morning.

Caroline was waiting for me just beyond passport control, sitting on a bench alongside Viola, who was safely stashed away out of sight in her made-to-measure black case. While it was not quite a Stradivarius, Viola was still much too valuable to have traveled across the Atlantic in the aircraft hold.

"Where do we go from here?" she asked as I sat down next to her.

"What do you mean?" I said.

"Do you think it's safe to go back to my place?" she said.

"When do you have to be back with the orchestra?" I asked her.

"Wednesday, lunchtime," she said. "We have a couple of

days off now before rehearsals for the concerts on Thursday and Friday at Cadogan Hall. But I've got to do some personal preparation before then."

"We are going to stay with my brother for a couple of days," I said.

"Are we indeed? And where does he live?"

"East Hendred," I said. "It's near Didcot, in Oxfordshire."

I had no intention of using my cell for a while, so I called Toby on an airport pay phone in the baggage area to tell him we were coming today.

"Will it be safe?" Caroline said.

"I don't know." It worried me that it might not be totally safe for my brother's family either. But it was a chance I had to take. "I don't know if anywhere could be totally safe," I said to her. "But I can't hide forever. I need to find out why Komarov is trying to kill me."

"If you're sure it's him," she said, "don't you think it's time you talked to the police?"

"I will," I said. "After I've spoken to my brother and showed him the metal balls. Then I'll call the police."

So it wasn't the Boys in Blue I called next from the pay phone. It was Bernard Sims, my irrepressible lawyer.

WE COLLECTED first our luggage and then the rented Ford Mondeo from the airport hotel parking lot, where I had left it the previous Wednesday. Fortunately, it had an automatic gearbox, and driving mostly one-handed was relatively simple, so we joined the crawl-crawl, non-rush rush-hour traffic along the M4 into London. Caroline insisted on going to her flat to get some fresh clothes even though I wasn't very keen on the idea, if only because East Hendred was in the opposite direction. I personally didn't have any fresh clothes. Other than a couple of items I had abandoned at Carl's house, all the clothes I owned were here in my suitcase.

"I absolutely have to go home," said Caroline. "I also need some fresh strings for my viola, I have only two left."

"Can't we just buy some?" I asked her.

She just looked at me for an answer, her head to its side, her mouth pursed.

"OK, OK," I said. "I'll take you home."

So we went to Fulham, but I insisted on driving up and down Tamworth Street at least three times to see if anyone was sitting in any of the parked cars, watching her flat. Neither of us could spot anyone, so I stopped the car on the corner, and Caroline went into her flat while I sat outside keeping watch with the engine running. No one came, and there were no shouts, but I felt uneasy nevertheless.

I was beginning to think that Caroline had been rather a long time when she reappeared and came sprinting back to the car. She threw a carryall onto the backseat as she jumped in. There was something urgent about her movements.

"Go," she said, slamming the door. I didn't need telling twice, and we sped away. "Someone's been in my flat," she said.

"How do you know?" I asked.

"I thought it was a bit odd when I went in," she said, turning her head to see if we were being followed. "There was a dirty footprint on one of my letters on the mat under the letter slot. I told myself that I was being paranoid. That footprint could have been on the letter before it was pushed through the door. But I am also certain someone's been in my bathroom, in my medicine cabinet."

"How?" I asked again.

"My bathroom cabinet is so full of stuff that it tends to all fall out when you open the door. It takes a knack to stop it happening, and someone didn't have it. Everything in there is now in a slightly different place."

"Are you sure?"

"Absolutely," she said. "Trust me. I know exactly what's in my bathroom cabinet and where. I went to get some aspirin, and everything had definitely been moved. Only slightly, mind, but I'm sure." She looked around again. "Max, I'm scared."

So was I. "It's fine," I said, trying to sound calm. "There's no one in there now, and no one's following us." I was repeatedly looking in the rearview mirror to make sure I was right. We pulled down another quiet residential street, and I stopped the car. We both looked back. Nothing moved. We waited, but no one came around the corner after us.

"Why would someone have been in my flat?" she asked. "And how did they get in?"

"Maybe they wanted to find out when you were getting back."

"How would they do that?" she said.

"I don't know," I said. "Perhaps they planted something to tell them." It all sounded so James Bondish. It was all so unlikely, but why else would anyone go into the flat?

We drove westward out of London and back onto the M4 motorway. I stopped at a service station at Heston, and Caroline called her upstairs neighbor using a pay phone outside while I sat nearby in the car.

"They said they were sent by the landlords," Caroline said, getting back in the car. "Checking for water leaks, or something. Mrs. Stack—that's her, upstairs—says she let them in all right, but at least she did wait there while they checked the kitchen and bathroom. There were two of them. Well-dressed men, and not very old, she said, but she's half blind and anyone to her is not old if they are under seventy-five. She seems to think that I'm still in primary school. She keeps asking me about my mummy and daddy." Caroline rolled her eyes.

"I wonder how they knew she had a key," I said.

"I asked her that," said Caroline. "Apparently, they didn't. Seems they knocked on her door and asked her if she knew where I was. She asked them why they wanted to know, and that's when they said something about a possible leak in my flat. That's when she told them about having a key. Apparently, they didn't bother checking her flat for anything, though."

"Then we shall assume that one of them was Mr. Komarov, or, at least, that he sent them even if he wasn't there himself," I said. "I wonder who the other one was."

BY THE time we reached East Hendred, my wrist was hurting badly again, and I could hardly keep my eyes open due to tiredness. I had driven down the motorway watching the cars behind me almost as much as the road in front, and Caroline had gone to sleep in spite of promising that she wouldn't. I, meanwhile, had continually speeded up, then slowed down, all the way from London, and had even left the motorway at Reading to go twice around the roundabout at Junction 11 to ensure that no one was following us.

I wakened Caroline as we approached the village, and Toby came out to meet us as the car scrunched across the gravel driveway in front of the house. It was always a strange experience for me to come back here, my childhood home, to find that it was my brother and his family, rather than my parents, who were the residents. Perhaps it was another reason why Toby and I saw so little of each other.

"Toby," I said, climbing out of the car, "may I introduce Caroline, Caroline Aston."

They shook hands. "You're so alike," Caroline said, looking back and forth at us both.

"No we're not," I said, purposely sounding offended. "He's much older than me."

"And more distinguished," said Toby, laughing. He put a hand on my shoulder "Come on in, little brother."

It was as good a greeting as we had shared in years.

I went in through the so-familiar front door and was greeted by Sally in the hallway. We kissed, cheek to cheek. Politeness only.

"Sally," I said, "how lovely to see you. This is Caroline."

They smiled at each other, and Sally, ever well mannered, leaned forward for a kiss.

"Max," she said, "how lovely." I didn't know whether she meant it was lovely to see me or whether Caroline was lovely. I didn't particularly care just as long as we weren't fighting. "I'm so sorry to hear about your house," she said almost sincerely. "And your arm." She looked at the end of the cast sticking out below the cuff of my shirt. I smiled my thanks to her. I had told Toby on the phone that I had a broken wrist but not how I came by it.

"Where are the children?" I asked, looking around.

"At school, of course," said Sally. "Philippa, our youngest, is now six."

"Really," I said. It must have been a long time since I was there. My niece had been a toddler on my last visit.

Toby jumped into the awkward pause. "Well, I expect you two would like to lay your heads down for a few hours." I had explained to him coming from the airport that we had both hardly slept on our flights.

"Thank you," said Caroline, "I think we would."

On my way upstairs, I looked briefly into the room that had been mine for the first eighteen years of my life. It didn't really appear much different. My elder nephew was the current occupant, as was clear from the JACK'S ROOM plaque screwed firmly to the door. His bed was in the same position as mine had always been, and his chest of drawers in the corner was the very same one that had held my clothes for so long. It made me yearn for my childhood, for the happy years spent growing up in this house, and for the assurance of youth that nothing nasty can ever happen. That utopia had lasted only until the brick truck had broken the spell.

Caroline and I went to bed, and straight to sleep, in the guest bedroom.


I SLEPT sporadically, for a couple of hours or so, before the discomfort of the cast woke me up for good. I dressed quietly, left Caroline sleeping peacefully and went downstairs in my stocking feet. Toby was in his office, off the main hallway. I stood silently in the doorway watching him as he studied the *Racing Calendar,* as my father had done every single day of the year without fail. The *Racing Calendar* was the industry bible for trainers, allowing them to look at the terms and conditions of every upcoming race so that they could determine which of their horses to enter and where. In my father's day, it had been a weekly broadsheet printed on yellow paper that he would spread out wide on his desk and study for hours on end. Now Toby sat looking through a smaller, stapled booklet, with blue type on white paper, yet it performed much the same function as the old newspaper version. But the computer age was taking over, and no doubt the booklet version would soon be consigned to history as well.

"Hello," said Toby, looking up. "Sleep well?"

"Not really," I said. I lifted up my arm with the cast. "Too bloody uncomfortable."

"How did you do it?" he asked, looking back down at the calendar.

"I didn't move out of the way quick enough," I said.

"Of what?" he asked, not looking up.

"A polo mallet," I said.

He glanced up at me. "I never realized you played polo."

"I don't," I said flatly.

"Then why . . ." He tailed off and leaned back in his chair. "Are you telling me that it was deliberate? Someone broke your arm on purpose?" He looked suitably horrified.

"I don't think they would have stopped at my arm if I hadn't run away."

"But that's terrible," he said. "Have you told the police?"

"Not yet."

"But why on earth not?" he asked. It was a good question, I thought. Why didn't I just leave everything to the police? Because I was very afraid that if I did, I would end up dead before they found out who it was who was trying to kill me. But I couldn't exactly say that to Toby right out of the blue, now, could I?

"I want to explain everything to you because I need your help," I said. "I need your knowledge of horses. I know I grew up in this house and some of it rubbed off on me, but you have forgotten more about horses than I ever knew and I believe I need that knowledge now. That's why I've come here."

"Explain away," he said, putting his hands behind his neck and testing the tilt mechanism on his office chair to the limit.

"Not yet. I want Caroline there too. And, I hope you don't mind, but I've asked a lawyer to come down here later this afternoon to listen to it as well."

"A lawyer?" he said slowly. "This is serious, then?"

"Very," I said. "I've never been more serious in my life." And Toby knew that in my life, especially since the death of my father, I had always been serious. It had often strangely annoyed him.

"OK," he said, looking carefully at my face. "What time is this lawyer arriving?"

"He said he'd try to be here by four," I said. "He's coming down from London." I was suddenly not sure if it had been such a good idea. A lawyer might make Toby rather wary. He had fought long and hard with them over the terms of my father's will. Lawyers were not Toby's favorite people. But, then again, he'd never met a lawyer like Bernard Sims. In truth, I hadn't met him either. It was a pleasure yet to be enjoyed by us all.

BERNARD PROVED to be everything I had expected him to be. He was large, jovial, with a mop of wavy black hair and a huge, double-breasted pin-striped suit doing its best to hold it all together.

"Max," he said expansively when I greeted him in the driveway. He advanced towards me with a hand outstretched that seemed to me to have far more than its fair share of fingers. Perhaps it was just because each finger was twice the width of my own. I held up my cast and declined the handshake.

"How did you do that?" he asked.

"I'll tell you later," I said. "Come on in."

"But is she here?" he asked in a half whisper, almost conspiratorially.

"Who?" I said innocently. I too could play his little game.

"The viola player, of course."

"She might be," I said, not able to resist smiling.

"Oh good," he said, rubbing his hands together. But then he stopped. "And bad."

"Why bad?" I asked.

"I'm not sure I should be meeting her socially," he said. "It might produce a conflict of interests in the poisoning case."

"Bugger the poisoning case," I said. "And, anyway, this is definitely not a social visit."

"No," he said. "But I don't know that, do I? You didn't actually tell me why you were so insistent that I came down here this afternoon."

"I will. I will," I said. "All in good time."

"A matter of life and death, you said."

"It is," I replied seriously. "My life, and my death."

# 18

We all convened in Toby and Sally's drawing room at four-thirty like characters in an Agatha Christie novel, with me playing the part of Hercule Poirot, except that unlike him I didn't know all the answers, I wasn't at all sure who done it and, for the most part, I didn't have a clue of what it was they had done in the first place.

There were five of us in the room. I had thought that Sally would be busy caring for the children, but, after school, all three of them had gone to have tea with her sister, their aunt. So Sally sat on the settee with Toby, while Caroline and Bernard sat in armchairs on either side of them. I stood by the fireplace. All I needed, I thought, was a little mustache and a Belgian accent to complete the illusion.

I had previously threatened Bernard with excommunication from the Law Society if he misbehaved, and, to be fair, so far he had been propriety personified. He hadn't even made any snide remarks to me when I had introduced him to Caroline. In fact, quite the reverse. He had been unusually effusive in his comments, with not a single mention of dropping the lawsuit in time with her knickers.

So now the four of them sat with expectant faces, waiting for every one of the facts to be revealed in front of them. They were going to be disappointed.

"Thank you all for being here," I said by way of introduction. "And thank you, Toby and Sally, for allowing Caroline and me to stay here. And also, thank you, Bernard, for coming all the way from London."

"Just get on with it," said Toby a little impatiently. And he was right. I was procrastinating because I really didn't know how or where to begin. Everyone laughed, and it lightened the mood.

"Sorry," I said. "I don't quite know where to start."

"Try at the beginning," said Caroline helpfully.

"OK," I said, and took a deep breath. "The night before the 2000 Guineas, I was engaged by the Newmarket race-track caterers to be the guest chef at a gala dinner. They also engaged all my restaurant staff to be there as well, so the restaurant was closed that night. There were other staff too from a catering agency, but I was in charge of both the ordering of the food and the cooking of it."

I smiled at Caroline. "Caroline was also at the dinner, as part of a string quartet." She smiled back at me. "Well," I went on, "nearly everyone who was at that dinner suffered from food poisoning during the night. I did, Caroline did and most of my staff did. One even ended up in hospital. Tests have since shown that the cause of the poisoning was undercooked kidney beans in the dinner." I paused. "Now, everyone involved in food knows that undercooked kidney beans are very nasty, even though I didn't realize that just one bean per person can be enough to cause terrible vomiting, and that's what we all had. But there shouldn't have been any kidney beans in that dinner. I made it from raw ingredients, and there were no kidney beans included. But the tests were conclusive, so someone else had to have put them there."

"Are you saying that it was done on purpose?" asked Bernard.

"Yes," I said. "You can't accidentally add enough kidney beans to a dinner to make over two hundred people ill. And the beans had to be ground or finely chopped, otherwise they would have been visible in the sauce, which is where I think they must have been put."

"But why would anyone do that?" said Toby.

"Good question," I said. "And one that I spent days and days trying to find an answer to, and I still haven't." I looked around at the faces in front of me, and no one came up with any answer. I hadn't expected one. "Let's move on. The following day, I was again a guest chef, this time in the sponsor's box at the races. We all know what happened there, and I was extremely lucky not to be killed along with the nineteen others who were, one of whom was a young waitress from my restaurant." I paused again, thinking about Louisa's funeral, remembering the pain of loss for her parents and friends, recalling the awful ache in my jaw. I took a couple of deep breaths and went on to describe just a little of what I had seen in the box that day without delving too deeply into the worst of the gory details. I could have left it all out, but I suppose I wanted to shock them a bit. They needed to be fully aware of what some people can do to others. They would later need to believe that my life, and maybe theirs, were truly in danger.

"I never realized you were so close to it," said Toby. "Mum had said something about you being at the races, but nothing about . . ." He petered out. I decided that I must have successfully created the mental image I was after.

"It's horrible," said Sally, shivering. "I don't want to hear any more."

"And I don't want to wake up in a cold sweat having had another nightmare about it either," I said quite forcibly. "But I know I will. And I will because it was real, it happened and it happened before my eyes to people I knew." Sally looked quite shocked.

"The papers have all been saying that the bomb was aimed at an Arab prince," said Bernard, bringing us all back from the brink. "So what has it got to do with the dinner?" He was one step ahead of the others.

"What if the bomb was not aimed at the prince but at those people it really hit?" I said. "And suppose the poisoning of the dinner was done to stop someone being at the races the following day so they wouldn't get blown up."

"But if someone knew there was going to be a bomb, then surely they could just have not turned up to the lunch," said Bernard. "Why would they have to poison everyone the night before?"

"I don't know," I said almost angrily. I wasn't angry with him, I was angry with myself for not knowing. I couldn't be angry with Bernard. After all, that's why I had asked him to come. I knew he would be skeptical and would argue. It's what I wanted.

"But," I said, "I do know that when I started saying this out loud and asking around about who was meant to be at the lunch but didn't actually show up, someone tried to kill me."

"How?" asked Bernard in the sudden silence.

"They caused the brakes to fail in my car and I hit a bus."

"It's a bit hit-and-miss, if you'll excuse the pun," he said. "Not the best way to kill someone."

"It was designed to look like an accident," I said.

"Are you absolutely sure it wasn't?" he asked.

"No, I'm not," I confessed. "For a while, I thought I was just being paranoid. I couldn't think why anyone would want to do me harm. But then someone burned my house down with me in it. And I am certain that was another attempt on my life."

"Have the fire brigade confirmed that it was arson?" Bernard asked.

"Not that I'm aware of," I said, "but I know it was."

"How?" he asked again.

"Because someone went into my house and removed the battery from my smoke alarm before they set the house on fire and I know for sure that there had been a battery in there. And I'm also sure that the fire was started at the bottom of the old wooden stairs to prevent me getting out." In my mind, I could still see the flames roaring up the stairwell, cutting off my escape route. "It is only due to luck, and a few hefty blows on my bedroom window frame with a bedside table, that I am here now. And I wasn't sure how much longer my luck would last, so I ran away to America."

"Unlike you to run away," said Toby. I was surprised, and pleased. It was indeed unlike me to run away, but I hadn't expected him to know it, let alone to say it.

"No," I said, "but I was frightened. I still am. And with good reason, if what happened in America is anything to go by."

"What did happen?" asked Sally.

"Someone broke my arm with a polo mallet," I said.

"What, surely not on purpose?" said Sally.

"I think you could say that," I said. I told them about the maniac with the mallet and about the damage he did to the rental car.

"But why?" said Bernard.

Instead of answering, I removed the shiny metal ball from my pocket and tossed it to Toby.

"What is that?" asked Sally.

"I don't know," I said. "I was hoping one of you might be able to tell me. I know it's significant. Having one probably contributed to my broken arm, and it might have cost me a lot more if I hadn't managed to escape."

Bernard looked me in the face.

"Life and death," he said slowly, half under his breath.

They passed the ball back and forth between them, and I gave them a couple of minutes to examine it in silence.

"OK," said Toby. "I give up. What is it?"

"Hey," exclaimed Sally, "it unscrews. It comes apart." She triumphantly held up the two pieces. She leaned over and showed Toby what she had done . . . She then put the ball back together and tossed it to Bernard. He struggled with his pudgy fingers, but finally he too was able to open the ball.

"But what is it for?" asked Toby again.

"I really don't know," I said. "But I feel it must be part of the key to all this."

"Max and I think it must have been made to hold something," Caroline said. "It fits so tightly together that we wondered if the contents mustn't leak out."

"And it might have something to do with polo ponies," I added, as if another clue might help solve the riddle.

"Polo ponies?" said Bernard.

"Yes," I said. "It may be to do with the importation of polo ponies."

"From where?" asked Toby.

"South America, mostly," I said, remembering what Dorothy Schumann had said. "Argentina, Uruguay and Colombia."

"Drugs?" said Sally. "There's an awful lot of cocaine in Colombia. Could this be used to hold drugs?"

They all examined the ball again, as if it would give up the answer.

"Like condoms," I said.

"What?" said Bernard.

"Condoms," I said again. "You must have heard of people who are paid to carry drugs in condoms through customs. They tie the end up and swallow condoms with drugs inside them. Then they fly to England, or somewhere, wait for nature to take its course and—hey, presto—you have condoms full of drugs."

"Mules," said Caroline. "They're called mules. Lots of women do it from Jamaica or Nigeria. For the money."

"Sounds rather dangerous to me," said Toby. "Don't the condoms burst?"

"Apparently not," Caroline said. "I saw a television program about it. Some of them get caught by customs, using X-rays, but most of them don't. And they're desperate for money."

"Are you suggesting," said Bernard, "that metal balls like this could be somehow filled with drugs and swallowed to smuggle the stuff here from South America?" He held the ball up to his open mouth. It might have just about gone in, but his expression said that swallowing the ball would be another matter altogether.

"Not in humans, you fool," I said, laughing at him. "In horses."

"Could a horse really swallow something this big?" he asked, serious again.

"Easily," said Toby. "They can swallow an apple whole. I've seen it. You twitch the top lip, hold the head up and throw the apple down the throat. It used to be done quite often to give pills. You hollow out an apple, fill it with the medicine and chuck it down. No problem."

"What do you mean you twitch the top lip?" asked Caroline.

"A twitch is a stick with a loop of strong twine on the end," he explained. "You put the loop round the animal's top lip and twist the stick until the loop gets tight."

"It sounds dreadful," said Caroline, holding her own top lip.

"Well, it is," said Toby. "But it works, I can tell you. It will control even the wildest of horses. They usually just stand very still. We sometimes have to use a twitch on one of ours for shoeing. Otherwise, the farrier gets kicked to hell."

"So you could get a horse to swallow one of those," I said to him, pointing at the ball.

"Oh yes, no problem. But I don't think it would ever come out the other end."

"Why not?" I said.

"Horses eat grass, we don't," he said.

"What's that got to do with it?" Bernard asked.

"Grass is very indigestible," said Toby. "Humans can't live on it because everything goes through us so fast, the cellulose fibers of grass coming out much the same as they went in, so we wouldn't get much nutrition from it. Horses have a system for slowing the process down, so there's time for their system to break the cellulose down."

"Like cows?" said Bernard.

"Well, not exactly," Toby went on. "Cows have multiple stomachs, and they chew their cud, which means they constantly regurgitate their food and rechew it. Horses have only one, fairly small stomach, and once food is down there it won't come back up due to a strong valve at the stomach opening. This valve also means that horses can't vomit. So they have another method of breaking down the grass. It's called the cecum, and it's like a great big sack nearly four feet long and a foot wide that acts as a fermenter. But both the entry point and exit of this sack are near the top, and I think this ball would simply drop to the bottom of the sack and stay there."

"What would happen then?" I asked him.

"I don't know," he said. "Unless you can be sure the ball would float in the cecum, I don't think it would ever come out. God knows what would happen. I suspect the horse would eventually get seriously ill with colic. You would have to ask a vet. All I know is that surprisingly little actually comes out the back of a horse compared to the amount you put in it at the front, and I really think the ball would be most unlikely to ever be emitted with a horse's dung. And it would certainly be far too chancy to try it."

"That puts the kibosh on that theory, then," I said. "I somehow don't think that Mr. Komarov leaves anything to chance."

"Komarov?" said Toby. "Not Peter Komarov?"

"Yes," I said, surprised. "Do you know him?"

"I know of him," said Toby. "He sells horses."

"Yes," I said. "Polo ponies."

"Not just polo ponies," he said. "He also sells lots of racehorses at the bloodstock sales. I've bought a few of them myself. For my owners, of course. Is it him you think is trying to kill you?" He sounded somewhat skeptical.

"I think he has something to do with it, yes."

"Blimey," he said. "I always thought of him as a pillar of racing society."

"Why exactly?" I asked him.

"I don't really know," he said. "I suppose it's because he seems to have given a bit of a boost to racing. At least, he's given a bit of a boost to me!"

"How?"

"I've bought some reasonably priced horses from him," said Toby. "Some of my one-horse owners have been talked into buying a second. Good for training fees." He smiled.

"Do you know where the horses came from?" I asked.

"Now that you mention it, I think they did all come from Argentina. But that's nothing special. Lots of racehorses trained here are bred in Argentina. What makes you think Komarov's responsible?"

"A number of things," I said. "The most important one being that when I mentioned his name and showed someone

one of these balls, I got my arm broken for my trouble. Also, Komarov and his wife were invited to the lunch at Newmarket when the bomb exploded, but they unexpectedly didn't turn up."

"That's not very conclusive," said Bernard.

"I know," I replied. "But his name keeps popping up. And he seems somehow connected with lots of what's been going on." I paused. "If I was dead certain that it was him, then I'd be telling this to the police. But, I have to admit, I'm slightly afraid they might just laugh at me. That's one of the reasons I wanted to try it out on you first." I looked at Toby, Sally and Bernard, but I couldn't read their minds. I knew that Caroline believed me.

"It does all seem a bit far-fetched to me," Sally said. She turned to Caroline. "What do you think?"

"I know it's true," said Caroline with certainty. "You might ask how I can be sure, so I'll tell you." She looked up at me and smiled lopsidedly. "I have been badly frightened by what has happened to Max over the past ten days. I was at the poisoned dinner and was dreadfully ill that night, and we have all seen the photos of the bombing and have heard Max's description of what it was like after the explosion. There can be no doubting that those things did happen."

"No," said Bernard. "No doubt whatsoever."

"And Max's car did collide with a bus, and his house did burn down."

"Yes," said Bernard. "We don't doubt those things happened either. The question is whether they were genuine attempts to murder him."

"I presume," she said, "that there's no question that Max did have his arm broken by someone wielding a polo mallet just for mentioning this man Komarov's name. I saw the mallet."

Bernard looked around at Toby and Sally. "I think we can agree that Max had his arm broken, but was it because he mentioned Komarov's name or because he had one of these balls?"

"Both," I said. "But I was definitely threatened with the mallet before I even showed them the ball. The Komarov name was the key."

"And," said Caroline, "someone went into my flat when I was in America."

"What do you mean?" said Bernard.

"Two men told my neighbor a pack of lies and managed to convince her to let them into my flat. I don't know why, but we think they must have planted something there that would let them know when we got back."

"But how did they know where you live?" said Bernard.

"Whoever it was must have followed me there," I said.

"But why?" said Bernard.

"I don't know," I replied. "If someone could fix the brakes on my car the night I had dinner with Caroline, then they only had to follow me to the restaurant to know who I was seeing."

"But that doesn't mean they know where she lives," said Bernard.

"I don't know," I said again. "If they saw me with her, they could have found out where she lives. Perhaps they followed her home."

"That's surely very unlikely," said Bernard.

"It was surely unlikely that someone would bomb Newmarket races," I said, "but they did." I stared at Bernard. "And you were able to find out where Caroline lives."

"That's different," he said.

"How exactly did you do that?" asked Caroline accusingly. "And you got my telephone number as well. How was that?"

Bernard went bright red, but he refused to say how he did it. He mumbled a bit about databases and so on, and about the data-protection act. As I had suspected, what he had done wasn't entirely legal.

"But you are sure someone was in your flat," he said, trying to get us back on track.

"Absolutely positive," she said. She told them briefly about things being moved in her medicine cabinet. Sally nodded. It must be a girl thing, I thought.

They all sat silently, digesting what Caroline and I had just told them. But were we getting anywhere? I wondered. There were so many questions, and I was far too short of answers.

"Sally," I said, "do you think we could have some tea?"

"Of course," she said. She seemed relieved to be able to get up and move. She went out to the kitchen. It somehow broke up the formality of the gathering. Bernard started apologizing to Caroline. Now, that had me worried.

Toby sat and turned the ball over and over in his hands. "I suppose . . ." he said, almost to himself. "No, that's ridiculous."

"What's ridiculous?" I asked him.

He looked up at my face. "I was just thinking aloud," he said.

"So tell me your thoughts," I urged him. Caroline and Bernard stopped talking and looked expectantly across at Toby.

"No, it was nothing," he said.

"Tell us anyway," I said.

"I was just wondering if it could be used for marbling."

There was a brief silence as we thought about what he had said.

"And what the hell is 'marbling'?" asked Bernard in his best lawyer voice.

"It's not the proper name, but it's what I call it," Toby said.

"Call what?" asked Sally, coming back into the room with a silver tray, with teapot, cups and so on, plus some chocolate biscuits that clearly caught Bernard's eye.

"Toby was just saying that this ball could be used for marbling," I said.

"What's that?" she asked, setting the tray down on a table.

"Yes, what is this marbling?" implored Bernard.

Toby looked at Caroline and he seemed a bit embarrassed. "It's placing a large glass marble in the uterus of a mare to simulate a pregnancy."

"But why would anyone do that?" asked Caroline.

"To stop her coming into season," said Toby.

"Sorry," said Bernard. "You've lost me."

"Suppose you don't want a filly or a mare coming into season at a certain time," said Toby. "You place a large marble or two through her cervix and into the uterus. The fact that there is something in the uterus already seems somehow to fool the animal into thinking that she is pregnant, so she doesn't ovulate, come into season or go into heat."

"Why would that be a problem anyway?" I asked.

"Well, sometimes it may be that you want the mare in season at an exact moment—say, for breeding on a specific day to a stallion—so you could marble the mare for a few weeks, then remove the marbles and—hey, presto—the mare comes into heat almost immediately. I don't know it all; you'd have to ask a vet. But I do know it's done a lot. Some show jumpers are kept off heat for major competitions. Otherwise, they can go all moody and don't behave properly. Just like a woman." He laughed, and Sally playfully smacked his knee.

"Or a polo pony," I said. "I doubt you would want a female polo pony to be in season during a match, especially if there were some male ponies playing as well."

"Certainly not if any of them were full horses," said Toby.

"Full horses?" asked Bernard, munching on a biscuit.

"Stallions," said Toby. "As opposed to geldings."

Bernard seemed to wince a little, and he put his knees tightly together.

"So you think this ball could be used instead of a glass marble?" I asked.

"I don't know," he said. "They're about the same size. But it would have to be sterilized. At least on the outside."

"How many did you say could be inserted?" I asked.

"One or two is normal, I think," he said. "But I do know that at least three have been used. Maybe more. You would have to ask a vet."

"Wouldn't they just fall out?" asked Caroline, amused.

"No," said Toby. "You need to give the mare an injection to open the cervix to get them in. The marbles are placed in the uterus through a tube that looks like a short piece of plastic drainpipe. When the injection wears off, the cervix closes and keeps them in. Easy. I've seen it done."

"But how do you get them out again?" I asked.

"I've never actually seen them come out," he said, "but I think you just give the mare the cervix-opening injection and the marbles are pushed out naturally."

"But surely this ball wouldn't be big enough to smuggle drugs," said Bernard. "In horses or otherwise."

"I was told that Peter Komarov imports horses by the jumbo jetful," I said. "How many horses could you get on a jumbo?"

"I'll try and find out," said Toby, and he went out of the drawing room.

"We shall assume that each horse would have a minimum of three balls placed in it," I said.

"Only the female horses," said Caroline.

"True," I said. "But wouldn't they all be females if that is what he wanted?"

"Wouldn't it depend on which horses were due to be imported?" said Sally.

"Not if Komarov owned the horses as well," I said.

Toby came back. "According to LRT, the transport people who take and collect horses from Gatwick and Luton, there can be up to eighty horses on a jumbo."

"Phew," I said. "That's a lot of horseflesh."

"Eighty horses times three balls each," said Caroline. "Two hundred and forty balls' worth. How much is that?"

I remembered from school that the formula for the volume of a sphere was $\frac{4\pi r^3}{3}$. The balls were about four centimeters across. I did a quick mental calculation. The volume of a ball was about thirty cubic centimeters. 30cc per ball × 240 balls = 7,200cc.

"Just over seven liters," I said.

"And just how much is that?" asked Bernard. "I don't work in liters."

I did another rough calculation. "It would fill a bit more than twelve pint beer glasses."

"And how much would that volume of cocaine be worth?" he asked.

"I've no idea of the price of cocaine," I said.

"I expect it will say on the Internet," said Toby. "I'll go ask Google." He disappeared again.

We sat and waited for him. I drank my tea, and Bernard sneaked his fourth chocolate biscuit.

Toby came back. "According to the Internet, cocaine is worth about forty pounds per gram at a sort of wholesale price," he said.

"And how many grams are there in a pint mug?" asked Bernard, holding out his chubby hands with the palms up.

I laughed. "My brain hurts. If it was water, there would be a thousand grams in each liter. So there would be seven thousand grams in all. I don't know whether cocaine powder is more or less dense than water. Does it float?"

"It can't be much different," said Bernard. "Say seven thousand grams at forty pounds at a time is"—he paused— "two hundred and eighty thousand pounds. Not bad. But not that much for all the risks involved."

"But that's not the half of it," said Caroline. "For a start, you probably import cocaine at one hundred percent purity, and then you 'cut' it—that is, you add baking soda or vitamin C powder, or even sugar. At least a third, and sometimes as much as two-thirds to three-quarters, of what is sold on the street is the cut."

I looked at her in shocked surprise. She smiled. "I once had a crackhead as a boyfriend. It lasted for a week or two, until I found out about his habit. But we stayed friends for a while longer, and he told me all about buying coke, as he called it. Users mostly buy it as a twist of powder or a rock of crack. That's just enough for a single dose. A twist of cocaine powder may only contain fifty milligrams of pure cocaine. So you can get at least twenty twists from a single gram. That puts the potential street value of each gram hugely higher. In all, a jumbo jetload would be worth millions, and how many jumbo jetfuls are there?

"Plus, of course, the profit from the sale of the horses," I said.

"If there is any," said Toby. "He would have to buy them in South America and pay for the transportation. I don't suppose there would be that much profit. Unless horses are very cheap in Argentina."

"How would we find out?" I asked.

Toby went out again, and I thought he was going to somehow find out the answer to my question. But he didn't. He came back with a book. It was like a large, thick paperback. "This is a catalog from the Horses in Training sale at Newmarket last October, when I bought a horse from Komarov. I thought I'd look it up." He flicked through the pages. "Here it is." He studied it. "It says here that it was sent to the sale by a company called Horse Imports Ltd. But I know it was Komarov's horse. He was there. He congratulated me afterwards on my purchase."

"You mean you spoke to this man?" said Sally, disturbed. "Does he know who you are?"

"Not really," said Toby.

"I hope not," she said to him. "Not if he's trying to kill your brother." She looked at me. "You shouldn't have come here." I could see that for the first time she really did believe I was in danger, and, consequently, so was she, and so was her family.

Toby was actually my half brother. We shared the same mother, but my father had been her second husband. Toby was the son of a newly qualified accountant who had died of kidney failure when Toby had been two. Toby's surname wasn't Moreton. It was Chambers.

"Komarov won't know that Toby is my brother," I said.

"I hope you're right," Sally said.

So did I.

# 19

Toby spent much of the evening going through the sale catalog page by page. He came up with the fact that sixty-eight of the fifteen hundred or so horses sold at that sale were from Horse Imports Ltd. And every single one of them was female, either a mare or a filly. And that couldn't be a coincidence.

That sale was just one of eleven similar sales held each year at Newmarket. There were also many major bloodstock auctions at Doncaster, and at Fairyhouse and Kill in Ireland, not to mention many others around the world. Then there were the horses sold privately. The horse-selling business worldwide was enormous. Lots and lots of jumbo jetfuls, each producing millions.

As Toby had studied the catalog, Caroline and I had sat in front of his computer screen and run searches on Horse Imports Ltd on the Internet. It was a British subsidiary of a Dutch company. It had an annual turnover that ran into tens of millions, but it seemed to have liabilities to its parent company equal to its gross profit and so it showed no net profit and hence paid no UK tax. I didn't know how many horses it sold each year, but if they were all as reasonably priced as Toby had said there must have been thousands of them. I wondered if they all had a uterus, and whether they had all arrived in the UK with it containing drug-filled metal balls. And those were just the British-bound horses. I knew he also sold horses in the United States, and I suspected he did too in his native Russia, if only to his polo club. Where else? I wondered. Would there be enough female horses in the whole of South America?

I tried to use the computer to trace the parent company into the Dutch system, but without any success. I was fairly confident that the Dutch company would, itself, prove to have a parent company, and so on. I suspected that the overall parent, the matriarch company at the top of the tree, would prove to have a Dutch Antilles base, to be an offshore entity where such considerations as corporate taxes were not a worry.

Bernard had made an interesting little speech before he had taken himself back to London. "One of the major problems for drug dealers," he had said, "is what to do with the vast amounts of cash generated by the trade. Nowadays, governments have wised up and put anti-money-laundering measures in place. You know how difficult it is now to open a bank account? Well, that's because the banks are required to prove not only who you are but that funds in your accounts are come by in a legal and tax-reported fashion. These days, you can't buy things with cash, not really expensive things like cars and houses. Even bookmakers won't take a large bet in cash anymore, and they certainly won't pay you out in cash if you win. It has to be by bank transfer or credit card. So cash is a problem. It's all right if it's only a few hundred or even a few thousand. That's easy to spend. But millions, in cash? You can't just buy your luxury Mediterranean yacht with suitcases full of cash. The yacht broker won't take it, because then he has the same problem."

"Can't you take the suitcases of cash into the Cayman Islands or somewhere and put it in a bank?" I had asked.

"No chance," he'd replied. "It's now more difficult to open a bank account in the Cayman Islands than it is here.

They are subject to all sorts of regulations laid down by both the United States and the European Union."

"But I thought they were an offshore center for saving tax. What have the U.S. and Europe got to do with it?"

"If the offshore centers don't comply with the rules, the U.S. won't allow its citizens to go there. It would be like Cuba," he had gone on. "And the Cayman Islands rely on the tourism industry to survive, and nearly all their tourists come from the United States, mostly on cruise ships."

I sat playing with the computer and thinking about how I would deal with millions of pounds in cash if I had been Mr. Komarov.

"Suppose," I said to Caroline, "he sends the cash back to South America along with the empty balls. The customs don't care about cash leaving. They're too busy looking out for drugs arriving."

"So," she said, "what good would that do? Bernard said you can't transfer large amounts from South America to banks over here without having to prove first it's not drug money."

"I know," I said. "But how about if you don't transfer it back. How about if you use the cash to buy horses as well as drugs."

She sat there looking at me with her mouth open.

"No one," I went on, "is going to worry about being paid in cash for a moderately priced horse or two in Argentina, Uruguay or Colombia. I bet that Komarov has hundreds of small horse breeders who regularly provide him with the horses for cash in hand. You simply send the profit generated from the drug smuggling back to South America as cash to buy more female horses to continue the trade in a never-ending cycle. It's self-perpetuating. Remember, Toby said he doubted that the sale of the horses would make much profit. It doesn't have to. It's not there to make a profit. It's there to launder the cash. In the end, you have legitimate money from the legitimate sale of the horses at the prestigious Newmarket Bloodstock Sales, where Mr. Komarov is seen as a pillar of society, and is, no doubt, welcomed with open arms and a glass of champagne because he brings sixty-eight horses to every sale."

"But we don't actually know he smuggles drugs," Caroline said.

"It doesn't matter what he's smuggling," I said. "It could be anything of high value that can fit into those balls. Provided someone is prepared to pay, it could be computer chips, explosives or even radioactive materials."

"Wouldn't that injure the horses?" she said.

"Not if they were alpha particle sources," I said. "Alpha particles can be stopped by a piece of paper, and the horse would easily be shielded from them by the metal of the ball. But they are very deadly if they enter the body without any shield at all. Remember that ex–KGB spy who was murdered in London with polonium-210? That stuff is an alpha source, and it had to have been smuggled here from Russia or somewhere in Eastern Europe. These metal balls easily could have been used to smuggle polonium-210 here without any harm being done to the horse."

Caroline shivered. "It's scary."

"It certainly is."

"But surely the balls would show up if the horses were X-rayed," she said.

"I expect so," I said. "But they don't X-ray the horses. X-rays can damage a developing embryo or a fetus, and many horses are transported after they are pregnant. It would be far too risky."

"But," she said, smiling, "if someone was to anonymously whisper to Her Majesty's Customs that Mr. Komarov's next jumbo jetful of horses from South America might just be worth X-raying, then Mr. Komarov might find himself in a bit of hot water, not to mention in the slammer."

I kissed her. Perfect.

"But something is still worrying me," she said. "Why did Komarov bomb the box at Newmarket? Surely that was stupid and dangerous."

"I wonder if it was a punishment," I said.

"For what?"

"Maybe Rolf Schumann was not paying his dues to Komarov." I thought for a moment. "Perhaps he'd been using the cash from the drug and horse sales to support his ailing tractor business instead of passing it on. Maybe the bombing was a demonstration to warn Komarov's associates in other countries around the world that he means business, and he won't stand for anyone robbing him."

"You mean he killed innocent people just to send a warning?" she said.

"Komarov wouldn't care about the innocent," I said. "Drugs kill innocent people every day, one way or another."

TOBY WAS very moody in the morning. He snapped at the children over breakfast, and even swore at the dog in front of them. It was out of character.

He had been out on the gallops with the first string of horses at six, an unusually warm May driving them out earlier and earlier. Breakfast with the family was between the first and second lots, before the three little ones were packed off to school in the car with Sally. They were at an age when the coming and going in this house washed over their world of school, parties, television and computer games.

"Bye, Uncle Max," they all shouted to me as they clambered into Sally's people carrier, and then they were gone. I had left Caroline in bed, catching up on six hours' time difference, and I had dragged myself from between the sheets only because I felt I had neglected the children the previous evening.

I went back inside and found Toby at the kitchen table trying to read the *Racing Post*. However, he obviously wasn't concentrating on the newspaper, as I saw him restart the same article at least three times.

"What's the matter?" I asked, sitting myself back down with a mug of coffee.

"Nothing," he said, and set about reading the article for the fourth time.

"Yes there is." I reached across the table and dragged the paper away from him. "What is it?"

He looked up at me. "Sally and I had a row."

"I can tell," I said. It had been obvious the whole time Sally was getting breakfast. "What about?"

"It doesn't matter," he stated firmly, standing up.

"It clearly does," I said. "Is it about me?"

"I told you, it doesn't matter."

"So, it was about me," I said. "Tell me."

He didn't answer. He turned to go out of the door, back to the stables.

"Toby," I almost shouted, "for God's sake, what is it?"

He stopped, but he didn't turn around. "Sally wants you to leave here this morning," he said. He now turned and looked at me. "She's worried and frightened. You know, for the children."

"Oh, is that all?" I said with a smile. "We'll go as soon as we're ready."

"You don't have to," he said. "I put my foot down. You're my brother, and if I can't help you when you're in trouble, then who will? What good am I as a brother if I throw you out of my home?"

I could hear in his voice that this was an argument well rehearsed during his row with Sally.

"It OK," I said. "She's right. Perhaps I shouldn't have come here in the first place." But I was glad I had. Toby's knowledge of horses had been the key to everything.

"But where will you go?" he asked.

"Somewhere else," I said. Perhaps it would be better if he didn't know. "We'll be gone when you get back from second lot. I'll call you later. And thank Sally for me, for having us."

Surprisingly, he walked across the kitchen and gave me a huge hug.

"Be careful," he said into my ear. "Be a shame to lose you now." He suddenly let me go, looked away as if in embarrassment and went straight outside without saying another word. Maybe he was too emotional to speak. I was.

CAROLINE AND I were packed up and away by nine-thirty. She hadn't been too happy when I had woken her from a deep sleep, but she hadn't protested much either.

"Where are we going?" she asked as we drove out of the gate.

"Where do you suggest?" I said.

"Somewhere with a nice soft bed." She yawned, leaned back in the passenger's seat and closed her eyes.

I thought about my mother's cottage down the road. I didn't have a key, but I knew, as I expect everyone else in East Hendred knew, that she always kept a spare under the third geranium-filled flowerpot to the left of the back door. I decided against it. If, before I went to Chicago, I had believed that it was too risky for my mother to stay there, then surely it was too dangerous for me and Caroline now.

I drove aimlessly for a while along roads I knew so well from my childhood. Maybe my conscious mind thought my driving was aimless, but subconsciously my brain took the Mondeo unerringly the twelve miles from East Hendred to the establishment overlooking the river Thames that had once been owned by my mother's distant widowed cousin and where my passion for cooking food had been first awakened.

The place had changed during the six years since I had left. It was no longer the elegant sixteenth-century inn with restaurant that I remembered. There was a new, twenty-first-century glass extension reaching down towards the river, over what had been a well-tended lawn when I last saw it. A long brass-fronted bar had been built down one side of the old dining room, and the only food now offered was what my mother's distant widowed cousin had always referred to with distaste as "bar snacks."

Caroline, Viola and I sat down at an outside table with benches, set up on what once also had been part of the lawn but was now a concrete patio. Viola could not be left in the car, Caroline explained, as she was too valuable. Quite apart from the fact, Caroline added, she felt lost without her close by, to pat. At least Viola was out of sight, in her case.

It was too early for what my father had always called a proper drink, so Caroline and I had cups of coffee, while Viola just sat there. I didn't recognize either the barman who took the order or the waitress who delivered it. I suspected that none of the happy team from six years ago would remain. But what hadn't changed was the restful view of the ancient six-arched stone bridge that spanned the river, the endless sounds of gurgling water and the seeming calmness of a mother duck gliding along in the sunshine followed by a line of six tiny, fluffy chicks.

"What a beautiful place," said Caroline. "Have you been here before?"

"This is where I learned to cook," I said.

"Really." She was surprised. She had looked at the menu while I had ordered the coffee.

"It's changed a lot," I said. "Where the bar is now is what used to be the restaurant. I'm rather sad to see that it's all gone a bit down-market. The place was taken over by a chain that was obviously more interested in selling beer than in fine dining."

"So why did we come here now?" she asked.

"I don't know," I said. "I suppose I wanted somewhere peaceful to think, and to plan."

"So what is the plan?" she asked eagerly.

"I don't know that either," I replied. "But first, I'm going to make a few calls."

I turned on my cell phone and used it to call the car-rental company in Newmarket. No problem, they said, keep the Mondeo as long as you like. They took my credit card details and told me that I would be charged weekly. Fine, I said, and hung up.

The phone immediately rang in my hand. It was my voice-message service.

"You have six new messages," it told me, and then played them. One was from Clare Harding, the news editor, belatedly thanking me for dinner, and the other five were all from Carl. He needed to speak with me, his disembodied voice repeatedly told me. Over the five successive messages, he became more and more agitated that I hadn't been in touch.

I rang him. He was relieved and delighted that I called, but I was hardly delighted with what he told me. "I need you back here," he said urgently. "And now." Things had clearly gone downhill quickly since we spoke on Saturday.

"What's the matter?" I asked, concerned. It was not like Carl to be in a panic.

"I've had to fire Oscar," he said. "Gary caught him in the office going through the papers on your desk, and some of the petty cash was missing too. Oscar denied it. But, then, he would, wouldn't he? But that's only the half of it. He was disruptive in the kitchen with Gary all last week. Then the two of them had a stand-up row on Saturday. I thought Oscar was going to stick Gary with a fish filleter at one point." A fish filleter was a very sharp, very thin, eight-inch-bladed kitchen knife. Sticking anyone with a fish filleter was likely to prove very terminal, very quickly. I was very glad that Oscar had gone.

"But surely you and Gary can cope without him for a few days?" I said.

"We could if Gary was here," he exclaimed. "He's now got bloody chicken pox, and the doctor's told him to stay at home for the next ten bloody days."

"Can't you get another chef from the agency?" I asked him.

"I've tried that," he said. "They've got their back up over Oscar. They say we didn't treat him right. I tell you, he was nothing but a bloody menace."

"Apart from all that," I said to him, "is everything else all right?"

"No, not really," he replied. I wished I hadn't asked. "Jean wants to know when we are going to replace Louisa. She claims she is being worked too hard in the dining room. I told her to shut up or get out, and now she has her back up too."

I wasn't surprised. Staff management had never been Carl's strong point.

"OK," I said. "Is everything else fine?"

"No it's not," he said. "Jacek says he wants more money. He says that the other kitchen porter gets more money than him and it's not fair." Jacek's English must be getting better, I thought. "I also told him to shut up or get out," Carl continued. "He's still here today, so I presume he's shut up. But when are you coming back?" Soon. I feared that if I didn't get back there quickly, the whole business would be destroyed.

"I'll call you again later to let you know," I said.

"Please come back," he was pleading. "I don't know how much longer I can go on like this." He sounded almost manic.

"I said I'll call you," I replied, and hung up.

"Problems?" asked Caroline, who had only been able to hear my end of the conversation.

"The ship is foundering on the rocks without the captain," I said. "One of the chefs has been fired for threatening another with a knife, and now the threatened one has caught chicken pox. Carl, my number two, is basically on his own." Julie, who prepared the cold dishes, wouldn't be much use in the heat of the kitchen.

"Can he cope on his own?" she asked.

"Not really," I said. "Not if the restaurant is more than half full."

"And is it?" said Caroline.

"I didn't ask," I said. "But I hope so. And if it's not tonight, it certainly will be towards the end of the week. But that's not all. Carl has upset some of the other staff, and I can imagine the undercurrents running through the place. They will all be waiting for me to get back before the volcano explodes, and the longer I'm away, the worse will be the eruption when it finally happens."

"Then you must go back there now," said Caroline.

"I couldn't be much help one-handed," I said, holding up the cast.

"Even a one-handed Max Moreton would be better than most," she said.

I smiled at her. "But is it safe?" I said. "Or is it precisely what someone wants?"

"Who?" she asked. "Komarov?"

"Maybe," I said. "Or Carl."

"Carl? Don't you trust your number two?"

"I don't know who I can trust," I said. I sat there, thinking, as I watched a boat chug upstream through the bridge with two pasty-white sunbathers lying on its roof. "Yes, I think I probably do trust Carl."

"Right," she said. "Then we go back to Newmarket and

save your restaurant. But we don't tell anyone we're coming before we get there, not even Carl."

CAROLINE TOOK Viola for a walk down the riverbank into the meadow below the pub while I sat and made the rest of my calls. I could hear the mellow tones of her playing as I rang first my mother, to ensure she was all right, and then the police—the Metropolitan Police Special Branch, to be precise.

"Can I speak to D.I. Turner, please?" I asked.

"Can you hold?" said a female voice. It wasn't so much a question as an order. Eventually, she came back on the line. "D.I. Turner is off duty until two p.m."

I left him a message, asking him to call me. I told him it was urgent. I was promised that he would get the message. I wondered if I should have spoken to someone else. But D.I. Turner knew who I was, and he was less likely to dismiss my information with a laugh.

Caroline continued walking the riverbank towpath and playing sweet music for about forty minutes before she returned, flushed, smiling and happy.

"Oh that's great," she sighed, sitting down. I looked enviously at Viola. I wished I could make Caroline feel like that in the middle of the day, and with jet lag.

"Don't you need to read the music?" I asked her.

"No," she said. "Not for this piece. I know it so well. I was just making sure my fingers knew it as well as my head does."

"I thought orchestras always have music," I said. "They have music stands. I've seen them."

"Well, we do. But soloists usually don't, and often the music is there just as an aide-mémoire rather than being absolutely necessary." She slipped Viola lovingly back into her case. "Are we staying here for lunch?"

"No," I said. "I'd rather go. It's been over an hour since I first used my phone here and it's time to move on." And, I thought, the food wasn't very inviting.

"Can someone really find out where you are from your cell?" she asked.

"I know the police can," I said, "from your phone records. I've heard about it in trials. I'm just not taking any chances that Komarov has someone at the phone company on his payroll."

"Do you want to go back to Newmarket?" Caroline asked.

"Yes and no," I said. "Of course I want to go to the Hay Net and sort out the mess, but I have to admit that I'm wary."

"We don't have to go, you know," she said.

"I can't go on running forever," I said. "I'll have to go back there sometime. I've left a message for the policeman I spoke to at the Special Branch, and I'll tell him what I think has been going on and ask him for some police protection. It'll be fine."


WE STOPPED just north of Oxford and enjoyed a leisurely lunch in a pub garden, sitting under a bright red sun umbrella that made our delicious stilton and broccoli soup appear pink when it should have been green. The closer we came to Newmarket, the more nervous I became, and, when we arrived in the town at about six o'clock, I felt lost, like a fish out of water. I had no home to go to, nothing but a pile of blackened stones and ash, which I drove slowly past, in each direction, as Caroline sat silently staring at the devastation.

"Oh, Max," she said after our second pass. "I am so sorry."

"I can always rebuild," I said. But that little cottage was the only home I had ever owned, and I could remember clearly the excitement on that July day nearly six years ago when I had first moved in, the joy of discovery of unknown cupboards, and the sounds made by the structure as the hot summer day had cooled towards evening. It had been built from local stone in the last decade of the eighteenth century, and although I currently owned the freehold I had always considered myself a temporary tenant in its long and endless existence. But now its life had been burned away. Murder had been done here, not on a human being but on a member of my family nevertheless. What remained was dead, and silent. Would rebuilding ever bring it back its soul? Perhaps the time was right, after all, for me to grieve for my loss, and to move on.

"Where exactly are we going to sleep tonight?" Caroline asked after I had finally driven away from the disaster.

"Do you remember when I first talked you into coming to Newmarket, I promised you a night at the Bedford Lodge Hotel?" I said. "And the best-laid plans were somewhat disrupted by a certain car crash. Well, tonight, my dear, you shall finally have your night in Newmarket's finest hotel."

"I am honored," she said.

"Don't get too used to it," I said. "They have a room only for tonight. They're full tomorrow."

"I have to be in London tomorrow night," she said.

I hadn't forgotten.

To say Carl was pleased to see me would be rather an understatement. He almost cried when I walked into the Hay Net kitchen at seven o'clock.

"Thank God," he said.

"I won't be much use," I said, tapping the hard shell on my right arm.

"What did you do?" he asked. His shoulders sagged. His joy was rapidly turning to disappointment.

"Fell and broke my wrist," I said. "Stupid. But I can still help a bit."

"Good." A little of his joy returned.

I didn't bother to change. I just slipped one of my chef's tunics over my shirt and set to work, assisted by Caroline, who did the two-handed jobs.

I wouldn't exactly claim that the kitchen service was back to normal, but we coped with the seventy-two covers. I decided not to go out to the dining room at any time as I really didn't want to be seen by any of the customers. The staff saw me, of course, but I asked them to keep it to themselves. I held up the cast and told them my doctor had forbidden me to work, and I didn't want him finding out that I had. They smiled at me knowingly and promised to keep the secret. But did I trust all of them to do so?

Finally, the rush was over, and we had a chance to sit down. It had now been nearly two weeks since I had worked and I was out of shape. I slumped, exhausted, into my chair in the office.

"I never realized it was so hot in a kitchen," said Caroline. Throughout the evening, she had gradually removed articles of clothing until removing any more would have been indecent. Marguerite, my mother's distant widowed cousin's fiery cook, who had first nurtured my love for cooking, had regularly worn nothing but a pair of knickers under a white, lightweight cotton doctor's coat.

"You should try it on a blazing June day," I said.

Carl came into the office from the bar with beers for us all. "OK?" he said to Caroline, handing her one.

"Lovely," she said, taking it.

"Do you want a job?" he asked her, smiling. He had the look of a prisoner reprieved from the gallows. Seventy-two dinners was more than he would have been able to do alone, at least to any decent standard.

"I've already got one," she said. "Although I might lose it if I don't do some practice soon."

"Practice?" Carl asked. "What do you do?"

In answer, Caroline reached down for the ever-present Viola and took her out of her case.

"I know who you are," said Carl suddenly. He looked at me. "She's the bitch that's suing us." We laughed. Even Caroline, the bitch, laughed.

"I'll try and see about that," she said. "Perhaps I've just been paid off." She held up the beer and drank deeply, leaving a white mustache on her upper lip that she wiped away with her forearm. We laughed again.

I tried calling D.I. Turner. This was the fourth time, and once again I was told he was not available. I again asked if I could leave a message, but I was beginning to think that he wasn't receiving them. I told the person at the other end of the line that it was really urgent. "Can I help?" this person asked. I started to tell him that it was about the bombing at Newmarket races. He told me that I should contact the Suffolk police, not the Special Branch. I told him that I feared my life was in danger, but I don't think he believed me. He repeated that I should contact my local police station. So I did, and I asked for the senior officer on duty, only to be told that the inspector was out at the moment and would I like to leave a message. I sighed and said I would try again later.

Richard came into the office to say that most of the customers had gone and only one table remained, and they were having their coffee.

"Mrs. Kealy was asking after you," he said to me.

"Were the Kealys here tonight?" I asked. "It's not Saturday."

"Last night and tonight," he said. "Mrs. Kealy said something about wanting to support the restaurant after the difficult times with the poisoned dinner and all."

How nice, I thought. I needed more customers like the Kealys.

"Most of the staff can go home now," I said. "And you, Carl, if you like. I'll lock up." I wanted to be the last to leave so as not to be followed. "Richard, can you finish up?" He would ensure that the last table paid their bill, and then he would see them off the premises.

"No problem," he said, and departed back to the dining room.

"Where are you staying?" Carl asked.

"We're booked into a hotel," I said.

"Which one?" he asked.

I wondered just how much I trusted Carl. "The Rutland Arms," I lied.

I hoped he didn't check. Moreton would not be on the guest list for tonight at the Rutland Arms. But, then again, Moreton wasn't on the guest list for the Bedford Lodge either. I had booked our room in the name of Butcher.

"Well, I'm pooped," said Carl, standing up. "I'm going home to bed." The office usually doubled as a changing room, but, no doubt out of deference to Caroline, Carl took himself off to the gents' to change out of his work clothes. I had always intended putting in a proper changing room, including a shower, but we had never quite got around to it.

Caroline placed Viola on her shoulder and played softly. It was wonderful. I watched her, and she stopped playing. "Don't stop," I said. "It's beautiful."

"I'm embarrassed," she said.

"Don't be silly," I said. "On Thursday night, hundreds of people will be watching you."

"That's somehow different," she said. "They won't be just two feet from my nose."

I pushed my chair away until I was at least four feet away. "Better?" I asked.

She didn't answer but again placed Viola on her shoulder and played sweet music.

Carl came back into the office, changed. Caroline stopped, and he smiled at her. "Someone's left a cell phone in the gents'," he said, placing it on my desk. "Silly bugger. I'll deal with it in the morning. Good night." He turned to leave.

"'Night, Carl," I said. "And thanks for holding down the fort."

"No problem," he said, and departed. I couldn't actually say to him tonight that he needed to work on his man-management skills. I would deal with that in the morning too.

"Are we off?" said Caroline.

"Soon," I said. "We'll wait until Richard has finished up and gone too."

The forgotten cell phone on my desk rang. Caroline and I looked at it.

"Hello," I said, answering it at the fourth ring.

"Hello," said a male voice at the other end. "I think that's my phone."

"Who is this?" I asked.

"George Kealy," said the voice. "Is that you, Max?"

"Yes, George," I said. "You left your phone in the gents'."

"Thought so," he said. "Stupid fool. Sorry. I'll come and get it, if that's OK."

"Sure," I said. "But we'll be locked, so knock on the front door."

"Will do," he said, and he hung up.

Richard came back in to report that all the customers had now gone, and he was going too. "Oh," he said, turning back, "Jacek is still here. He wants a word with you. He's waiting for you in the kitchen."

"Tell him to go home," I said. "I'll see him in the morning."

"OK," he said hesitatingly. "I've already told him that once, but he seemed very intent on waiting."

"Well, tell him again," I said. "He's to go home now." I had no intention of going alone into the kitchen with Jacek there. I wasn't at all sure I could trust him.

"OK," he said again. "I'll tell him."

"Come back to tell me when he's gone," I said. "And, Richard, please make sure he leaves completely." I knew that Jacek rode a bicycle to and from his digs in the town. "Check he leaves on his bike."

Richard looked at me somewhat strangely but nodded and went out.

There was a loud knock on the front door.

I went out into the entrance lobby between the bar and the dining room. I looked through the window into the parking lot. As expected, it was George Kealy. I had his phone in my hand.

I unlocked the door, but it wasn't George Kealy's foot that crashed it open, sending me reeling backwards. It was another man, and he held an automatic pistol in his hand and he was pointing it right between my eyes. Mr. Komarov, I presumed.

"George tells me that you're a very difficult man to kill, Mr. Moreton," he said, advancing through the door.

# 20

I retreated back from the door into the entrance lobby. Komarov and George Kealy followed.

Richard came out of the dining room, carrying a tray of dirty glasses from the last table. Komarov and I saw him at the same instant, and before I had a chance to shout a warning Komarov swung the gun around and shot him. The noise of the retort in the enclosed space was startling, and I jumped. A crimson star appeared on the front of Richard's white shirt, and there was a slight look of surprise on his face as he pitched forward. The bullet had caught him in the center of his chest, and I was convinced he was dead before he hit the floor. The metal tray he had been holding clattered noisily to the floor and all the glasses shattered, sending hundreds of fragments in all directions across the stone tiles.

The gun came unerringly back to point at me, and I thought that this was it. He would surely kill me just as easily. Why shouldn't he? He had tried twice before, why not a third time? The anger that I had channeled into my survival in my burning cottage rose again in me. I wasn't going to just die without a fight.

Komarov saw the anger in me and read my intentions. "Don't even think about it," he said in almost perfect English, with just a hint of his native Russian accent that made the "think" sound like "sink."

I stood my ground and looked at him. He was a thickset man in his mid-fifties, of about average height, with a full head of thick gray hair, well-coiffed. I realized I knew him from before. He had been George and Emma Kealy's guest here at the Hay Net the first Saturday after the bombing. I remembered that George had called Emma to get going, "Peter and Tanya are waiting," he had said. Peter and Tanya, George Kealy's friends, were actually Pyotr and Tatiana Komarov, smugglers, bombers and murderers.

I found it difficult to believe that George was not the friendly regular customer I knew so well. I looked at him, but he didn't seem to be embarrassed one bit by my predicament. He didn't even seem shocked by what his friend had done to my headwaiter. I continued to stare at him, but he refused to look me in the eye. He simply appeared determined, and resigned to the necessity of such actions.

"I am going to kill you," Komarov said to me. I didn't doubt it. "But before I do," he went on, "I want back what is mine that you have."

"And what is that?" I said, finding it quite difficult to talk. My tongue seemed to be stuck to the roof of my mouth.

"You know what I want," he said. "You obtained it in Delafield."

Oh dear, I thought. He must have spoken to Mrs. Schumann, or perhaps it was Kurt and his polo mallet–wielding chum who had paid her a visit. I didn't want to think about what they might have done to that dear, devastated lady.

"I don't know what you're talking about," I said. I had raised my voice a little. I was very conscious that Caroline was still in the office, and I was trying to somehow warn her of the danger, although she had to have heard the shot and then the crash of the tray and the glasses. I had no doubt whatsoever that Komarov would kill her as easily as he had killed Richard. Or worse, he would use her for leverage to get back the metal ball. I thought about that ball. I didn't actually have it with me, so I couldn't have given it back to Komarov even if I had wanted to. It probably was still on Toby's desk where I had left it, for him to show to his vet. And I had no intention of putting my brother or his family in danger again.

"George," said Komarov, keeping his gun pointed straight at me, "go check that we are alone."

George Kealy produced another pistol from his own pocket and went into the dining room. I could hear him going into the kitchen beyond. After a while, he came back. "No one else here," he said.

"Check in there," said Komarov, waving the gun towards the bar and the office beyond. The office actually sat between the bar and the kitchen, with a door at each end, and was more like a wide corridor than a proper room.

I went on staring at Komarov but slightly bunched my muscles, ready to try to rush him if George cried out that he had found Caroline. But he didn't call out. He just came back and reported that we were all alone.

"Where's your girlfriend?" said Komarov.

"In London," I said.

"Where in London?" he asked.

"With her sister," I said. "In Finchley."

He seemed satisfied with the answer and waved his gun towards the dining room. "In there," he said.

I had to step around Richard's body. I looked down at his back. There was no exit wound; the bullet was still in his body. Did it make things better or worse? Neither. It was horrible either way.

I walked ahead of Komarov. Was he going to shoot me in the back? Unlikely. Not that I thought it would make any difference to him. Or, I suppose, to me.

"Stop," he said. I stopped. "Pull out the chair, the one with arms." I reached to my left and pulled the armchair away from the table. I realized that it was the Kealys' usual dining table. I wondered if George noticed. "Sit down facing away from me," said Komarov. I did as he said.

He and George moved around me so that they were again in front.

I heard someone crunching across the broken glass in the lobby behind me. I thought it must be Caroline, but Komarov looked over my shoulder and he didn't seem alarmed. The new arrival was obviously his ally, not mine.

"Have you got the stuff?" he asked the newcomer.

"Yeah," said a male voice. There were more crunching steps as the man moved nearer to my back. "Shame you had to shoot Richard," he said.

I recognized that voice. Much suddenly became clear.

"Tie him up," said Komarov.

The man who had been behind me walked around in front. He was carrying a dark blue canvas carryall.

"Hello, Gary," I said.

"Hi, Chef," he said in his usual casual style. There was not a chicken pox scab to be seen. But, then, there wouldn't be. It had been so simple, and I had walked right into the trap. Gary didn't have chicken pox, and, no doubt, Oscar hadn't been going through my papers in the office and hadn't stolen any of the petty cash. Komarov had needed me back at the Hay Net, and the best way to do that was to create a manpower crisis. Get Oscar fired through Gary's false accusations, then simply get Gary to call in sick. Hey, presto, I came running. Like a lamb to the slaughter.

"Why?" I said to Gary.

"Why what?" he said.

"Why this?" I asked, spreading my arms out.

"Money, of course," he said, and smiled. He seemed not to realize how deep he was in, or the danger.

"But I pay you good money," I said to him.

"Not that good," he said. "And you don't provide the extras."

"Extras?" I asked.

"Stuff," he said. I looked at him quizzically. "Coke."

I hadn't figured him as an addict. Drugs and kitchen heat don't normally go together. I supposed that it did explain some of his mood swings, as well as his current actions. A drug habit can be very demanding; cravings and addiction usually dispel all logic and reason. Given certain circumstances, Gary undoubtedly would do anything for his next fix, and George must have had quite a hold over him.

He took a roll of brown packing tape from the carryall and used some of it to bind my left wrist to the arm of the chair. Komarov moved off to the side, to make sure that Gary never came between me and the gun, but I had no doubt that Komarov would shoot Gary as easily as sneeze if he thought it was necessary to his plans.

Gary moved to my right wrist.

"Hey," he said, "he's got a plaster cast under this tunic."

"Kurt claimed that Walter must have broken his wrist," said Komarov. He came close to me. "You broke Walter's arm," he said into my face. Good, I thought. I wish I'd broken his bloody neck. "You'll pay for that," he said. Then he stood up and smiled. "But Walter always was such an impetuous boy. He probably tried to bash your brains in with a polo mallet." He smiled at me again. "You might wish he had." I felt cold and clammy, but I smiled back at him nevertheless.

Gary taped the cast to the other arm of the chair. Then he taped my ankles to the chair legs in the same manner. I was trussed up like a turkey waiting for the knife to cut my throat. Then Gary took some more stuff from his bag. It looked like putty—soft, white putty. It was in a long plastic bag and looked like a white salami. If possible, I felt even colder and more clammy. Gary had removed a couple of pounds of plastic explosive from his bag.

He taped the white sausage to the chair between my legs. Oh God. Not my legs. MaryLou's legs, and the awful lack of them, haunted me still. Now, it seemed, I was to live my nightmare. Next, Gary delicately took a cigarette-sized metal tube from the bag and very carefully pushed it deep into the soft white explosive, like pushing a chocolate chip into an ice-cream cone. The tube had two short wires coming out of the top that were connected to a small black box. The remote-detonator system, I concluded. I sweated more, and Komarov clearly enjoyed it. For the first time, I became really terrified, absolutely certain that I would die, hopeful that it would be quick and easy and frightened to the point of despair that it would not. Would I be able to not tell him where the balls were? Would I be able to die without giving up that information? Would I be able to keep those I loved safe no matter what was done to me? The same questions that every Gestapo-tortured spy or resistance fighter had asked themselves more than fifty years ago. Neither I, nor they, would know the answer, not until the unthinkable actually happened.

"Where is it?" Komarov asked.

"Where is what?" I replied.

"Mr. Moreton," he said, as if addressing me in a company board meeting, "let us not play games. We both know what I am talking about."

"I left it with Mrs. Schumann," I said.

George appeared slightly uneasy.

"I am informed," said Komarov, "that that is not the case. Mrs. Schumann gave two of the items to you. One has been recovered, but the other has not." He walked around behind me. "Mrs. Schumann should not have had any of the items in the first place. They have all now been recovered, other than the one you still possess." He came around in front of me again. "You will tell me where it is, sooner or later." He smiled again. He was obviously enjoying himself. I wasn't.

There was a noise from the kitchen. It wasn't particularly loud, but it was clear, like a metal spoon falling onto the tile floor. It must be Caroline, I thought.

"Can't you do anything right?" Komarov said, cuttingly, to George Kealy. He was irritated. "Watch him." He pointed at me. "If he moves, shoot him in the foot. But don't hit the explosive or we might all end up dead. You"—he gestured towards Gary—"come with me."

Komarov and Gary went from the dining room into the kitchen through the swinging door that was more often used by my waitstaff than by a gun-toting murderer. I prayed that Caroline would stay hidden.

George stood nervously in front of me.

"How on earth did you get involved in this?" I asked him.

"Shut up," he said in reply. I ignored him.

"Why did you poison the gala dinner?" I asked him.

"Shut up," he said again. I ignored him again.

"Was it so you didn't have to go to the Guineas?" I asked.

"I told you to shut up," he said.

"Did Gary add the kidney beans to the sauce?" I asked him. He didn't say anything. "Now, that was really stupid," I said. "Without that, I wouldn't have worried. I wouldn't have asked any questions." And, I thought, I wouldn't be here, tied up and waiting to die.

"Don't *you* start," George said. I must have touched a raw nerve.

"In trouble, are you? With the boss man?" I said, rubbing salt in the wound. He was silent, so I taunted him more. "Messed up, did you? Was George not such a clever boy after all?"

"Shut up," he said, waving the gun towards me. "Shut up!"

"What does Emma think?" I said. "Does she know what you're up to?"

He turned and looked towards the door through which the other two had disappeared. He was hoping for reinforcements, and I was obviously beginning to get to him.

"Was it Emma who prepared the poisonous kidney beans for you?" I asked.

"Don't be bloody stupid," he said, turning back to me. "The beans were only there to make her ill."

"To make Emma ill?" I said, astounded.

"Emma was insistent that we go to that bloody box at the races," he said. "I couldn't talk her out of it. She and Elizabeth Jennings had been planning it for weeks, ever since we were first invited. I couldn't exactly tell her why she shouldn't go, now, could I?"

"So you poisoned the dinner to stop her going to the races?"

"Yes," he said. "That damn Gary was only meant to poison Emma's dinner and those of the Jenningses. Stupid idiot poisoned the whole bloody lot, didn't he? He even made me ill, the bastard."

"Serves you right," I said to him, just as Caroline had said to me.

I supposed it was easier for Gary to poison the whole dinner rather than just three plates and then somehow ensure they went to the correct people. That would have involved a conspiracy with one of the waiters. The mass poisoning also gave him the excuse he needed for not being in the kitchen himself at the racetrack on the Saturday.

"But Elizabeth Jennings went to the races anyway," I said to George. "How come?"

"I didn't realize she was allergic to mushrooms," he said. Elizabeth would have eaten the chicken without the truffle and chanterelle sauce. "I was sorry about that."

Not so sorry, I thought, to have kept him away from Elizabeth's funeral. Not so sorry to prevent him offering Neil Jennings his bloodied hand in comfort at the church door.

"You should have just left it," he said to me, looking me in the eye for the first time.

"Should have left what?" I said.

"You seemed so bloody determined to find out who had poisoned the dinner."

"Well, of course I was," I said.

"But I couldn't let that happen," said George.

I stared at him. "You mean it was you who tried to kill me?"

"I arranged it," he said rather arrogantly. There was no remorse in his voice.

I had liked George. I had always considered him to be a friend, and yet he had apparently twice arranged to have me killed. He had caused my car to be written off, he had burned my home and all my possessions and here he was standing in front of me with a gun in his hand and murder on his mind. Last week, I had told Dorothy Schumann that lots of people were murdered by their friends. I hadn't expected that fact to be so manifestly demonstrated quite so soon.

"But you weren't very good at it, were you?" I said, again goading him. "I bet Komarov wasn't too pleased with that either, was he? You couldn't even bump off a country chef, could you? Can't you do anything right?" I echoed Komarov.

"Shut up," he shouted again. He was becoming very agitated. "Bloody Gary couldn't organize a proverbial bloody piss-up in a brewery."

"So it was Gary who tried to kill me?" I said.

He ignored me and walked over to look through the circular window in the door to the kitchen.

"Why did Komarov bomb the box?" I asked him, changing direction.

"I told you to shut up," said George, waving his gun at me.

"Was Rolf Schumann the target?" I asked, ignoring him.

"I said shut up," he shouted, walking right up to me and pointing the gun at my head from about twelve inches away.

I ignored him again. If I made him angry enough, then perhaps he would do me a favor by killing me quickly. "Why bomb the box?" I said. "Surely that was out of all proportion. Why not just shoot Schumann, if he wanted to kill him? Nice and quiet, down some dark alley in Wisconsin?"

"Komarov doesn't do things quietly," said George. "Make a statement, that's what he said. Show everyone he meant business. Schumann was stealing from him, and Komarov doesn't like thieves. An example had to be set." George was clearly repeating to me exactly what Komarov had said to him.

Strange logic, I thought. Schumann was a thief, so Komarov tried to murder him, and killed nineteen innocents instead, including the lovely Louisa and the conscientious MaryLou, and all in such horrific circumstances. Komarov was truly evil.

There was a shout from the kitchen. Then a shot. I was frantic. Please, God, I prayed, let it not be Caroline who was shot.

George backed away from me and again looked through the circular window in the swinging door and beyond into the kitchen. There was another shot, then another, followed by more shouts. Pity we had no near neighbors, I thought. Someone might have heard the shots and called the police.

Komarov came back quickly through the door.

"There's someone outside the back," he said to George. "I think I hit them. Go out and finish them off. I've sent that

Gary out as well, so don't shoot him." George seemed to hesitate. "Now, George." George moved through the door, his body language screaming that he didn't want to go. Messing about in the dark with guns was not really his scene. But he should have thought of that before he became involved with a man like Komarov.

"Now, Mr. Moreton," said Komarov, coming right up to me, "where is my ball?"

I almost laughed. If my legs hadn't been taped to the chair legs, I would have kicked him in his balls. Then he'd have known where they were. He seemed to spot my amusement and his anger rose. He clearly expected me to be frightened into submission. Little did he realize that I was.

"I will give you one last chance to tell me, then I will shoot your left foot," he said. "Then I will shoot your right foot, then your knees, your wrists and your elbows." As he spoke, he ejected the partially used magazine from his gun and snapped in another from his pocket. I assumed it was fully loaded. "Now, time is passing. For the last time, where is it?" He leaned down towards my face. I wondered if it would help if I spat at him. Perhaps he would become so angry that he would kill me quickly. I tried it. He just laughed and wiped his face with his sleeve. "That won't help you," he said. "You will tell me what I want, I promise you. Then I will detonate the bomb and blow you and your restaurant to smithereens." His Russian accent made it sound like "*smis-ereens*," but I understood his meaning. Another example to be set, no doubt.

He stepped back and raised the gun. I wondered how much it would hurt. I wondered if I could stand it, and whether I would be able to stand the pain of both feet, my knees, my wrists and my elbows. I just couldn't tell him to go to East Hendred, to Toby and Sally's house, with their three lovely children. Whatever happened, I kept telling myself, I must not talk. I must not rain death and destruction down on my brother.

Komarov aimed his gun at my right foot.

"Wait," I cried. His arm dropped a fraction.

"Yes?" he said.

"Why do you need it back anyway?" I asked. "You must have more, hundreds more."

"Why would I have hundreds?" he asked, clearly curious to learn how much I knew. What should I tell him? Did it matter?

"To put inside the horses," I said. "Full of drugs."

The effect was quite startling. He went very pale, and his hand shook a little.

"Who knows this?" he said in a higher pitch than usual.

"Everyone," I said. "I told the police." I didn't expect this comment to save me; quite the reverse. But I hoped it might now be a quicker, less painful death.

"That was very careless of you," he said, returning somewhat to his normal voice. "For that, you will die." I was going to die anyway. No change.

He started to walk around behind me. Good, I thought, he is going to shoot me in the back of the head. Much cleaner, and much better not to see it coming. I would just be . . . gone.

As Komarov passed my shoulder, Caroline stepped through the open doorway and hit him squarely in the face with her viola. She swung the instrument through the air with both hands, using the neck and fingerboard as a handle. Such was the force of the blow that poor dear Viola was damaged beyond repair. Her neck was broken and her body shattered, but, more important for me, Komarov went down to the ground semiconscious. Caroline herself was both hyperventilating and crying at the same time.

"Quick," I shouted at her, "get a knife." She looked at me. "From the sideboard," I shouted. "Top drawer, on the left." She went straight to the sideboard and came back with a nice sharp, serrated steak knife. I didn't usually give my customers steak knives, as I thought it was an admission that my steaks were tough, but we kept a few just in case. Thank goodness we did. Even so, Caroline had difficulty cutting through the tape around my wrist. But she managed out of sheer desperation, hurried along by the imminent reawakening of the terror at our feet.

Finally, she freed my left hand.

"Quick," I said again. "Grab his gun and give it to me."

Komarov had fallen, but he had not let go of his pistol completely. Caroline went down and grabbed it out of his hand just as he was beginning to recover. She gave it to me, smiled wanly and went on trying to free me from the chair. Suddenly, I remembered the explosive. Where was the remote-detonator switch? Was it in Komarov's pocket?

Caroline sawed away at the tape around my legs, but she was too slow. Komarov was fully awake and watching, a line of blood running down from his nose, across his mouth and on down his neck. He put his hand up to his face and winced. I think Caroline must have broken his nose.

"Stay where you are," I said, pointing the gun at him.

He leaned on the floor with his left elbow and put his right hand in his pocket.

"Keep your hands where I can see them," I said.

He pulled his hand out again, but I could see that he now held a small, flat black box with a red button in the center of it. Oh God, I thought, my legs. Would he push the switch? But he would surely kill himself as well. Should I shoot him? If I did, would he detonate the bomb? Would he detonate it if I didn't?

I watched him, and I could sense that he was weighing up his options. If I had indeed told the police, his empire was about to come crashing down. Perhaps he could escape back to Russia or to South America, but maybe the escape routes had already been closed. Life imprisonment in a British jail would almost certainly mean just that, the rest of his life behind bars. There would be no parole for such an act of terrorism as the Newmarket bombing.

I quite suddenly sensed that he was going to do it. He was going to blow us all up and end it here.

I leaned down between my legs, grabbed the wires and pulled the cigarette-sized detonator out of the explosive. I threw it across the dining room. Komarov pushed the red button, but he was too late. The detonator exploded in midair with a harmless pop, like a very loud champagne cork exploding from the bottle.

Komarov looked cheated, and he was in a rage. He began to stand up.

"Stay where you are," I repeated. He ignored me and rose to his knees. "I'll shoot you," I said. But he continued to rise.

So I shot him.

I was surprised how easy it was. I pointed the gun in his direction and squeezed the trigger. It wasn't even as loud as I had expected, since the dining room was less confined than the lobby where Komarov had shot Richard.

The bullet caught him in the right leg, just above the knee. I hadn't been aiming for his leg particularly. I was right-handed, but the cast had forced me to shoot with my left. I had simply pointed the gun at the middle of the target and fired. If I'd aimed at his leg, I would probably have missed. Komarov dropped the detonator switch, grabbed the wound with both his hands and fell back to the floor. Blood poured out of his leg, and I wondered if I had hit an artery. I didn't particularly care about him, but he was ruining my dining-room carpet. I thought about shooting him again, in the head, to stop the bleeding. There had been so much blood—bright red, oxygenated blood. I decided to just let him bleed. At least the blood spilt here would not be from the innocent, and my carpet could be replaced.

Caroline was down on her knees behind me. She had finally cut through all the tape and I was free of the chair, so I went to her, keeping half an eye on Komarov and another half on the door from the kitchen. There were still George Kealy and Gary to contend with. Caroline cradled Viola in her arms and sobbed. It was only the four strings that were keeping the pegbox and the scroll attached to what remained of the body of the instrument. The neck and fingerboard had broken through completely, and the soundbox was cracked apart along its full length. The damage reflected the ferocity of the attack Caroline had made on Komarov. I was actually surprised that he had recovered from it as quickly as he had.

"Be careful, my darling," I said. "There are still two of them about. I'm going to find them. Go to the office and call the police."

"What shall I tell them?" she said, visibly in shock.

"Tell them there's been a murder," I said. "And the murderer is still here. That should bring them quickly."

Caroline went through the lobby and into the bar beyond, gently carrying Viola's remains in her arms.

Komarov was struggling to his feet. The bleeding from his leg had eased to a trickle, and I wondered if I should shoot him again. Instead, I grabbed him by the collar and thrust him ahead of me through the swinging door into the kitchen with the gun in the small of his back. If George Kealy was going to shoot me, he would have to miss his boss to do it. But the kitchen was empty. George and Gary must still be searching outside.

I pushed Komarov right across the kitchen and banged him up against the wall next to the stainless steel door of the cold-room. I bashed the back of his wounded leg with my knee, and he groaned. It felt good, so I did it again.

I used the lever handle to pull open the cold-room door and then I thrust Komarov in and sent him sprawling across the slatted wooden floor. The room was about ten feet square and seven feet high, with four food-filled wide stainless steel shelves running all around the walls, with a space about seven by four feet down the middle to walk. It had cost a fortune to install, but it had been worth every penny. I slammed the door shut. There was a push rod to open the door from the inside, to stop people getting trapped, and there was a place on the outside to affix a padlock, if desired. I didn't have a padlock handy, so I slipped a foot-long metal kebab skewer through the hole, thereby imprisoning Komarov.

I went into the office to find Caroline standing by the desk, shaking. She was sobbing quietly and close to hysteria. I held her close to me and kissed her neck.

"Sit and wait here," I said in her ear. "I have others to find." I pushed her into a chair. "Did you call the police?" I asked her. She nodded.

I went back into the kitchen, and I could hear George Kealy outside the back door, shouting for Gary. I removed the skewer and held the gun up as I carefully reopened the cold-room. Komarov was still there, sitting on the wooden slats and leaning up against the bottom shelf. He looked up at me, but the broken nose, the bullet wound and the loss of blood had taken the fight out of him.

I could hear George coming back in through the scullery. So could Komarov.

"George," he tried to shout, but it was little more than a croak.

I simply stepped behind the door and held it open as far as I could. I sensed, more than saw, George come into the kitchen and walk over to the cold-room. His gun appeared around the edge of the door, then withdrew when he spotted Komarov inside. Then he walked in and I slammed the door shut behind him. I quickly replaced the skewer.

I heard George pushing the rod to try to open the door, but the skewer held it closed with ease. He fired the gun, but there was about three inches of insulation between the stainless steel sides of the door and there was no chance of a bullet from a handgun penetrating that.

Now I only had Gary to deal with.

It took me a while to find him. He was leaned up against one of the trees on the far side of the parking lot. He was no trouble. In fact, he wouldn't be any trouble to anyone ever again, except perhaps the undertaker. A fish filleter was embedded in his chest the full length of its thin, eight-inch, razor-sharp blade. There was virtually no blood, just a slight trickle from the corner of his mouth. The knife looked like it had pierced his heart and had probably stopped its beating almost instantly.

Who, I wondered, had done that? Surely not George Kealy. He wouldn't have had the strength.

I spun around. There must be someone else here.

Caroline suddenly screamed from inside, and I hared across the parking lot, back into the building via the scullery door and through the kitchen. She was standing, wide-eyed in the center of the office, and she was not alone.

Jacek was standing in front of her, and he too was bleeding. Large drops of blood dripped continuously from all the fingers of his left hand onto the wooden floor below and made a bright red pool by his foot. Would this bloodletting ever end? I raised the gun, but it wasn't needed. Before I could say anything, he dropped to his knees and slowly rolled over onto his back. He had been shot in the shoulder.

Jacek, the man I hadn't trusted, the kitchen porter of whom I had believed there was more to than met the eye, had been one of the good guys all the time, and he had undoubtedly saved my life.

THE POLICE arrived, in the end. And an ambulance. Caroline had indeed called the emergency number but she had apparently been too shocked to make herself understood properly. The operator had finally traced the call and dispatched help.

First Jacek, then Caroline were conveyed to hospital. I was assured by the paramedics that they would be fine but that both definitely would be admitted overnight. Caroline was suffering badly from shock, and, it appeared, would again miss out on her stay at the Bedford Lodge Hotel.

The police who had arrived in the first patrol car had no real idea how to proceed, and, it seemed to me, they spent most of their time winding blue-and-white plastic POLICE— DO NOT CROSS tape around everything while they waited for reinforcements.

I tried to leave in the ambulance with Caroline but was prevented from doing so by a policeman, who took a break from his taping long enough to insist that I stay at the restaurant to make a statement.

So, instead, I went through the office and the bar to the lobby. Richard was still lying facedown on the stone floor. I moved some of the glass fragments and kneeled down next to him. I was sure he was dead, but I felt his left wrist just to make sure. There was no pulse, and his skin was already noticeably cold to the touch. How could such a thing happen to my caring, reliable headwaiter? I knelt there for a while, resting my hand on his back, as if I could give him some comfort in death, until one of the policemen came in and told me to please leave.

The police reinforcements, when they finally arrived, took the form of some senior plainclothes detectives, a firearms squad and the bomb-disposal team from the Army.

Understandably, none of them was too eager to open the

cold-room door. There was still the issue of the loaded gun inside. They decided to leave the occupants where they were for a while to cool off, literally. Three degrees centigrade would have been pretty uncomfortable even if they'd been wearing thick coats, gloves and hats. As it was, it had been a warm late-May evening, and Pyotr Komarov and George Kealy had both been in shirtsleeves. Was I bothered?

The senior officer present interviewed me briefly, and I tried to explain to him what had happened. But it was complicated, and he seemed preoccupied with the men still in the cold-room. I would be reinterviewed, he explained, at the police station later. In the morning, I hoped, yawning.

Both the police and I were required by the bomb-disposal team to leave the building while they removed the explosive, so I sat on a white plastic chair on the gravel in front of the restaurant. One of the ambulance staff came over, wrapped a red blanket around my shoulders and asked me if I was OK.

"I'm fine," I said. It reminded me of being at Newmarket racetrack on the day of the bombing. But, this time, I really was fine. The nightmare was over.

# EPILOGUE

Six months later, I opened Maximilian's, a modern and exciting restaurant on the south side of Berkeley Square in Mayfair serving mostly French food but with an English influence.

The opening night was a grand affair, with lots of invited guests. There was even a string quartet playing at one end of the dining room. I looked over at them, four tall, elegant young women in black dresses. I took particular notice of the viola player. She had shoulder-length light-brown hair tied back in a ponytail, bright blue eyes, high cheekbones and a longish, thin nose above a broad mouth and square-shaped jaw. She was playing a new viola—at least, it was new to her. As her left hand glided up and down the fingerboard, I could see a diamond engagement ring glistening in the light. I had given it to her on my bended knee in the kitchen just before the first guests had arrived.

"I'd always thought your name was Maxwell," said a booming voice in my ear. It was Bernard Sims. "I hear you've decided to make an honest woman of the plaintiff," he said, shaking his head but with a smile.

"Guilty," I pleaded with a grin.

The prosecution of me under section 7 of the Food Safety Act 1990 had been dropped, and the civil poisoning case had been settled out of court with the plaintiff accepting undisclosed damages from the defendant. Caroline's agent had tried to claim his fifteen percent of the amount, which was confidential, but Bernard had explained to him that he was entitled to commission only on her earnings and the damages had been offered and accepted not for loss of earnings but in recompense for distress caused. He hadn't been best pleased, but, then again, it would have been very difficult for Caroline to play only eighty-five percent of an 1869 Stefano Scarampella viola.

D.I. Turner had finally returned my calls, and had come eagerly in person when I'd told him I knew who had committed the racetrack bombing at Newmarket. Since then, he had kept me up-to-date with progress in the case. Komarov had survived both the bullet wound in his leg and the hypothermia brought on by the cold-room, and had been charged with a total of twenty murders, including the cold-blooded killing of Richard, my much-missed headwaiter. Further charges of conspiracy to set off explosions and traffic drugs were expected to follow. George Kealy had also been charged with Richard's murder, although Turner was pretty sure that he would eventually be convicted only of being an accessory to the murders because George was singing for his freedom, or, at least, for a shorter sentence. A police search of the Kealy residence had discovered boxes of the metal balls in a locked storeroom, and a similar exploration of Gary's flat had turned up a certain silver key fob, complete with the key to my now-burned cottage front door. Many of the details had been widely reported in the newspapers, and especially by Clare Harding in the *Cambridge Evening News*.

As I had expected, George Kealy was Komarov's man in the UK, just as Rolf Schumann had been in the U.S. George had been the official link between Horse Imports Ltd and Tattersalls, the bloodstock auctioneers in Newmarket, and he had even been the chairman of the East Anglia Polo Club.

Like Rolf Schumann, George had apparently been a busy

boy in the drugs market, supplying some big players with a steady stream of high-quality cocaine. The coke was then cut before being passed down the chain to the street dealers and the users, with the proceeds passing back up the line. Rolf had been skimming off about half of this drug cash to keep his business afloat. It took precisely three months from the Newmarket bombing until the tractor factory closed for good. The lady in the Delafield embroidered-cushion store wouldn't be happy.

Unlike Rolf Schumann, George it seemed had remained loyal to Komarov, at least until he had been arrested and charged with murder.

As a result of the information George was giving to the police, several big-time drug barons had received a dawn visit from one of Her Majesty's constabularies, and they were now languishing in one of Her prisons awaiting trial. A number of other leads he had provided were also being investigated by various police forces around the world. I reckoned that the horse-breeding business in South America was about to suffer a major downturn.

Kurt and Walter, meanwhile, had been cornered by the Delafield sheriff's department, who had wanted to question them concerning criminal damage and a vicious assault at the home of Mrs. Dorothy Schumann. Walter, the impetuous boy, had apparently tried to brain one of the sheriff's men with a polo mallet and had been shot dead for his trouble. It was not a great loss.

I stood by the bar and surveyed my new domain. Mark Winsome had been as good as his word, but I think he'd had to write a check rather larger than he had originally intended. But the money had been well spent, with acres of glass and a forest of beech wood visible to the customers, and a further mass of stainless steel out of sight in the well-equipped kitchen. There were more than twice the number of tables than at the Hay Net, and I was confident that, with the longer dinner service in the big city, we could serve at least three times as many covers on a busy night.

In spite of opening the London venture, I had decided not to close down in Newmarket. Carl and I had worked together on his people management skills, and then I had appointed him as chef de cuisine at the Hay Net, with three new assistants, one of whom was Oscar, who had accepted our profuse apologies, a substantial one-off cash payment, and a permanent position as Carl's number two. Ray and Jean had decided to go elsewhere, but there had been no shortage of capable staff to fill their shoes and breathe new life into the freshly recarpeted dining room. Jacek, however, also didn't stay.

I had been right about him, at least in one respect. There was, indeed, much more to my kitchen porter than had first met the eye. When he had arrived from his native Czech Republic, his English had been so limited that he had been categorized by the local job center as suitable only for unskilled restaurant work. But Jacek proved to be highly skilled. At home, he had been not a scrubber of cooking pots but a user of them. He did not remain at the Hay Net because, now joined by his wife and daughter, he came with me to Maximilian's as an assistant chef. After all, one never knew when a bodyguard might come in useful.

I felt a hand on my arm and turned to find Sally standing there. She and Toby had eagerly accepted my invitation to the opening, and they had brought my mother with them in their car.

"It's lovely, Max," said Sally with a genuine smile. "Absolutely lovely."

"Thank you," I said, and I leaned down and kissed her on the cheek.

I had seen more of Sally and Toby over the past six months than I had during the previous six years. Caroline and I had been invited to stay with them on several occasions, which was great since their house still felt like home to me, and was, for the moment, my only home. I had, by now, become quite accustomed to my nomadic existence, living constantly out of a suitcase. My cottage had been completely bulldozed, the heat of the fire having rendered the walls unsafe to reuse. The plot of land on which it had stood, complete with permits to build a new dwelling, was currently on the market at a price that I thought was unreasonably high but one that my real estate agent was confident of obtaining.

Over the past months, when in Newmarket, I regularly stayed with Carl, except when his wife and children were there, which was increasingly often. On those occasions, I took a room at the Bedford Lodge Hotel, where I had finally managed to entertain Caroline the night after she was released from the hospital.

My temporary London address was a certain ground-floor flat in Tamworth Street, in Fulham, where two miniature listening devices had eventually been discovered, one in the cupboard under the kitchen sink and the other hidden among the packages in the dark recesses of the medicine cabinet.

Caroline hadn't made it to the Cadogan Hall for her solo, and neither had Viola, whose remains had been lovingly borne to a top violin restorer. He had tut-tutted over her condition for some time and had declared that she was beyond reasonable repair. I had asked him what he meant by "reasonable repair," and he had replied that he could easily make Viola look all right but was highly doubtful that she would ever again sound as she should. The belly and the back had been split right through, he had explained, and bits of the ribs were missing altogether, as was the sound post—no doubt rolled up and thrown away with the bloodied Hay Net dining room carpet. He would have to replace the missing ribs and to add reinforcing materials to the inside of the body that would permanently and adversely affect the tone. So we had taken her home as she was and had laid her on a shelf as a constant reminder to us of her sacrifice.

Caroline, meanwhile, had quickly been restored to perfection, and she had even wooed the orchestra directors into adding the Benjamin Britten Concerto for Violin and Viola, the piece she had missed at Cadogan Hall, into a Summer Soirée concert in St. James's Park. It had been a wonderful, warm late-June evening, and I had been spellbound by her talent.

I looked again across the restaurant at her and smiled. She smiled back. Miss Caroline Aston, violist and proud of it, my fiancée and my savior.

Between them, Jacek and Caroline had given me back my life. I had been reborn after I had fully expected to die. That fateful night, as I had sat waiting for the bomb squad to remove the explosives from the Hay Net, I had resolved to grab life by the horns and hang on.

I was going to live my second life at full throttle.